The Refrain Within

MUSIC OF HOPE SERIES

Book Three

The Refrain Within

MUSIC OF HOPE SERIES

Book Three

A WWII Women's Fiction Novel

LIZ TOLSMA

GILEAD PUBLISHING

The Refrain Within, book #3 in the Music of Hope series

Copyright © 2020 by Christine Cain
Published by Gilead Publishing, LLC
Grand Rapids, Michigan, USA.
www.gileadpublishing.com

 **GILEAD** PUBLISHING

Scripture quotations are from the King James Version of the Bible.

This is a work of fiction. Names, characters, places, and incidents are products of the author's imagination or are used fictitiously. Any similarity to actual people, organizations, and/or events is purely coincidental.

Library of Congress Cataloging-in-Publication Data
Names: Tolsma, Liz, 1966– author.
Title: The refrain within : a WWII women's fiction novel / Liz Tolsma.
Description: Grand Rapids : Gilead Publishing, [2020] | Series: Music of hope; book 3
Identifiers: LCCN 2020022473 (print) | LCCN 2020022474 (ebook)
Subjects: LCSH: World War, 1939–1945—Hungary—Fiction. | GSAFD: Historical fiction. | Christian fiction.
Classification: LCC PS3620.O329 R44 2020 (print) | LCC PS3620.O329 (ebook) | DDC 813/.6—dc23
LC record available at https://lccn.loc.gov/2020022473
LC ebook record available at https://lccn.loc.gov/2020022474

ISBN: 978-1-68370-044-9 (paperback)
ISBN: 978-1-68370-045-6 (ebook)

Cover design by Sarah Slattery

Printed in the United States of America
20 21 22 23 24 25 26 / 5 4 3 2 1

To my dad

I love you more than words can say. Thank you for all the love and laughter you have brought to my life and for encouraging me in whatever I did. I will always be your little girl.

One needs something to believe in,
something for which one can have wholehearted enthusiasm.

—Hannah Senesh, 1921–1944, Hungarian-Jewish
soldier and WWII rescue mission volunteer

Since thou wast precious in my sight, thou hast been
honourable, and I have loved thee: therefore will I give men
for thee, and people for thy life. Fear not: for I am with thee:
I will bring thy seed from the east, and gather thee from the
west; I will say to the north, Give up; and to the south, Keep
not back: bring my sons from far, and my daughters from the
ends of the earth.

—Isaiah 43:4–6

Glossary of Foreign Words

Hungarian Words

A múzsám (ah MEW-zham) – my muse

Anya (AHN-ya) – mother

Apu (AH-poo) – father

Asszony (AH-soyn) – Mrs. (as in some Asian languages such as Korean and Japanese, it comes after the surname)

Buda (BOO-duh) – the more residential side of the city

Csillagom (CHEE-la-gome) – dear

Édesem (EE-deh-shem) – sweetheart

Gundel palacsinta (GOO-dell paula-CHEEN-tuh) – crepes with ground walnuts, raisins, and rum and topped with dark chocolate sauce

Halászlé (HAW-lass-lee) – soup loaded with carp and paprika

Igen (EE-gen) – yes (the number of times it is said in a row indicates a level of excitement)

Jó napot kívánok (Yo nuh-POTE kee-VAN-oke) – good day, formally

Köszönöm (KOO-sih-num) – thank you

Langosi (LAHN-go-she) – fried dough topped with cheese

Lecsó (LEH-cho) – vegetable stew

Nem (NEM) – no

Nyuszikám (NEW-see-cam) – my bunny

Pálinka (PAH-lean-kuh) – Hungarian fruit brandy

Pengő (PEN-gyou) – Hungarian currency from 1927 until 1945; in June 1944, 1 USD = 33.51 pengő

Pest (PESHT) – the more commercial side of the city

Szent Istvan Bazilika (ZENT ISHT-von BOZ-eel-ih-kah) – Saint
   Ivan's Basilica, a famous Budapest church
Szerelmem (Suh-RELL-mem) – my dear
Tiyul (tee-YOOL) – an exodus or journey
Ulti (OOHL-tee) – a trick-taking card game for three players
Úr (OOR) – mister

As with most Asian languages, in Hungarian the family name comes first and then the Christian name. For example, I would be Tolsma Liz. The heroine in the story is Bognár Éva. Titles also come after the family name. *Úr* means "mister," so when referring to Éva's father, he will be called Bognár *Úr*, or Mr. Bognár.

Chapter One

Budapest, Hungary
Late April 1944

I'll see you next week, Miss Bognár." Ten-year-old Ferenc flashed Éva a dimpled smile as he turned to leave the bright music studio.

"Don't forget to practice your scales. They're very important to playing the clarinet well."

Ferenc gripped his small, square case embossed with the Bognár clarinet-maker seal and grimaced.

"Now, now. We talked about this during the lesson. No one likes them much. Just do them at the beginning of your session and get them over with."

"Fine." The boy harrumphed and made a hasty exit before Éva could instruct him further.

He had so much talent. If only he would be more disciplined, he would have a bright future as a musician.

As she stared out the window after Ferenc, a black-booted Nazi soldier strode by like he owned the world. Right now, he and his countrymen did own this part of it and had since they'd invaded almost a month ago, after President Horthy attempted to make peace with the Allies.

She put the kettle on the coal stove to boil. What would remain once the Germans left? If they ever left.

She shook away the thought as if she were shaking a cramp from her hand from too much practicing.

Her clarinet. Other than her fiancé, Patrik, the only distraction these days from the Nazis. She retrieved her case from the back room and assembled the instrument, the greased corks sliding together as she tongued the callus on the inside of her bottom lip. Not taking much time to warm up, she launched into Brahms's Hungarian Dance no. 5. The vibrant Cossak, Eastern tone of the piece took her from the bottom to the top of the register, her fingers flying over the keys.

As she played, her body swayed, almost as if she danced to the tune. The music transported her from this storefront to a celebration on the Hungarian plains, conjuring women in dark blue dresses with crimson embroidery swirling around the floor while men in tall black boots slapped their knees.

Some notes she drew out, while for others, she allowed her fingers to skip over the instrument. With her tongue relaxed, she tapped out the staccato on the reed. By the time she reached the end of the short piece, she was breathless.

Then she flicked her gaze to the window. A German in his olive-green uniform stared at her through the glass, his blue eyes narrowed, his arms crossed over his chest. She swung around, swabbed out the ebony clarinet, and shoved it into its case. By the time she glanced up again, the Nazi was gone.

She breathed a sigh of relief and spun from the window to straighten the disheveled sheet music for sale on metal racks in the front of the shop. A page slipped from her fingers and fluttered to the ground.

The bell above the door tinkled, and a blast of chilly air rushed through the room. Good, her next student was here. She picked up the fallen sheet of music and turned to greet her student. But instead of another pupil, her sister-in-law Zofia dashed in and locked the door.

"What are you doing?" Éva clutched the paper to her chest.

Zofia's breath came in short spurts. "Someone is following me."

"Following you? Why?"

With a flourish, Zofia pointed to the yellow star sewn onto her blue coat.

"Oh." Zofia had been such a fixture of Éva's life for the past several years, she often forgot her best friend was a Messianic Jew. "Come on back and sit down. You're pale and shaking. I'll make you some tea. I already have the kettle on."

"Don't waste the precious leaves on me. We have so few left."

Éva guided Zofia to the break room behind the glass case displaying instruments and accessories for sale. She pulled out a chair and motioned for Zofia to sit at the table. "Tomorrow we can drink ersatz coffee. Today, you need the tea."

The kettle whistled as the water boiled, and Éva poured a cup before sitting across from Zofia. "Tell me what happened."

Zofia drummed her fingers on the tabletop as if playing the piano she so loved, her dark red hair falling across her cheek. "I was on my way back from Hansi's audition with the Youth Philharmonic. She performed very well, by the way. Your Patrik, the great conductor, was impressed." For a moment, her eyes brightened.

Éva giggled at the way Zofia referenced her fiancé.

Dimness overtook Zofia's eyes once more. "On the way back, I had this, this feeling. I can't describe it. Like pinpricks on my skin. When I turned around, I didn't see anyone. Not out of the ordinary. People going about their usual day. So I kept on.

"The feeling ate at me all the way here. That's why I locked the door. Whoever was following me might be on the street waiting." She lowered her voice. "Waiting to arrest me."

Éva's mouth dried out. "You don't think this is because of Károly, do you?" Could the man she had once loved still be causing her friend problems?

Zofia straightened. "He's dead, no longer a danger to me or anyone. What I'm more afraid of, though, is that despite the fact the Nazis aren't rounding up Jews en masse in Budapest like in the country, they will arrest anyone who steps out of line."

"There you go, then." Éva returned to the table with the steaming mug. "Nothing to worry about, because you don't step out of line." Besides, they had Zofia's husband and Éva's fiancé to keep them safe. "I'm sure the incident was nothing more than your imagination"

"What incident?" The deep voice behind them sent Éva rocketing out of her chair. She hadn't heard the bell above the door. Her fiancé, Kedves Patrik, leaned against the door jamb, his hands in his pockets, cool as you please.

"Patrik, you scared me half to death." Éva steadied her trembling legs. "If you keep doing that, I'm going to have to take away your key." She crossed her arms and tried to pout but couldn't stop a smile from breaking out.

He dangled his key chain. "Come and get it."

She leapt for it, but he jerked the key behind his back. When she reached to snatch it, he pulled her close and kissed her soundly.

"That isn't a fair fight." But she kissed him back. "Alright, you win. This time."

"You wouldn't want the key. Then you'd have to keep lending it to me for the evening deliveries."

She brushed away a lock of his dark, wavy hair from his forehead. "No, we wouldn't want that. We might end up seeing each other even more than we already do."

With a gleam in his dark brown eyes, he held out the key to her. "You may not win with brute force, but you do make a persuasive argument."

"Ha, ha." She stepped from his embrace. "Just make some more noise next time."

"I will. I'll clomp in like a bear. Or an elephant." He grinned, lumbering around the room and stomping loudly enough to alert everyone in Budapest of his presence. "How's that?"

She laughed, heart fluttering, and kissed him on his clean-shaven cheek. "Much better, thank you."

Oh, he was a good man. As true and honest as he was hand-some, and someone who had helped her forget the past.

He dropped the key into his pocket. "Why is the door locked in the middle of the day anyway?"

"It's my fault." Zofia traced the rim of her teacup, her piano-playing fingers long and delicate. "I'm pretty sure someone followed me here after I left the concert hall."

"Pft." Éva waved away Zofia's concern, more to reassure herself than anything. An idea shaped in her mind and settled her stomach. "This answers the question. Patrik was behind you."

He shook his head. "Not that close. She must have left at least fifteen minutes before me. One of the flutists stopped me to ask a question, and then I straightened the chairs."

Maybe they were making too much of a single incident. True, there were those Hungarians, her own countrymen, who hated and persecuted the Jews. She shuddered when a picture of Károly, sandy brown hair, laughing blue eyes, a cleft in his chin, flashed through her brain. As she always did, she dismissed it. Sent it to the furthest reaches of her mind, unwilling to relive that part of her life. Unwilling to suffer that pain again.

But his haunting presence hung over her, a specter whose shadow hounded her. Visible in each and every German who now walked the streets of Budapest.

"Did you see anyone suspicious behind you?" Patrik sat at the table, his gaze intent on Zofia.

"Not that I noticed." Zofia played with the cup's delicate curved handle. "Just this feeling I had. I still can't shake it."

The same one Éva had now. She returned to her seat. "Why don't we talk about more pleasant subjects? Like our wedding. Not too many more weeks—"

"Think harder, Zofia. Try to remember who was behind you. Did you see the same person more than once?"

"*Nem*, not that I can remember. Like I said, it was nothing more than my gut speaking to me."

The room darkened, the light from the front window dimming as the sun slid behind Buda's buildings. "If you remember anything at all, let me know right away. But do be careful. Both of you."

Though he included Éva in his warning, he directed his narrow-eyed stare at Zofia.

The whir of the printing press as Patrik cranked the machine inspired a song in his head. He paused in his publishing of the anti-German pamphlets, grabbed a piece of paper and a pencil, and before he forgot, scribbled out the tune's melody.

The back-alley office of this branch of the Zionist Youth was peaceful tonight. No meetings. No planning sessions. No one here forging documents. With the solitude and quiet, he got a good deal of the composition written.

He whistled quietly to himself to hear the refrain, to avoid drawing the attention of the authorities.

Not quite right. Something in the rhythm of the notes was wrong. He put aside his music and ran off another stack of pamphlets. The steady *whish* as he fed the paper through the machine took on a life of its own. He tapped his toe to the pulse of it.

A smile spread across his face. Ah yes, that was better. The correct rhythm. Giving his tired, aching arm another rest, he reworked the problem spot and completed the rough sketch of the tune. He would present the music to his symphony in a couple of weeks, but he already knew what it sounded like. Typically Hungarian with its Asian influence and haunting, minor melodies. Inspiring. Rousing.

Something the Germans were sure to hate.

He grinned wider.

He picked up one of the pamphlets and checked it. The words outlined the severity and gravity of the situation for Hungarian Jews. Many of them in the countryside had already been rounded up and herded into ghettos, like sheep ready for the slaughter.

People like his younger sister. His older sister and her husband. All living in Nagyvárad, on the Romanian border. He'd urged them to cross. Get out while there was time. Go to Palestine, where his mother had always dreamed of going. She would never get there, but they could start over in the promised land.

Time might have run out, though.

Only Budapest remained relatively safe. Even that wouldn't last forever. Already it was changing. The incident earlier today with Zofia troubled Patrik. Her writings for the Zionists, one of which he printed now, must have drawn the attention of the authorities. They were hunting her. Of that, there was no doubt.

Her affiliation with Éva had him pacing the floor. The two women owned the music studio. But technically, only Éva owned it now. Jews could no longer possess businesses. Not much longer and she wouldn't be able to employ Zofia either.

Not only did they work side by side, but Zofia was married to Éva's brother, illegal in itself, and the couple lived with Éva and her parents. The ties were close. And dangerous.

If only the Soviets would hurry up and arrive.

Patrik patted his false identity booklet tucked in his suit coat, which hung over the room's lone chair. He was safe, safer than his people, safer than his kin. He'd tried to create new identities for them. His sisters, though, took after their father, the stubborn old goat, and would hear nothing about it.

Patrik hadn't been able to protect them. He couldn't allow anything to happen to his precious Éva. His muse. His life.

God, when will this all end? He rubbed his gritty eyes. These late nights, working the printing press into the wee hours of the morning and then going to his job as conductor for the Budapest Youth Philharmonic, were brutal. He needed some sleep.

Before he made a crucial error.

If only he could turn off his racing thoughts.

A soft knock sounded at the door, the syncopated rhythm just right. Someone from their organization who knew the code.

He opened the lock and ushered in Varga Bram. "What a surprise. I thought you headed home hours ago."

"I did, but I couldn't sleep." Bram bounced on his toes, his curly blond hair keeping time.

"What's on your mind?" Patrik yawned.

"Just excited for Zofia's latest treatise. We're fortunate to have her, you know. No one can match her writing style. Fantastic. Good enough to awaken the people from their pathos. I want to grab a handful and pass them out to everyone I meet."

"Hold on. That isn't the best idea, you know. The Gestapo wouldn't appreciate your gesture. Especially since she was followed today."

"We've all been shadowed. She'll have to watch her step, but she's a smart woman."

Being smart hadn't been enough for many people Patrik knew.

Bram rambled, circuiting the stuffy room as he did. "There are too many people in this city, in this country, who have closed their eyes to anti-Semitism for too long. President Horthy awakened the sleeping giant by trying to make peace with the Allies, and now reality is here. Time for us to shake off our slumber and push back. To fight what is happening."

"I agree with you. But is it too little too late? And at too great a cost?"

"Never too little. Never too late. Always worth whatever price we have to pay."

Thoughts of what the Nazis might do to Éva in retaliation sucked out what little air there was left in the room. Everyone knew how ruthless and brutal the Nazis were, though no one spoke about it. If he was caught, if Zofia was caught, everyone associated with them would pay the price. Patrik leaned on the table to steady himself.

"Why don't you go home and get some rest?" Bram slapped Patrik on the shoulder. "You look like you could use it. Since God gave me a motor that runs all the time, and I'm already awake, you might as well take advantage of my offer. It will probably be the best one you get all day."

Patrik's eyes were heavy, and the page's print swam in front of him. Bram was right. Nothing sounded better to Patrik at this moment than a mattress and a feather pillow. Perhaps tonight he would manage to fall asleep. Perhaps tonight his dreams wouldn't haunt him. His flat was a few blocks from here, down a couple of alleys and across a single street. He'd snuck around past curfew plenty of times.

After a last farewell to Bram, he exited the room. Bram clicked the lock shut behind him.

Tonight, the moon scuttled behind clouds that dropped a light mist. At least it wasn't the snow they'd had earlier in the month. April in Budapest. Would spring ever arrive? Maybe not. Maybe with the Germans, winter was perpetual.

He scurried down the alley and took a left at another back street. In the dim light, he made out his building up ahead, the many tall windows dark. All he had to do was cross this street and he would be home.

He set out.

His foot slid on a small remaining patch of ice.

In horrible slow motion, he flew into the air and landed hard on the ground.

His hands throbbed. White-hot pain raced from his tail bone up his spine.

For several seconds, he sat without moving. He couldn't stay here forever, but every breath, every flinch of his muscles was excruciating. He mustn't cry out. He bit his tongue until he tasted blood.

"Hey, you there. It's after curfew. What are you doing out?"

A German soldier dressed in a long, dark coat and tall, dark boots marched toward him.

And Patrik was in no shape to run.

Chapter Two

$\mathcal{P}$atrik lay on the ground, incredible pain shooting up his back and down his legs.

The German soldier advanced.

Patrik's pulse pounded in his ears, drowning out the man's shouts. It didn't matter. He understood the rifle that the thin but muscular soldier shrugged from his shoulder. Germans had shot people for far less provocation than being out after curfew.

And they didn't bother to ask questions.

Biting the inside of his cheek to stifle his scream, Patrik jumped to his feet. Half limping, half running, he tore down the street.

The Nazi's boots sounded on the pavement behind him, pounding a tympanic beat, driving, relentless, drawing closer.

The pain drove Patrik's breath from his lungs. He would never outrun the soldier, not in this condition. A plan, that's what he needed. He gasped for air, his mind racing faster than his legs.

The blackout darkness might be his best defense. That and his knowledge of Budapest's side alleys might give Patrik a fighting chance.

There—a narrow, dark crevice between the Baroque-style buildings. Patrik darted into it and down an alley that reeked of rotting cabbage and spoiled eggs.

His skin tingled, a sure sign the soldier tailed him. What Zofia must have felt earlier today.

Near the end of the alley, Patrik stubbed his toe on something, perhaps a piece of wood. He clenched his fists, digging his fingernails into his palms. Now his foot throbbed too. But there could be no pausing. Onward he hobbled, his chest heaving, dodging left down another of the city's back streets as rats scurried in front of him. Behind him, the German puffed. Good. Perhaps he was tiring. Patrik's own legs burned. He wouldn't be able to keep going much longer.

A thin shaft of light from the upper story of a building shone into the alley, illuminating an oversized construction garbage bin. Perfect.

Avoiding the light, Patrik slipped behind the metal container, breathing through his mouth, making as little noise as possible.

Footsteps. Patrik closed his eyes. The steps halted in front of him.

Tick, tock, tick, tock. Patrik covered his Swiss watch to dampen the sound. How long before the soldier searched behind the bin? Patrik scooted farther into the shadows, his tail bone screaming in agony as his backside hit the rough brick of the building.

In a deep voice, the Nazi swore. The footsteps moved on. Not toward Patrik but away from him.

When he opened his eyes, Patrik couldn't make out a thing. The light from above had been extinguished. God's providence.

Still he stayed planted in place. The German might be trying to lure him into a false sense of security, ready to pounce on him the minute he moved from his spot. So even though he needed an ice pack on his backside and another on his toe, he didn't twitch a muscle.

The adrenaline drained from his body, and sleepiness overtook him.

Patrik nodded off.

When Patrik awoke, still squatting behind the stinking refuse bin, light brightened his surroundings. Above, in the narrow opening between the buildings, was blue sky. Patrik drew his coat around himself, his fingers stiff with the cold.

Perhaps it was time for the monkey to jump in the water. The soldier wouldn't have waited for hours to catch a lone man breaking curfew. Still, Patrik hesitated. He peered around the corner of the bin. The only creature stirring here at this time of day was a scrawny rat.

His back in agony, Patrik crawled from hiding. No movement at either end of the lane. Fire raced through his aching body as he stood up.

Though he wasn't sure of his exact location, he was familiar with the area in general. He'd never make it home in this condition. Where could he go to rest and maybe procure a few aspirin? Someone he could trust.

Ah. Éva and Zofia's music studio wasn't far. If he couldn't depend on his fiancée and his future sister-in-law, whom could he trust? Perhaps they had aspirin. At least they had a waiting room with a comfortable chair.

The odor of spoiled milk and ripe fish clung to him as he crept down the main street. The few early morning commuters steered a wide path around him.

Up ahead was Éva's ground-floor studio. A large plate-glass window, decorated with flowers constructed from sheet music, occupied the storefront next to the door.

He shuffled up and tried the knob. Locked. Of course. It was far too early in the morning for anyone to be here. He fished his key from his pocket.

"Excuse me, sir. Can I help you?"

He startled at the sound, then relaxed. It was his beautiful Éva, the loveliest woman he'd ever seen. Tall and slender, she gazed at him with her warm brown eyes, her wavy, golden hair brushing her shoulders. The deep purple of her long wool coat complemented her fair skin. "Good morning, *a múzsám*." His muse.

He kissed her lips, lingering, desiring to stay here and forget the war, the Nazis, his night in the alleyway.

When she broke away with a sniff, his lips tingled.

She drew back and covered her wrinkled nose. "While this is a wonderful surprise, you stink, and it's barely after sunrise. What happened?"

"Well, I was in the neighborhood . . ."

She raised her fair eyebrows. "Really?"

"Really."

Éva fumbled with the key before opening the door. "I'm not a fool. How about the truth, Patrik?"

The truth. One of the few things she demanded of him. One of the few things he was unable to fully give her. "It was late last night. I got caught up in my work at the concert hall and was hurrying home when I fell. I slept in an alley."

"An alley? My poor dear. You have to watch the time better."

"I do. You're right." She believed his story. He was getting a little too good at lying. But he couldn't tell her. She didn't know what he did during the hours he wasn't with her or at work. For both their sakes, he aimed to keep it that way.

He stepped into the studio, Éva forging ahead of him. To his left, racks of music. In front of him, a long counter over a glass display case filled with instruments from flutes to trumpets. On his right, a grouping of chairs and a table holding a couple of magazines. Behind that, a hall with a row of doors. The lesson rooms.

"How about some tea and an aspirin?"

"That would be perfect."

He trailed her into the kitchen behind the counter. In short order, she brought him a warm cup of tea and the pill and settled him on a chair, rolling up her own coat to provide a bit of cushioning.

"What would I do without you?" He pecked her on the cheek.

"Let's hope you never have to find out."

That was his constant prayer these days.

He sipped the spiced liquid. The warmth spread through him, driving away the last vestiges of the chill that had permeated him.

A small bell chimed, and a minute later, Zofia joined them. Her mouth opened into an O. "Patrik, what are you doing here?"

"Dracula was chasing me, and I fell." A code she would understand and something that made Éva laugh as intended. "I came here because I knew I'd get proper care."

"Of that I have no doubt." She patted a strand of red hair back into its roll and nodded to Éva. "We received that new shipment of music books yesterday. Would you mind sorting through them? I'll be along in a moment to help you."

After a glance between Patrik and Zofia, Éva left the room. Zofia leaned on the table near him and spoke in a low voice. "What really happened?"

He gave her the details. "Do you think they're on to us?"

Early May 1944

Zofia shrugged into her blue coat, cringing at the sight of the yellow star sewn onto the lapel. The symbol that marked her as one to be feared. Hated. Killed.

Her husband, Ernő, stood in front of the apartment door, his arms crossed in front of him. "Why do you have to go out tonight? You weren't feeling well not that long ago."

She pecked him on the lips. "I'm fine now. Something I ate for lunch must have upset my stomach. You know this is for a private lesson. This student is frail and can't leave her home, but she loves to play the piano. Her one joy in life. And I'm thankful they continue to employ me, even at great risk to themselves. Not many people do anymore. Business at the shop has dropped off a great deal."

"Just stay home this evening. You can phone and cancel. Under the circumstances, I'm sure they won't mind. I don't like the idea of you being out alone. Not after you were tailed the other day."

"I'm sure that was nothing more than my imagination." She should never have told Éva, who in turn had told Ernő. She had caused him worry and had made it more difficult on herself to slip out to meetings.

"I could see it shook you up."

"I'll be fine. Quit fretting." He didn't understand the importance of where she was going.

"Let me walk you there."

That was the last thing he could do. "No need. I wouldn't be good company. You stay home where it's warm."

"I'd rather be cold than have you in danger. You aren't involved in the same sorts of activities as in Poland, are you?"

Another thing she should have never told him. His suspicion wasn't good, not good at all. She touched both his cheeks. "Of course not. You are my life now. My previous activities cost me everything. I wouldn't put you or your family at risk."

But wasn't that exactly what she was doing?

Even after what had happened, though, she had to help her people any way she could. The cost of action was high. The cost of inaction was higher.

All she could do was trust herself and those she loved to God. That's what Mama would tell her.

"I hope not. You've done your part."

"You're overprotective, and I love you for it, but now it's time for you to let go." She kissed him again, stroked his blond hair and his square jaw, and slid outside, shutting the door before he had a chance to protest further.

Once down the steps and on the street, she released a breath she hadn't realized she'd held. In truth, there was no student and no in-home lesson. Instead, she headed toward Bram's flat and a meeting of their branch of the Zionist Youth.

Her illness and Ernő's reluctance to let her go put her behind schedule. She scurried as fast as she could down the damp street and slipped by the sentry at the door and into the apartment just as the meeting got underway. So many Jewish young people crowded the room, it was almost impossible to pick out the black lacquer Chinese-style furniture covered in bright designs.

Patrik stood beside Bram, a head taller than the man who was always in motion, Bram's green eyes always twinkling. No chairs were set up. Instead, most of the guests held glasses of fruit brandy, *pálinka*, so that in case of a raid, the meeting would appear to be nothing more than a cocktail party.

Before she even shed her coat, Bram motioned her forward. "Here is the lady of the hour. That pamphlet you wrote calling the citizens of Hungary to throw off their apathy and come to their senses about the senseless, just brilliant. A masterpiece."

At the round of polite applause, she shuffled her feet and studied the floor. "All I did was share my thoughts."

"And so eloquently. Please tell me you have more inside you dying to be written."

She nodded. Indeed, several ideas swam in her head. If she had more privacy at the studio or at home, she would be able to produce many more pamphlets for their organization.

"Good, good, so glad to hear that. With Jews being rounded up all over the country and shipped to Poland, it's more important than ever that we give a rallying cry to the rest of the nation. The time for sloth and indifference is over. The time for action is now."

"Hear, hear." Several members raised their glasses.

The teenage boy posted at the cracked-open door closed it and shushed them. "German voices. Coming up the stairs."

The party-like atmosphere fizzled. A tickle settled into the bottom of Zofia's stomach. Were these the men who had been following her earlier? Must be. She'd brought them here. Ernő had been right in warning her not to go out. She should have listened to him.

Zofia slipped to the piano and opened the lid. "It's a party, remember, everyone." Without any other fanfare, she touched the keys and brought forth Lizst's Hungarian Rhapsody. Her fellow Zionists gathered around the piano.

Before she finished the song's introduction, before she came to the rolling, rocking melody, without so much as a knock, the door flew open and three armed Germans strode inside. "All of you, into the corner."

All twenty or so of them?

"Move it. Now."

As one, they scuffled toward the far corner. Bram moved a painted silk screen, so everyone would fit.

Zofia huddled close to Patrik and whispered to him, "This must be who was following me."

He shrugged.

"Turn the place upside down." A lanky Gestapo officer, as tall as Patrik and as fair as Patrik was dark, marched over and stood toe to toe with him. "Do you have something to say, Jew boy?" He slapped Patrik.

Patrik didn't flinch.

"Answer me."

"I'm not Jewish. Check my papers."

"Then a Jew lover, at the very best." He slapped Patrik once more.

Zofia's throat swelled. What was going to happen to them? Would they all be arrested?

What had she done?

Some of them, like Patrik, had false identity papers. Others, like her, didn't. A careful search would turn up that fact and jeopardize their entire operation.

Bram left the corner, ambled to his ebony drink cart, and poured three glasses of *pálinka*. He turned to the agent in charge and clapped him on the back. "Have a drink and join the party."

The officer eyed Bram.

"Come on. There's no harm in a single glass. Your superiors don't even need to know. There's nothing for you to find, so you might as well enjoy yourselves while you're here. Warm your insides before you head out. Chilly spring we're having."

The German grabbed the proffered glass, downed the liquid in a single gulp, and handed the tumbler back to Bram.

"See, I only keep the finest. I'll get you another one."

A tall, fair-haired man, almost Aryan in appearance, grabbed the glass from the German. "Let me do it, Bram. Keep the others calm."

"Thank you, Simon. I'm grateful to you."

Simon slid past Zofia, and she shivered. The man had been to several of their meetings, and Bram acted as if he trusted him, but something about his lazy smile was as oily as a Danube eel.

After the tall Nazi drank two more glasses, the two soldiers under his command returned from their search. "Nothing out of place here, sir. Do you want us to bring some of them in for questioning?"

The officer waved them away. "That's enough." He slurred his words. "There's nothing here. A few Jews we'll deal with sooner or later. And a man with the best bottle of *pálinka* I've had in a long time."

The Nazi's two comrades steadied him as they exited the flat.

A din filled the room, and a wave of nausea overtook Zofia. She swayed, and Patrik steadied her. "That was too close."

"Bram has a way of falling into a manure pile and coming out smelling like a rose. Though if they had searched me, they would have found this." From the inside of her coat pocket, she pulled a sheet of paper.

Her latest writing.

Titled "In Defense of Those Who Assist Jews."

Chapter Three

Mid-May 1944

Patrik held tight to Éva's hand as they strolled down the Danube Promenade along the sparkling blue-green river that separated the residential area, Buda, from the commercial and retail area known as Pest. The dying light illuminated the Chain suspension bridge, and beyond it, the green-domed Buda castle. The early evening air was cool but not as cold as it had been.

With the ever-present threat of Allied bombing attacks, any quiet evening such as this needed to be enjoyed.

Patrik squeezed Éva's hand. "I'm sorry I've been busy these past few weeks. I've missed you."

She gazed at him. "What's been keeping you so preoccupied?"

He kissed the back of her soft hand. "You, *a múzsám*." Adding to the list of lies. In fact, his work with the Zionists took up much of his time.

"Me?" She widened her deep brown eyes.

"*Igen*, you. As I look forward to our wedding, my heart is filled with music, consuming me. All these melodies play in my head, light, bright, happy songs. Ones you could dance to. My fingers can't form the notes on paper fast enough."

"I'm sorry to have caused you such trouble."

"You are the best kind of trouble I could ever have."

He ushered her into a small, quiet café and drank in the odors of paprika and fried potatoes and onions. They evoked memories of his mother's cooking. No one rivaled her in the kitchen.

What he wouldn't give for one more of her home-cooked meals. A black-suited waiter met them at the door. "Good evening. Since you're early, you have your pick of tables. One near the window, perhaps?"

Patrik nodded, and the waiter led them to their seats. With the blackout shades yet to be drawn, they had a magnificent view of the Danube, the sunset's brush painting it red and gold.

After they settled in and placed their orders, Éva leaned forward. "Speaking of trouble—"

"That's never what you want to hear at the beginning of a conversation."

"*Nem*, but Patrik, she's in trouble."

"Who? Zofia?" Just like Éva to run ahead and finish a story before giving all the details.

She furrowed her brow. "Why would you think Zofia?"

"Because she was followed. If it isn't her, I need more information, *a múzsám*."

She fiddled with the pristine white napkin in her lap. "Székely Ersebet."

"Ah, your prized pupil and the star of my youth orchestra."

"She never, ever misses a lesson. I haven't seen her since the invasion two months ago. Has she been at practice?"

"*Nem*, I haven't seen her. But that doesn't mean you should go searching for her. She's Jewish. And she lives in Kistarcsa."

"What does that mean?"

"You haven't heard?" He leaned forward.

"*Nem*."

An example of what they had been talking about at the meeting the other night. Ignorance. Apathy. "She won't be coming anymore."

Her brown eyes clouded. "I don't understand."

"You've heard about the roundup of Jews outside of the city? Trains leave there every day, full of human cargo bound for a place much worse than the camp at Kistarcsa."

"That's what they say."

"It's the truth."

"Have you seen those camps?"

"*Nem.*" He couldn't. Prayed to God that he never would.

"Then you don't know for sure. I'm going to find her. If I need to bring her to the city, I will."

He banged on the table. The few other patrons in the café stared at them. "You won't. Do you hear me? Don't go anywhere near there." His mouth dried at the possibility of losing her too. He would lock her up somewhere safe if he had to.

She pushed her chair back, her shimmering eyes wide. "You're frightening me."

He forced himself to relax and keep his voice calm. "Good. You should be afraid. This isn't a game. This is life. I don't want anything to happen to you. We're about to get married and, Lord willing, have children. What would I do without you?"

"You could come with me to find her."

He couldn't. The images in his mind of what his family was suffering haunted him as it was. Taking Éva to one of these camps would only intensify his nightmares.

To protect the identity he'd constructed with such care, he couldn't let her discover his secret. "Neither of us will go. I understand you and your heart, and that's why I love you. But I'm too busy right now. You should be as well, with the last-minute arrangements for our wedding."

"But—"

"For now, stay out of trouble. Please. I can't lose you so close to when I can make you my wife." He kissed her hand, so soft and smooth.

Éva made no reply, but he read her silence. She was bent on tracking down her student. "Promise me—"

"Éva, my dear, what a surprise to see you here." A chunky, fair-haired woman clad in a black coat with a rose pin on the lapel stood at their table. "And who is this handsome fellow with you?"

Éva smiled, her grin tight and stiff. "This is my fiancé, Kedves Patrik. Patrik, this is an old schoolmate of mine, Lakatos Reka."

Reka grimaced. "It's nice to meet you, Patrik. But we aren't old."

"I only meant that we've known each other for a long time."

A dimple appeared in Reka's full cheek. "Of course we have, but it's been a while since I've seen you. Not since I moved to Nagyvárad. Now I'm back in the city on business. I travel here every Monday and then back to the border on Thursdays. How are you doing? And that handsome brother of yours?"

"He and his wife are wonderful. Very happy together."

Reka bent over and whispered, "Too bad she's Polish. And Jewish. He could have done so much better for himself."

Éva stiffened. Patrik squeezed his hands together. Reka was so typical of many Hungarians.

The two women chatted for a couple minutes more about people he'd never met, so he tuned them out. At long last, Reka waved and headed to her own table.

"You're friends with her?"

Éva shook her head. "She always did have a crush on him."

"On who?"

"Sorry. Guess I jumped ahead again. She always had her eye on Ernő. I never have been friends with her. We attended school together, but that was the extent of it. Ever since Ernő became involved with Zofia, she's popped back into our lives, despite the fact she lives in Nagyvárad."

Nagyvárad. The city where he'd been born, where his sisters still lived. A haunting melody arose in his mind, accompanied by images of his siblings' faces, of their lives in the ghetto.

Nem. He would not think of these things. Not now. He shut off the memories and concentrated on the woman in front of him.

An air raid siren blasted the evening's stillness.

Éva hunched over. "I hate those things."

Though their food hadn't yet arrived, Patrik laid a few *pengő* on the table, then assisted Éva out of her chair. Her face was as white as the Carpathian snows, and she bit her lower lip.

"Don't worry." He grasped her by the elbow. "We'll be fine."

"Do you even know where a shelter is?"

The waiter picked that moment to scurry to the front. "Get down! Get down!" He shoved Patrik and Éva to the ground. The roar of bomber engines crescendoed above the whine of the sirens.

Patrik blanketed Éva with his own body, then covered his head.

Whistling noises filled the air.

Explosions shook the café.

The window above them shattered.

Splinters of glass rained down like hail.

Beneath him, Éva shuddered.

"Hush now, I'm here. Everything will be fine. God will take care of us." *Please, Lord, do just that.*

The whistles and rumbles surrounded them for half a lifetime. The building shook a few more times but remained intact.

Then, as suddenly as the raid came, the bombers turned and headed home. Not until the all-clear sounded did Patrik move. He stood, shaking the glass from his back and his hair. He helped Éva to her feet and checked her for injuries. None visible.

She turned around so he could brush her back. "Oh God, *nem! Nem!*"

He followed her gaze.

There on the ground lay the black-suited waiter, his white shirt steeped with blood, an enormous, icicle-shaped shard of glass piercing his heart.

Patrik stepped between Éva and the waiter's lifeless body and wrapped her in the cocoon of his embrace. She trembled as she leaned against him. Bombs ripping apart homes and lives. Hunger. Fear. Pain. When would it all end?

"Hush now, it's over. You're fine." Patrik spoke the words into her blond hair as he rubbed her back. The action eased her thumping heart. After a while, her breathing returned to normal.

"Let's get you out of here."

"Shouldn't we alert the authorities?"

He bent and kissed her cheek. "The police will find him when they search the buildings. Right now they're busy giving aid to those who will benefit."

Reka rushed to them, her blue eyes standing out in her pale face, the red of her rose pin the same shade as the waiter's blood. "Oh my, oh my. That bomb almost killed us. Did you feel that? I've never been so scared in my life." She glued herself to Patrik's side and batted her eyelashes.

Éva swallowed the hard lump rising in her throat. "Are you injured?"

"My ears are ringing, and I think I twisted my ankle when I rushed over here. Could you take a peek at it, Patrik?"

"If you could run, then there's nothing wrong with it."

"But it's throbbing."

"I'm not a doctor."

"Please." Reka's nasal whine was worse than the screech of the air raid sirens.

Patrik crouched and palpated Reka's bare ankle. "No broken bones. I don't even see any bruising." He stood up again. "My prognosis is that you'll live."

Éva couldn't stop the smile that spread across her face. Good for Patrik.

"I don't know how I'm going to make it home." Reka pursed her full lips into an inelegant pout.

Éva sighed. "Her parents live around the corner."

"We'll walk you home." Patrik acted the gentleman while Éva longed to wave a magic wand and make Reka disappear.

"How gallant of you, Patrik. If you weren't engaged to a friend of mine, I'd snatch you for myself."

Éva fought to tamp down the heat rising in her chest. Not that she didn't trust Patrik. Still, when they were alone again, he would get an earful from her about his gallantry.

The three of them crunched their way through the café and out the door, Reka's limp almost convincing. Their walk wasn't far, five minutes at most, but the destruction along the way was unbelievable. Buildings that had weathered centuries of war and turmoil lay in heaps of rubble. One explosion had knocked a streetcar from its tracks. Éva averted her gaze from the bodies of passengers strewn about.

Patrik rubbed her shoulder. He could read her thoughts.

"Why didn't the alarm sound in time?" Eva shuddered. "No one had a chance to take cover."

"Who knows?" Patrik shook his head.

"Do the Germans want to see us all killed?"

Reka gave a hyena-like laugh. "Of course not. We have been loyal to them from the beginning. If not for that coward, President Horthy, our country would still be at peace. The Allies wouldn't be bombing us."

Patrik sighed. "I doubt that. The Soviets are land-hungry and eager to spread their ideology to the world. Hungary would be one tiny bite for their voracious appetite."

"Oooh." Reka sidled closer to Patrik. "Handsome and intelligent. I agree with every word you say about those fascist dogs. The Russians won't be satisfied until they've gobbled up every country in their way. That's why we need Germany."

Éva fisted her hands but held her tongue. Only by divine strength. Thank goodness, they arrived at Reka's parents' building in short order.

"How can I ever thank you, Patrik? You saved me."

"Hardly. No thanks are necessary."

Reka planted a big, noisy kiss on his cheek and hobbled into the building.

As soon as the door shut behind her, Patrik burst into laughter.

Éva huffed. "What do you find so amusing?"

"She is quite something."

"I'm happy you recognize it. To top it off, she's smitten with you. I'm glad you're all mine."

"Good thing, because she's just my type."

"You know how to lighten my mood." What had she done to deserve such a man in her life?

They set off for the main road toward the bridge. More destruction. Homes. Businesses. Places of worship. Lives lost. Other lives that would never be the same. Jew or Gentile, it didn't matter.

"Do you see my point now about how dangerous times have become?" He gestured at the devastation.

"It's just as dangerous sitting on the davenport in the living room."

He clamped his lips shut. What she said was true. Nowhere was safe now.

And the Allies had bombed Budapest, not Kistarcsa. She might even be safer in Kistarcsa.

Igen, she would search for Ersebet.

Chapter Four

Éva leaned out the trolley's window as it clanged through Budapest toward the outlying towns. Buildings bursting with amazing architecture from Baroque to Art Nouveau to charming, pastel-colored homes lined the tracks. This was the home of her birth, the city she loved. The place devastated by the arrival of the Nazis.

No longer the haven it had been a mere two months before.

Éva sat back against the seat and closed her eyes, but that only elicited images of German tanks rolling through her beloved Budapest and people cheering their conquering heroes. Thank goodness she had *Apu* and Patrik to keep her safe.

She shivered, opened her eyes, and focused on today's task while the overweight man next to her snored. Éva was off to search for Székely Ersebet. Every week for years, the girl and her mother had traveled into the city for lessons with the daughter of Bognár László, the famous clarinet maker.

Then she'd just stopped coming. Every attempt Éva had made to contact Ersebet or her family had met with failure.

The trip didn't take long. Soon the trolley slowed, then ground to a halt in Kistarcsa. Éva climbed down the steps, crossed the tracks, and searched for the address she had for Ersebet.

Tree-lined streets and whitewashed houses with red tile roofs greeted Éva. Such a charming place. An old woman with a colorful scarf on her head was sweeping her front step. Éva stopped and asked her for directions.

In short order, Éva located the Székelys' home. As she knocked on the door, it pushed opened.

"Hello? Is anyone here?"

No answer. What should she do? To walk in would be an invasion of privacy. But the door had been left ajar.

She stepped into the dank interior, and as her eyes adjusted to the dim light, she gasped at the sight. Dark spots on the gold-flecked papered walls marked where pictures had been removed. Almost no furniture remained but a battered armchair, its floral upholstery shredded, stuffing popping out. Papers littered the tile floor.

What had happened here?

Behind her, someone cleared his throat. Éva startled and spun around. In the doorway stood an older man, a few wisps of gray hair covering his head. He held a carved wood cane, his hand trembling. "Are you looking for the Székelys?"

"Do you know where they are?"

He nodded and took three or four steps into the home, crooking his gnarled finger for her to come closer. Her pulse pounded in her neck, but she crept closer to him anyway.

When he spoke, he kept his voice low. "Maybe a month or so ago, the Gestapo rounded up all the Jews in the town. There weren't many, but the few there were are all gone. Each and every one of them."

"Gone?" Éva swallowed hard.

"Disappeared into the night."

"Do you know where?"

"I don't like to say."

"Oh, sir, it would mean the world to me if you would let me know. I'm so very fond of Ersebet—the entire family, really—and I'm concerned for them."

"Well you should be." The old man straightened, his eyes flashing. "Those Nazis don't care one whit about those people. They're holding them at the camp at the edge of town."

"*Köszönöm* so very much." She pushed by him to get to the door.

"Where are you going?"

"To see Ersebet. She's missed several clarinet lessons and needs to catch up. If she can't come to me, I'll go to her."

"Ah, so you're the one who teaches her to play that thing." He flashed an almost-toothless grin. "I remember the squawking from this house in years gone by. My oh my, what a racket. But now she plays such beautiful music. Moves you. Stirs the soul."

"You understand, then, why she can't stop. In years to come, she'll have a brilliant career."

"But you can't go to the camp." He hobbled after her.

She stopped short. "Why not?"

He grabbed her by the arm, a little too tight for her comfort, pulled her close, and whispered, his words whistling in the gaps between his teeth. "Because those who go in never come out."

Éva stumbled backward. "You must be wrong."

"Where have you been the last five years? You know what the Germans are like."

If they were anything like Károly, with his hatred for the Jews . . .

Éva wrenched herself from his grasp. "Again, I thank you for the information. But I aim to find out for myself where Ersebet is, and I will see her." She had to do something to help her student.

"Don't say you weren't warned. You might be running to your own death."

Éva raced from the residence and down the street. The old man's demeanor had unsettled her more than anything he said. After several blocks, she stopped and caught her breath. Good thing she'd worn her flat-heeled oxfords. And good thing she had the lung capacity of a clarinetist. No matter what that man said, she would go to the camp and find Ersebet. See for herself what the Germans were up to.

After strolling to the outskirts of the town, she stumbled onto the prison. Rows upon rows of barracks filled the field, with a parade ground anchoring them. A high fence surrounded all of it. Armed guards in watchtowers kept track of the scores of prisoners.

Well, it would be a challenge to locate Ersebet. But nothing was impossible. Éva marched to the soldier in a yellow-green uniform at a brick guard gate. "Excuse me, I'm looking for Székely Ersebet."

He narrowed his hard, blue eyes. "What do you want with a Jew like her?" He softened his gaze. "You're a pretty young thing. With your blond hair, you could almost be German."

Perish the thought. She rubbed her arms as if to wipe away his leer. "I'm Ersebet's clarinet teacher. She's missed several lessons, and I was told I might find her here."

The guard chuckled, but it was not a pleasant sound. More like the grating of the metal trolley wheels against the steel tracks. "Pretty and naive. Only Jews go in. And those who help them. No one goes out."

She backed away. "So sorry to have bothered you."

"I get off duty at six."

"*Nem*, I must be home by then. Good day." She spit out the words as she dashed around the corner and out of the man's sight. Then she leaned against the fence to compose herself. Ersebet was in true danger. And so was Zofia. Just as before. Maybe even worse.

She was startled out of her thoughts by a tug at her sleeve. A little girl in a dark maroon coat had slipped her hand through the narrow gap in the fence. She grasped Éva's wrist. "Please help. We're so hungry."

Bognár *Úr* pulled out his tall dining room chair with scrolled arms and took his place at the head of the mahogany table. The rest of the family, including Éva's mother, her brother Ernő, and his wife Zofia, sat in their designated spaces. Patrik settled himself beside Éva and clasped her soft hand for prayer.

At least she hadn't spoken any more about her crazy idea to find Ersebet. A fruitless mission it would be. The girl wouldn't be playing her clarinet again for a long time. If ever.

Éva squeezed his hand. He closed his eyes as the words of the prayer floated over him, and his mind wandered to a few weeks from now when Éva would be his wife. *Lord, thank You for giving her to me, such a great blessing. She's all I have. Keep her from harm.*

The slightly spicy, tantalizing aroma of Bognár *Asszony*'s goulash set Patrik's stomach to rumbling. No one had made a better pot of it than his mother. But Éva's mother's was very good. He tightened his shoulders. He would never taste *Anya*'s cooking again.

A gentle nudge on his shins brought him from his musings, and he blinked his eyes open. The rest of the family was digging into the meal. Polished silverware clinked against the delicate china hand-painted with purple violets. He glanced at Éva. "What was that for?"

"You know." She winked.

Caught in the act.

"So, how did today's rehearsal go?"

Éva's question caught him with a full mouth. He chewed a tough piece of beef. At least it was meat. They didn't have that every day. "Fine, fine. I thought I told you about it."

"*Nem.* You're still preoccupied, I guess."

He was. Day by day, circumstances grew harder for the Jews. New laws. New regulations. And new word of packed trains heading north. "I suppose I am. Only a little while until the wedding." He flashed her a smile.

She returned it, her oval face flushed. These weeks couldn't go by fast enough.

"From what Patrik said, Hansi is doing well." Zofia pushed the meat around her plate.

"She is. She's making a fine addition to our symphony."

"That's wonderful." But none of Zofia's usual sparkle colored her words. In fact, she pushed away from the table after only a few bites. "Will you excuse me? I'm not feeling well." She rushed from the room and up the stairs where, a moment later, a door slammed shut.

"I'll check on her." Ernő dropped his napkin on the table and scampered after his wife.

Éva concentrated on her meal, also picking at her meat. "I had an interesting day today."

From beneath his bushy eyebrows, Bognár *Úr* studied Éva. "You don't say."

Patrik picked up his glass to sip his water.

"I traveled to Kistarcsa in search of one of my students."

Patrik spluttered and coughed, his cut-crystal glass still in his hand. "I told you not to go." He loved her spunk, but her head-strongness would get her in trouble.

She spoke to her father instead. "Ersebet is very talented, but she hasn't been to a lesson since the invasion."

Bognár *Asszony* dabbed her lips with her napkin. "So you poked around there? Patrik was right to warn you."

"She's in the camp the Nazis have set up," Éva continued. "Those places are real. They aren't figments of our imaginations or products of Allied propaganda."

The rich goulash that had sent Patrik's stomach rumbling moments ago now churned in it. What she must have seen. He set down his glass.

"Oh *Apu*, it's terrible what they're doing to the people. They're half-starved, even after just a few weeks, and many of them don't have coats or proper shoes."

Patrik didn't want to hear. His sisters in Nagyvárad lived in such a place. From his sources, the ghetto there was overcrowded, infested, unbearable. So many died, there weren't enough places to bury them.

Éva wiped her mouth with her napkin. "While I stood against the fence—"

"What were you doing against the fence?" Patrik gripped his silver fork and knife so hard his knuckles turned white.

"You should have seen her. She had such a sweet, round face, brown curls, and the biggest soft brown eyes you've ever seen."

Patrik blew out a breath. "Who?"

"The young girl who slipped her hand through the fence and took mine. She asked if I had any food." Éva turned to Patrik. "We have to help her. If we pool our ration coupons, I could return there with a few loaves."

"Absolutely not." Bognár *Asszony* shot to her feet and grabbed Éva's plate, even though she hadn't finished her dinner.

Patrik set his fork on the side of his dish. "I forbid you to put your life at risk."

"You can't forbid me. We aren't even married."

"But I'm still your father, and I forbid you." Bognár *Úr's* voice was soft, but it filled the room.

"What if Zofia were in that situation?"

"She's not." Éva's mother removed more plates from the table.

"We've heard the rumors. Now we know they're true. The Jews are going to places they'll never return from. We have to help them. Don't you agree, *Apu?*"

"Your mother has spoken. You will not disobey her."

"I'm twenty-three. Quit treating me like a child."

"I, for one, agree with both of your parents." Patrik threw his napkin on the table and stood, fighting to keep from raising his voice. "If you had been caught, what do you think would have happened to you?"

"Nothing. Because a guard did see me."

"What?" Bognár *Úr* and Patrik bellowed at the same time.

"He . . . he . . ." She pushed away from the table. "It doesn't matter. He did me no harm. The Jews inside, they are the ones being persecuted. All I want to do is bring them a little bread.

Maybe it's not much, but it's something. A bit of Christian kindness in the middle of a world gone mad."

Ernő rejoined them in the dining room, his jaw tight. "Keep the noise down. Zofia isn't well."

She rushed to her brother's side. "Tell them to allow me to bring food to the Jews in the camp at Kistarcsa."

"Why would you want to do such a thing?"

"To help people like Zofia."

"It's too dangerous. Didn't you learn anything from Károly? Stay away from people like him, people bent on destroying the Jews and anyone associated with them."

"We are already associated with a Jewish woman, and I wouldn't want it any other way. If Zofia was in danger, you would want someone to give her aid."

There was no way Patrik was going to allow Éva to return to the camp. By doing so, she would put her life in jeopardy. And he would lose what little good he had left in his life.

"Turning our faces from the problem has gotten us in this situation to begin with. Too many Christians never spoke up about the anti-Jewish laws Hungary enacted over the years. Too many of them, like Károly, hate the Jews. Now look what's happening." Éva stomped from the room, the heels of her dark brown pumps clacking on the parquet floors.

When she got to her bedroom, she slammed her door. Patrik cringed at the noise.

She was right. Much, much too right.

And, stubborn as she was, she would do something about it.

Next time, though, the guard wouldn't let her get away.

Chapter Five

The trolley halted at the corner near Éva's home, a crowd of people already on board. She ascended the metal steps, holding to the cold rail with one hand and the handle of her large, cumbersome bass clarinet case with the other.

Once in the car, she banged her way down the aisle. A broadly built middle-aged man with a handlebar mustache clinging to one of the straps stopped her. "Would you like me to hold that for you, madam?"

She tipped the case so it was vertical and clutched it. "*Nem, köszönöm.* I'm fine."

"Are you sure? I'm happy to help."

"It's the only instrument I have. I don't want it to get damaged or to fall if the trolley makes a sudden stop."

"Very well."

Éva placed her instrument against the window and plopped onto the seat beside it. Though the tram was almost full, it was best that she sit alone for this trip and not have anyone asking too many questions.

Before long, the trolley clanged down the street. Éva had told Zofia she had to take her instrument to her father to be repaired. With any luck, she would return home before Zofia did and asked *Apu* questions.

And before she raised any suspicions with Patrik. Imagine him saying she couldn't come here. She loved that he watched out for her, was protective of her, took care of her. She trusted him and relied on him. Couldn't he see, though, how important this was to her?

For two weeks she'd saved her bread coupons, enough to buy several loaves. Loaves now tucked inside her instrument case. She leaned against it and closed her eyes. Could anyone else smell the yeasty goodness contained within?

The ride didn't last long. Before she knew it, they'd arrived at Kistarcsa. This time, she didn't need to ask for directions.

The barbed-wire fence enclosed hundreds of people, maybe thousands, their eyes vacant. More than just Jews from Kistarcsa. The Germans must have brought them from other villages.

How had it come to this? Just months ago, these people had been living life. Loving. Laughing.

Now? Every vibrant fiber of their being had been sucked from them. Even their clothes were dark and hung lifeless on their scrawny bodies.

As she drew near, she gagged at the stench of body odor, feces, and decaying flesh. Yet her fellow countrymen turned a blind eye to what has happening. They had done so for years.

What good would her little loaves do for this mass of people?

Five loaves. If Jesus could use such a small amount of bread to feed five thousand men, then He could use what she brought to help someone. Even one person.

Remaining some distance from the fence, she ambled the length of it, searching for the brown-haired girl in the dark maroon coat. No sign of her.

Éva spun around and made her way in the opposite direction. Wait, that was her. The cherub's not-quite-as-round face lit up when she spotted Éva, and she waved in recognition.

Checking to make sure no guards were watching, Éva slunk toward the girl.

"You came back." They spoke to each other through the fence, barbed wire separating them, the blood of one condemning her to remain inside, the blood of the other allowing her to live her life.

"I made a promise, and I always keep my promises."

"What's that?"

"It's the case from my bass clarinet. It's much bigger than my B-flat clarinet, the one I usually play."

"Why did you bring that?"

Éva leaned in closer, so the child would hear her quiet answer. "Because I have a special surprise inside."

"I love surprises." The young girl's eyes widened, and her loud response drew attention from the other prisoners.

Éva glanced at the guard. He stared in the opposite direction. That was a relief. "Shh, you must be very quiet to get it."

She nodded.

Éva opened the case and drew out the bread. The child gasped. "Is that all for me?"

"I hope you'll be generous and share with your family, at least."

A woman not much older than Éva herself stepped up, her brown tweed coat hanging on her thin frame, her cheekbones jutting from her narrow face. "Who are you?"

"My name is Éva. Is this your daughter?"

"What do you want with us?"

"To help you."

The woman studied the bread in Éva's case. "You think that pittance of an offering is going to do us any good?" She spit on the ground.

Éva's shoulders slumped. Of course, it had been silly of her to think she could do some good here. Jesus may have multiplied the loaves, but he was the Son of God. She was nothing more than a music teacher. "I wish it could be more, but it's all I can come by right now. I'll return as often as I can with as much as I can. Even if I help just you and your daughter, it's worth it."

The woman smacked her lips. "It does look good."

"And no worms, *Anya*."

Worms? They ate infested food? "I promise to do what I can for you."

"And she always keeps her promises."

"By the way, do you know Ersebet? She was a pupil of mine, and I understand she's a prisoner here."

"I knew the Székelys."

"Knew them?"

"They left on the transport yesterday or the day before. I forget which."

Transports. Her breath hitched. "Headed where?"

"The whispers are that the trains go to Auschwitz."

Nem, not Ersebet. All her talent gone to waste because of what? The blood that flowed through her veins. None of this was fair. *God in heaven, don't You care about Your people anymore?*

"You there, what are you doing?" A guard yelled in perfect Hungarian from the tower on the corner closest to them.

Her heart rate kicked up to a nice allegro tempo. "I have to go. I'll return soon."

Éva backed up a half dozen big steps, and even though her hands shook, with all her might she chucked the bread over the rounded loops of barbed wire at the top of the fence. Then she closed her case and, not bothering to latch it, tucked it under her arm, and sprinted for the tram, praying all the while that no one followed.

The bell in the music studio announced Patrik's entrance. Gorgeous, velvety, deep notes floated from one of the lesson rooms. He stopped for a moment, drinking in the flowing, rolling melody of the clarinet. Éva was talented, no doubt, and the sound her father's clarinets produced was unrivaled. The piano, probably played by Zofia, provided a beautiful accompaniment.

He strolled toward the room and stood in the doorway, the music washing over him. When the piece ended, Éva peered up at him from the sheet music and smiled. "Hello. We didn't hear you come in."

"Hello yourself. I was enjoying the performance." A residual tension hung in the air like a morning mist. Patrik hadn't seen Éva since the night she had announced she'd gone to Kistarcsa to search for Ersebet. She hadn't come out of her room until he was ready to leave that evening. Even then, her hug was wooden, her kiss nothing more than a peck.

"I'm sorry for being sore at you." She turned her mouth into a frown.

He maneuvered into the small room, the piano almost filling it, and wriggled to her side. "I am too."

"We shouldn't be disagreeing so soon before the wedding. Not ever, really. It was wrong of me to run to my room and pout like a child."

"I understand. We're all on edge. So much is happening in our lives and in our world."

She snuggled against him. "So you understand why I had to go to Kistarcsa?"

He stepped away. "Please tell me you didn't go back. How can I keep you safe if you don't stay put?"

"I did go." She stared at the black-and-white tile floor and bit her lip. "You were right. Trains are leaving there, emptying the camp. Ersebet and her family were among those who left."

The news was what he feared, what he had tried to deny. If he didn't believe it was true, even though deep inside he knew it was, then it couldn't be happening. But it was. Not thinking about the atrocities didn't make them go away. Somehow, someway, he had to convince his sisters to leave. Before it was too late. Before the Nazis emptied the ghetto they occupied.

Why wouldn't Éva listen to him? Was she bent on getting herself killed? "I told you not to."

"You said yourself we shouldn't argue, so let's not."

She spun around, her back to him, but he turned her to face him. He drew her close, so close her heart beat against his, pounding a rhythm that would find its way into his next composition.

She fisted her hands and beat on his chest. "It was awful. So much suffering. Why, why do humans commit such unspeakable crimes against innocent people?"

"Because they are evil. One day they will receive justice."

"How long will that take?"

If only he had an answer. "God knows. Don't you see? I couldn't bear it if one of them hurt you in any way." They had already hurt too many he loved.

She clung to him for a long while. "I want to help. I'm going back."

Just a few weeks remained until their wedding. Perhaps then she would forget about Kistarcsa. He kissed her sweet, warm cheek.

"That's enough, you two." Zofia rose from the piano bench. "I've sat here long enough and let you have a moment. You're off early today, Patrik."

He released Éva. "I couldn't concentrate. Not when I'm about to marry this beautiful woman."

"Always the charmer." Éva giggled.

"Ah, young love." Zofia shook her head. "Why don't you head home? I'm sure you must have plenty of wedding details to discuss. I'll lock up and be along in a few minutes."

"We'll wait for you." With Germans patrolling the streets, keeping watch for Jews to harass and arrest, it wasn't safe for Zofia to be out by herself, especially this late in the day. Patrik wouldn't forgive himself if anything happened to Zofia either.

"Nonsense. You don't want me tagging along. I remember how it was just before Ernő and I were married. We wanted no one else but each other." She winked at Patrik.

Perhaps she needed some time alone to work on one of her pamphlets. Not that it was safe for her to do so.

Éva kissed Zofia on the cheek. "You're right. But don't be long. *Anya* is sure to have dinner ready soon." She dismantled her clarinet and set the pieces in the case.

"I won't be. Just one or two more things to take care of before I'm done here."

Things Patrik knew about but Éva didn't. "If you're sure you'll be fine without us."

"I'll be less than a block behind you. Now scoot before it gets any later."

Patrik held out Éva's purple wool coat for her, then from the shelf above picked a small blue hat with a brown feather jutting up.

Éva laughed. "Don't you know me at all?"

"What?"

"Just like a man. That's Zofia's hat, not mine." She grabbed her own red one and set it on an angle on her head.

Ushering Éva into the chilly Budapest twilight, Patrik spied four or five Nazi soldiers in olive drab uniforms down the street ahead of them. Men with eagle eyes. Perhaps he and Éva should wait for Zofia. If she was stopped and the Germans discovered who she was, her life would be worth nothing.

Éva touched his arm, drawing him from his thoughts. "You might as well be on the moon."

"I'm sorry. Were you saying something?"

"Just hoping the weather warms before Saturday."

"*Igen*, I hope it does."

"Still so far away." Éva's voice was soft and lacked indictment.

How easily he could tell her about the enormous weight that pressed on his shoulders. To share it with her would be freeing. For him, anyway. But if he did, she would only worry and might want to join him in his high-risk mission. "I have a lot on my mind. Nervous about the wedding, I suppose."

"What do you have to be nervous about?" She stared at him with those puppy-like eyes he couldn't resist. Had never been able to. Never would be able to.

He focused on the bustling street in front of them. "I want to make you happy. I suppose that's what has made me apprehensive. More than anything in the world, I don't want to disappoint you. You are *a múzsám*, you know. The inspiration for the music I write." He turned to her once more. This much was true.

"You could never disappoint me." She pulled him to a stop and caressed his cheek, her fingers soft and warm against his skin. "I only hope I won't let you down."

"What could ever make you think that?"

"I am a little bossy. And I don't know how to cook very well. And I tend to be messy. I'd rather practice my clarinet than clean the house."

"I already know those things, and I love you anyway. Although I do wish you could cook as well as your mother." He worked to appear serious.

She batted at him. "Such a tease you are. At least our life together won't be boring."

"*Nem*, that it will not be."

Boring? Definitely not. Dangerous? He was going to do everything in his power to keep it from being that.

Zofia meandered around the small music studio, pushing in the piano bench in one room and tidying the music books in the racks in the store area. If Ernő's mother wasn't waiting for her to eat dinner, she would stay and get some writing done. More pamphlet ideas swirled in her head. So many, she couldn't write them fast enough.

But Ernő already questioned her going out in the evening. There wouldn't be a good enough excuse for missing the family supper tonight. She jotted a few ideas on a slip of paper and hid it underneath a loose floorboard.

Music haunted the space. Even though she was the only one here, the sounds of plinking piano keys and the warmth of clarinet tunes filled her mind.

At least it loosened the knot in her stomach, the ever-present apprehension that someone had their sights on her. Followed her. Knew all about her.

She shook her head. She couldn't give in to these imaginations.

Just because it had happened before in Poland didn't mean it would happen again here. Still, she hadn't slept well since the invasion. When the Germans marched across the border, the small bubble of security around her had burst.

With a sigh, she switched out the lights and locked the door. After she deposited the keys in her coat pocket, she started down the street toward the home she shared with her husband, his parents, and his sister Éva.

Like ants on a picnic blanket, Nazi soldiers teemed on the sidewalk. She huddled deeper into her coat and quickened her steps. Her skin crawled, like someone was watching her. Just like the other day. Her heartbeat soon matched the rapid tempo of her footfalls.

Up ahead, there they were, Éva and Patrik. They stood in the middle of the walk, young lovers oblivious to the world around them. If she could reach them, she might be able to breathe again.

And then someone grabbed her around the waist, pulled her tight against his solid chest, his arms bulging as he pinned her against him. The stench of stale beer on his breath choked her sob. "Good evening. If you want to live, you'll be quiet."

Chapter Six

Warmth flooded Éva as she and Patrik entered her family's tidy, well-appointed home. He helped her slip her coat from her shoulders and hung it on the hook by the door. Hand in hand, they trekked down the long hallway that opened into a large, white lounge with soaring ceilings and tall windows overlooking a courtyard.

Apu sat on the yellow, floral-print settee, the evening paper spread in front of him, while Ernő had pulled the matching chair against the radio in the corner, the volume turned low. He must be listening to the forbidden BBC. Patrik shook *Apu's* hand and settled himself in the green armchair across from her father. "What's the news from the world?"

Apu smoothed his graying mustache. "From the world, Ernő is listening to find out. According to the Germans," he rattled the newspaper in his hand, "all is well."

"And we know that's not the case." Patrik sighed.

"Éva, is that you?" *Anya* called from the kitchen.

Let the men talk politics. Éva left them discussing the new Jewish laws that would soon affect Zofia and found her mother bent over the stove, the aromas of paprika and onions wafting from it, sending Éva's stomach to rumbling.

Anya spun, and slight crinkles appeared around her eyes as she raised her lips in a half smile. "There you are. My, your cheeks are red. I hope you aren't getting sick."

Perhaps the flush lingered from Patrik's attention to her on the street. "*Nem*, but it is rather chilly. Still not much of a sign of a true spring."

"If you would set the table, I'm almost finished here." *Anya* stirred the contents of the bubbling pot.

"Okay. Zofia was closing up when we left."

"I hope she hurries, before dinner gets cold."

The warm, mildly spicy scent of chicken paprikash filled the air. Éva shared *Anya*'s hope. "She said she would be right behind us. I expect her any second."

"Good. After we eat, I'd like you to try on your wedding dress so I can see if there are any last-minute alterations I need to make."

A thrill rushed up Éva's spine, like her fingers up her instrument in a run. "Can you believe the wedding is just a few weeks away?" Finally her dream would come true. She could put her nightmare behind her and live her life with a wonderful, trustworthy man.

Anya returned her attention to dinner preparations, her voice husky. "My little girl, all grown up into such a beautiful, fine young woman. And so talented too. It has been nice having my entire family under one roof. There is nothing so happy as for a mother to see her children grown and well, and at the same time, nothing so sad as they leave and life changes."

Éva hugged *Anya*, then grabbed a handful of forks from the drawer. "Patrik and I will only be a few blocks away. You'll probably see as much of us after the wedding as before. You know I don't cook as well as you."

"You'll learn. Whatever you put your mind to, you work toward it with your entire being. Even with the rationing, I have no doubt you and Patrik won't starve."

They would have to see about that.

Anya pulled a serving bowl from the cabinet next to the stove, and Éva completed setting the gleaming mahagony table.

"That's everything. Will you please call everyone to dinner?"

"Oh, did you hear Zofia come in?"

"*Nem*, I assumed she was here since you said she was right behind you."

"I'll see." Éva straightened a couple forks on her way out of the dining room into the lounge. The men huddled around the radio. "Ernő, is Zofia home? Has she gone to your room?"

All three men turned and stared at her. Her brother shook his head. "I haven't seen her."

Éva laughed. "Too engrossed in current events to even notice your wife walk through the door. Let's promise never to be like that, Patrik."

Patrik didn't respond to her joke. Rather, he furrowed his forehead and clasped his hands together. The smooth sounds of the English words were the soft background music to the silence. Men. *Igen*, what was happening in the world was important, but so was your wife.

She left them to worry about current events, climbed the stairs, and because the door stood ajar, peeked into the bedroom Ernő and Zofia shared. The large bed occupied most of the space, the pale blue spread pulled over the pillows. Their wedding picture, both of them with sparkling eyes, kept watch from the small bedside table.

No Zofia.

Where could she be? She should have been home. The bathroom door was open, the room dark. The house wasn't large enough for Zofia to disappear.

Éva scurried down the steps and returned to the lounge. The men had risen and were making their way to the dining room. "She's not here."

Everyone turned to her. Ernő frowned. "What do you mean, she's not here? I thought you said she was right behind you."

"She was. That is, she was supposed to be. She said she was going to lock up and follow us. There isn't that much to closing the shop." Éva's stomach clenched.

Patrik's brown eyes widened. "I agree. Something about this isn't sitting right."

Ernő's face drained of all its color, and his voice shook. "We have to find her. Who knows what those Germans might do? How could you leave a Jewish woman alone on the streets?"

"She practically shoved us out. Told us she'd be fine." Éva stepped toward him, but he backed away, closer to the dark, quiet radio.

"Fine? Is this fine? This is my wife we're talking about. My vulnerable wife."

Anya came behind Éva and rubbed her shoulders. "He's just worried."

"We shouldn't have left without her." How could they have done that? They knew better.

Patrik and Ernő headed for the door, shrugging on their coats as Ernő turned the knob. Éva broke from *Anya*'s hold and hurried after them. "Wait for me. I'm coming with you."

Patrik grasped her by the upper arm and stopped her. "You are doing no such thing. We don't know what we're going to find. Stay with your parents. Perhaps she will come home while we're out."

"Please, let me. She's my sister-in-law and my best friend. If something has happened to her . . ."

"Do as I ask." He brushed his lips against her cheek and, like a prayer, added a near breathless "please."

Ernő stepped into the hall. "We're wasting time. Let's go, Patrik. Éva, ring the shop and all her friends. Perhaps one of them detained her."

"Have dinner warm and ready for us when we return. I'm sure we won't be long." With that, Patrik ducked through the entrance and shut the door behind him.

The sound reverberated in Éva's pounding head. For the longest time, she stood and stared at the door. She had no other choice but to put her hope in Patrik and her brother. They were good, strong, smart men. They would find Zofia. No doubt about it.

Apu came behind her and gathered her to himself like when she was a child afraid of a thunderstorm. "Standing here won't bring them home any faster. Come into the living room. They'll be back before you know it. God is watching over her."

She believed that, but it was comforting to have Patrik and Ernő searching for her and *Apu* here beside her, taking care of things at home. "Of course, you're right. But we were just talking about how dangerous times were getting for Zofia. Anything could've happened to her." Éva straightened her shoulders as if she were getting ready to perform a clarinet piece. "*Nem*, there's no use in thinking the worst. After I make the calls, I'll start warming the water for a bath. She's bound to be frozen through when she gets home."

She would come home. She had to.

The German pressed Zofia against his well-muscled body. She repressed the scream that bubbled in her throat and begged for release. This had been bound to happen, had been coming. But not this soon. Not now. Not when she harbored a secret she was about to reveal to Ernő.

She wriggled as he held her firm in his grasp. While she wouldn't yell, she wouldn't go with him without a fight. A fight for Ernő, a fight for Éva, a fight for all those she loved.

A fight for the secret life she carried within her.

The man stuck something cold and hard into her side. The fight flooded from her. She stilled, apart from forcing her feet to move forward. Right now, this is how she had to fight.

He pushed her down a side street and, after a couple of blocks, led her into an apartment building's courtyard. Very little light filtered into this hidden square in the middle of the city. With a shove, he threw her into an even darker corner behind a group of still-leafless trees. A cold breeze blew a strand of loose hair into her mouth.

"What do you want with me?" She spit out the hair and the words.

The man stood toe to toe with her, his black pistol jammed into her chest. "I want you to tell me everything."

The cold metal of the weapon pressed on her flesh and sent a shiver through her. "I don't know what you're talking about."

He narrowed his steel-gray eyes. "But you do. I know who you are and what you've been doing."

"If you know it all, why do I have to tell you anything?"

Her smart remark earned her a slap across the face. Her eyes watered.

"You are Katona Marika, are you not?"

"I have never heard of her." How had they figured out the connection? Who had tipped them off? Did they have Patrik and Bram too?

"Liar. I want names and places and specific activities. Provide me with that information, and it may go well with you. Refuse to cooperate to your own detriment."

Her knees shook and she collapsed to the ground. She couldn't. She just couldn't. But if she didn't . . .

Her stomach rolled about in her midsection. She couldn't be sick. Couldn't let him see that he affected her. Then again, she already had.

What about Ernő? He had to be missing her. Perhaps he was even out searching for her. He'd never find her here. It would be better if he didn't. But maybe she should have told him her news. At the time, with what she had planned, she thought it best to keep her secret. To tell him at the right time, in a special way. If only she had. Now it might be too late.

The German tapped his foot, the brown loafer beating out an irregular rhythm.

One that matched the pounding of her heart.

A muscle in his cheek jumped. "I'm tired of waiting. Give up the information. Now."

She glanced at the scrolled iron balconies that ringed the three-story-high courtyard, jutting out from dirty yellow brick. The wind rattled the bare branches together. If she screamed, would anyone in those flats hear her? Would anyone care?

Károly had committed unspeakable acts against Jews. Was this man like him?

The Nazi smirked. "Don't look for your salvation to come from the people living here. We rid the place of Jews the night after we arrived in the city. Nothing but Germans residing in the complex now."

She swallowed hard and scrunched her forehead. She had to think. There had to be a way out. If only she could put a plan together. But her muddled brain couldn't concoct a reasonable escape. Not one that would work. *God, help me!*

The man stepped toward her, his gun still trained on her chest. "I've been patient long enough. It's time you start talking."

"Imrédy Miklós. You'll find him in the flat on the corner of Dohány and Rózsa Streets. Lists of names, printing presses, the information you're after, it's all there."

The man worked his mouth, as if trying to decide whether to believe her. Zofia prayed he would. Imrédy Miklós was a figment of her imagination. Perhaps her little lie would buy her the time she needed to make an escape.

"Get up." The Nazi yanked her to her feet by her hair, pain shooting throughout her scalp. She bit her lip to avoid crying out. "Let's go." He thrust the gun into the small of her back, and she stumbled ahead of him to the street.

What had she done? Her story wouldn't check out, and her life would be forfeit. She should have never told him anything. Wasn't that the first rule she learned when she joined the Zionist Youth? How stupid was she?

When this German got to the building, he would make a search and find nothing. As far as she knew, no Jews lived in that area. Especially no one involved in forging documents and printing pamphlets. Not that she would purposely lead him to any of her compatriots.

Could she make a run for it? Why had she worn her favorite pair of pumps today? There was no way she could outdistance him.

"Show me the way. And hurry up about it."

What else could she do? She headed in the general direction of the address she had given him, acting like she was out for an early evening jaunt. In a few short minutes they crossed the Danube River and arrived at the intersection. "Which building is it?" The German's words were a low growl.

She pointed at one of the stone buildings with arched windows, her hand shaking. As fast as possible, she lowered it and held it to her side.

"Take me to the flat."

He shoved her, forcing her forward, and they crossed the street to the building. Inside? She had to go inside with him? She couldn't do this. *Nem.* What would he do to the occupants? Was she about to sacrifice a stranger's life to save her own?

She couldn't allow that to happen—again.

They stepped through the entry into the hall, and Zofia edged near the first door on the left and knocked. A young, brown-haired woman not much older or taller than Zofia herself answered. Before she could draw in a breath to say anything, the Nazi thrust her into the apartment ahead of him, slamming the door behind them.

He released his grip on Zofia and moved around the living room, pulling out the drawers from the little desk in the corner and dumping the contents onto the floor. Papers fluttered, ink spilled, pens clattered.

The young woman backed up a few steps. "Who are you? What are you doing here?"

The German waved the gun in their direction. "Shut up. You know what this is about. I will find what I am looking for. Sit over there and be quiet."

Zofia sat on the plain blue couch next to the woman. She attempted to mouth words of explanation, but the woman shook her head. She didn't understand. How could Zofia apologize?

A wave of nausea rushed over her. She jumped to her feet, darted down the hall to the bathroom, and was sick. She clung to the porcelain toilet bowl, shaking so much she couldn't stand.

From the living room came the Nazi's harsh voice. "Where is she? Where did she go?"

The woman answered in a trembling voice. "I don't know. I don't know who she is. I don't know who you are or why you're in my home. Please, go away. I don't have anything you want. I'm innocent."

"Silence. Tell me where she is."

Zofia had to get out of here. Now.

She struggled to her feet and willed her legs to hold her upright. She was trapped in this tiny room. No way out.

She glanced around. The window just to the right of the toilet. Could she fit through it? Could she even get it open? They were on the first floor, so the fall shouldn't be far. It was her only chance.

Ever so quietly, she slid open the lock and tugged on the sash. The window stuck for just a moment before a rush of spring air burst in. Zofia slipped off her shoes, stepped on the toilet lid, and wriggled through the opening. *Oomph.* She dropped to the ground and fell to her knees.

From inside the apartment, shots rang out.

Nem, nem! God, nem! What had she done?

An innocent life sacrificed to save her own. And it wasn't the first. The memory of the last time haunted her. *Please, God, let there be no more.*

Chapter Seven

*E*rnő led the way down the street overflowing with people heading home after a long day's work, weaving in and out of the crowd, setting a frenetic pace. Patrik scurried along, bumping into people on the street, mumbling apology after apology.

Ernő turned to speak over his shoulder. "Let's check the music studio. Perhaps a student came in late and delayed her. Or maybe she wasn't feeling well. She hasn't been herself the past couple of weeks."

They reached the storefront in record time. The late afternoon sun glinted off the spotless window, but inside it was dark. Ernő scrubbed his stubbled face. "The door is locked."

Patrik clapped him on the back. "That doesn't mean she's not in there."

Ernő drew the key from his pants pocket. His hands shook as he worked to insert it into the lock. Patrik snatched it from him and opened the door. Ernő glanced at him and bit his lip. "What if—"

"There's no reason to think the worst." Just to be sure, though, Patrik pushed by Ernő, stepped in first, and allowed his eyes to adjust to the dimness. The racks of music, the chairs arranged in a little waiting area, the sales counter along the back of the room—everything was in its place.

Ernő crept in behind him. "Zofia! Zofia! Are you here, *szerelmem?*"

Silence hung over them. Ernő called out again with the same result.

They searched the back room where Éva and Zofia took their breaks and completed their paperwork. Again, not a cup remained in the sink or a paper on the table. Nothing was amiss.

Ernő grabbed the back of one of the kitchen chairs. "She left here just fine. So where is she? What happened to her between the studio and home?"

"We'll retrace the routes she might have taken. Maybe she fell and twisted her ankle. We'll find her. Don't worry."

"It's far too late to tell me that. Even if she met up with a friend, she would have phoned. Something is wrong. I feel it deep in my bones." Ernő mussed his curly blond hair. "Since the day we married, I've never not known where my wife is. She's my everything. You don't understand."

But Patrik did understand. If Éva had disappeared, Patrik would be frantic, beside himself. Unthinkable not to have his muse, his love, his life. Ernő was calmer than Patrik would be under these circumstances. Patrik wouldn't be able to breathe. He might lose his mind.

"I keep imagining her out there alone. Is she hurt? Scared? Still alive?" Ernő's eyes, the same eyes as Éva's, shimmered in the dull light.

Patrik had no reply. A few afternoons ago, while Éva was out, he and Zofia had discussed this very scenario. What to do when the Nazis caught up with her. What to do when they discovered her truth.

Because, despite his assurances to Ernő, what happened to Zofia was clear.

They would not find her sitting on the sidewalk with a twisted ankle.

The Nazis had figured out her secret.

But he couldn't tell Ernő what was happening. Couldn't clue

him in or suggest where to search. If Ernő knew what Zofia had been up to, he would discover Patrik's own secret.

There was one spot he wanted to check that Ernő couldn't come. "To save time, let's split up. You take one of the possible routes home, and I'll take the other. We'll meet at your place in thirty minutes. I'm sure one of us will locate her in the meantime."

Ernő nodded, his face drawn.

"We will find her." *Please, God, let us find her.*

They exited the studio, securing the door behind them. Ernő hustled to the left, winding through the crowd, craning his head to search for his wife.

When he had disappeared into the throng, Patrik started in the opposite direction. He didn't want to go there. Didn't want to find Zofia there. But the Gestapo headquarters was her likeliest location.

The sun dipped lower as he picked his way down the busy sidewalk. If God blessed them, there would be no bombing raids tonight, at least not this early.

He had gone several blocks when he noticed a commotion up ahead. His height afforded him a good view. A woman wearing a dark blue hat with a brown feather was weaving among the people, shoving them aside, moving as fast as possible.

Wait a minute. Wasn't that the hat he'd tried to hand to Éva? The one she'd teased him about? That meant it belonged to Zofia. He thrust his way through the throng in her direction. A moment later and he reached her and strode alongside her. "Zofia."

She either didn't hear him or ignored him.

"Zofia." A little louder this time. Thank goodness for his long legs. Fast though she was moving, he easily matched her pace.

"Zofia. It's me. Patrik."

She stopped right in his path. He bumped into her and grabbed her in a hug. "You're safe."

With her bare foot, she kicked his shin, but without a shoe, she did little damage.

"Zofia, stop. Whatever happened, it's over. I'm here. No one is going to hurt you now."

She stilled in his arms. "Patrik?"

"*Igen, igen.*"

"They found me. We have to get home. Have to warn the others."

He led her around the corner to a quiet side street but kept his voice low. "Who found you?"

"This German grabbed me right on the street, demanding information about our group. They know who I am. I denied it and fed the man false information. I took him to a location where I knew there would be no Jews. He was ransacking the building when I slipped out the bathroom window. I heard gunshots." Her eyes glazed over as if reliving the horror, both from tonight and from many years ago.

"Then you can't go home. That's the first place they'll search for you. You'll endanger everyone there."

"I have to warn them. This can't end like it did with my mother. It can't. I won't allow it. Ernő has to get away. All of them do."

"You're risking your life, and you might be leading the Germans straight to your family. Did you ever think you might be followed? They know where you work. How long before they figure out where you live?"

"*Nem.* I'm going home. My mother paid with her life because of me. Because I didn't tell her the Gestapo was after me. That will not happen again. Do you hear? I won't allow it. I have to tell them what is going on. Tell them to leave. Immediately. Even now, we're wasting time. The Gestapo might be on their way to the house at this moment."

She wrenched from his grasp and raced away from him toward home. Even sprinting, he couldn't keep up with her. Sheer determination must have fueled her.

But by the time they arrived at the Bognárs' house, it was too late.

Ernő paced in front of his family's three-story home. Where was Patrik? And Zofia? When they parted, he said they would meet here in thirty minutes. Why hadn't they returned?

Sweat soaked the back of his shirt despite the chilly temperatures. He climbed the steps to the house, ready to turn the doorknob. Footsteps clicked on the street, and he turned, praying to see Patrik and Zofia. But it was only an old man out walking his little dog before the nightly air raids.

Still, Ernő bounded down the stairs, glanced both ways down the road. Empty. This time, he flew into the house. Éva, *Apu*, and *Anya* sat in the living room, Éva studying her fingernails, *Apu* with his nose buried in the paper, *Anya* with a serving fork in her hand.

"Any word? Did anyone ring?"

All three gazed at him and shook their heads.

Anya brandished her fork, waving it like a surrender flag. "What I don't understand is how Éva and Patrik could have left the studio without Zofia. You know how dangerous it is for her on the streets." She tapped *Apu*'s paper with her utensil. "You must tell her not to do such a thing again."

Anya peered above the page. "She knows."

Éva rubbed the back of her neck. "We shouldn't have done it. But she assured us she was right behind us. She was giving us some time alone."

Ernő strode the length of the entry hall and back toward the door again, cracking his knuckles. "I don't care what she told you or how nice she was being. The two of you shouldn't have left her wandering the streets alone." How could they have done it? What were they thinking? They weren't, that was the problem. Weeks away from their wedding, they had their heads in the clouds.

Éva stood, a blush rising in her fair cheeks. "She went out alone the other night. To that lesson, remember? You wanted to escort her, but she insisted on going by herself."

"And this is why she shouldn't be out at night at all, much less alone." Ernő puffed out a breath. "Why, why did this have to happen?"

"What's done is done. From here on, Zofia will be accompanied at all times. Finding her is what is most important right now." *Apu's* gentle words sliced like a blade.

"After the rain comes the raincoat." Ernő pounded on the wall, the sting in his hand far less severe than the pain in his heart. "My wife is missing, possibly deported to a place where hundreds of thousands like her have been killed. I'm frantic about her. We can't change the past, but this should never have happened."

Anya came at him. Was she going to spear him with the fork? Instead, she embraced him, the warmth of her flowing into him. "Focus on what you have to do. Frustration won't get you anywhere."

"You're right." He stomped out the door and onto the street. Still the road remained quiet. Deserted.

Until a shiny black car hummed down it. Stopped in front of their house. A large swastika was emblazoned on the side.

Ernő's stomach sank to his toes.

He dashed inside. "The Gestapo is here."

Anya and Éva blanched. *Apu* folded his paper as if a friend had come to call, and they were getting ready for a night of playing *ulti* cards.

The Germans pounded on the door. "Open up, open up." The gutteral voices barked their demands.

Ernő swallowed. Shaking, he unlatched the door. As soon as he turned the knob, three Gestapo officers burst into the flat, silver bars on their shirt collars.

Ernő backed against the wall, digging his fingernails into the soft plaster. "What is the meaning of this? What do you want?"

"We're searching for Bognár Zofia. I presume you are her husband."

He wiped the beads of sweat from his forehead. "She's not here."

The biggest, burliest of the men, muscles bulging under his too-tight green shirt, pinned Ernő to the wall by the neck. *Anya* gasped. "Don't try to fool us." The soldier turned to his comrades and motioned with his head. "Search this place from top to bottom. She has to be here."

Ernő couldn't draw much air into his lungs. Despite the Nazi's choke hold, he slipped out a few words. "Not here."

The German kneed him in the crotch. He refrained from crying out, but only the man's hands around his neck kept him from slumping to the ground. From the corner of his eye, he saw *Apu* holding back Éva.

If they were going to kill him, they might as well get on with it. But not in front of his family. *God, not in front of my parents.*

The Nazi kneed him again. Excruciating pain shot through him. This time, he didn't have the breath to cry out.

"Where is she?"

"Don't know."

The German held him with one enormous hand and waved his pistol in the direction of the rest of Ernő's family. "Do you need a little help remembering? Would seeing your father or mother die jog your memory?"

Nem, he couldn't allow this man to harm his family. "Don't know." Ernő struggled for breath to speak. "Where she is."

"Liar."

Again the knee. And again. How many more times, Ernő didn't know. He lost count when the pain became unbearable.

After an interminable length of time, the two other goons returned from ransacking the flat. "Nothing. But her clothes and possessions are here."

"Well, well, well, isn't that interesting?" The officer's hot breath blew across Ernő's cheek. "I have all kinds of questions for you."

Where were they taking him? He didn't care as long as they

stopped this torture. The Nazi yanked him away from the wall, and the cold, hard steel of a revolver touched the back of Ernő's head.

"Let's go."

"*Nem, nem.*" *Anya* and Éva's cries faded as they marched him down the steps to the street and into a sleek black car parked at the curb. The other times Ernő had witnessed arrests, the detainees had been herded into trucks.

Special treatment? More likely, special torment.

The big thug shoved Ernő into the auto, the pistol still trained on his skull as he slid in. The other two jumped into the front seats, and the car roared away into the Budapest twilight.

They didn't travel far before they reached the hotel that served as Gestapo headquarters, its many windows glittering pink and yellow in the dying light.

Between the pain in his groin and the mush of his legs, he could barely walk. The Nazis half carried him up four flights of back stairs to what had probably once been a janitor's closet, now stripped of everything save for a metal chair.

Blood spatters covered the sterile white walls.

The beefy soldier shoved Ernő into the seat and at last holstered his weapon. "Now, Bognár *Úr*, would you mind clarifying something for us?" He drew a paper from his coat pocket. "This is an interesting piece I ran across published by some underground organization. Very curious. The author is named as Katona Marika. We have reason to believe she is your wife."

Ernő kept what he hoped was a neutral expression that would not give anything away. But hadn't Zofia teased him that if she changed her name to a Hungarian one, it would be Marika? It meant rebellious.

Trembling, Ernő grasped the proffered page. "In Defense of Those Who Assist Jews" by Katona Marika.

His pulse quickened.

What was his wife involved in?

Chapter Eight

Zofia stood at the corner, transfixed by the long black sedan parked in front of the Bognárs' house. She fell to her knees on the hard ground and covered her face. *Nem, nem,* this couldn't be happening again. *God, don't let it be so.* A brisk wind blew down the street, striking her tender cheek.

Patrik helped her to her feet and whispered in her ear, "We have to get out of here. You'll be arrested if they see you."

"What does it matter when the entire family is sure to be taken away? I should be with them." But his vice-like grasp on her upper arm held her in place.

Several soldiers burst through the front door, dragging Ernő behind them. He couldn't stand. What had they done to him? She inhaled to scream for him, but Patrik covered her mouth, muffling the sound.

She fought him as hard, maybe harder, than she had fought the German. This time not for her life but for her husband's. He was an innocent man. He had no idea of the activities she'd been involved in. No matter what they did to him, he wouldn't be able to tell them anything.

That's the way she had wanted it, but perhaps it hadn't been for the best.

Patrik didn't release his hold on her. She struggled and writhed and attempted to bite him, all to no avail.

"Stop fighting me. I'm not the enemy."

Perhaps if she relaxed, he would too, and she would have the chance to get away. She stilled.

"We have to talk. But not here. *Szent Istvan Bazilika.*"

She glanced around, her gaze settling on the dark gray Gothic church nearby that stood above almost every other building in Pest, its spires reaching to the heavens.

Like a prayer offered to God. Would He listen? Did He still care?

"We can go in the side chapel where it will be quiet. And private."

The Nazis shoved Ernő into the car. His shrill cries of pain pierced her soul. What were they going to do to him? Was this the last time she would ever see him?

The Germans slammed the car doors and sped down the street. She didn't move her gaze from the car until it turned the corner and disappeared.

Patrik pulled her to her feet and led her away from the Bognárs' home. He held tight to her until they passed through the church's massive oak doors carved with saints and gargoyles. The interior was pure grandeur, all gold and dark red-brown and blue, a dome above the altar. The sweetness of burning incense greeted them. A few people knelt in the pews, mumbling their evening prayers. At the end of the aisle, tiers of candles flickered on a metal stand. Signs of prayers. How many of them remained unanswered in the wake of the Nazis?

They slipped into the small, quiet chapel behind the altar, the place where *Szent Istvan*'s bejeweled, mummified hand was displayed in the 1800s. Patrik kept his voice low. "You aren't going near that house."

Her hat slid down her head, and a stray lock of hair brushed the back of her neck. "Why not? They took Ernő away, and I want to be with him. Don't you want to be with Éva?"

"Without you at home, it may be they will let the others go."

"But it may not be." Her voice cracked.

"If you step foot into that house, if either of us do, they are sure to arrest everyone." Patrik pursed his lips as he studied the stained glass windows depicting Hungary's most famous saints. The evening light sent beams of reds, blues, and greens scattering across the marble tile floor. "Don't you see? We've brought danger to them. How did they find you? What did you do?"

His last words echoed in the small space accusing her over and over, and she fought against the rising guilt. "You know as well as I do that even with the greatest of care, sometimes the Gestapo catches up to us. Do you think that after what happened to me in Poland, I was going to get sloppy and endanger my husband? A man I love as much as you love Éva?"

"You can't go back to the house. Right now we have hope that the Gestapo will only take Ernő. Once they find out he knows nothing, they will release him. Return home and you crush any chance."

Every part of her cried out for Ernő. She ached, a real, tangible pain. But what Patrik said made sense. If only it didn't. If only she could be with her husband. Tell him her secret. Share in whatever fate awaited him.

By staying away, however, she offered him a prayer of escape.

Patrik rubbed his temples. "You know what this means."

"*Nem*. I won't go into hiding. I won't be separated from him."

"You will. For all their sakes."

"By staying away, I'm not protecting them." Staying away hadn't safeguarded her mother.

"You are. The Gestapo won't discover anything incriminating in the home, will they?"

She shook her head. "I was meticulous. There is nothing there they can find."

"Good. That's the best news so far. They will watch the house, though. You know they will. The moment you return, all of you will be spirited away. You have to disappear. For your sake. And for theirs."

Zofia nodded, tears clouding her vision. "I didn't even get a chance to tell Ernő good-bye." *Or that I am pregnant with his child.* Again that stabbing pain in her chest.

As she sat in *Szent Istvan Bazilika*'s Holy Right chapel, the organ in the main sanctuary swelled to life. The deep tones resonated inside her, tickling the soles of her bare feet and filling her lungs with air. The music. No matter what else she lost, she would have that. But without Ernő, it wouldn't be enough.

Patrik gazed at her, his stare hard and penetrating. "You have to do this. Have to disappear without telling either your husband or your best friend."

Could she do it? Leave all those she loved without a backward glance? Oh *nem*, she would be looking behind her for however long they were separated. Remembering all she once had.

Patrik touched her hand. "You know I'm right."

"I lost one family because I refused to bow to the Nazis. But I will leave my love and my heart so that they can live." She choked on a sob. "You have to tell them, though. Let them know I had to leave. That the Gestapo will be watching. I don't want them to worry about me. Tell them I'm safe."

"And what shall I say when they beg me for your whereabouts? If I give away your location, they will come to find you, bringing the Germans with them."

Now she held to him with both hands. "Please, promise me you will let them know I haven't come to any harm. That I will return as soon as possible. Promise me."

He gave a single nod, and she relaxed her shoulders.

Zofia rose from her pew and paced the small room, the marble floor cold beneath her feet. If only she could be so cold, so unfeeling as the stone. "*Köszönöm.* When I walked into the Zionist Youth building and saw you there that day, I couldn't believe my eyes. At the time, I didn't understand why you would be involved, what your interest was in the group. But you've proven to be a godsend."

"I'm happy to help. I told you that from the start."

"Sometimes we are asked to do the impossible. You questioned if I could do this. I'll prove to you I can. But only if the rest of my family knows I'm safe. And as long as they are protected." She turned to face him.

Patrik was grim. "I've heard enough about the atrocities the Germans are committing against the Jews in other countries to know your life is worthless to them. But your life is worthy of being saved. And so are Ernő's and Éva's and everyone else's."

Zofia hugged herself and glanced over her shoulder. How long before they discovered her here? Minutes, if they were lucky. "We have no time to waste. I don't have anything with me."

"I'll find a way to get you what you need."

"What I need most is one of those documents from Switzerland granting me safe passage. Then I can be reunited with my husband, and this nightmare will come to an end." *Please, Lord, let that happen soon.*

"I'm working on it. I'll do everything in my power to make sure you get those papers. Fast."

"Press Bram. Press him hard. I know so many others are in need they can't print the documents fast enough. But let him know how dire my situation has become."

"I will, I will." Patrik's jaw was firm.

He would try. Please God that it would be enough.

The organ music rose and fell like the waves on the ocean, and it swept her away. Was this God's way of telling her He was watching out for her? That He would protect her and take care of her? Oh, how she prayed it was.

Still, she was helpless as a few tears rolled down her bruised cheeks. From his coat's breast pocket, Patrik pulled a handkerchief and handed it to her. She dabbed her eyes and forced a small smile to her face.

Patrik stood and linked his arm through hers. "We are going to stroll out of here as if nothing is amiss. Just stay calm and relaxed."

Zofia nodded. She kept her expression neutral, but her stomach churned, and not from the pregnancy. Her child, her sweet, sweet child. Would he ever know his father? Would his father ever know him?

They kept to the shadows of the side aisle and headed for the main doors, she trailing him as he pulled her along, his pace impossibly rapid. She stumbled, and he slowed down, but only a little.

The few congregants scattered among the carved pews sat with their heads bowed and their eyes closed, the women with lace scarves covering their heads.

Once outside, they descended the long stone stairway to the walk. Patrik nodded at her. "It won't be too far. I'm sure your feet must be sore. We'll find you some shoes."

"I'm fine."

Before long, they arrived at an old Baroque-style apartment building, its stones yellow with age. He led Zofia up three flights of stairs and stopped in front of one of the doors, where he knocked with a syncopated rhythm.

A woman about her mother's age opened the door. An ache consumed Zofia at the site of her welcoming smile, graying hair, and work-worn hands.

Mama. Gone because of her.

Patrik motioned her into the apartment ahead of him and shut the door. "Zofia, this is Tóth *Asszony*." He turned to the older woman. "I'm sorry to come unannounced like this. We have an unexpected situation."

Tóth *Asszony* drew Zofia farther into the tiny flat and examined her from head to toe. "We'll see about getting you new shoes. In the meantime, I'll put on the kettle for tea and pull out a pair of warm socks. Don't worry, dear. You'll be fine. We'll talk a little more when you've warmed up."

Patrik glanced at his watch. "I'm going to return to the house and see if I can find out what's happened. Are you going to be okay?"

Zofia bit her lip. Would she? Would she ever be okay again? Not until this awful war ended and she and Ernő were reunited. And had their child. She nodded. "I'll be just fine."

He turned to go.

"Patrik, wait."

He faced her. "What is it?"

She brushed a kiss across his cheek. "That's for Ernő. If you can, find a way to tell him I love him."

Patrik kissed her hands. Then he left. The door clicked shut behind him.

Zofia's old life was over. Her new one had begun.

❧

"Ernő, no!" Éva screeched as the car holding her brother turned the corner. She strode two steps toward the door before *Apu* wrapped her in a bear hug so she couldn't move.

"Stop. You can't help him."

"How can you stand there and allow them to take away your son? What are they going to do to him?"

"Nothing more than question him." As always, *Apu* didn't even waver. How could he be so confident?

Anya brandished her fork. Did she realize she still held it? "This has something to do with Zofia, I just know it."

"And where is Patrik? He hasn't made it back either." Her heart raced like a sixteenth-note run. He called her his muse, but he was her refrain. The best part of the song. The highlight. Would there be anyone left at all by the time the Nazis were done with them?

She paced the living room, glancing at the door with each circuit. Nothing. Nothing at all. Throughout the long evening, as bombings on the other side of the city lit the sky, the door remained shut. No one walked through it. How could everything have gone so wrong so fast—as fast as the Germans had invaded Hungary?

"God, please bring them home safely." She whispered her prayer, wandering back and forth. "Keep them from harm. Don't let the Nazis hurt them. Protect them. And by your power, open that door right now. May the three of them be standing on the other side."

"Come here, Éva." *Apu* motioned for her to join him on the davenport.

"I'm not sure I'll be able to be still."

"Sit."

At his soft but firm word, she dropped to the couch.

"Praying is fine. It's what we should be doing. But pacing and fretting and watching the door are doing no good. You'll only work yourself into a lather and make yourself sick."

Anya had at last put away the fork, but now she sat under the reading lamp, her embroidery forgotten in her lap. "Listen to your father. He knows what he's talking about. What I don't understand is why all three of them are gone in one night. Somehow, this ties together. I believe Zofia and Patrik have much explaining to do."

"Alisz, *nem*." *Apu* narrowed his eyes as he stared at *Anya*. "That isn't helpful."

"But my boy is out there. Who knows what they are doing to him?"

With another pointed gaze, *Apu* silenced *Anya*.

Éva leaned against *Apu*'s shoulder, closed her eyes, and lifted a silent prayer. Each tick of the clock was a lifetime.

And then the most beautiful sound, more beautiful than the rich tones of a well-played clarinet. A knock at the entry.

Before either *Apu* or *Anya* could move, Éva had sprinted to the door. She threw it open. There stood Patrik, a half smile flitting across his face.

"Oh, Patrik, Patrik, *csillagom*, my dear. You're here. I can't believe it. We were wild with worry." She kissed his face over and over. Then stepped back to see behind him. "Where is Zofia?"

He took her by the hand, and together they shuffled into the house. "Let a man catch his breath."

Zofia was nowhere in sight. "You found her, didn't you?"

"Let's all sit down."

"Patrik, tell me now."

"Do as he asks." *Apu*, in charge again.

Éva obeyed him.

Patrik settled on the sofa's arm, his hands clasped in his lap. "I wasn't able to find her."

"*Nem! Nem!*"

He tried to draw Éva to himself, but she resisted. She needed answers, not comfort. "Where could she be?"

"I scoured the city. It's like she disappeared."

The worst word you could hear these days in relation to a Jew. Too many of them disappeared. None of them returned.

Ever.

"First Zofia and now Ernő."

Patrik pushed back. "Ernő?"

Anya jumped into the conversation. "The Gestapo was here. Searched the place. Threatened and beat my son, then led him away. God alone knows what's happened to him. It's because of Zofia. You know I love her, but she brought this trouble with her from Poland."

"*Anya!*" Éva sucked in a breath. How could she besmirch Ernő's wife and Éva's best friend that way?

"I'm only speaking my mind."

Patrik stood and scrubbed his face. "She has a point. I was afraid of this."

Éva embraced him. "What were you afraid of?"

He snapped his attention to her. "Nothing. Nothing at all."

She hugged herself. Most Hungarians were open. They didn't keep secrets. From the moment you met a person, you knew all about them.

Patrik was different. Closed off at times. Like now.

Was he telling her everything he knew?

Chapter Nine

By the time the Gestapo released Ernő, darkness once again covered the city. The Germans had held him for almost twenty-four hours. For a while he wandered the streets, his muddled brain working to recall where he was and how to get home. Soon, though, the Buda castle rose above the city, and he managed to orient himself.

In a short amount of time, he stood in front of his family's three-story residence, staring at it. How could he go inside if Zofia was still missing, out there somewhere? What might be happening to her if they still held her? Now he had something of an idea. If the Germans ever found her, they wouldn't be any gentler because she was a woman.

His Nazi interrogator's scorching breath still singed Ernő's cheek. He struggled to get air into his lungs, every expansion of his chest like knives ripping his ribcage open. Likely broken. Maybe all of them.

Had they broken Zofia's bones? Was she in pain? Suffering?

"Tell me where your wife is." The soldier's demands had reverberated in the dark, tiny room.

"I don't know."

The Nazi slapped him across the cheek, the sting of it no match for the pain in the rest of his body. "Fool. You're stalling, and I'm tiring of your game."

Ernő sat as straight as possible and clung to the edge of the chair. "I don't know where my wife is." Zofia had told him how the Nazis had killed her mother when she couldn't tell them where her daughter was. Would they do the same with him?

Let them do what they wanted with him. Just don't let them harm Zofia. His precious, precious wife. His everything.

The questioning, badgering, and beatings had lasted for hours. More than one officer took his turn with Ernő. In the rare moments they left him alone in the room, he caught a few seconds of sleep. But his body cried for more.

His heart cried for Zofia.

Then, just like that, they had released him. Was it because they had arrested her?

"Ernő! Ernő!" Éva's cries snapped him from his memories. She raced down the steps and stopped short. "I can't believe you're home. I was watching out the window for Patrik to come for dinner, and there you were." She touched his face, her fingertips soft and gentle. "What happened?"

He couldn't stop the laugh that escaped his lips. "I didn't expect such a homecoming. You'd think that I'd been gone for a year."

"Look at what those beasts did to you. An innocent man. Are you in much pain?"

"More worried about my wife."

"Zofia isn't here."

"I know. They wouldn't have released me if she were. Either they have her in custody, or they let me go in hopes I will lead them to her. Or that she'll come to me."

"At least you're home."

"I need to find her."

"Later. Please, come inside."

Patrik rounded the corner and grinned at Ernő. "Good to see you."

"When you didn't meet me last night, I thought they'd taken you too."

"I had a lead. Though it turned out to be nothing, I had to check it." Patrik toed the ground.

Interesting. He couldn't look Ernő in the eye. Why not?

The door opened, and *Anya* stood in the entrance. "There you all are. Ernő, my boy. Come in, come in. Allied planes are headed this way. They just announced it on the radio. We have to take shelter."

At that moment, the air raid sirens blared their warning, their awful screech piercing his eardrums. The rumble of planes sounded in the distance. But Zofia . . . she always froze when the sirens sounded, her face draining of its color. He had to push her to the shelter. What would she do without him? He had to continue searching. Couldn't give up.

Overhead, the roar grew louder, the whine of the engines and the howl of the air raid sirens filling his ears. Antiaircraft fire split the air, tracers and searchlights illuminating the deepening night.

"Ernő, you can't look for her now. What good will you be to her dead?" *Anya* motioned him inside.

She was right. With great reluctance, Ernő climbed the steps into the hallway and shut the door behind him.

While the rest of the family made their way down the stairs, Ernő stopped Patrik. "You know more about the situation with my wife than you are acknowledging. Tell me what's going on."

"Nothing, I promise you. You know as much as I do." Again, Patrik's attention was elsewhere as he spoke to Ernő.

"You're lying."

A deafening whistle cut off the rest of Patrik's words. The ground shook below them.

At that moment, someone pounded at the door. "Open up." Not German words but Hungarian.

Ernő turned the knob and three policemen burst into the house. What did they want? Who did they want? The pain in his ribs prevented him from taking a deep breath.

The tallest and heaviest of the bunch pointed his weapon at Patrik and Ernő. "Downstairs."

Ernő dragged himself down the stairs behind Patrik to the basement where the rest of his family huddled on a sofa in the cold, damp room. "There you two are." *Anya* crumpled a handkerchief in her trembling hands. "What is going on up there?"

"Just the air raid wardens making sure everyone is complying with the law to be inside." At least, that's what he hoped, though it didn't make sense. Wardens patrolled the streets to be sure they were empty but didn't enter homes. Their presence upstairs was both puzzling and troubling. Ernő's thoughts traveled upstairs, outside, wherever his wife was. He paced the small space until he reached the foot of the stairs. Zofia was out there. Alone. What would happen if—

Apu stepped in front of Ernő, blocking his path. "She would want you here."

Ernő stared at the low ceiling that was closing down on him and sagged in defeat. "Tomorrow I'm resuming my search for her." When these air raids occurred, they lasted most of the night. For now, he was stuck inside, helpless to find Zofia, to help her, to protect her.

"Of course. Tomorrow you look for her. Tonight you rest and stay safe. You'll do her the most good that way." *Apu* led him to the sofa as if he were a small child and squeezed him between *Anya* and Éva. Ernő twiddled his thumbs, wishing the Allied planes away.

The floors above them creaked. Boots stomped up and down stairs. Their hard, almost angry words said they weren't here for an innocuous compliance check. So what were they doing up there? Looking for something? But what? There was nothing that might interest them. They had to be searching for Zofia. Maybe, maybe it was best she wasn't here.

Nem, not best at all. If she were here, he would give his life to ensure she was safe. That was how much he loved her. How much he couldn't live without her.

After several more minutes, with a slam of the door, the police left the building.

For most of the night, Ernő and his family huddled together, quiet, deep in thought and prayer, until the all clear signal came. Could a person go crazy in that amount of time? Never had the hands on his watch moved with such maddening slowness. After an eon, Ernő and his family tromped upstairs and opened the door.

What a sight greeted them. Their visitors had overturned the couch and slit the cushions, had dumped the contents of every desk drawer on the floor, had broken the dishes on the table. Even the Germans hadn't been this thorough. If he had to guess, he would say the police had been here on the Nazis' authority.

Ernő swallowed hard. "They weren't here to check on us. They came looking for something."

Could it be true? Was Zofia caught up in the underground, writing the papers the Nazis accused her of writing? Is that what the thugs who barged in here were after?

He tried to catch Patrik's attention. But again, Patrik avoided his gaze.

May 28, 1944

Patrik blew out a breath as the train chugged into the station in Nagyvárad. A red roof covered the platform that led into a low, cheery yellow building. Rain splattered the window of his car, and he pulled up his trench coat's collar.

Despite everything going on with Zofia and with his impending wedding, he had to come. Had to see for himself, know for himself what had happened to his family.

The worst part was that he couldn't speak to Éva about any of this. He'd told her he had to go out of town to scout new talent for the symphony and wanted to get it done before the wedding so he wouldn't have to leave her right after their marriage.

He prayed he would return for the ceremony.

With a belch of steam and soot, the train halted. Along with many of the passengers, Patrik stood and retrieved his small bag. He had a few clothes inside but also a stash of money. Bribes, if he needed them.

The walk was long, but except for the Germans patrolling the streets, the city was beautiful. He'd loved growing up in this place, surrounded by amazing architecture. Every Sabbath, he, his parents, and his sisters had attended the Great Synagogue with its blue-ceilinged dome. A place of wonder and awe.

Now the place of worship sat on the very edge of the Nagyvárad ghetto.

After a warm, brisk walk of almost forty-five minutes, he arrived on Zarda Street. A wooden fence had been erected around the ghetto. Though it contained several blocks of homes, the place was nowhere near large enough to hold all Nagyvárad's Jews.

At the stench that reached him, Patrik gagged. The foul odor of human excrement. Of unwashed bodies. Of death.

So strong he tasted it and fought to keep his breakfast in his stomach.

He meandered the perimeter of the ghetto, always searching for his dark-haired sisters. Like him, they were tall and willowy. But he spied no one who even resembled them.

In fact, he spied no one at all. An eerie silence hung over the place. With tens of thousands of Jews crammed into this tiny area, with the heat of the approaching summer and open windows, he should have heard the sounds of everyday living. Clinking of plates. Laughter of children. Talk between friends.

Instead, there was nothing but silence. Heavy. Oppressive. Deadly.

He peered down one street. The doors to the houses hung open. Belongings were scattered about the road. Parcels and bags lay where they had been dropped and abandoned, and food rotted in the late-spring sun.

The dusty street was a confusion of footprints—scuffed, crazy patterns, prints of all sizes. Hundreds of people had passed through here not long ago.

Amid it all, a stuffed polar bear lay in the middle of the street, trampled, dirty, destroyed.

Goose pimples broke out on Patrik's arms. In his head, voices whispered, the voices of those who had marched down this road. The only voices he could hear.

Where had they all gone?

He moved on toward Rhedey Park. What he saw next almost brought him to his knees. He leaned against a tree for support. Thousands of Jews guarded by gendarmes and SS soldiers crowded around the train tracks that ran along the park.

Here at last there was sound. Moaning. Crying. Screaming. Armed soldiers herded groups of Jews, regardless of youth or age, into cattle cars, stuffing them inside one after the other. The soldiers maintained order, but chaos and confusion were in the eyes of the people. Patrik's people.

They had no idea of their fate. Or, like his sisters, they had chosen to ignore it for too long, certain that what was happening to other Jews throughout the Third Reich and even in their beloved Hungary would never happen to them.

Then, on the edge of the crowd, Patrik spotted them. For a moment, he forgot to breathe. Their dark hair, chopped at their ears, was unmistakable. They rose above the other women.

Róza, the oldest, bent over and straightened her son's cap while her husband held to the child's hand. Patrik's nephew, István, was just three years old.

He would never survive.

A lump formed in Patrik's throat and grew.

Then there was Magda, so much like Róza they almost might be twins. His effervescent sister, making friends from strangers, always attracting a crowd.

Now she shuffled along, her head bent. The Nazis had already snuffed the life from her.

"Róza, Magda." He shouted and waved. "Over here! Over here!"

Igen, igen, it was dangerous for him to call attention to himself. Crazy, really, if they realized who he was. But he had to see them. Try to help them. Freedom was just a short distance away.

Spurred by a burst of adrenaline, he rushed in the train's direction. "Róza, Magda, it's me."

They didn't turn one way or the other. Did they hear him? Or were they too frightened to answer him?

"Róza! Magda!" He screamed with all his might.

As Patrik surged forward, an SS officer, the silver bars on his collar glinting in the sunlight bursting through the clouds, advanced and, gun raised, stopped him. "Where are you going?"

Róza disappeared into the car. *Nem, nem!* The narrowing of his throat restricted his breathing. The world tilted.

"What do you want with them?" the German demanded.

"They are, were, my neighbors. I . . . I wanted to say good-bye."

"You cannot go there. Unless you are one of them."

István's father lifted him into the car, jumped inside himself, and pulled Magda inside.

They were gone. Forever.

Great, uncontrollable sobs tore from Patrik. *"Nem, nem!"*

"If you know what's good for you, you'll get out of here. Now. You don't belong." The soldier trained his rifle on Patrik's heart.

One of them had to survive. The Friemann family couldn't be extinguished from the earth. Shuddering, Patrik backed away.

Across the tracks stood a blond Aryan woman, concealing a smile behind her handkerchief. From a brooch on her dress came a glint of red.

Patrik knew that face. But from where?

Early June 1944

"Two days." Éva paced the small living room from the piano in one corner to the radio set in the other. "Zofia has been gone for more than a month, and there are only two days left until our wedding." She turned to Ernő and Patrik, who sat forward on the couch. "I can't get married without her."

Since Éva had become engaged to Patrik, she and Zofia had planned their wedding. A ceremony in a beautiful church, with stained glass splashing multicolored light across the stone floors. A lace gown with a cathedral-length train. An abundance of roses and orchids filling the space with their sweet aroma.

Above all, Patrik. Each other.

Zofia and Ernő flanking them.

Without Zofia, it wouldn't be Éva's dream.

On the other hand, she counted the hours until she became Patrik's wife. How could she bear another day without him as her husband? Their love was like a symphony reaching its pinnacle. To halt it now would be unthinkable.

Patrik rose and enveloped her in an embrace. Most of the time, his warm presence calmed and soothed her. Not today. She had hardly slept, hadn't eaten much since Zofia disappeared from the face of the earth.

Éva pushed away from him, her stomach in knots. "What are we going to do?"

Patrik stroked her cheek. "If you want to postpone the wedding, I understand. I'll continue to search, but don't get your hopes up." He leaned in and brushed a kiss across her lips. "Please don't make me wait too long to marry you."

She reached for him and gave him a proper kiss. "Don't worry, I won't. Just until we know for sure."

She glanced at Ernő huddled on the end of the couch, a

faraway look in his brown eyes. Several days' worth of stubble bloomed on his cheeks and chin. Even in such a short time, he had lost weight. She sat beside him and patted his hand. "She'll come home soon. Keep believing that she will." She said the words, but did she know them to be true? How long could she keep believing that nothing sinister had happened to Zofia?

A knock came at the door. *Anya* and *Apu* had gone to a friend's home for the evening, so Éva hurried to answer it. Each time someone showed up at the house, a little flicker lit inside her, the tiny hope that Zofia stood on the other side of the door.

But the flame sputtered out. It wasn't Zofia but a rotund woman, the string of pearls around her neck contrasting with her black dress, on which was pinned a red rose brooch. "Reka, good to see you." Éva forced herself to be polite as she had been taught from childhood. As every Hungarian had been taught. "Won't you come in?"

Éva stepped to the side so Reka could enter.

Reka embraced her. "I heard about your sister-in-law. What awful news. Is there somewhere we can speak in private?" She peered over Éva's shoulder and into the living room, her features hardening.

What did Reka have to tell her that she couldn't say in front of Patrik and Ernő? When they had been in school together, they hadn't been close. They had never shared secrets before. But perhaps she brought news about Zofia. Éva shrugged and led Reka down the hall and into her bedroom.

Éva shut the door and motioned for Reka to take a seat on the narrow bed with its pink spread. The small room contained only that and a walnut wardrobe. Éva clasped her hands together and sat beside Reka.

The woman fiddled with her necklace. "How have you been?"

This wasn't starting off like a private conversation. Or did Reka bring such awful news that she didn't know how to come out and say it? "Right now, worried about Zofia."

Reka jiggled her leg so hard that the bed shook like there was an earthquake. "It was nice of you to introduce Patrik to me when we met at the café a few weeks ago."

"I like to show him off. He's becoming quite well known as a composer."

"That's nice."

Silence stretched in front of them until Éva squirmed. Reka's leg jiggled again. Well, that was enough of this. "Is there something you need to tell me?"

Reka sniffled. "I can't seem to find the words."

"Just let them spill out." Although by this time, Éva had broken into a sweat. Whatever Reka had to tell her wasn't good.

"A few weeks ago when I was in the city, in the evening, I went to *Szent Istvan Bazilika* to pray. There were some things I had on my mind. As I was finishing and standing, from the corner of my eye, I caught a strange sight."

Éva was ready to burst. "Was it Zofia?"

Reka bounced her leg harder than ever. "It was. Her hair was disheveled, and she didn't have any shoes on. She was wearing a blue coat with a small matching hat with a brown feather. It appeared to me that she had a bruise on her face too."

"That was her. No one else has a hat like that. I don't know what it all means, especially that she looked like she had been through some kind of ordeal, but you saw her. And she was alone?" Wait until Éva told Ernő.

Reka shook her head, her fair curls bouncing. "She wasn't."

Éva's stomach sunk. "The Gestapo?"

"*Nem.* It, it was . . ."

"Who?" Éva's voice was nothing more than a whisper. "You can tell me."

"It was Patrik."

Éva must have heard wrong. "Not Patrik. Someone who looked like him. He said he didn't see her. He'd been out looking for her. He wouldn't lie to me." This was all a terrible, terrible mistake.

"He was leading her by the arm. She lagged behind him, almost like she didn't want to go with him. I'm so sorry to be the one to have to tell you."

"You must have confused him for someone else. You barely know him."

"He was wearing pinstripe pants, a blue and white sweater vest, and a white shirt."

Éva shook her head. "Those are the clothes he had on that day, but hardly unique. Most businessmen wear similar attire." Did Reka have it out for Éva? Why would she tell such a lie?

"That's not all." Reka dug through her black pocketbook. "He dropped this on the way out." She pulled out a photograph and handed it to Éva.

Her own eyes stared back at her, shining and full of light as she laughed, the sun streaming behind her. The photo Ernő took of her and Patrik last fall on a countryside picnic.

The photo Patrik told her he always kept with his handkerchief near his heart.

As she flipped it over, she held her breath. Penned on the back, in her own handwriting, were the words she had written. *My darling Patrik, I'll be your muse forever. Your loving fiancée, Éva.*

Her hands trembled, and the picture floated to the rug. *Why?* "There has to be a reasonable explanation." She worked to keep her voice strong and steady as if to convince herself of that truth.

"I saw him drop it."

Reka's voice startled Éva. She'd almost forgotten the other woman in the room.

"He pulled something from his breast pocket, I didn't see what, and this fell when he did. As soon as they were out of sight, I picked it up."

Éva closed her eyes and expelled the air she'd been holding. Though theirs had been a short courtship, he'd never done anything to make her question his goodness, his forthrightness, his truthfulness.

But there were those mysterious meetings he attended at night. And the way he evaded her questions. His mumblings the night Zofia disappeared.

None of this made sense. "Patrik was with me when she vanished. He couldn't have been involved."

Reka tilted her head and shrugged. "I only know what I saw. I'm positive of what I'm telling you. He was with her, dragging her away."

"Was she fighting him?"

"Possibly. That might be why her face was battered."

On the way home, had Zofia stopped at the church to pray? Like them, she belonged to the Hungarian Reformed Church, but maybe she had needed the cathedral's solitude. Had Patrik found her there, alone, and taken the opportunity to be rid of her? Had Patrik arranged to meet Zofia there on false pretenses, planning her capture the entire time?

Possibly.

But *nem*, not her Patrik. Her beloved. Her man of God. The one who always protected her.

The picture. There was only one in existence. It belonged to Patrik.

Her Patrik.

Her thoughts tumbled over each other like a stream over a pile of rocks.

This was too much like Károly and his deep betrayal. The same nightmare all over again.

The pain ripping apart her insides was unbearable. She had brought Károly to her family, and he'd almost destroyed it. Had she done the same with Patrik?

She couldn't breathe. Because it couldn't be true. It just couldn't be.

She staggered to her feet and stumbled to the door. Shaking all over, she opened it. "Please, leave."

Reka lumbered to the entryway, then turned. "Don't be blind to the truth. He was with her. He's involved."

Éva answered through clenched teeth, "I said get out now."

"Think about what I told you." Reka exited the room, and shortly after, the door to the house clicked open and then shut.

Éva bit the inside of her cheek. Patrik couldn't have harmed Zofia. Could he? What reason would he have? And why would he lie to her and to Ernő?

She crumpled the photograph and sobbed.

Chapter Ten

As Éva's friend marched down the hall and through the Bognárs' living room, she flashed Patrik an icy stare. "You ought to be ashamed of yourself." Her words dripped with venom.

What had he done? He didn't even know the woman save for their one brief encounter in the café. Though he'd seen her somewhere else. No doubt about it. When she left, he blew out a breath and turned to Ernő. "Are you acquainted with her?"

"She attended school with Éva. I wouldn't call them friends or anything. I have no idea why she was here." Ernő's words were tight. Since his interrogation, he had been withdrawn, as if he had curled into himself and didn't trust that he was safe. And, of course, his heart wasn't. To him, Zofia was very likely dead or in the hands of the Gestapo. *Nem.* None of them were safe.

The atmosphere here was strange, but maybe it was Patrik's imagination.

He returned his attention to the BBC radio broadcast, fixated on news about the Soviet advance in Romania and always alert for the nightly air raid warnings.

Then through the din of the announcer's words, from the direction of Éva's room, sounded a low, keening cry, like that of an injured dog. Patrik jumped to his feet. "Is that your sister?"

Ernő stared at the floor in front of him. "Who else?"

Patrik sprinted up the stairs, his mind running as fast as his feet. What had happened? He knocked on the door but didn't wait for an answer before entering.

His beautiful Éva huddled on the blue-and-pink flowered rug

covering the hardwood floor. He bent to scoop her up, but she fought him. "Don't touch me."

Her words sent him stumbling backward. She had been insane with worry about Zofia. The grief must have gotten to be too much. "It's okay. I'm here for you."

She peered at him, her eyes red and puffy, tear stains marring her flawless cheeks. In her hand, she held out a piece of crumpled paper. "Do you recognize this?"

He took it from her. His picture of her from last fall. So that's where it had gone to. "I've been searching for this. I must have dropped it here when I took my handkerchief out of my pocket."

She rose to her feet. "You didn't drop it here." Her words were soft but caustic.

He sagged. Could she know? "What do you mean?"

"You dropped it at *Szent Istvan Bazilika* a few weeks ago."

All the feeling left his body. He had to act innocent. "I was never there."

"Not even to hunt for Zofia?"

"Perhaps. In the franticness, I don't remember everywhere I searched."

"Reka saw you there with her. Dragging her out against her will. While there, you dropped our picture."

They had been so careful, or so he had thought. Apparently not. He should have known the church wasn't a good place. Too public. They should have found a more private area. A place no one could have seen them.

Éva couldn't know. For Zofia's safety, for the safety of them all, she couldn't find out. But what could he tell her? What was right in this situation—to put all of them in danger or to lie to Éva? Which sin was worse—murder or lying?

Patrik drew near her, but she backed away and thumped on her bed. "I didn't find Zofia. I don't know what her motivation might be, but Reka is lying." *God, let her believe me.*

"What about the picture?"

"It's possible I went there and dropped the photo."

"So you knew it was missing?"

"*Igen*." He patted his heart. "With the hubbub over Zofia, I never thought to mention it."

"Reka knew what both you and Zofia were wearing."

Patrik rubbed his sweaty hands on his pants. Stupid, stupid. He and Zofia should never have been anywhere in public together. He should have waited until the dead of night to spirit her away.

"How she would know that, I can't explain. But who are you going to believe? Someone you barely knew years ago or the man who you're about to pledge your life to?"

"Did you hurt her?"

"You have to know I would never hurt anyone. You know me."

She shifted her gaze away from Patrik and then back to him. Good. He was building doubt in her mind.

"But you do stand out in a crowd."

His cursed height. Always a giveaway. "There are others in Budapest as tall as I am, with similar build, and the same color hair. If I wished harm to Zofia, would I have searched for her? That woman has filled your head with craziness."

The floorboards in the hall creaked, and Ernő appeared in the doorway. "What are you two arguing about?"

Éva pointed at Patrik. "Reka accused him of being with Zofia the night she disappeared. She said she saw him at *Szent Istvan Bazilika* with her, dragging her out. And she gave me this." She grabbed the photograph from Patrik and handed it to her brother.

Ernő stared at the grainy picture. "You did what?"

The odds were not in Patrik's favor here. "Nothing. I did nothing."

Ernő lunged for him, but Patrik sidestepped. "You are believing someone you don't know very well over the word of a man who loves your sister and your entire family more than anything. I can't understand how you would find her more credible than me."

"If you did anything to my wife—"

"Trust me. I wouldn't lie to you." Except that he was. "Right now, you're thinking with your emotions. You'll see how wrong Reka is. I may have dropped the picture at the church the other night, but I was not with Zofia. If I had been, I would have brought her home."

As she hugged herself, Éva rose and paced in small circles, glancing his way every so often. How could he hurt her so? The truth danced on his tongue, but he reined it in. Zofia had begged him to tell them she was unharmed, but that would send Éva and Ernő on a search. A search that might well bring more danger to this house.

The picture of his sisters boarding the train in Nagyvárad flashed through his brain. Everyone in Hungary had heard about Auschwitz and what happened there. By now, they had arrived. By now, they were dead.

He replaced the image of his sisters with that of Éva and Zofia. *Nem.* He refused to allow that fate to befall them. He stomped the words of truth back down his throat.

After several silent minutes, Éva came to a halt in her pacing and stared at him. "I don't know, Patrik. After everything I've been through, you know how I value the truth. How do I know you aren't lying to me?"

He knew all too well how honesty was the number one virtue in her book. She'd shared her past with him. But lying to her was the only thing he could do. "How can you not believe me?" Hadn't he been convincing enough? Or had she never loved him as much as she proclaimed she did? The thought struck him as hard as a fist to the gut.

"I want to, I truly do. But she said she saw you. She knew details."

"Maybe she's involved and is trying to pin the blame on me."

"What about the photo?" She pointed to the picture Ernő crushed in his bear-sized hands.

"I did drop it somewhere. She must have found it. Don't make it out to be something it's not." How would he bear it if she didn't believe him? She wasn't supposed to find out about this. None of them were.

She covered her face, her voice muffled. "Please, Patrik, give me some time to deal with everything that's happened. I must think and get things straight in my mind. Give me a few days, I beg you. Then we'll talk again."

What else could he do for the woman he adored? "I'll leave both of you in peace. But use your logic. Reka is twisting the truth to make me guilty. You were about to trust your life to me. Can you throw that away?"

Zofia paced the length of the tiny living room crowded with furniture, covered in doilies, and filled with knickknacks. Tóth *Asszony* hummed in the kitchen as she prepared borscht for dinner, but the smell of the beets simmering did nothing to calm Zofia's stomach. Much as she wanted to help with making the meal, she couldn't get near food right now.

She crossed to the corner of the room by the single, small window whose curtains were drawn against watchful German eyes. Against men who hunted her. And did unimaginable things to her husband.

When Patrik had brought her here the night her world turned upside down, all she knew was that the Gestapo had arrested Ernő. Patrik hadn't been back since. Every minute of every day, she had to stifle the screams that threatened to erupt from the depth of her soul. No German torture could be worse than this not knowing. Not knowing if her love was in prison. Not knowing if her heart and soul was alive or dead.

She understood that Patrik couldn't visit every day. She understood that he couldn't communicate with her on a regular basis. But couldn't he get word to her on the fate of her husband?

In this room sat a pretty little parlor piano, its walnut case polished to a mirrorlike finish. The most torturous part of her confinement. She'd longed to touch it for days but hadn't dared. Until now. She could no longer stop herself. She opened the lid and, not making a sound, ran her fingers over the ivory keys.

"Do you play?" Tóth *Asszony* stood in the doorway, wiping her hands on an apron yellowed with stains.

"I'm part owner of a music studio. Whenever I'm not teaching, I'm sitting in front of my spinet, losing myself in the beauty of the tunes."

"My husband used to play so well. Such an ear he had. He couldn't read a lick of music, but what came from his memory was incredible. All he had to do was hear the melody once, and he could play it to perfection. I'd sit for hours and listen to him."

At the mention of a husband, Zofia's eyes burned. She blinked several times. "Has he been gone long?"

Tóth *Asszony* fingered the long gray braid that hung down her back. "Nearly thirty years now. We'd only been married for three years when he passed away. They didn't know why. One minute he was here, the next he was gone."

Three years. Just as long as she and Ernő had been married. Would that be all the time the Lord would give them together? *Nem, Lord, just a little more than that.* She rubbed the spot where her child grew.

"If you'd like, you're welcome to use the piano. Since my husband has been gone, it hasn't been touched except by the piano tuners. I don't need it, but I can't bear to part with it. How lovely it would be to hear its tone again."

Zofia shook her head. What was the woman thinking? "Any music coming from this flat after so many years would raise suspicions. Remember, I'm not here. I can't make a sound."

Tóth *Asszony* covered her mouth. "Oh dear, that was careless of me. Please, I wasn't thinking. When I saw you there, I got carried away to another time, and longing for my husband and his music overtook me."

Would that be Ernő thinking of Zofia thirty years from now? She shut her mind to all thoughts of him.

"Supper is almost ready."

"I hope you haven't made too much. I'm not very hungry."

Tóth *Asszony* marched toward Zofia and patted her cheek. Such a motherly gesture. Again, someone else it was best not to think about. "You do look a little peaked."

"Would you mind if I laid down for a while? Perhaps later I'll feel up to eating."

"Of course, dear. I do hope you aren't coming down with something."

Before Zofia could turn for her room, the shrill wail of air raid sirens pierced the air.

"Oh dear, oh dear. I have to go to the shelter, but you aren't supposed to be here." Tóth *Asszony* clasped her hands together and squeezed them tight. And so began the conversation they had almost every night.

"You go ahead. I'll be fine here."

"But what if we're bombed?" All color fled the older woman's face. Tóth *Asszony* fretted so much.

"Then no shelter is going to save me."

"Or what if the Nazis come?"

That was a bigger concern.

The low drone of plane engines and antiaircraft fire drowned out the sirens. "I have my hiding spot. Go, go." Zofia just about pushed Tóth *Asszony* out the door. But as she did so, Patrik bounded up the stairs. Finally. What had kept him all these weeks?

"You'd better get to the shelter, young man."

"You go down. I'll catch up with you later." He slipped into the flat and locked the door. His face was flushed and warm as he kissed Zofia on both cheeks. "How are you faring?"

She plastered on a smile. "Fine. We're getting along well. Everything here is comfortable. But what about Ernő? And the others?"

"Have a seat." He didn't smile, and his eyes didn't hold their usual shine.

She dropped to the red brocade couch, her knees unable to support her. "What's happened to him?"

"He was released. A little battered but safe."

Every muscle in her body lost its stiffness, and she slumped against the back of the couch.

"So you see, I was right in making you come here. We have a bigger problem, though."

"Have you been followed?"

"They aren't tailing me. They don't know about me. To be on the safe side, I didn't approach this building until the sirens sounded."

She crossed her arms in front of her. "They are watching this place. Sometimes I see the soldier on the street. Always the same one, young, blond, with a jagged scar along his cheekbone. Unless it's an emergency, you shouldn't be here. One of these days the Nazis will grow suspicious and come after you. Then you would be the one bringing trouble to the house."

"Reka saw me dragging you out of the church."

Zofia bolted upright. "What?"

"I dropped the photo Éva gave me. She . . . they think I may be responsible for your disappearance."

"Surely Éva knows you better than that."

"The evidence points at me. If these were normal circumstances, I'd be hauled off to prison and charged with your kidnapping."

"And my husband?"

"He knows. Like his sister, there is doubt in his mind."

"They know I'm in hiding, though. You told them, so why would they believe a word she said?"

"I . . ." He rubbed the couch cushion.

She sprang to her feet. "You didn't tell them, did you?"

"It was for the best. If I told them, I would have to reveal my secret. About who I am. I refuse to do that."

"Because you cherish this precious world you've built more than me, more than Ernő, even more than Éva, whom you claim to love. Isn't that it?" The sirens' screech blasted through the window.

"I value my life. And theirs. Even above my love for her."

"You're afraid to tell her."

"That's absurd. If I don't tell her, I lose her too." He pinched the bridge of his nose. "Either way, my dream of making her my wife is gone."

"I want Ernő to know. Everything. You can't subject him to this torture of not knowing what happened to me." She understood that torture.

"He's already been brought in for questioning once. Next time, they won't release him. I won't put them under further risk. Or you. Did you think about what might happen if they go looking for you? Following me to find out? They'll lead the Gestapo straight to you."

"What if I'm willing to risk it?" A headache pounded behind her right eye.

"I'm doing this because I love all of you." Patrik's words stabbed her heart.

There were wrinkles around his eyes that hadn't been there a few weeks ago. None of this was easy on any of them. He stood beside her and took her by the hand. "In time, we'll tell them. We won't lie to them forever. When we reveal our secrets, they'll understand. They'll know why we did what we did."

She rubbed her aching temple. "I know. But—"

An ear-splitting screech cut off the rest of her words, followed by a concussion that shook the building. She covered her ears and huddled into herself.

Patrik enveloped her in an embrace for a long while until her trembling ceased.

She understood Patrik's reasoning. But she didn't agree with it. Maybe she would have to go to Ernő herself.

Chapter Eleven

Ernő held fast to the leather strap hanging from the streetcar's wood ceiling. The bell clanged at regular intervals along the route home. Buildings of every architectural style from the past few hundred years edged the street. A chilly, foggy drizzle obscured the Buda castle rising high above the city.

Bognár's Clarinets didn't produce many instruments these days. Importing wood and getting metal and felt to make the keys was impossible. The company refurbished and rebuilt what they could, but business was hurting.

The motion of the car rocked him into a teenage girl sitting beside him. He peered down to apologize, and the redness of her hair caught his eye.

So much like Zofia's.

For yet another day, he'd awakened without her beside him. Her disappearance hadn't been a bad dream. It was reality. Every morning that truth punched him in the gut.

For yet another day, he was going to the home he'd shared with her. And she wouldn't be there.

The streetcar slowed and came to a stop not far from the residential area where his family lived. Stepping to the street, he paused to remind himself that Zofia wouldn't come to the door and greet him with a kiss. Because sometimes, when he walked into the house, he expected just that.

"Hello, Ernő, is that you?" *Anya* called to him as he arrived inside. "You have a note on the table there. I came home from the market and found it in the letter box. Very odd, if you ask me. I hope it's not more bad news. This family can't stand any more."

Ernő tuned out the rest of *Anya*'s words as he picked up the paper. His heart pounded in his ears. The writing, though shaky, was familiar, like the love notes Zofia would stick in his lunch box. Could this be from her? Was he about to get answers?

He couldn't breathe. He broke the seal on the paper.

I have reason to believe your wife is alive and in hiding.

That was the entire length of the letter. He slammed it on the table. Nothing. No real information about Zofia such as her location or her well-being. It couldn't be from her. If it had been, she would have written more. Been more specific.

She would never have gone into hiding without informing him.

Anya emerged from the kitchen, wiping her hands on her apron. "What's wrong?" A few more crinkles appeared in her already-wrinkled brow.

"This." He shook the paper. "It says Zofia is in hiding."

Anya raced forward and gave him a gentle embrace. "What wonderful news."

He broke her hold and stepped away. "Not really. Who is it from? How does this person know for sure? Where is Zofia? All it has done is add more questions to the ones I already have."

"But it's hope. You can't deny that."

"You're right. And I know who can answer those questions." He turned to leave the house.

"Where are you going?"

"To find Patrik. Deep inside, I know he's the key. This time, I intend to find out what information he has."

After all, what did they really know about Patrik? He'd come into their lives just a year ago and won his sister over. The man had no family and hailed from another town. Was he a spy? When he met Zofia through the symphony, had he known her background or suspected it? Had he then used Éva to get to her?

It had happened before with Károly. He had used Éva to get information on Zofia, to dig into Zofia's background when she worked with the Polish underground. Éva had fallen in love with him, a man with a deep-seated hatred of the Jews. One he'd kept hidden from them until it was almost too late. If not for . . .

No time to dwell on that now. Ernő hurried in the direction he'd come from, avoiding the clanging streetcar, and traversed the few blocks from his house to Patrik's flat.

As soon as Patrik answered the door, Ernő stormed in, slamming it behind him. "What is the meaning of this?" He thrust the note at Patrik.

Patrik grabbed the piece of paper and read it, his eyes widening. "How did you get this?"

"So you do know something about it?"

"*Nem*, I don't. But who brought it to you? Who is it from?"

"At first, I thought Zofia, because the handwriting is similar to hers. Now I'm convinced it's not. She wouldn't drop me a single line and not tell me more."

Patrik shook his head. "You're right. If she were going to contact you, she wouldn't be this cryptic."

"So you do believe she's alive?"

"I can't say." Patrik turned his back on Ernő before facing him once more. "I just can't say."

"Can't or won't? From the time she disappeared, you haven't been able to look me in the eye. What is that about?"

"My friend . . ." Patrik's gaze flicked to Ernő's and then away again.

"Do you have any idea who this is from? Who might have information about my wife?" He resisted grabbing Patrik by the neck. Barely.

Patrik gave a slow shake of his head, his mouth turned down. "I am sorry for you. For Zofia. I'm sorry I . . . I can't look at you because every time I do, I see what could happen to me, to Éva."

Was his disappointment genuine? Was Ernő reading something into Patrik's behavior that wasn't there? Who knew anymore? He hadn't been part of their lives long enough for Ernő to read him well.

Ernő leaned in, close to Patrik though still half a head shorter than him. "If I find out that you had anything to do with my wife's disappearance, anything at all, I will come after you. What the Nazis did to me will be minor in comparison to what I will do to you. Do you understand?"

Patrik stood to his full height, towering over his friend, but his eyes were soft. "Of course I understand. You would protect your wife as I would Éva. I know you miss Zofia. We all do. How is Éva?"

"Confused. Hurting."

"Perhaps I'll stop over later tonight. I need to see her, speak to her. Tomorrow is supposed to be our wedding day."

"That's not going to happen."

"But I'd like to be with her."

"That's not a good idea."

"I understand it's difficult to know who to trust these days. But you have to believe me. She can't sort through her feelings without me there to answer her questions, if nothing else."

"Just leave her be."

"If you think it's best." Patrik sighed and rubbed his forehead. "I understand what you're going through, though, missing Zofia. So you know why I'm anxious to see Éva."

Why did his words ring hollow? Ernő left Patrik's flat and started for home. *Anya* would have dinner waiting. And one thing you didn't do was make her wait to serve a meal.

Just as he was about to step onto the walk, he bumped into someone. The scent of lilies filled his nostrils, the same scent Zofia wore.

He tightened his arms around the woman. Before he could kiss the top of her head, she shoved him away and pummeled him with her pocketbook. The metal clasp bruised his flesh, and a shock of pain ripped through his not-quite-healed ribs.

"What do you think you're doing, accosting a woman like that?"

Ernő covered his face and stepped away. "My apologies. I thought you were someone else."

The hail of blows halted, and he glanced up. He squinted to be sure he saw right. Before him stood a plump, fair-haired woman in a black coat, a rose-shaped pin on the lapel. "Reka?"

"Ernő, what are you doing here?" Red flooded her round cheeks.

"I could ask you the same question."

"I asked first."

"I needed to speak to Patrik. Your turn."

"Oh, this is Patrik's building? I didn't know that. What a co-incidence. I'm on my way home from a friend's house. I'm in town on business. Has he told you where Zofia is?"

"You think he has something to do with her disappearance?"

"I saw them. With my own two eyes. On the night she disappeared."

"He denies it. Says he could have dropped that picture any-where." He hated to believe that a member of their family had betrayed them.

"How would I have known what they were wearing? Did he deny being in the church?"

He hadn't.

She shifted her considerable weight from one foot to the other. "These are the days when you can't trust anyone. Not even your spouse." With that, Reka flounced away.

Strange, bumping into her at Patrik's flat. Very strange.

June 10, 1944

Éva slid the clarinet's mouthpiece between her lips, drew in a deep breath, and blew through the instrument. The reed vibrated against her lips, the tickle of it familiar.

She threw herself into Carl Maria von Weber's Concerto no. 1, the complicated runs and deep, haunting emotion of the composition lifting her from this world to one of music.

Nothing but music.

Her fingers ranged over the keys as her tongue tapped the reed during the staccato sections. The walls of her bedroom fell away. She didn't see anything. Only heard.

Heard with her ears.

Heard with her heart.

She sprinted with the runs, cried with the melody, somersaulted with the turns.

At last the piece ended with a flourish. All of the sudden, the walls were back. The room, her bed, her small wardrobe in the corner.

And her worries.

Today would have been her wedding day. Should have been. How could it have only been a few weeks since she'd been happy? Since everything in her life had changed?

On the corner of her desk sat the crumpled picture. She turned her attention from it. Was the man in the photo who he said he was? Or did he hide a dark secret?

Despite sleepless nights and restless days, she'd come to no conclusions. That's why there was no wedding today. No joyful start to a new life. Just questions and more questions.

With everything in her, she longed to believe in Patrik's innocence. But maybe Reka was correct. How well did she know him? Their courtship had been so brief, as had their engagement. Just a year from the time they met until the wedding. Was that enough time to get to know someone, or did the war make life move faster, like a movie reel in fast-forward?

With their like faith and their similar interest in music, their relationship came without much effort. They spoke for hours upon hours at a time.

But Reka had nothing to gain from discrediting Patrik. She had no obligation to come to Éva and share what she saw.

Was everything he said a lie?

Whom did Éva believe? A lifelong acquaintance or the love of her life?

She swabbed out her clarinet, pulled it apart, and placed the pieces in the blue-velvet-lined case, closing the lid with a click. What she needed to do was to speak with Patrik.

After informing *Anya* she was going out, she grabbed her coat and made her way toward Patrik's apartment. What would have been her home after today. Already some of her clothes and other belongings were there.

As she neared the neoclassical building with its straight, true columns, what might have been a swarm of bees infested her stomach. Why was she nervous to speak to Patrik? She'd been ready to marry him, might still do so. What held her back?

As she stood down the block from his flat, he exited the building and strolled down the street, hands in his pockets, as if he didn't have a care in the world.

"Patrik? Patrik!"

He didn't turn around. She scurried to catch up to him, but then he turned the corner onto the main street, and she lost him in the crowd.

Nem, wait, there he was, head and shoulders above everyone else. Though she attempted to wind her way through the maze of people, she couldn't catch him.

"Patrik!" Just as she shouted his name, the bells of the nearby church chimed the hour and drowned her out. Before she could call again, he turned down a side street and picked up his pace, his stride long and determined.

She remained behind him, too distant now. He was focused on something and not likely to respond to her call.

Before long, he reached a building much like his own. As he started up the steps, a German soldier departed the building, a creased cap on his head, a black belt cinched around his waist. The men stopped and spoke to each other.

Éva ducked behind a tree so neither one would catch sight of her. If only she could understand what they were saying.

Patrik laughed at something the Nazi said. Inconceivable. Patrik didn't usually have much positive to say about the occupiers. Both men then turned, and Patrik held the door open for the other man as they disappeared inside.

Éva's head swirled. What Reka had told her was true. All of it.

Patrik had been with Zofia. This jovial conversation with a Nazi proved he was collaborating with the occupiers and likely had been involved in her disappearance.

She tore down the street, not caring where she ended up or whom she bumped into. Her breath came in short spurts when it came at all.

She pumped her arms and legs, blinded by tears.

Then came the screech of brakes.

The shriek of an auto's horn.

An awful thump and searing pain.

Blessed blackness.

Chapter Twelve

A warm wind caressed Patrik's cheek as he hurried down the busy main street. Not wanting to draw attention to himself, he resisted the urge to turn around, but he couldn't shake the tingling of his skin that told him someone was following him.

He was being ridiculous. The end-of-the-day rush was on, and many of Budapest's residents were homeward bound. With everything going on with Zofia, he had turned paranoid.

He arrived at the side street he needed and broke off from the main throng, picking up his pace. After a minute or two, he dared to glance over his shoulder. See? He had been imagining things. No one was behind him.

Soon he came to his destination and climbed the single step to the dark-brown building, carved scrolls above the long windows on each of the three stories. Just as he was about to enter, the door swung open and a German soldier exited. He doffed his creased cap. "*Jó napot kívánok.*"

"Good day to . . . Bram? Is that you? I almost didn't recognize you." Patrik eyed him up and down. "What on earth are you wearing?"

Patrik's fair-haired compatriot grinned, dimples appearing in each cheek. "Don't you like it?"

"Have you gone mad?"

"Hardly, my friend. This is our latest Zionist Youth uniform."

Patrik chuckled. "Sure it is. And next, we'll all grow mustaches like Hitler."

"You never know."

Again, laughter exploded from Patrik's lips. "Never lose your sense of humor. It may serve you well in the days to come."

"I'm on my way out for some supper at the café. Would you care to join me?"

"What I have to discuss with you is better said away from the public. Can we speak in private?" Patrik opened the door and motioned for Bram to step inside.

"I'd prefer to converse with a good meal in my belly, but let's go up to my flat. A *pálinka* and a cigarette will have to do."

They ascended the two flights of stairs to the top floor. "Why would you wear that outfit if you're on your way out to eat?"

"We all know the Germans get the best seats, the prettiest waitresses, and the fastest service." A gleam lit Bram's green eyes.

The world may be crumbling around them, but Bram would forever be the jester of the bunch. They crossed into his well-appointed flat, Chinese-style furniture standing on top of Oriental rugs. "Honestly, I managed to come across this uniform—"

"Don't tell me—"

"And I wanted to try it out. See if I could fool people into believing I was a Nazi." He slid the red armband with the black swastika from his bicep and shivered. "You never know when it might come in handy."

Bram crossed the large, airy room to a brass beverage cart under a window accented by heavy red velvet drapes. He lifted the lid on an ice container, plinked two cubes into a glass, and poured liquid from a tall decanter. He turned to Patrik. "I'd offer you some, but I know you'd decline."

"Much as I would like it to be, this isn't a social call. We've had some trouble."

Bram took a swig of the liquor. "I heard about Zofia. Nasty business, but she's a smart woman. Now that she's stashed away, she'll be fine. With a good head on her shoulders like that, I imagine there will be no more problems."

Patrik sat on the edge of the sofa and leaned forward. "The hitch is that the Gestapo searched the Bognár apartment the very night she went into hiding."

Bram settled himself in an out-of-place brown leather armchair and crossed his legs. "Did they find anything incriminating?"

"I don't believe so." Patrik shifted his gaze to the scene outside the window, a light drizzle falling as dusk covered the city. Not far in the distance, an ambulance siren wailed. "Zofia told me she didn't keep any paperwork at the house."

"Then we have nothing to worry about." Bram set his drink on a black-stained end table and lit a cigarette.

"She needs papers."

"And she'll get them. Eventually."

"Eventually?" Patrik jumped to his feet. "That's not good enough. Zofia has a husband she needs to reunite with. She already sent him one note, anonymously, saying she was alive and in hiding. How long before she dares to step out and go to her husband? The Germans will be on her like ants on candy. And I've lost Éva over this mess."

"What aren't you telling me?" Bram raised one eyebrow.

Patrik drew in a deep breath. Bram would be furious, but Patrik owed him the truth. "An old school friend of Éva's saw me with Zofia the night she disappeared."

"What? Why weren't you more careful? This certainly is a problem."

"Apparently, in the church, I dropped a picture Éva had given me as Zofia and I left. This woman told Éva she believes I am responsible for Zofia's disappearance."

"You are."

"Éva isn't supposed to know that. Now my relationship with her is threatened."

"I'm more concerned about this woman who spotted you with Zofia and found the photograph. That's where your carelessness might get us in trouble. How much does she know?"

"Nothing. As I said, she told Éva she thinks I'm involved with the Germans."

"All the better for us. Better than having them think you're part of the Zionist Youth."

Couldn't the man see Patrik's point? "Zofia needs those papers. Now. Then she and her husband can get out of the country before she does something stupid."

"I'll do the best I can, but I make no guarantees." Bram ground the butt of his cigarette into a brass ashtray.

"Why?"

"Because she's already in hiding. There are others not so fortunate. Those are the ones who need the most help."

The wail of an ambulance siren interrupted their conversation. Patrik rose and peered out the window. A group of people huddled together at the end of the street. He could make out nothing else. "But Zofia's husband."

"She has to stay away from him. They're watching the house, in all likelihood."

But Zofia might just be desperate enough to do more than send Ernő a note.

Anya came and touched Ernő's shoulder as he sat in the living room staring out the window at the light rain deepening the gathering dusk. The warmth of her fingers penetrated his cotton shirt but didn't reach the chill that had permeated him since Zofia disappeared.

The numbness was a blessing. If he dared to think or feel too much, the pain was unbearable.

"How are you, son?"

He clenched his jaw and shook his head. "How am I supposed to be? My wife is missing. And Patrik isn't telling the truth about it. No matter what that note said, I have no confirmation Zofia is alive."

"That Patrik. I never did trust him."

Ernő glanced sideways at her.

"He wanted to get married so fast and take Éva away. Maybe in the country, that's how it's done, but not here. Families stay together. Plus, Éva wants to believe him, you can tell. All he's done is upset her and the rest of the family. But if he's not being truthful with you, then she shouldn't marry him. Too many people have too much to hide these days."

Ernő stared at his hands, the hands which God had gifted him to create some of the most sought-after clarinets in Europe. With the way they shook now, he couldn't carve the wood the way he needed to produce the fine-quality sound musicians all over the continent demanded. "Maybe we all were fools." Ernő spun around and stared into his mother's soft blue eyes. Were those new crow's feet?

She rubbed his upper arm. "I know."

"Has he betrayed us? We trusted him. Éva almost married him. Has he duped us all? Did we allow another Nazi sympathizer like Károly into our lives?"

"I don't know. I suppose it's a good thing it happened now and not after Éva wed him."

"So you think he was part of it?"

With a shrug, she turned toward the kitchen, then called to him over her shoulder. "Please tell *Apu* and Éva that dinner is almost ready."

He lumbered down the hall and was about to knock on his parents' bedroom door when the telephone rang.

"Could someone answer that? I can't leave the gravy right now."

"Sure, *Anya*." Ernő hustled to the living room to the phone on the little stand beside the couch and lifted the black receiver. "Hello."

"Is this the Bognár residence?" Noise in the background made it difficult for Ernő to pick out the tinny voice.

"It is."

"Are you a relative of Éva?"

"She's my sister." Ernő clutched the receiver with all his might.

"I'm calling from St. John's Hospital. Your sister was struck by an auto this evening."

"That's impossible. She's in her room. I was about to call her for dinner. I'll show you." He held the phone away from himself and shouted up the stairs. "Éva. Éva! I need you now."

Apu and *Anya* wandered in from opposite ends of the house. "What is the commotion for?"

Ernő covered the mouthpiece. "This woman says Éva was in an accident. But she's in her room. Isn't she?"

Anya furrowed her brow and hustled to the stairs. Ernő set down the receiver and sped after her, up the steps to Éva's door, and flung it open. *Anya* gasped.

The room was empty.

God, nem.

"She's not here." *Anya*'s voice warbled. "She told me she was going out earlier, but I thought she'd returned."

Ernő raced down the stairs and spoke to the woman on the line once more. "Which hospital did you say?"

"St. John's."

"We'll be there as soon as possible."

Apu already had his suit coat on and was helping *Anya* slip on her sweater.

No sooner had they left the house than the air raid sirens blared their nightly call. Already fires burned in other parts of the city, the flames licking at the darkened sky, casting a ghostly glow over all of Buda. Ernő turned to his parents. "Go back. I'll check on Éva and ring you with news."

Anya stomped her laced-up oxford. "*Nem.* My daughter needs me. I want to be with her."

"The patrols will catch you. The planes are coming ever nearer." Not too far in the distance, flashes of light brightened the early evening.

"And what about you?" *Apu* shrank into his over-sized black blazer.

"You know I run faster than a thoroughbred. I'll outsprint anyone who dares to stop me."

"I'm coming with you." *Anya* set her shoulders, and her page-boy haircut swayed as she shook her head.

"I'll run faster alone, and I won't have to worry about your safety if I know you're at home."

Apu tugged on *Anya*'s arm, even though she rose at least fifteen centimeters above him and outweighed him by a good number of kilos.

"Promise me you'll find shelter if the planes get too near." *Anya* shook her finger in Ernő's face.

"I promise."

They returned inside, and he trotted down the street. His loafers weren't designed for running, and the shock of every step jarred his bones. But he had no choice. He had to stay ahead of the air raid wardens and the Germans and get to Éva as fast as possible.

Within three blocks, his lungs burned. The rumble of planes and the whine of falling bombs broke the silence of the streets. Still he raced, willing his legs to carry him with all speed. The dark shadow of an air raid warden loomed in front of him and Ernő careened around the corner.

The dash wasn't the sole cause of his rapid heartbeat. He'd already lost Zofia. Now this had happened to his precious Éva. "Not her too, Lord!" He shook his fist at the heavens.

Up ahead stood the hospital, a red brick building with its grand, arched doorway and arched windows. Sirens wailed as ambulances delivered patients, perhaps bombing victims. Gasping for air, Ernő burst through the doors into a chaotic scene.

Men, women, and children, probably brought in from all parts of the city, lay on stretchers in the lobby, the floor slick with blood. White-coated doctors and capped nurses triaged the wounded and dying.

Ernő covered his mouth but couldn't block the metallic odor of blood. Was Éva among these patients?

A young blond nurse, a swastika pin on the collar of her white dress, pushed through the wounded toward him. "Can I help you, sir?"

"Bognár Éva."

"I'm sorry. We haven't identified everyone." She appraised him, and he stood taller under her scrutiny. Perhaps if she believed he was an important person, she would assist him in locating his sister. "Did you come with the victims?"

"*Nem*, she was in an accident earlier this evening. Hit by an auto."

"Fourth floor." The woman pointed to the stairs at the far end of the lobby.

Averting his eyes from the mass of suffering humanity was impossible. Instead, Ernő tried his best to ignore the weeping, the cries of anguish, the moans of the dying as he made his way to the stairs.

Once he reached the fourth floor, another nurse pointed him to Éva's bed, under the window near the end of the ward. The nurse in her white uniform reminded him of an angel robed in pure raiment.

But this was not heaven.

Ernő rushed to Éva's side. Bandages covered her head, the flesh around her eyes was black-and-blue, and her cheeks were swollen. She was almost unrecognizable. Only her honey-colored curls gave away her identity.

As he clasped her by the hand, she convulsed.

Ernő's own heart seized. "Nurse! Nurse! Help us! Please save my sister."

♪♫♪ ♪

Chapter Thirteen

atrik!" Zofia restrained herself from leaping into his arms when she opened the door to him. His special knock had informed her he was here before she even saw him. Tóth *Asszony* was kind, but a familiar face buoyed her spirits more than summer sunshine.

Then again, if he had spoken to Ernő, he would know about the note she sent her husband. She'd labored over each word so she didn't leave any clue to her whereabouts. Just a little something to ease his mind.

Patrik kissed her on both cheeks, and she led him into the old-lady-styled living room.

"I'm surprised to see you here so late. Tóth *Asszony* has already retired for the evening. She goes to bed early every night there isn't an air raid."

"And that leaves you lonely."

"Terribly. But let me take your coat and get you a cup of tea. She has a few leaves left. She claims to have had some clairvoyant sense that war was coming, and so she stocked up."

He waved her off. "I just came for a quick peek to make sure you were getting along." His words were clipped, stiff, formal.

He must know.

She motioned Patrik to the sofa and sat, her leg tucked underneath her. "Besides the loneliness and homesickness, I'm fine." That and the morning sickness that lasted all day. "But you look like you were dragged through the Danube and then run over by a truck."

"Lonely for Éva, I guess."

"And working long hours with the Zionists. How is everyone there? Can't I do something? I've already written a couple more articles. Take them with you and get them printed."

He nodded.

"Of course, I won't be here very long, because my new identification will come soon."

He reached out and touched her forearm, his dark eyes unreadable. "Zofia."

The way he spoke her name sucked the air from her chest. He was about to scold her for writing that note. "What?" She whispered the word and scrunched her eyes shut.

"Look at me."

She dared to peer at him through her eyelashes. What she saw etched in the tautness of his mouth wasn't good.

"I spoke to Bram the other day. There won't be papers for you, not any time soon."

"What?" This had to be a bad dream she couldn't claw her way out of. "Why not?"

"The Gestapo is on the lookout for you, especially since you slipped through their fingers once already. There is no way you can return to your family, not without leading the Germans straight to them. We've been through this already. No need to rehash it."

"Of course, but I thought—"

"And they've been to your residence twice."

"So I can't go home until when?"

"Very likely not until the war is over. And no more notes."

She tamped down her reaction, working on keeping her face neutral. "What do you mean?"

"Don't pick now to start being coy. It doesn't become you. Ernő came to my flat and showed me what you sent. Not only was it crazy to contact him, it was crazy for you to be out."

"Tóth *Asszony* dropped it in their mail slot. Did Ernő know it was from me?"

"I persuaded him it wasn't you who wrote it."

She blinked back the tears that rose to her eyes. "Why would you do that? Give the man hope that he'll see me again one day."

"I'm trying to keep him alive. Even sending Tóth *Asszony* was risky. Anyone watching the house might have traced her back here."

"How long will I have to remain in this confinement?"

"The Russians aren't far away."

Too long. She would have to figure out a way to see her husband. Sooner rather than later.

She rose and sauntered to the piano, pulled out the bench, and grasped the open keyboard cover. If only the peace, the comfort of the music would flow from the instrument into her body.

She slammed the lid shut. She couldn't play. "I'm going to go crazy."

"I have a story to cheer you up." He shared with her Bram's attempt to get better restaurant service by impersonating a Nazi officer.

She couldn't bring herself to laugh.

"Come on, what will make you happy?"

"Other than being with Ernő or being able to play the piano?"

"Whatever it is, I'll do my best to make it possible."

"Lipstick." Sure, it sounded shallow, but she had to have something to brighten her days. "I don't have any with me, and I need some. I feel unkempt without it."

"I thought you might ask me for chocolate."

Her stomach churned at the imagined aroma. Once it was her favorite candy, but since her pregnancy, she couldn't stand even the thought of the stuff.

"Or your Bible."

"Tóth *Asszony* has one I read every day. Don't fret about that. But a girl has to have lipstick."

"You're asking the impossible, you know. The shops don't carry it anymore."

"You're a bright man. You'll figure it out."

Patrik slapped his knees and came to his feet. "I'll do my best. Is there anything else?"

"So I can play the piano, can we start a rumor that I'm Tóth *Asszony*'s niece come from the countryside? I'm begging you."

"Not possible. Too suspicious. No one, and I mean no one, can know you're here. Behave yourself and stay put."

"What if you snuck Ernő out the back window of his house and took a circuitous route here? Just so I could see him for a while." She was being ridiculous. Crazy. Reckless. Her presence endangered him, much as it had her mother. But just to touch him . . .

In reply, Patrik raised his eyebrows. That was a *nem*. "You have to promise not to go to him. Promise me you won't get everyone in that house arrested."

"Fine. I promise."

As soon as he had that assurance, he was gone.

She should lie down and get some rest before another air raid sounded, but she couldn't make herself go to bed. Instead, she drew a sheet of paper, a pen, and a pot of ink from the middle desk drawer. She pulled her chair closer to the radio and turned it on, so low she almost had to press against the set to hear the Wagner opera that was playing.

Across the top of the sheet, she wrote, "'The State of the Persecuted in Hiding.' By Katona Marika."

That was her. The rebellious soldier. One who would see her husband.

Absolute silence filled Éva's head. All around her was still. No talking. No sirens. No music.

She couldn't open her eyes, no matter how hard she tried. What was wrong? Why was there no noise? Why couldn't she wake up?

A downward force tugged on her, dragging her lower, further into the silence. She pressed against it, fighting it. Without being told, she understood it was someplace she didn't dare venture.

She tried to inhale and exhale deeply, like she'd practiced in her quest for superb clarinet tone, but the pain was excruciating. However, it broke the hold of whatever was drawing her down.

"*Nyuszikám.*" My bunny.

The voice was familiar. She struggled to place a name with it.

"Don't move. You've been injured and had a seizure. I told the doctors to give you stronger pain medication, but they don't listen to me. They think they know it all, telling me it's being used in the war effort. I'll call for the nurse."

Anya. That's who it was. Her faithful, constant *Anya.*

Anya, don't go. I need you. I can't wake up.

Éva tried to speak but couldn't move her lips. But *Anya* was here. Was *Apu* too? And Patrik?

Nem, not Patrik. The memory of the past few weeks rushed back. Not him, never again.

"There now, it's just like I told you. She's struggling. Give her more pain medication."

"Bognár *Asszony*, she isn't due for more for two hours."

"My daughter is in pain. Give her some kind of relief."

Was that what had caused that strange downward sensation? If so, Éva would rather bear the agony. With all her might, she managed to get one of her eyes to crack open.

Anya's round face and pinched lips settled into focus. Éva blinked at the light.

"Éva. Éva, darling. You're awake."

"What—"

"Now, now, don't speak. You were hit by an auto, over in the Seventh District. What on earth were you doing there? We all thought you were in the house until the call came from the hospital. And that crazy German driver didn't even stop to help."

"Pat . . ."

"He's not here, and you don't want him here. Don't you remember?"

She did. All too well.

"*Apu* and Ernő went to get a bite to eat. Don't worry. They'll be back soon. You gave us quite a fright. You have several cracked ribs and a nasty bump on your head, and you had a seizure that scared us all to death. But praise the Lord, and only by His goodness, you have no internal bleeding. The doctor says it's nothing short of a miracle."

A miracle. *Nem*, this was a nightmare, not a miracle. No one here to protect her, to take care of her. She had no hope for the future.

"Stu-di-o." The effort required to pronounce the word left her exhausted. But without either her or Zofia, what would happen to their business?

"No need to concern yourself with that now. Your students will understand. Think of how well they will know their lessons when you return. Though it will be awhile before you'll feel like playing your clarinet again."

Nem, she needed its solace, especially now when she'd lost everything.

"Where is that doctor? He said he'd check you this afternoon, but it's nearly four, and I haven't seen him yet. He's not anywhere in the ward. By the time he gets to you, it will be well past supper time. Oh dear, you must be so hungry and thirsty. Let me get that nurse to get you something."

Éva tried to protest but didn't have the strength to call after *Anya*.

Éva turned her head, fire shooting through her brain and settling in her temples, sending them pounding. Her mother hustled down the aisle lined with beds, maybe twenty or so on each side, most of them occupied.

Anya had mentioned something about an accident, but Éva couldn't bring the event to mind. An image of Patrik speaking to a German soldier flickered through her brain. At that, her chest burned.

He'd betrayed her. And Zofia.

Someone appeared in the doorway *Anya* had exited—a dark, blurry figure, no more than a shadow. The shadow made its way down the aisle. The person's towering height, lean body, and confident stride left Éva no doubt as to who it was.

Patrik held his black Hamburg hat in his hands, a feather in the hat band, and spun it around. He flashed her a brief smile before occupying the chair *Anya* had vacated. "How are you feeling?"

Her tongue tingled, but she couldn't form the words she wanted.

"I would have come sooner, but I only found out about the accident today."

Sooner? How long had she been here? Hadn't it only been a few hours?

"I'm sorry this happened to you. On top of everything else. Don't worry. After this, I'm going to speak to your father about keeping your music studio open. We can use students from the university as temporary teachers."

"*Nem.*" She managed to croak out the word. Why would he be interested in the studio? Did he want to use it as a front for something? Of course. Before the occupation, they'd had many Jewish students. Perhaps he wanted to get his hands on their information so he could have them arrested too.

Then again, he already had a key. Maybe he possessed the information he needed.

"*Nem.*" She spat out the word with as much force as she could muster.

"I know you're upset about what Reka said, but you have to know her allegations are false. I would never, never do anything to harm Zofia. Please, believe me."

"What I believe, young man, is that you've come here while

my daughter is seriously injured and upset her." *Anya* stood behind Patrik, legs apart, her eyes glinting with the fierceness of a mother lion about to pounce.

He shot to his feet, knocking the chair over with a clatter. "Bognár *Asszony*, I didn't hear you coming."

"You should be ashamed of yourself. How dare you show your face here."

"I . . . I . . . I was concerned for her."

"How did you even find out about it?"

"There was a write-up in the paper. I only wanted to see for myself how she was and to tell her I'll be praying for her speedy recovery."

"That's not what it sounded like you were saying. Leave. Now. Before I have to get one of the orderlies to throw you out. And don't come near my daughter ever again."

Patrik picked up his hat, which had tumbled from his lap when he stood. "Feel better soon, Éva."

He hadn't walked more than a few meters before *Anya* started in. "Can you believe that man's audacity to show up here? He had no right to upset you in such a manner. Good riddance."

Anya chattered on, but Éva kept her attention on Patrik.

He'd betrayed her, just like Károly had. Károly had almost destroyed Zofia.

Patrik may well have succeeded where Károly failed.

There he went—down the aisle, through the door, and out of her life forever.

Chapter Fourteen

The small meeting room in the back-alley flat was crowded with men of varied attire. Some were dressed in smartly creased slacks, pressed white shirts, and colorful sweater vests. Others wore pants with worn hems and scuffed shoes that barely held together.

Patrik squeezed his way into the warm, overcrowded lounge where several women were as well, most dressed in simple wool skirts and plain blouses.

For the mass of humanity crammed into the tiny space, there was a remarkable lack of noise. And for good reason. If the Gestapo found out about this organization and its activities, they would all be as good as dead.

Flóra Simon, an elegant, well-bred young woman with dark hair, puffed on a cigarette in a long holder and leaned over to whisper in Patrik's ear as he passed. "How is Zofia holding up?"

"She wants those papers, and not in a few months like Bram promised."

Flóra widened her gray eyes. "She won't do anything rash, will she?"

"She's too sensible." At least, that was his hope. He had no guarantee of it. Already, she'd sent that note. What might she do next?

He rubbed his aching neck as he threaded his way toward Bram. In the two nights since he'd visited Éva in the hospital, he'd slept very little. The paper mentioned the location of the accident. It had occurred just a few blocks away, about the same time he was at Bram's. Had she tailed him?

Standing by her hospital bed earlier, gazing into her beautiful but bruised face, it had taken Patrik every gram of his willpower not to blurt out the truth. But to keep her from ending up in the hospital again, or worse, he had to keep his secret. He could not risk revealing who he really was or let Zofia see Ernő and put all the family in peril.

Saving Éva's life might mean he'd have to spend his own life without her. Nothing but difficult decisions these days.

Before Patrik could reach him, Bram called the meeting to order. Today he sported a long trench coat and knee-high boots, his ever-present glass of *pálinka* in his hand. "Recent developments underscore the danger each of us faces, especially those who don't possess Gentile identity papers."

A murmur spread throughout the tiny space, grumblings from those who weren't owners of the coveted IDs. Patrik patted the pocket of his light-blue dress shirt where he kept his false identity papers. They proclaimed him to be 100 percent Aryan, even though he was nothing of the sort.

Patrik stepped to the front beside Bram, raised his hand, and the group quieted. Then he turned his attention to Bram. "If we are going to be effective in our work, we all must be able to move about the city without worrying about being picked up. Because she didn't have the right identification, Zofia is in peril. She's only alive by God's grace and her quick thinking."

Bram swallowed a draught from his snifter. "I'm well aware. But we can only process so many papers at a time. There are limits to what our presses can do."

"Then we have to do better."

Bram nodded, a blond curl falling over his right eye. "I agree. Right now, the situation in the countryside is the direst. Almost all the Jews outside of the city limits have been rounded up into ghettos. The Allies have bombed the train lines to the extermination camps, but the Germans aren't deterred. They're forcing old and young alike to march into Poland."

A pang gripped Patrik at the news. *My sisters.* He pushed away the thought. "How long before they start mass roundups here? Once they begin, it won't take them long to cleanse the city. We all know about the yellow-star houses. Not ghettos, necessarily, but concentrations of Jews nonetheless."

Bram drained the last of the liquid in his glass and shrugged. "With the Germans, who knows what their next move could be? They could start emptying Budapest tomorrow or next week or next year."

Flóra swore. "God forbid this war lasts that long."

Bram brushed the hair from his face. "Not likely. The Russians are already on the Hungarian border."

Such news did nothing to calm Patrik. "That only makes the Nazis more dangerous. They're staring defeat in the eye, but they'll accomplish as much of their evil mission as they can before their downfall arrives."

The meeting droned on, the discussion revolving around their course of action in the coming weeks. After hours of debate, Bram motioned for silence. "The best we can do right now is process as many false birth certificates and passports as possible, both for our own members and for those Jews outside the movement. Though it poses greater risk of exposure, we'll have to bring in more people to work for us."

The meeting adjourned, and at last, Patrik managed to corner Bram. "Is it wise to increase your staff?"

"The Germans believe I run a harmless little glassware company, nothing they look at too hard. The size of my employee roster isn't a concern of theirs. Right now, their interest is focused on a single objective."

"Ridding Hungary of each and every Jew."

"Correct."

"We may have a problem, though."

Bram cocked his head.

"Éva was struck by a car the other night and sustained serious injuries. The accident happened a few blocks from your flat at around the same time I was there."

"You think she came after you?"

"I can't be sure. She couldn't speak well, and her mother chased me from the ward as soon as she spotted me. But it's possible."

"Be extra careful."

"She would never knowingly do or say anything to put me at risk, especially since she believes I'm working with the Germans."

"You just never know. Watch your back."

The dim evening light streamed through the window at the end of the ward, near where Éva lay. *Anya* had gone home to make supper for *Apu* and Ernő. Éva was here alone with her thoughts.

Still no word from Zofia.

That could only mean one thing. Patrik, working with the Germans, had her. And likely Éva and her family would never see Zofia again. Éva's physical discomfort didn't begin to match the pain deep inside her. Patrik had betrayed her. Betrayed them all.

She stared out the window until the sun dipped behind the church steeple. Then she allowed sleep to overtake her and, for a little while, bring sweet release.

"Éva, dear, are you awake?"

Someone's breath tickled Éva's ear. Though she brushed it away, the sensation didn't dissipate. She opened her eyes and rolled over, taking it slow, and found Reka hovering.

"Good, you are. I'm glad to see you are healing."

"How nice of you to come." But seeing Reka's face only engulfed Éva in the memories of her last, awful visit. The pain in her soul ran deeper than any physical ache. An agony that played a melody in a minor key.

"I brought you flowers." Reka held up a bouquet of yellow roses. Where had she gotten them? In a time of war, flowers were a frivolity few could afford.

"Thank you. Will you put them on the table there for me?" Éva pointed to a small nightstand between her bed and the one beside her.

Once she had done so, Reka seated herself at Éva's side. "I was terribly sorry to hear about the accident. I had planned to visit you anyway when I was in the city, to find out how you were doing after that blow I was forced to deliver." She opened her black patent-leather pocketbook, pulled out an embroidered handkerchief, and dabbed her dry eyes.

"You were right. I saw him." Éva whispered the words, still so difficult to believe.

"He was part of it? What did you see?"

"*Igen.* Much as I want to deny it, much as I want to close my eyes and turn the clock back, I can't. The day of the accident, I trailed him and caught him speaking and laughing with a German."

"Oh, my dear." With her pudgy fingers, Reka grasped Éva's forearm, her red mouth open, almost in surprise. "This is one case when I wish I would have been wrong."

"I have to thank you."

"Whatever for? I wish I could have spared you the pain of the truth."

"But you kept me from marrying a man who is involved in horrible, vile activities against the Jews, against Hungary. All along, he plotted against Zofia, even while he acted the part of a kind and loving Christian man. He used me to get to her."

"They have acid in the nice apples."

"That's all too true."

Reka straightened, and a smile lit her face. "Now I have a surprise for you." She reached to the floor and grabbed a portable wind-up phonograph player. "A little music to cheer you."

"Won't it disturb the other patients?"

"Nonsense. We'll keep it soft. Music has healing properties, you know, so it would be good for them too."

In no time at all, she cranked it and placed the needle on the record. Brahms's Clarinet Sonata no. 2 in E♭ filled the air, the melody washing over Éva like warm bathwater. She closed her eyes and reveled in the velvetlike smoothness of the sound. Her body relaxed, and the suffering subsided.

Reka kissed her on both cheeks. "I'll leave you now to rest. There is a stack of other records here for you. When you've recuperated, you can return them to me."

Éva flicked her eyes open and smiled at Reka. "You're a good friend and a blessing to me in this difficult time."

"You can always depend on me. Though there is one favor you could grant me."

"I don't know what I'm capable of from this hospital bed, but I'll do my best, because I owe you a great debt."

"I am troubled about Patrik. Do you remember where you witnessed him speaking to that German? There has to be something we can do to punish him for what he did."

"Like what? We can't go to the authorities, because the Nazis control everything. They would reward him for his actions."

"If you'll let me, I'll investigate Patrik further. See what he's been up to. Then perhaps we'll come up with something. Maybe a way to warn other Jews to stay away from him."

"I don't know." The music pulled her in, lulling her to slumber.

"Just tell me the location, and I'll take care of the rest."

"Right now, I truly can't remember. While I followed him, I didn't pay attention to where we were going. I need to sleep."

"Of course, my dear. I'm sorry to have disturbed you. Rest is the best remedy. We'll talk another day, perhaps earlier when you're fresh and can remember details. Focus on getting better."

"Thank you for everything."

"My pleasure." With that, Reka left, the rhythmic tap of her shoes fading down the hallway, the cloying scent of rose perfume trailing behind her.

The phonograph played on, but the melody didn't transport Éva back to sleep.

Chapter Fifteen

$\mathscr{P}$atrik wound his way through the streets of Budapest, the Buda castle rising above him. No direct route for him to Tóth *Asszony*'s flat today. Bad enough that Éva had tailed him. He couldn't risk anyone nefarious doing so.

After numerous twists and turns, he set course for the apartment building. Even before he rounded the corner onto the street, he glanced over his shoulder several times to be sure no one stalked him.

Good, all was clear. He slipped into the building and climbed the stairs to the flat.

Zofia opened the door before he had a chance to knock.

"How did you know I was coming?"

She ushered him inside to the lounge, with its collection of crocheted lace doilies covering every chair and table, and they sat. "I spotted you from the window." She pointed to the lace-covered panes in the center of the main wall.

"I thought I told you to behave."

"No one in this sleepy neighborhood saw me."

"What about that soldier who was watching the building?"

"I haven't seen him for the past couple of days."

"You can't be too careful. The people in this building may have nothing better to do than to snoop on others."

"Where's my lipstick?"

"Trying to change the subject, I see." He pulled the tube from his pants pocket and handed it to her. "One Éva left at my place a few weeks ago. A little used—"

"But a tube of lipstick." She jumped up and scooted to the gilded mirror above the ornate fireplace. As she did so, the green dress Tóth *Asszony* had provided for her clung to her midsection. Did Patrik detect a slight bulge?

He got up and stood behind her as she colored her mouth. Come to think of it, she was pale and the rest of her was thinner than usual. "Zofia, do you have something to tell me?"

She smacked her lips. "What do you mean?"

"Are you . . ."—how did he ask such a delicate question?—"are you with child?"

If possible, she paled further, the red of the cosmetic standing out even more.

"You are." A pregnancy was usually a happy event, but this was a complication that they didn't need. If all went well, the Soviets would liberate them before the child made his appearance in the world. If not, hiding not only Zofia but also an infant might be next to impossible. Bram needed to speed up those papers.

Zofia spun to face him but couldn't look him in the eye. "This is especially why I must see Ernő. He doesn't know. I was going to tell him but then I had to hide. I can't keep him from his child. Imagine the joy I'm depriving him of."

"If the Gestapo finds you and knows you are with child, that gives them even more leverage to get what they want. Your pregnancy has made matters worse, not better."

"What if you bring me to him on some dark and stormy night? One when the police and patrols won't be out. Or won't be interested in anyone who is."

"They'll be particularly curious as to why someone isn't inside by their cozy fire. *Nem*, it's bad enough about Éva. We don't need Ernő coming to harm too."

"Éva?" Zofia clung to the back of the davenport.

He related the information. She collapsed in his arms, and he led her to the settee.

"Will she make a full recovery?"

"I hope so. I've told you all I know, and I don't expect to hear much more. Bognár *Asszony* has banned me from seeing her daughter. My guess is that's fine with Éva."

Zofia shook her head, a red curl escaping from the pins that held it rolled against her scalp. "See, even without us in their lives, bad things happen to Ernő and Éva. My staying here isn't going to change their circumstances one way or the other."

"Never."

Zofia fanned herself. "Could you do me a favor and get me a glass of water?"

He rose from the chair and rummaged in the kitchen until he found a glass then filled it from the tap. When he reentered the lounge, Zofia stood in the middle of the room, grasping a bunch of papers in her hand.

She passed them to him as she took the water. "I've been working on this during my free time, which is all my time. Tóth *Asszony* does nothing more than nap and go out to play cards with her friends."

He glanced at the title, "The State of the Persecuted in Hiding."

"A little light reading for those who find themselves in the same situation as me."

He skimmed the content. Well written. Sympathetic. Obviously composed by someone with a price on her head. "What is it you want me to do with it?"

"Take it to be printed, of course." She rubbed her small, round belly.

He thrust the papers in her direction. "*Nem*, I won't do it."

"Why not?"

"What happens if the Gestapo finds this? They will double or triple their efforts to locate you."

She didn't take back the pages. "It's a risk I'm willing to take. Especially if I have to be cooped up in here."

"Think about this unborn child. That needs to be your primary concern. For the baby's sake, you must do everything in your power to survive and make sure his father lives."

She licked her red bottom lip, then bit it. "I must have something. My husband and my music have been taken from me, leaving me with nothing."

"This child isn't nothing."

She drew in a deep breath and let it out little by little. "What about the world my child will grow up in? What about all the Jewish children huddled out there now in the elements, nothing to eat, no one to care for them, their lives disposable? Someone has to do something for them. Why not me?"

True. All true. But at what cost? Was the price too high? Was there a point at which you had to say no to the greater good for your own good? "You are the most stubborn, most frustrating woman I've ever met. How does Ernő put up with you?"

"He loves me as much as you love Éva. Don't you want to make the world a better place for her and the family you will have someday?"

The thought almost ripped his heart from his body. "We will never have children together. I've lost her, Zofia. I've lost her." His throat swelled.

"All you have to do to get her back is tell the truth."

"*Nem.*" He croaked out the word.

"Then do this for me." She gestured toward the papers he clutched. "Print that, and have Bram distribute it to the Jews and the trustworthy Christians in the city. Give them hope."

"And if you're caught?"

"Then I trust myself to God."

Early July 1944

Éva sat in the yellow-flowered chintz armchair beside the tall window, the summer sunshine warming her shoulders. After a dismal and chilly spring with far too much snow, summer had come in all its glory.

She snuggled into the chair and relished her homecoming as much as she could, even though she was already bored, which made it difficult to ignore her headache. Her cracked ribs had yet to fully heal, so playing her clarinet was out of the question. It was still hard just to take a deep breath, let alone push air through an instrument. She had music playing on the portable phonograph Reka brought, but it wasn't quite the same as making the music herself.

A slip of paper on the end table beside her drew her attention. What was this? She unfolded it.

"What would you like me to make you for lunch?" *Anya's* call came from the kitchen. "I've been saving my coupons the entire time you've been in the hospital, so I can make you something wonderful for your homecoming. *Gundel palacsinta*, perhaps?"

Walnut- and raisin-filled crepes with chocolate sauce. Éva's favorite. But she was exhausted from the trip home. "Maybe something later. Right now I'm not hungry."

"Are you sure? I'd been planning to make it for Zofia's homecoming, but now that we know she's in hiding, she won't be back anytime soon."

Éva sat up as straight as she could. "How do you know she's in hiding?"

Anya entered the lounge. "Oh dear. Perhaps I said too much. Your brother received a note. Just a line in what appeared to be Zofia's handwriting saying she was safe and in hiding."

"What does it mean?"

"I don't know. Zofia is alive, apparently, and didn't bother to tell anyone she was going into hiding. Ernő went to talk to Patrik about it. He believes your former fiancé has something to do with this. You'll have to ask your brother more about it."

Anya spun toward the kitchen, probably to cook, even though Éva had said she wasn't hungry.

But that note.

Éva clutched the chair's scrolled armrest.

When he'd visited her in the hospital, Ernő hadn't said a word about it. Did he know what Zofia was involved in? Whisperings swirled on the streets about a Zionist Youth movement, Jews with Aryan papers laboring to spirit as many of their brothers and sisters as possible out of the country and to Palestine.

What did this mean for Patrik? Perhaps he had been telling the truth when he said he had nothing to do with Zofia's disappearance. Or maybe he helped her into hiding.

Could that be it?

But what about that German she saw him with?

Other than the clanging of pans and the scrape of a whisk against a bowl, the house fell silent. Once upon a time, the place had been filled with love, laughter, and music. Now, it was nothing more than an empty shell.

If only she could play her clarinet. Its sweet richness would help her forget the topsy-turvy world they occupied.

One thing was for sure. She would no longer sit here and do nothing to aid people like her sister-in-law. As soon as she healed, she would return to Kistarcsa with more bread. Would the little girl in the maroon coat still be there? Or had she left for Poland weeks ago?

Well, sitting here like this wouldn't help her regain her strength. Little by little, she raised herself from her chair and shuffled in the direction of the stairs. How good it would be to sleep in her own bed tonight. No more lumpy hospital mattress. No more nurses waking her in the middle of the night. No more crowds of moaning, dying bomb victims.

She hadn't gotten very far when the front door opened, and a burst of fresh air filled the room.

Ernő stood on the threshold. "Welcome home, little sister."

"Ernő!" She closed the distance between them, and he wrapped her in a gentle hug. "I have a question for you."

"Can't you let a man get all the way in the door?"

She allowed him to enter, and he stooped to untie his shoes. Once they were off and he had settled in the chair she had vacated, she pounced on him. "What about the note you received?"

"*Anya* shouldn't have told you. It's not from Zofia, if that's what she said."

"It's not?"

"I believed it to be at first. But she would have given me more information. Told me what was going on with her, where she was. The handwriting may be a little familiar, but the words aren't hers. Someone trying to forge her writing, perhaps."

"I'm not convinced." She sat on the davenport, in the spot closest to his chair. "Maybe that's all she was able to tell you. All Patrik allowed her to say."

"The note didn't come from him. He's the one who convinced me it wasn't from her." He gasped.

"Of course he would say that. Don't tell *Anya* or *Apu*, because they would only scold me for sleuthing about, but I snuck behind Patrik the day I had my accident. I saw him speaking to a German soldier. Laughing with him. Following him into a building. He's connected to Zofia's disappearance. All we have to do is figure out how."

The entire mess intensified her headache. Patrik wouldn't have helped Zofia if he were involved with the Nazis. But how else could she be alive and well, since they were spotted together the night she disappeared? Maybe she had escaped from him.

"*Nem.*" Ernő's brown eyes darkened. "You will rest and recuperate. Already, you've been injured while spying. Let me handle it."

Éva reclined a bit more, a position that didn't cause her ribs so much discomfort. "I have to be able to help her. Please, don't shut me out."

"You are in no physical shape to handle this."

"What about Patrik?" Éva's tongue raced ahead of her thoughts.

Somehow this all must be connected. She just couldn't put the puzzle together.

Ernő shook his head. "I have no idea."

Well, Éva had every intention of finding out.

Chapter Sixteen

August 1944

*Z*ofia sat at the little writing desk Tóth *Asszony* had allowed her to move from the living room into her bedroom. She peered up from her papers and gazed through the wispy white curtains to the courtyard below. A couple of children were kicking a ball around.

How much longer until her baby kicked? What an amazing feeling that would be. If only Ernő . . .

Nem, best not to think about that. Because each time she did, a knife sliced through her heart.

She examined the paper in front of her. Today's topic was the plight of those unable to obtain either false IDs or Swedish or Swiss passports. People like her. Bram had promised. So far, he had yet to deliver.

Tóth *Asszony* knocked on her door and waltzed in with a tea tray, the fine china cups dotted with purple violets clinking together as the older woman's hands shook.

Zofia leaped to take the tray and set it on the nightstand beside the narrow bed.

"I thought I'd bring you a treat. You've been working so hard. And you've been on edge. That's not good for a woman in your condition."

"I guess I can't hide it anymore."

Tóth *Asszony* shook her head. "We may have to alter that dress soon. I'll be on the lookout for a few with more room as you grow."

"Will I be here that long?"

"Only God knows, my child. We can't worry about that. All we can do is be prepared for whatever the Lord might have in store."

"You've been so kind. Someday, I will repay you."

With a wave of her age-spotted hand, Tóth *Asszony* brushed away Zofia's words. "No need. Just take care of yourself and have a healthy baby."

Then came the sound Zofia had dreaded hearing for the months she'd been holed up here. German voices at the door and a banging that would rouse even the deaf old woman downstairs.

Tóth *Asszony* nodded, her hands now steadier than a surgeon's. Zofia's midsection tightened in fear.

She gathered her papers, scooping up a few she dropped, and slid them into her portfolio. Then she grabbed her suitcase containing her few dresses, a handful of undergarments, and some toiletries, including the lipstick Patrik brought.

Jackboots struck the door. How much longer would the lock hold? Her pulse throbbed in her neck. If she could just take a deep breath, she might keep from fainting.

Once she had everything in order, she stepped into the large cherry wardrobe and fought her way between the fur coats to the back. With a little maneuvering and jiggling, she managed to raise the furniture's back panel and slide into the narrow space behind it.

Wood splintered, and the door crashed in. Though muffled, Zofia made out the German voices. "Where is she?"

"I don't know." The old woman's voice didn't waver.

Thwack. Zofia bit her hand to keep from crying out. What were they doing to Tóth *Asszony*? Not another person suffering because of her. The same smacks of hands meeting flesh. The same harsh, guttural words. The same cries of pain and helplessness.

"We know she's here."

How had the Nazis discovered her location? Had they spotted her in the window one day? Maybe she should have taken more precautions. Patrik had been right. She'd been too careless.

"I don't even know who you're talking about. I'm an old woman who lives alone. My husband has been dead for years, and I have no children. I don't even own a cat."

Another smack. Zofia's own eyes watered. *God, protect her. Please, don't let them hurt her.*

"Spread out. I can feel she's here."

Silence for a moment, then the crashing of drawers being yanked open and turned upside down, the tinkle of glass breaking, the ripping of a mattress being torn open.

The voices progressed toward her, now in the same room as Zofia's hiding place. Not much in here for them to destroy, just a bed, the empty, drawer-less desk, and the wardrobe.

The cabinet's doors clicked open. "Nothing in here but a bunch of coats." The soldier's words cracked, as if his voice was changing.

"Move it." This Nazi was in charge and demanding.

Zofia locked her knees to keep from bumping around as the soldiers slid the wardrobe from the wall. She held her breath, not that she'd been inhaling much.

"Nothing, sir. No doors behind here. It's heavy for being filled with just coats."

"Oh, cherry is a very dense wood," said Tóth *Asszony*. "That piece is sturdy and well-made. The way they used to craft furniture to last."

Bless Tóth *Asszony*. For an elderly lady, she had a quick mind. Zofia would have frozen and not been able to form a word.

"She's here," the German soldier roared, his words not even muffled now. "We cannot let her escape through our fingers. We aren't leaving until we locate her. Keep searching. Punch holes in the walls if you must. Ferret her out. That is an order."

Dear God, dear God, dear God.

"Haul the old woman to the hotel. We'll find a way to make her talk."

Nem, this wasn't the way it was supposed to happen. There wasn't anything incriminating in the flat. They'd seen to it.

What should she do? Should she give herself up to save Tóth *Asszony*? But what about her unborn child? Wasn't his life worth rescuing? What was the right thing to do?

Buzzing filled her ears. She went numb.

With the toe of her shoe, she slid open the panel.

Éva sat in the café overlooking the Danube Promenade and spun the china teacup in the saucer. The scene before her was grim. Allied bombing raids had reduced some sections of the city to rubble. Across the street, one building was nothing more than a pile of stones. A huge crater gaped in the next lot.

She stared into the rosy liquid, the steam rising and warming her cool cheeks. Despite the summer sunshine, she pulled her gray cardigan sweater around her shoulders.

Then came a sight that stole her breath. Still a head taller than everyone else, still straight and regal in his bearing, still confident in his stride, came Patrik.

Why had she agreed to meet him? This was crazy. Zofia may very well be alive, but Patrik had been involved in her disappearance. In all likelihood, he knew exactly where she was and refused to disclose her location to her family.

That answered her question. Though Ernő had warned her against detective work, she had to know the answers. For once and for all, she needed the truth.

She clasped her hands in her lap to keep them from shaking. Her heart drummed—whether from nerves or excitement, it was impossible to tell. Patrik sauntered through the door, and right away, a smile lit his long, thin, aristocratic face. He wandered to the table, neat as always in a green and yellow sweater vest and a white dress shirt. "Éva." His voice was husky, and he cleared his throat. "I can't tell you how happy I am to see you."

The words "You too" teetered on the edge of her tongue. Unsure of their veracity, she pulled them back. "Won't you have a seat?"

He slid out the straight-backed wooden chair and settled across from her. "I'm glad to see you've recovered well from your accident."

"*Köszönöm*." She paused, then stared him in the eye. "What I want from you is answers."

The waiter came and took Patrik's order for a cup of ersatz coffee, then left them alone.

"I told Ernő what I know. I'm in the process of tracking down Zofia."

"That's a lie." Like all the lies men who loved her told her.

His brown eyes widened at her announcement.

She leaned forward, nose to nose with the man she had almost married. Her traitorous heart somersaulted in her chest. "I want to know how you're connected to her disappearance. What did you know about it? How, exactly, were you involved?"

"Don't tell me that note wasn't from her. Ernő showed me. She tried to disguise her handwriting but wasn't successful. I've seen it too much on receipts and orders for the studio. I know the note came from her. And that you're connected. It's time you gave us some real answers."

He gazed out the window. "Those are questions I can't answer."

"Look at me."

He did so, his brown eyes soft. Maybe even sorrowful. "What is it you want from me?"

"The truth. After what Károly did to me, the way he betrayed me and Zofia as well, for you to do the same thing to us is . . ." The word eluded her.

She would never forget finding those papers in Károly's flat after word reached them that he'd been killed on the Eastern Front. Papers filled with hate for the Jews. For people like Zofia. Filled with love for Hitler and his ilk. For the pure race.

How could she have loved someone who harbored such hate in the depths of his soul?

She studied Patrik's eyes, as if she could discern from them what lay hidden inside him. Was his heart as black as Károly's?

Károly's diary had revealed his involvement in the rape and murder of an eighteen-year-old Jewish girl and her eighty-year-old grandmother. When he was sent to the front, he was planning even more atrocities, each more vicious than the last. Éva hadn't been able to discern the truth then. Would she recognize it even if Patrik told it to her?

Which way was up and which way was down these days?

She didn't break her gaze with Patrik. If only she knew. If only she could tell.

When she first met Patrik, she had resisted his charms. She hadn't spoken to him when he'd come to the music studio, had refused to go out with him. But the more he talked to her, the more at ease he put her, until he washed away the bad taste Károly had left.

Until she believed she could trust a man again.

Had she been wrong to do so?

He had brought her from the brink of despair and hopelessness. Now he drove her toward it again.

The waiter brought Patrik's coffee, and he took a long sip. "Much as I long to, *a múzsám*, I can't give you what you want."

"Why not? Whatever happened to the truth setting you free?"

He picked up his napkin and rubbed at an imaginary spot on the white tablecloth.

She sighed and glanced at the tin ceiling, studying the complicated swirls so much like her life. "Why can't you tell me the truth? Actually, it's not that you can't tell me, is it? It's that you won't."

"The truth would do anything but set you free. Or anyone

else, for that matter. Despite how it appears, the situation is much more complicated."

"Enlighten me. I'm an intelligent woman."

"By complicated, I mean there are certain things I can't share with you."

"Why don't you start with the night she vanished. Everything was fine until she didn't show up for dinner. Except for you. You were nervous about something."

"And as you recall, I was with you the entire time."

"But Reka saw you."

"Why are we rehashing this?"

"Because I'm racking my brain, going insane attempting to figure out what happened, how you are involved and with whom. Because of your bullheadedness, you are blocking me at every turn."

"Are you here for yourself or for Ernő?"

"For all of us, of course. Me, Ernő, my parents, Zofia, everyone who loves her. You know how close we were."

"Were. That's the key word, isn't it?"

She nodded, breathing hard, a knife stabbing her chest. "What disturbs me the most is . . ." She drew in a deep breath, every muscle in her body quaking. She might even be sick. "Is that I saw you with that German."

Patrik crinkled his forehead. "What German?"

"You know full well." She spun the teacup another rotation.

"I have no idea what you're talking about."

"The day I had my accident, I followed you. Saw you talking, laughing, being chummy with a soldier. I know you're involved with them."

For a long moment, he worked his mouth. He knew what she was talking about.

"You shouldn't have done that. See what happened to you?"

"You're not answering my question. Who are you involved with?"

"As soon as I have information I'm able to share, I will. Right now, you need to trust me. Trust that I wouldn't keep this from you if I didn't have to, and that I only have your best interest at heart. Trust that I'm doing this because I love you."

She gave a single-note laugh. "That's something that will never happen. You corrupted everything good about our relationship. I believed us to be close enough that we could share anything. Everything. I cannot love a man who could do less."

He squeezed his eyes shut, then opened them. "I understand. I truly do. Someday everything will be clear."

"See, I knew it. You are withholding information."

"Please, Éva, don't make this more difficult than it already is."

"I'm making it difficult? You're the one refusing to share the whereabouts of someone we dearly love. Possibly acting as a traitor to us and to our country." She pushed away her teacup, the water gone cold.

"We've been through this."

She clenched her hands. Why did it have to come to such a point? "Then we have nothing more to say to each other. Asking for this meeting was a mistake on my part. *Köszönöm* for coming."

He pulled his black leather wallet from the back pocket of his dress pants and withdrew several *pengő*. "The tea is my treat."

"That's not necessary." Why did he have to be such a gentleman?

"My feelings for you, Éva, haven't changed and never will. I'll love you forever. All I pray is that you'll be able to forgive me." This time he made eye contact with her.

Those feelings she suppressed for these months stirred inside her. She fought to maintain her composure. Several long seconds passed before she managed to find her voice. "That's not possible. I cannot love a man who lies."

"I'll earn that trust back."

"I don't see how. Please, leave now." She swallowed hard to keep the tears at bay. "Don't contact me until you have concrete information about Zofia. And when you can share with me how you and she fit into this puzzle."

Before she knew what was happening, he kissed the back of her hand and slipped from the café.

If only he would slip so easily from her heart.

♩♫♩

Chapter Seventeen

With the toe of her sling-back shoe, Zofia worked to lift the secret panel behind the wardrobe, her hands clammy, sweat soaking the back of her dress.

"Take this old woman from here." The Nazi's voice was harsh.

Zofia slid the panel higher.

"Don't show her any mercy until she tells you the truth."

Higher and higher she lifted the false back. If only there was the room to bend down. She had to hurry, before they took Tóth *Asszony* away.

"Wait. Wait." Tóth *Asszony*'s words were strong and sure.

Zofia held her breath. Was Tóth *Asszony* going to turn her in when doing so would mean forfeiting her own life?

"I know where the woman is you're looking for."

What was she doing?

"But she's not here."

Zofia released her breath in a silent whoosh.

"You will show us the way."

Nem, they weren't going to let her go. Zofia fiddled around, at last grasped the bottom of the panel, and yanked it up.

"I'm a very old woman and would only slow you down. I'll give you her location, but I can't leave my flat anymore."

"Carry her down, Abt."

"Oh, my." Tóth *Asszony* squeaked.

Zofia squeezed through the narrow opening, the bottom of the musty fur coats soft against her skin.

"I'm not afraid to go with you. I've lived my life to the full, and if it comes to an end today, I'm not afraid." Tóth *Asszony* spoke louder now.

Zofia reached to open the door with a special handle Patrik had installed inside the wardrobe.

"I know where the woman is, because she always stays put. She never does anything rash, so I know she wouldn't leave this place."

Zofia froze. Was Tóth *Asszony* trying to send her a message?

"She won't go anywhere. I can count on knowing just where she is."

She sat back among the coats, trembling from head to toe.

The door slammed shut, and the flat fell silent.

Zofia covered her face and sobbed. Tóth *Asszony* would never return to this apartment. She had given her life for Zofia. Her tears fell fast and furious.

Another human sacrificed for her.

What kind of person would do that for another? Was her life worth saving?

She wept until she was spent. With a handkerchief Tóth *Asszony* had embroidered, Zofia wiped her face.

When the Germans got to the place Tóth *Asszony* took them, wherever that might be, and discovered Zofia wasn't there, they would return here. She had to leave. Now.

But where would she go?

That was a problem to deal with later. Right this minute, she had to flee. Anywhere but here.

She crawled from the wardrobe, her legs stiff, her back aching, and reached into the small crevice for her valise and her papers. In her stocking feet, she crept across the floors, avoiding the spots that squeaked. If the neighbors heard noises from here after they'd seen Tóth *Asszony* carted away, they would be suspicious.

Someone knocked on the door. Her ears ringing, Zofia scurried toward the wardrobe.

"Tóth *Asszony*. Tóth *Asszony*, are you home?"

Patrik. *Köszönöm, Lord.*

Zofia opened the door, motioned Patrik inside, then bolted it. "We have to talk."

"There isn't time. They've been here and taken Tóth *Asszony*. She's pretending to know where I am. When they don't find me, they'll be back. Get me out of here." She squeezed his arm.

He pushed her away, and her nails left impressions in his flesh. "This complicates everything. I told you not to be so rash." His words were soft, but his face was crimson.

"There isn't time to waste arguing. We need a plan."

"I've had one for a while, afraid you might be compromised. Put on one of Tóth *Asszony*'s coats and her scarf."

Zofia obeyed.

"When we walk out of here, stoop like an old lady. Take her cane, if it's here."

Zofia located the gold-tipped walking stick carved with roses and doves, topped with an ivory handle.

"Where are we going?"

"My place. For now, anyway."

"But—"

"You said no time for arguing. Let's go."

Once on the street, Zofia blinked in the bright sunshine. Patrik held her back from breaking into a full-blown trot. They hurried as fast as an old woman could possibly walk.

Patrik gripped her by the elbow and guided her down the street. As they stopped to wait for traffic, he leaned over to whisper in her ear, "That hunch also hides your stomach."

She nodded but didn't dare gaze at him.

The streetcar passed, and they crossed the road. They said nothing more to each other until they stepped into the lobby of Patrik's apartment building. "You're my elderly aunt come to stay with me because your son has been called up to the service."

Together they climbed the stairs until they reached Patrik's flat. As soon as he shut and latched the door, she dropped onto the piano bench and allowed herself to relax.

Patrik brought her a cup of warm water to drink. He probably was out of tea leaves and ersatz coffee. "I had a visit with Éva today."

Zofia peered at him through her lashes. "That's interesting. Is she still angry with you? Or did you manage to patch up your relationship?"

"Far from it. She's demanding answers. Ones she's working to get on her own. The day of her accident, she was following me."

"Following you? She knows about Bram?"

"*Nem*. Once again, I lied to her. Or rather, ignored her question altogether. But you know how stubborn she is. She doesn't tolerate lying, so she won't let this go."

She set her cup beside her on the bench. "You're right, she won't. If she feels you betrayed her trust in you, she will go to the ends of the earth to discover the truth. The time has come to tell them. Keeping this from them isn't doing anyone any good."

"You were almost arrested today. Tóth *Asszony* was. Don't you see, the Nazis are still hunting you." Patrik paced a tight circle and mussed his dark hair. "Already Ernő was interrogated. How long before the Germans pressure him for more information?" He slapped his thighs.

"Knowing my whereabouts won't make a difference." She pounded her fist into her palm. "The Germans will do whatever they have to in order to get what they want. My mother didn't know anything about my underground activities in Poland or anything about my location. To them, it made no difference. They killed her anyway." Zofia shuddered. She could never wipe away those images of Mama, bloodied and battered, her body abandoned in their home.

As the child within her grew, so did her longing for the man she loved. She couldn't stand it much longer. She had to be with Ernő. Flesh to flesh. The way a married couple was meant to be.

Patrik slammed a palm against the wall. "I don't know. I don't know. My family is all gone, I'm sure of it. With the war winding down, the Germans, even with the rail lines cut, are finding ways to exterminate every one of Hungary's Jews. Éva is all I have left. She's everything to me. And if she's upset with me now, how much worse will it be when she discovers my lies?"

"She already knows you're lying, so I don't see how telling her the truth could make things worse."

"I don't know. I just don't know."

But Zofia could stand the separation no longer. "Whether you help me or not, I'm going to Ernő. One way or another, Éva will learn the truth."

Whatever the consequences, it was time to go home.

Bram lounged on the rounded-back dining chair in the middle of Patrik's living room, smoking one cigarette after the other and taking an occasional swig from the flask in his jacket pocket. With no sofa, the chair was the best Patrik could offer him. And Bram, dressed again like a Gestapo officer, sat as if he were on a tufted settee.

"Zofia's activities, and how close the Gestapo came to catching her, are a problem." Bram blew out a smoke ring.

"She wants those papers to get out of the country. Since she's insisting on going home, she must have them. Now. Her husband has been arrested once already."

Bram puffed twice. "As long as he doesn't know anything, he's not a concern."

"Not a concern?"

"He's not part of our organization. Low priority."

"What are you talking about?"

"We take care of our own first."

"But Zofia doesn't deserve to have papers? Is she too low a

priority?" Patrik banged his fist on the piano's closed cover, then winced. Zofia was napping.

"Sorry, old chum. Think of it as triage. We take the most critical cases first, then move to the ones who aren't in immediate danger. Zofia is safe here."

"But she's not going to stay here. And you said her activities caused a problem."

"They do." Bram stroked the Hitler-inspired mustache he'd grown. "What they've done is expose our group. Protecting the collective, that's what it's about."

"Don't tell me you've become a communist sympathizer."

"Fine, I won't tell you."

"Zofia needs those papers. Today. I'm going to attempt to get her out of the country to Palestine."

"The Romanian pipeline. Dangerous. Very risky."

Patrik repressed a sigh. How much should he tell Bram? Then again, the truth about Zofia's condition became clearer by the day. "That's why I prefer the papers. Especially since she's expecting."

"A baby?"

"*Nem.* Saint Nicholas."

Bram chuckled. "I knew you had a sense of humor in there somewhere. I'll see what I can do and how fast I can do it." Bram pointed at Patrik and came to his feet. "She's accomplished good work for us."

"That makes her worthy of the false identity now?"

"Something like that. What I need you to do is go to the registration office and get me a batch of names I can use for the documents."

"Your price for your services?"

Bram grinned. "Something like that."

Patrik ground his teeth. Typical Bram.

The telephone on the wall in the kitchen rang. "If you'll excuse me, I'd like to answer it."

"Sure. Maybe I'll have a chat with Zofia."

"Leave her to rest." Patrik scurried to receive the call.

"We're on to you." The voice on the other end of the line was muffled and yet feminine. A woman making threats?

Patrik's mouth dried out. "Who is this?"

"I've been watching you."

Though his heart beat an irregular tempo, Patrik did his best to keep his words calm and even. "This isn't a very funny joke."

"This is no joke. Yesterday, you brought an older woman home with you. But who was she really?"

Patrik sucked in a breath. Someone was watching him.

"I told you. I know all about you."

Everything about him? Even his closest-kept secret? "Who is this?" He spit out each word.

"Now, now, no need to get testy. Just watch your step."

Patrik reached out to place the receiver back in the cradle.

"Don't hang up."

He paused.

"And the stunning Bognár Éva."

He pressed the receiver against his ear, his hands clammy. "Leave her out of this."

"Wish I could. Too bad about your engagement being called off. You love her, don't you?"

He choked back his words.

"Don't you?" The woman screamed into the phone.

"What business is it of yours?"

"I'm warning you."

"What are you warning me of?"

"What we did to her brother, we'll do to her. Worse, if you don't stop your Zionist activities immediately, Kedves Patrik. Is that your real name?"

Patrik sank to the floor, the cord barely reaching.

"There won't be any more calls. Consider yourself fortunate to have gotten a warning at all."

The line went dead.

He might have sat there five seconds or five minutes. Time lost all meaning.

Bram burst into the kitchen. He pried the receiver from Patrik's hands and returned it to its proper place. "You look like you've seen Count Dracula."

"Worse."

Bram grabbed Patrik under the armpit and lifted him to his feet. "What could be worse than that?"

"I'm being watched. They know all about Zofia and Éva. Not to mention that they're suspicious of my own identity." Patrik blew out a breath. "We need those papers. Now. For everyone, including Éva and Ernő. There's not a second to waste. We all need to get to Palestine." In a strange way, he was fulfilling his mother's dream.

"All in good time."

Heat rose in Patrik's chest. He grabbed Bram by the uniform and pinned him against the kitchen cabinets. "Not good enough. You listen to me. I want them tonight. Do you hear me? Tonight."

"Then I need names. Today."

"Are you insane? I'm being surveilled."

"Lose them. That's the way it works. I can't be seen playing favorites."

Patrik growled and released Bram. "You play favorites all the time. That's why we've gotten into this mess. If you'd listened to me in the beginning, Zofia would be well on her way to Sweden or Switzerland or Palestine."

"By five this afternoon, otherwise I won't have time." Bram straightened his jacket and marched from the flat, his jackboots echoing in the hall.

Chapter Eighteen

Opening his flat's door a tiny crack, Patrik peered out, looking both ways as if he were crossing a busy street. No one about. He dare not breathe yet. Not until he and the others were out of the country.

Maybe not even then.

First things first. Bram demanded a list of names from which to forge papers. Simple enough. He'd done it before.

Not while being watched, though.

He descended the stairs, working to appear casual and unflustered by the telephone call. He couldn't allow the caller to know how she had affected him.

Hands in his pockets, he strolled down the street, whistling a jaunty tune. He nodded to the neighbors he passed. Coming to the main street, he attempted to blend in with the crowd and so lose his tail.

Drat his height. Impossible for him to disappear, even in a sea of people. Wait, up ahead was the café where he'd met Éva a few days ago. He remembered something important about the place.

Not pausing to weigh the pros and cons of his plan, he ducked into the restaurant. Before the maître d' could stop him, he broke into a sprint through the dining room, dodging tables and chairs, into the kitchen and past a gape-mouthed staff, and out the back door to a narrow alley.

Once outside, he broke into a full gallop, crossing streets, moving into other back streets, and through a couple more buildings. By the time he stopped and leaned against the brick exterior of a building in yet another alley, he was panting and sweating.

Catching his breath and listening, he stood there for the longest time. Not a sound other than the clanging of the trolley's bell on the street at the end of the alley.

He had to have lost whoever was following him. He had no sense of being watched. Not that his intuition was reliable, but it was all he had to go on.

Bram was out of his mind to send him on this mission. Didn't he realize Patrik's actions put the entire operation in great jeopardy?

Patrik crept toward the quiet residential street. Still in the shadows, he peered around. No one stirred.

Perfect. He slipped from the darkness and into the light, ramming his Hamburg hat farther over his eyes. If only it were cool enough for his trench coat.

He wound his way in a circuitous route through the city, passing more rubble than he cared to see. He cursed the war and those who took the lives of other humans. Those who treated people like animals because of the blood that flowed through their veins.

The same blood that flowed through his.

Finally, he arrived at the Population Registry office. He scrounged in his pocket for his own forged birth certificate, the folded paper crinkling when he touched it. For several years, it had protected him.

But no longer. Because someone out there knew the truth.

Today, praise be, there wasn't a long line, just two people ahead of him. Soon he stood in front of the brown-haired woman who peered at him over the top of her glasses. "Can I help you?"

He produced his birth certificate from his pocket. "I've lost my identity card."

The woman sighed. "This is a real problem, you know. So many are misplacing their cards." She shuffled a few papers on her desk until she found the book she was searching for. "Birth certificate."

He pushed the document forward.

"Let me get the paperwork you need to fill out."

Patrik glanced over his shoulder. No one waited behind him. Perfect opportunity. Once the woman left the room, he leaned over the desk and peered at the list of names in the book. As fast as he could, he noted them on a piece of paper, including addresses, birth dates, cities of origin, and so on.

Just as he slipped the paper and pencil back into his pants pocket, the woman returned to the room, the heels of her pumps clicking on the creaky wood floor. "I don't know why people can't hang on to their cards."

"I should have checked my pants before I washed them."

She glanced at him. "I thought you said you lost them."

"*Igen*, lost them in the wash."

She shrugged, and Patrik exhaled. Seating herself at her desk, she clacked away on the typewriter. Finally she handed him his new identity booklet. "Hang on to this one."

He gave her what he hoped was a cheerful smile. "I'll be more careful."

He exited the building and hurried toward Bram's flat, glancing over his shoulder from time to time. No one followed him as far as he could tell. His tail must have no idea where he'd gone. Just to be safe, though, he kept to the quiet streets and alleys, crossing and recrossing them, backtracking, strolling in circles. The walk took him twice as long as it should have.

Finally, he arrived at Bram's building. Just as he climbed the outside step to the front door, he caught sight of a woman in a black coat disappearing around the corner. A heavier woman.

He'd done all he could to be sure he was alone.

It wasn't enough.

With heavy feet, he entered the building and climbed the stairs to Bram's flat. Once inside, Patrik plunked the yellow sheet of blue-lined paper in front of Bram as he sat at the kitchen table. "I'll be back at ten tonight for the papers. You should know, I believe someone tailed me here. At the least, someone is watching the building."

"The time is fine." Bram sat back in the chair, no cigarette in his mouth or *pálinka* in his hand. "And you were followed."

Patrik thumped into the chair across from Bram. "I took every precaution. How do you know?"

Bram nodded toward the window. "I watched."

"That's not safe." Patrik crossed his arms.

"Don't worry. I'm not as sloppy as you."

"Who was it?"

"I didn't get a good look. A woman wearing black, a black scarf on her head. Appeared to be heavier."

"That's the woman I saw. Do you think it's the same one who threatened me?"

"Could be. When you leave, keep your eyes open and don't be stupid. Find me tonight at the house on Kastély Utca. I need to vacate this place. Then get the others and get out of the city as fast as possible."

"Bram, I—"

"Forget it. Just use your head. Mistakes like that while you're on the run could cost you your life. And everyone else's."

Only the clinking of silverware against the china broke the dinnertime stillness at the Bognár home. Éva pushed the *lecsó* around her plate, lacking any appetite for the vegetables in the stew. She glanced at Ernő across the table from her. Dark half-moons hung under his eyes.

Each day they waited for word on Zofia.

Each day ended in disappointment.

Ernő dropped his fork onto his plate, flung his napkin to the table, and stomped up the stairs to his room, slamming the door behind him.

Anya shook her head and shoveled in another mouthful of tomatoes, yellow peppers, and onions. "I don't understand why he spends so much time in there. It's not healthy for him to brood over her so. He needs to get out and get some fresh air."

Éva pushed her dish away. "That wouldn't help. How would you feel if someone knew *Apu's* whereabouts and refused to share the information with you? Why, it's like kidnapping. And I, for one, am furious with Patrik. He's caused this family nothing but heartache and pain." Her voice cracked.

"Éva, that is no way to speak to your mother." *Apu's* glare bore into her.

"I'm sorry, but it's the truth. He's not going to help us find her. It's up to us."

"You don't know what kind of—"

A knock at the door cut off *Apu's* words.

Éva pushed back her chair. "I'll get it."

When she opened the door, there stood Patrik, a weariness in his bloodshot eyes.

"Go away. We have nothing further to say."

She shoved the door shut, but he stopped it with his foot. "I have to speak to you. It's critical."

She shouldn't, she really shouldn't, but the urgency of his words drove her to step outside. "What is it?"

"Not out here. Too many prying ears. Please, can we speak inside?"

"I don't want my family to hear. Don't you know what you've done to them, especially Ernő? You promised us information, but you never delivered. We're through with you. Done."

"Why do you think I'm here?"

She drew in a breath and straightened like a clarinetist should stand. "You have details?"

His single nod was enough for her to allow him to step into the front hall. "Tell me first."

"I know where Zofia is. But even more pressing, your life is now in danger. Yours and Ernő's as well."

Her throat tightened. "What are you talking about?"

"There's not time to explain. By ten this evening, we'll all have new identity papers. From here, we travel to Nagyvárad, then to Romania and on to Palestine."

"Palestine?" Éva shook her head, more to clear her thoughts than from disagreement with Patrik.

"Get your brother. We'll waste precious time if I have to explain everything twice."

At least he knew about Zofia. She rounded up Ernő and her parents, and they met Patrik in the living room where he'd taken up residence on his favorite flowered armchair. They all settled into their seats.

For half a second, it was as if the past few months had never happened. They were back to the night a few weeks before their wedding, Patrik so comfortable in this home, a part of their family. Arguing politics, discussing the war, laughing.

Before that world changed forever.

This time, however, no smile graced Patrik's lips. Instead, he'd drawn them into a thin line. He glanced her way, then dragged his attention to the rest of her family.

Apu leaned forward in his chair. "You'd best have some true information about Zofia. And an explanation of your actions over these past weeks."

"Right now, there is a more pressing matter. One of life and death."

Even *Anya* sat openmouthed.

Patrik cleared his throat. "I received a troubling phone call this afternoon. The caller warned me that I'd been watched. You see . . ." He cleared his throat once more.

Éva scooted to the edge of the davenport.

"Zofia is at my flat."

Ernő's mouth fell open. *Anya* gasped.

A rush of heat raced from Éva's stomach to her face. "You've had her with you this entire time and couldn't find the words to tell us? Why was she with you and not home where she belongs?"

Patrik turned to her, his eyes soft. "You'll have your explanation soon. The caller, a woman, knew Zofia was with me. She made threats against us and against Éva. After his run-in with the Gestapo, I believe Ernő's life to be in an equal amount of danger. We leave for Romania and, eventually, Palestine, tonight."

A thousand other questions crowded Éva's mind, but *Apu* jumped into the conversation. "You believe these threats to be credible?"

"Very. The caller knew details. She trailed me as I secured false papers and met with one of my contacts with the Zionist Youth."

Éva hugged herself. "How can we trust you after what you put us through? After your sea of lies?"

"I didn't do it to cause you pain but out of necessity. Once you hear the entire story, you'll understand. And I have this." He held out a piece of paper.

Ernő grabbed it and opened the note. "It's from Zofia. This time, she signed it. All it says is to trust Patrik."

Patrik nodded. "Go now and pack a bag."

Ernő broke from his stunned silence. "What about my parents?"

"They are welcome to come, though I don't have new papers for them. I don't believe them to be in danger."

"Don't believe, or know?" Éva couldn't leave without an assurance that her parents would be safe.

Éva gazed at *Apu* and *Anya*, who stared at one another for a long while, carrying on a silent conversation that only people married for many years could.

At last, *Apu* broke eye contact and directed his attention to Patrik. "We'll stay. I have my business here to think about."

Éva's own business came to mind. What would become of it? What about her students? How could she leave them? She had returned to teaching lessons not long ago. And now? "I'm not sure I can flee either."

Patrik stood and wandered to the window, peering at nothing but the blackout curtain. "If you stay, they will find you and kill you." His tone was quiet but desperate.

A little of the ice around Éva's heart melted. She sidled next to him, not quite touching him. "Why?" She whispered the word.

He turned and addressed all of them. "Because of your association with Zofia and the group she's affiliated with. And because of my secret."

Chapter Nineteen

Goosebumps broke out over Éva's arms at Patrik's words. "Secret? What secret of yours could put us in harm's way?" What was Patrik talking about? With him it was always secrets and lies and more secrets. Had she ever really known him? Could she trust that Zofia had written the note of her own free will and not under duress?

The air raid sirens picked that moment to wail.

"Ignore it."

"*Igen*, I will. But I'm not going anywhere or doing anything with you until you answer my question. What secret are you still hiding?"

He faced her, his eyes so familiar. She could still read them, read the pleading, the begging for trust in them. "It doesn't make a difference in what is going on now. You still have to leave."

"Not until I have my answer."

"You will. Soon. I promise. But we need to go. We don't have a moment to lose." He swung his gaze to each person in the room, sending each of them wide-eyed glances, unspoken words of urgency tinged with panic.

Anya wiped her hands on her pristine apron. "We have to get downstairs before the planes get here. Hurry now, all of you. We'll sort the rest out later."

Éva scurried toward the basement steps. So what if Patrik had told them part of the truth? He was withholding information. He wasn't trustworthy. How did they know the note was from Zofia?

How did they know there weren't German trucks waiting outside to cart them away to those unspeakable places?

"Stop, everyone. We must leave this moment."

Patrik's command pulled her to a halt. She stood breathless on the steps. "If we go outside now, wouldn't that provide the Nazis you say are after us the perfect opportunity to nab us?" He did say it was the Germans they had to fear, didn't he? *Nem*, he didn't. "They are the ones after us, right?"

"Get a bag packed." Patrik's voice was firm and sure. Not commanding but serious.

Éva's determination faltered. If he was telling the truth about Zofia and the danger they were in, they would be wise to listen. From what he said, their lives were in jeopardy.

But if he was lying, they could be in another kind of danger.

She gazed at *Apu* and motioned him into the kitchen, dishes that needed to be washed stacked next to the sink, dinner's leftovers still on the stove. "What do you think? What should we do? Stay or go? How do we know what's right?"

Apu scrubbed his stubble-covered cheek. "What do you think?"

"Everything in me wants to believe him. But so much of me is scared to. He betrayed me. Could he be betraying me again? He could also be trying to save my life. It's like trying to play a sonata without the score. How do you know which notes are the right ones?"

With a gentleness that brought back a flood of childhood memories, *Apu* pulled her close and stroked her hair. Like he had after Károly's betrayal. "Where does your hope lie, sweetheart?"

She nestled against his chest, a place she had always been safe and secure. If she left with Patrik, would she ever see *Apu* again? "Hope for what?"

"Your hope for this life and the one to come?"

At his inquiry, the answer to the first catechism question

she had memorized as a young child sprang to mind. "That I with body and soul, both in life and death, am not my own, but belong unto my faithful Savior Jesus Christ; who, with his precious blood, hath fully satisfied for all my sins, and delivered me from all the power of the devil; and so preserves me that without the will of my heavenly Father, not a hair can fall from my head; yea, that all things must be subservient to my salvation, and therefore, by his Holy Spirit, he also assures me of eternal life, and makes me sincerely willing and ready, henceforth, to live unto him."

"You answer without error, but do you know what those words mean and believe them deep inside, in the very core of your soul?"

"Of course." She'd believed all her life, since she was a little girl. There wasn't a time when God hadn't been her heavenly Father.

"Then that is the hope you must rely on."

"You aren't answering my question. What do we do?"

"I have given you your answer." *Apu* kissed the top of her head and released her. Hand in hand, they strolled to the living room. Ernő wasn't with *Anya*.

"He's gone to pack, foolish boy. He'll put his own life at risk just to see his wife." *Anya* frowned.

So, her brother had decided to take the risk. Why wouldn't he? It was worth it for one more minute with Zofia.

If Patrik was indeed hiding her, as he said. "How do we know you didn't force her to write the note?"

Patrik sighed. "Please, get ready to go. There isn't time to waste. You just have to trust me."

The sirens screamed their nightly call. Overhead, the rumble of Allied planes intensified.

Anya grasped the wood back of the settee. "They're coming to this area tonight. We have to get to the basement. Now."

Patrik shook his head hard. "Not until Éva packs. As soon as the all-clear sounds, we must be on our way. I can't stress how imperative it is."

Anya grasped Éva by her upper arm and attempted to drag her to the basement door. "She's coming downstairs."

"*Nem*, I'm not." The decision solidified in Éva's mind as she spoke the words. "I'll go with Patrik. Give me five minutes." If he wasn't telling the truth about Zofia, she could always return home. Couldn't she?

She scurried to her room and yanked her suitcase from underneath her bed. *Apu* had bought it for her when he took her to Paris to hear clarinetist Louis Cahuzac play. Just the two of them had traveled there. Such a wonderful memory to carry with her. One to cherish, to hold close to her heart.

She flung open the wardrobe doors and pulled out several dresses, some lighter in weight, others heavier. Who knew how long it would take them to get out of the country? And what was Palestine like?

Palestine. The thought of it made her sick at heart. Would she ever come home to Hungary? From this moment on, her future, the one she had planned to the last detail, would be entirely different.

She stashed her underthings and both of her coats in the case and then climbed on the bed to reach the shelf *Apu* had built above it.

Here sat all her mementos, little snapshots of her life. The awards and ribbons she'd won for her clarinet playing. They couldn't come. But she grabbed the silver-framed portraits of her parents and of the grandparents she never knew.

A few toiletries filled the small case. Then she glimpsed her clarinet in its black case on the floor, a stack of music beside it.

Walking away from it would be like walking away from a part of her body. Impossible to do. She grabbed it and, after one last look at her cheery pink room, shut the door and made her way down the hall.

Ernő stood ready to go at the door, his suitcase in one hand, his own clarinet in the other. Without their music, neither of them would survive.

Patrik watched her and lifted one corner of his mouth in a half smile. She turned away.

Anya bustled to the door and shoved in front of Ernő. "Now can we go to the shelter?" The drone of planes almost drowned out her words. "They're on top of us!"

Éva couldn't hear anything other than the whine of the engines, the vibrations shaking the entire building. "We have to get out of here."

An ear-splitting, head-splitting whistle.

Silence.

The air sucked from the room.

And a deafening roar.

Zofia sat on the tufted bench at Patrik's spectacular ebony grand piano. Just sitting here and being this close to the music helped her to relax her shoulders and take a deep breath.

Patrik had been gone for a long while. When he left, he'd said he had important business but didn't go into details. He didn't mention how long he'd be gone. These days, you never knew.

The peace and tranquility of the place washed over her. For now, she was safe. Once again she'd come too close to being caught. How long would it be before the Gestapo closed in?

She stroked the lacquered wood, so smooth and soft beneath her hands. Even without her fingers on the keyboard, the music flowed through her body.

She lifted the lid and lost herself in the sensation of the cool ivory keys. Though no sound came from the instrument, in her mind she played Beethoven's *Moonlight* Sonata with its rolling left hand and its singing right hand. The C# minor key resonated in her bones.

Along with her, it wept for the life that once was but was no more.

She switched to "Clair de Lune," a softer, quieter tune. One she and Ernő might dance to. A calm lake to float in.

The wailing of the air raid sirens outside interrupted the serenity of the piece and sent Zofia crashing back to the here and now.

Since she wasn't supposed to be here, she couldn't go to the shelter with the building's other residents. She had no other choice but to remain in the flat. Overhead came the all-too-familiar rumble of Russian planes.

First the Germans claimed her country, then the Russians stood on the eastern door. She gave free rein to her fingers to fly just above the keyboard, Liszt's Hungarian Rhapsodies swirling in her brain, the music deep and dark and so very eastern European.

Perfect.

The roar of plane engines advanced, soaring above this neighborhood tonight. For many weeks, they'd been spared the wrath of Soviet bombs. Tonight it appeared they wouldn't be.

A barrage of whistles broke off her concentration, and the music in her head halted. Heart in her throat, she dove under the piano for all the protection it would provide.

The vibrations from the explosions shook the Baroque-style building. Though it had stood for a hundred years, it might not survive the night.

She covered her ears, willing the songs to come to mind again. They refused. Even with her ears plugged, the kabooms were loud enough to hurt.

Then one bone-splitting whistle. A moment of silence. A terrible, jarring boom-bang.

The floor beneath Zofia shuddered. The building swayed. Time hung suspended. She braced herself to fall to the cellar.

The lights flickered and extinguished.

The dwelling stilled. Time restarted.

In a rush, she expelled the breath she'd been holding.

Where had that bomb landed? Very nearby. She crawled from underneath the piano, stretched out her stiff legs, then staggered to the window.

With no electricity, she could open the blackout shades without the worry of spilling light into the street for the bombers to find her. She pressed herself against the length of glass. Blazes ringed her. The clang of responding fire trucks rang in the darkness.

She turned in the direction of the Bognárs' home. Her home. Flames shot from the buildings in that section of the city, just blocks from Patrik's flat.

Had they been bombed? She had to know if they had come to any harm. If any of them had been injured. Or . . .

Ernő, Ernő. She raked her fingers down the glass. If only she could know what had happened to him. Had their home been hit? Judging by the crimson sky above, it might well have been.

She turned from the window without bothering to draw the drapes and padded across the living room in her stocking feet, not caring when she tread on a squeaky floorboard.

God, give me a sign. Something to let me know he's not injured. Or worse.

She rubbed her expanding belly. "Oh, little one, why did you pick such a time as this to be born into a world gone mad?" Her child may never meet his father. Her child might never live to draw a breath.

Nem, nem. She couldn't allow that to happen. She had to do everything in her power to ensure her child's safety.

And let his father know of his existence.

Patrik was wrong. Staying hidden, away from Ernő, wasn't protecting anyone. They'd both been in the hands of the Nazis. Ernő had suffered brutality while in their custody.

When she and Ernő had married, they promised to support each other in good times and bad. Sickness and health. Though the vows said nothing about war and peace, it applied.

She had been wrong to leave her husband, wrong not to be at his side, fighting this oppression together.

Before she could change her mind, she grabbed her still-packed valise and slipped on her sensible lace-up oxfords. The all-clear siren blasted as she stepped from the flat. Everyone would be coming from the basement now. She slid back into the apartment and waited an agonizing fifteen minutes. The flickering light from nearby blazes illuminated the minute hand on her watch.

She had to know. Now. She slipped from the building.

Chaos reigned on the street. Rescue workers, the injured, the survivors, all clamored about. She raced down the road, dodging the litter of broken glass, crumbled bricks, and other things too horrible to think about.

On the Bognárs' street, just a few blocks from where she started, the destruction was much worse. The bombs had blown the facades from many buildings, exposing living rooms, kitchens, and bedrooms. Naked lives on display for the world to see. Through her splintered neighborhood she sprinted, until . . . *nem, nem!*

She slid to a stop in front of her residence.

What was left of it.

Zofia dropped to her knees, covered her face, and sobbed.

♪♫♪

Chapter Twenty

Ernő raced through the front door of their home, dragging Éva behind him, as the loudest explosion he'd ever heard shook the ground, the sky, the very air around him.

Like an earthquake, the ground trembled. In a single rush, the building collapsed. What had taken months to build, what had stood for years, was reduced to nothing in seconds.

He, his parents, Éva, and Patrik stood in front of what had been their house. The only one he'd ever known. The one he'd shared with his bride.

"Help. Help." The faint cry came from next door. Three stories' worth of rubble buried their neighbors. The rest of the street sat silent, as if holding its breath, awaiting the next attack.

Ernő glanced at *Apu* and Patrik. But Zofia. Had Patrik's building been struck? Was she hurt?

Apu motioned to Ernő. "We have to get the Nagys out."

Patrik shook his head. "Now is the time for us to leave the city, while all is in chaos. No one will stop to examine our papers."

Ernő gazed down the street. "I have to get my wife from Patrik's flat. What if she's buried under rubble too?"

Apu patted his shoulder. "You'll get to her. We can't leave our neighbors to die."

Éva set her bag and clarinet case on the brick-strewn walk. "Time is critical. Let's get to work."

Ernő spun on his heel and crawled on top of the mountain of debris. *Apu*, Éva, and Patrik climbed after him.

Together, without any equipment, they dug—through

splintered wood that had once been an elegant bedroom set. Shards of glass, the remains of cut-crystal water goblets that pierced Ernő's hands as he moved shattered bricks. Ripped and torn material that had once been a dress the owner had worn to the opera.

The voices below him faded.

"Hello. Are you still there? If you can hear us, make some sort of noise."

Dead quiet.

But he refused to quit. Though pain shot through his bloody hands, he worked and worked. If Patrik's building had been hit, perhaps the neighbors would be digging to save Zofia. Would sacrifice themselves to rescue her.

Apu, who labored beside him, stood and clapped the dust from his hands. "They're gone."

Ernő yelled louder. No response.

Apu grasped him by the shoulder. "You need to leave. Get Zofia and flee before it's too late. There's nothing more we can do for the Nagys, but there is something you can do for yourself and your family."

On his other side, Éva gasped. She elbowed Ernő in the ribs.

"Ouch. Stop it. We'll go."

"*Nem*." She pointed behind him. In front of what was left of their home, a figure huddled on the walk, her shoulders shaking. Or was that the flickering firelight?

Wait. That coat. That hair.

Zofia?

Éva nudged him. "Go to her."

Like a dream, it had to be too good to be true.

"What are you waiting for?" Éva nudged him.

He skidded down the pile of bricks and raced toward the woman. Over the stomach-churning odor of burning lives, he caught a whiff of roses.

Could it really be?

He reached out and touched her shoulder. For a moment she stilled, then uncovered her tear-stained face.

Her beautiful, wonderful, heavenly, tear-stained face. He knelt beside her. "*Szerelmem*. Is it truly you?"

"Ernő?"

He wrapped her in an embrace and kissed her salty lips. She cupped his cheeks and returned the kiss.

Breathless, they parted. "Why are you here?"

"I saw the fires, and I was afraid I would lose you. What is my life without you? I should have never left."

His throat tightened. "I'm just happy you're alive. I love you. I always will. Nothing will ever change that."

"I couldn't bear to be away anymore. I couldn't live knowing you didn't know . . ."

She grasped his hand and directed it to her stomach. A slight bulge. Had she gained weight while in hiding? Not likely, given the meager rations everyone had.

Then what?

Like the dawn, understanding broke over him. "You're with child?"

She nodded.

She was pregnant. With his child. His baby grew inside her. His breath rushed from his lungs. He pulled her close once more. Never would he let her go, never again. Not her nor their child.

He was going to be a father.

"You're squeezing the air out of me."

He released her. "I'm sorry. Did I hurt you or the baby?"

She laughed, the music of it rising above the mourning and gnashing of teeth around them. "We're fine."

Within moments, the rest of the family surrounded them. They came to their feet, and they all hugged each other. In the middle of death and destruction came life.

Patrik tapped him on the back. "I understand how joyous this reunion is, but we have to go. Right now. Zofia, I didn't even get a chance to tell you that we've been compromised. At this moment, our new identity papers are being produced. We're on our way to Romania."

Ernő kissed his wife's cheek. "Éva and I are part of this now. We're coming with you."

"This is the perfect cover." Leave it to Patrik to have a plan. "People will think Bognár *Úr* and Bognár *Asszony* survived the bombing of their home, but their children and their daughter-in-law were lost. It is crucial, though, that we leave now, before anyone sees you."

Éva clung to *Apu*.

Patrik tugged her from *Apu*'s side. "No time for good-byes. Let's get out of here."

Ernő now had a wife and a child to take care of. He clapped *Apu* on the back, pecked *Anya* on the cheek. Any more, and the tears now moistening his eyes would overflow. For Zofia, for their child, he had to be strong. He stopped a moment to study his parents' faces. How long before he saw them again? Would he ever?

In the center of the ring of fire that had been Éva's neighborhood, in front of what had been the only home she had ever known, Patrik ripped her from *Apu*'s arms.

"*Nem, nem*, I can't go without them."

Apu smoothed down her hair, in much the same way as he had when he had come to kiss her good night when she was a small child. "Go with God. And with Patrik."

"I can't do this without you." Her voice squeaked through a swollen windpipe.

He kissed her forehead. "We will put our hope in the Lord, that he will reunite us one day very soon. You must live in peace and security."

"Why won't you come?"

He shook his head. "I spoke to Patrik while you were packing. At four people, your group is already large enough. Six is too many to be fleeing together. It's not a journey without its dangers. *Anya* and I aren't young anymore. The trip would be difficult on us, as would leaving all we've ever known. We decided it's for the best that we stay."

"Tearing families apart? That's for the best?" How could she walk away from her parents? You didn't do that. Parents cared for their children until their children cared for them. Families lived together, generations of them under the same roof. They didn't divide themselves among countries.

Patrik tugged on her arm all the harder. "No more time for leave-taking."

Apu and *Anya* gave her one last hug. "We kiss your hands many times. And never forget, we love you." Tears raced down *Anya*'s cheeks, the same way they coursed down Éva's.

Patrik clapped *Apu* on the shoulder. "I'll take care of her."

With that, Patrik pulled her away from her family, the people who had given her life, nurtured her, loved her. Together with Ernő and Zofia, they raced into the eerie, haze-clogged darkness.

She steeled her spine.

One last glance backward.

In the fires' glow, there stood *Apu* and *Anya*, holding hands.

Then they disappeared in the smoke.

"Where are we going?" The haze was so thick, Éva fought to catch her breath.

"You'll see when we get there." Patrik didn't slow his pace.

Zofia and Ernő caught up. Her sister-in-law touched her shoulder. "He's a good man. After Ernő, the best. You'll understand in time. Go now." Zofia and Ernő resumed their half run, half walk.

Patrik grasped her hand all the tighter. "It's for the best. We must hurry. As soon as the Gestapo discovers we're missing, they'll be hunting for us. They already might be."

The word *Gestapo* was enough to drive Éva forward, her legs trembling, her heart beating at a furious tempo. Her lungs and legs burned. Finally, her feet aching, they turned down a back alley and arrived at a plain brick house. Its simple, flat facade held no charm or character. "What is this place?"

He released his hold on her, and she wiped her damp palm on her yellow dress. Her feet throbbed, even though she wore her low, soft-heeled, buckled oxfords. How much would they hurt by the time they crossed into Romania?

Romania. Of all the crazy places.

Without answering her question, he withdrew a key from his pocket, slipped it into the lock, and ushered the group inside, then latched the door.

The large building housed several offices, now closed and darkened for the night. They climbed the steep wood stairs up two flights to a tiny room that held nothing more than a row of almost empty bookshelves and a narrow pine desk. Not a single sheet of paper or even one pen graced the top.

Patrik reached behind the books on the bottom shelf, fiddled with something for a moment, then slid the shelves to the side, revealing a short door. He knocked, the rhythm irregular, perhaps a code.

A deep voice answered from the other side. "Come."

Patrik ducked through the doorway and motioned the rest to follow him. Éva crouched low and almost crawled through the opening, popping up once she crossed the threshold.

Cigarette smoke filled the large, blue-hazed room. With no air circulating, it was thicker in here than outside. A blond-haired man leaned over a printing press, a tumbler in one hand. His cigarette leaned against the edge of a ceramic ashtray. He turned to Patrik. "You're early."

"Suffice it to say, there has been a change of plans. How long until our papers are completed?"

"Patience, please."

Patrik circumnavigated the room.

Éva shifted her weight from one leg to the other and glanced from Patrik to Zofia and back again. "That gives you time to explain."

The man waved his glass, the liquid sloshing over the side. "They don't know?"

Patrik huffed. "Not everything."

"Start at the beginning." A wave of exhaustion swept over Éva, and she leaned against the wall. "I need to know. To understand."

Patrik embraced her, but she flinched, and he backed away. "This is a Zionist Youth building. We run a branch of the resistance out of here, printing false birth certificates, identity papers, and passports. That's what we're waiting for now."

Rumors had floated around about the Jewish men and women working to get other Jews either new identities or spirit them out of the country. "How do you know these people and this place?"

"Zofia and I work for them."

Éva stared at Patrik for a long moment then turned to Zofia. "You're involved? How long?"

Ernő caressed his wife's arm. "You've been part of this?"

She nodded. "Almost from my arrival. That's why I had to go into hiding. I was discovered and taken by the Gestapo."

"What did they do to you?" Ernő clung to Zofia.

"I'm fine. That's why I didn't come home that day. As soon as I escaped from the Nazis—"

"You escaped?" Éva leaned forward, her head pounding.

"A story for another day. What I don't know is why we need to get out of the country now." Zofia turned to Patrik.

His features hardened. "We warned you about that pamphlet. They figured out who wrote it and where you were. I received a call this afternoon threatening not only you and me, but Ernő and Éva as well."

Éva clutched her chest. How had she been dragged into this ugly mess? "One more question. I can see how Zofia would join the Zionist Youth. She's Jewish. But you? Why are you part of the organization?"

Patrik's face flushed. "I . . . I . . . it's not important."

Was *this* the secret he wouldn't share?

Chapter Twenty-One

*H*ow was Patrik to answer Éva's question? For years he'd hidden who he was. But to lie to her again would jeopardize any chance they had at reconciliation. "Listen to me."

Éva turned her attention from the parquet wood floors to Patrik, her brown eyes shimmering. Ernő's and Zofia's stares weighed him down. Even Bram stilled the printing press.

"I joined because I want to help these people. Too many of my orchestra members fled Germany, Poland, and Czechoslovakia because of what was happening to the Jews there. The stories they told were horrific. We can't imagine what happened to them, although Zofia's story gives us a good idea. Now, in this place where they believed they'd be safe, they're facing the same fate."

"I didn't think the organization allowed Gentiles to be part of it." Éva breathed the question.

"We don't." Bram slurred his words.

Patrik shot him a black look.

Éva turned away.

He grasped her by the shoulder and spun her around. "You have to believe—"

"So you are—"

"All finished." Bram slapped some papers on the small, rickety table.

"Thank you." Maybe now Éva would let the question of his Zionist Youth involvement die.

"No problem." Bram flashed a crooked smile. "I've done it for you before, Patrik. You get to be Orbán Bela this time."

Patrik could only pray that Bram would be sober when the Gestapo discovered him. His tongue wagged far too much after a few drinks. Although without a doubt, he was the best forger the Zionist Youth had.

"Let's get out of here." Patrik nodded toward the small passageway.

"Best of luck to you." Bram raised his glass. "A toast to your success."

They wormed their way through the small opening and into the empty office. Éva pulled Patrik to a stop. "Before we go anywhere, I want to know what the plan is. Every detail."

When it came to organizing the wedding, Éva's obsessive planning was a good thing. Now, not so much. "The less you know, the better for you."

"Does Zofia know what's going to happen?"

Zofia held her suitcase in front of her. "I don't."

Patrik breathed a sigh as the two women and Ernő stared at him. "There isn't a real plan. I know what to do. Others have been doing it for a while. But things can and do go wrong even when everything is laid out. We need to be flexible so we can deal with every contingency. We just can't foresee everything."

"No plan? You're going to get us out of Hungary and to Palestine, but you have no idea how you're going to do it?"

"The *tiyul*, this exodus across the border, has been well orchestrated by the Zionist Youth. You're going to have to trust me."

"Trust you?" Éva snorted.

"You don't have a choice." Patrik moved toward the door.

Ernő beat him to it and held it closed. "We can't run into the streets. There's this thing called a curfew."

"Look at your identity papers."

The other three flipped open the covers on the booklets Bram had printed.

Éva's eyes widened. "I'm a physician."

Ernő chuckled. "Same as me."

"We all are." Patrik opened the door. "It's already much later than I wanted it to be when we got our start."

Ernő and Zofia filed by him. Éva stopped. "So if the Germans question us about being out after curfew, we're on some kind of medical mission?"

"Something like that. With all the bombings tonight, it's not so far-fetched. The perfect cover, really. Either that or you'd have to be a firefighter. I thought you'd prefer doctor."

"What about our suitcases?"

Good question. He hadn't thought about wandering the city with their luggage. "We were on our way to the train station to go to a conference in Nagyvárad when the bombers came."

"Let's go, then."

Good, she'd finally come to her senses. The four of them wound down the stairs and out the door to the deserted street. Off in the distance, the screech of ambulance sirens cut the still-ness of the night. The putrid odor of cordite and death hung in the air.

Patrik led the way through the dark streets lit only by the fires burning throughout the city. For Éva's sake, he'd made this sound like a simple proposition. Stroll through the city in the middle of the night past curfew while enemy planes flew overhead, take a train to the border, and before you know it, you're in Palestine.

He turned left, in the opposite direction of the station, just in case someone followed them. What would the promised land be like? No longer was it flowing with milk and honey, that much was sure. Most of it had reverted to desert. He also understood from some clandestine messages the Zionists had received that there were oases, places of peace, tranquility, and beauty.

A sweet foretaste of heaven itself. No matter the outcome of this journey, he would end up in paradise.

After several minutes, Patrik doubled back, this time moving in the station's direction. Glass crunched under their feet as they drew close to a section of the city hit by bombings.

The streets here were not empty. Rescue personnel bustled to and fro. Patrik and his group turned the corner and almost ran headlong into a younger woman holding a dirty rag to her eye, blood rushing down her face.

Behind her marched three soldiers, their dark green uniforms covered in dust, their rifles trained on the woman's back. Patrik glanced away. It was wrong to leave her when she needed help, but he couldn't save everyone.

If only . . .

He marched forward.

Zofia averted her eyes from the woman the Gestapo was leading away. How easily that could have been her. Should have been her. Smoke from the fires all about them clogged her throat. She coughed and stumbled.

Patrik hastened toward the station, Éva right by his side. Zofia held Ernő's hand as they brought up the rear. How good it was to be near her husband once more. To have his flesh touch hers. They had been apart too long.

By the time they arrived at the railway, Zofia was panting from the brisk walk. Ernő squeezed her shoulders. "How are you doing?"

She mustered her best smile. "Fine. I have been sitting around and not going anywhere, so I'm out of shape. And growing our baby has taxed my strength."

"Are you up to this?"

"I don't have a choice. Don't worry about me. I'll be okay."

He squeezed her upper arm, conveying the strength of his commitment to her.

They burst into the station and descended the stairs to the public shelter, Patrik banging on the door as the air raid sirens wailed yet again. A warden admitted them. Once inside, Zofia drew in a deep breath and sank onto the end of a bench beside a rotund man who reeked of onions and sweat. Nausea, which she had thought herself past, swept over her. She fanned her face.

Ernő, who had no room to sit, leaned over her to speak to the man. "Could you please move elsewhere? My wife is pregnant and needs air."

Some of her discomfort eased at her husband's words. Even though they'd spent the last months apart, he could still read her, knew what she was thinking and feeling before she expressed herself.

How had she ever lived without him?

"I was here first. Find somewhere else."

Ernő's face reddened. "How can you—"

She touched his forearm. "We'll find another seat." At least she didn't have that horrible star on her coat or dress any longer. Her new identity enabled her to rip it off. That action allowed her to enter the shelter, where Jews were not permitted. She smiled. Freedom, just a small taste of it. Down here, she could relax. No hiding underneath the piano wondering if she would survive the hail of bombs.

"Where? The place is full."

Éva waved from farther into the shelter. "Ernő, Zofia, over here." They wound their way through the narrow tunnel lined with benches and discovered a spot beside a woman with a sleeping baby on her shoulder. For the second time, Zofia settled into place. Now there was enough room for Ernő.

She rested against him, warm and secure for the moment.

He kissed the top of her head. "Why didn't you tell me? Why leave without me?"

"Not here, not now. Too many prying ears."

"Of course," he whispered in her hair. "I didn't think."

"Let's enjoy our reunion."

Ernő rubbed the gentle rise of her belly. "You knew you were pregnant when you left." Not an accusation as such, but a statement.

"There wasn't a chance to tell you. Oh, how I wanted to. I was planning to make the announcement special. But then—" Were they saying too much? They spoke in low tones, and the mother beside them had her eyes closed, but she might be listening to their conversation. "Let's not talk anymore. I'm exhausted."

"Of course, *szerelmem*, you sleep now. I should have thought. But I don't understand."

"You will in time." She sat up. "Do you hate me?"

A brief, heart-stopping moment went by before he answered. "*Nem.*"

"You're angry, though."

"Hurt, disappointed, grieved. All of those things."

"I'm sorry. Can you forgive me?"

"In time, I'm sure I will."

"Not now?"

"I need to figure this out. Can you understand?"

"I can." Though it didn't ease the pain in her heart. All along, Patrik had believed and had convinced her that not telling her family was the right thing. The only thing to keep her husband and his family from harm. In the end, it was for naught, and the Germans had hurt and harassed her family anyway.

Whatever it took, she would mend what she had broken.

She pecked his cheek and resumed her position against him. Being near him for now satisfied her. No matter if the Lord gave them just this night together or fifty years of marriage, it was enough.

She must have dozed, because the next thing she knew, the all-clear sirens sounded. The shelter's denizens stood and stretched and sauntered to the entrance.

The foursome brought up the rear of the group, making their way forward little by little. Éva stood beside Zofia, who caught her by the arm. "Don't hate me for what I did."

"Hate is too strong of a word for what I feel."

"I know how I hurt all of you."

"What I don't comprehend is why Patrik didn't tell us where you were."

"He felt it was for the best so that I didn't endanger you. He did it because he loves you."

Éva nodded. "The situation is like a tangled ball of yarn that's going to take time to unravel."

Time. How much did they have? Zofia had heard about the *tiyul*, the exodus of Jews from Hungary to Palestine. Some escaped to Romania and beyond. Others did not survive.

Hungary was supposed to be her safe place, her shelter after her flight from Poland. But she hadn't awakened from the nightmare. Now her decisions might have spoiled the beauty that had come from that pain.

August 10, 1944

Patrik led the little group up the concrete stairs to the train platform, blinking against the early morning light. He rubbed his gritty eyes. Twenty-four hours ago, he had no idea this was how today would begin.

Hordes of humanity crowded the station—Germans fleeing the Soviets, businessmen in and out of the city, and probably a few Jews like himself and Zofia, doing their best to escape an impossible situation.

The four of them gathered near the top of the steps. "Éva and I will buy the tickets." He fingered the money Bram had given him in his pocket. Enough to see them through for a while. "Ernő and Zofia, why don't you get us breakfast?" He handed a few of the bills to Ernő.

Zofia took the cash, and they soon melded into the crowd. Patrik turned to Éva. "Are you coming?"

"How convenient you would send off the others so we could be alone."

He shrugged. "Not my intention, but I don't have a problem with it. Unless you do."

"Actually, I do. After what you did—"

"What did I do?" He leaned over her, close to her. "Saved your sister-in-law's life. And probably Ernő's and yours. That's what I did. You're angry with me for that?"

She deflated a bit. "Not for that but for the lies that accompanied it."

"This is neither the time nor the place to get into everything, but I can say it's Reka who turned you against me. She twisted what she saw and made you believe it."

"You're crazy."

He gave a wide shrug and sighed. "However we got here, the fact is that we're here. We have to deal with the present. Rehashing the past will have to wait for another day. Let's get those tickets."

His chest heaving, he stomped off in the direction of the ticket counter. He hadn't meant to raise his voice to Éva. None of this was her fault, except maybe believing Reka over him, her own fiancé. How had such a wedge come between them?

He slowed to allow her to catch up as they maneuvered through the maze of people. "My apologies for getting angry."

She harrumphed. Not exactly forgiveness, but he'd take it for the time being.

A long line snaked from the counter, where multiple agents sat behind barred windows. More than an hour went by before they reached the head of the line. "Four tickets to Nagyvárad, please."

With the slips of paper tucked inside his jacket pocket, he and Éva trekked in the direction of Ernő and Zofia.

"Stop."

Though the German words sent a chill up and down Patrik's spine, he moved forward.

"I told you to stop."

Éva spoke low to Patrik. "I think he means you."

"He may, but I'm not going to obey."

"You. The tall one. I order you to halt."

Not willing to have a bullet pierce his skull, Patrik stopped. "Keep going." He nudged Éva forward.

"*Nem.* I'm staying with you."

Before he could question her further, the square-jawed German came even with Patrik. "Identification."

Concentrating on keeping his breathing steady and even, he produced the booklet from his pants pocket and handed it to the sandy-haired man who stood as tall as him.

The Nazi bit his lower lip as he examined the identification. He peered back and forth between it and Patrik. "Dr. Orbán?"

"That's me."

"What is your specialty?"

"Podiatry."

"Hmm. Interesting. I know I recognize you from somewhere."

Patrik stared harder at the man. He would remember someone as tall as himself, because they were an oddity. Wait a minute. *Igen.* He was the man from the Zionist meeting. Simon. He'd come only those few times. "We've never met."

"I don't forget a face. A non-Aryan appearing one at that."

"You must have me confused with someone else."

"Wait a minute."

Éva grasped Patrik by the arm. "Sir, we must catch this train. We're on our way to a medical conference in Nagyvárad, and since we're both presenters, we cannot miss it."

Patrik ground his teeth. What was Éva doing?

The officer glared at her, but she didn't break eye contact with him. "You are?"

She retrieved her identity booklet from her black pocketbook and handed it to the Nazi. "You can see that everything is in order. Now, if you would permit us to leave."

"And what is your relationship to this man?"

"His fiancée." She flashed her hand where the sapphire ring he'd presented her on their engagement glittered on her finger. "And a colleague."

"And you practice what kind of medicine, Miss . . ." he glanced at the card, "Molnár?"

She yanked it away from him. "That's Dr. Molnár. I'm an obstetrician. One of the best in the country."

"Are you now? And it's my experience that such professionals are also Jews."

Patrik piped up. "True that many are, but not all. There are a few of us Hungarians in the field of medicine." He gave a wry chuckle. "Now, as Dr. Molnár said, we must be on our way." He took three steps.

"Not so fast. I have just remembered where I've seen you before. You'll be coming with me. Both of you."

Chapter Twenty-Two

*E*rnő stared at his wife as she slumbered on his shoulder while they rested on a bench in the train station. Her red hair cascaded over her cheek. What he had missed without her by his side.

But her deception cut him to the quick. She should have been able to come to him and share what was going on in her life. Patrik knew more about her, and had so much influence on her, that she had agreed to not tell her own husband where she was.

Too much pain to deal with right now. Their main objective at the moment was to get to Romania.

She stirred in her sleep, and his body warmed. Despite everything, he loved her. Always would. Especially now that she carried his child.

Yet another secret she'd kept from him.

Where had Éva and Patrik gone? They should have been back with the tickets already. He and Zofia had procured a few *langosi*, fried dough topped with cheese, quite some time ago. Zofia had already eaten hers, needing to keep food in her stomach to hold the morning sickness at bay.

While Zofia's lying hurt him a great deal, Patrik's was almost worse. He knew where Zofia was, and even though his family had begged Patrik for information, he didn't tell them the truth. Instead he allowed them to believe she was out there alone and frightened.

How many nights' sleep had Ernő lost, frantic over his wife's whereabouts? Patrik could have given each of them comfort. He chose not to.

All of it could have been prevented.

All of it should have been prevented.

He glanced over the crowded station. Well-dressed business-men in sharp three-piece suits mingled with country folk clad in simple pants and skirts with frayed hems. Ah, there was Patrik. Even if you tried, you couldn't lose him in a throng. He spoke with a similarly sized Nazi, medals glinting on the soldier's drab green uniform. Ernő didn't spot his much more petite sister, but she must be beside Patrik.

Nothing good could come from that situation. He shook Zofia. "Wake up. I think Patrik is being questioned."

She sat, yawned, and rubbed her green eyes. "What? Where are they?"

Ernő nodded in their direction.

Zofia gasped. "I know that man."

"You do?"

She covered her mouth, her eyes twitching, then released a long breath. "It all makes sense now. How they found out about me, my involvement in the organization, where I was."

"You'll have to explain."

"There isn't time. But I believe he's a spy who infiltrated our branch of the Zionist Youth. We knew him as Simon. I only saw him at a few meetings, but that must have been enough. We have to help them. He'll recognize Patrik too."

Ernő's head throbbed. "What can we do?"

Zofia turned to him, biting her lip. "I don't know, because he'll know who I am. I'm sure I spoke to him."

So when she said she had to teach late, she was really going to meetings? Ernő rubbed the back of his neck. "But my face wouldn't be familiar to him."

"I suppose not."

"Then it has to be me who handles the situation."

"What are you going to do?" She really chewed her lip now.

"I'll think of a plan on the way. It's going to take me a while to swim through all these people."

He rose to leave, but she grabbed him by the hand. "Be careful."

He almost chuckled. His wife, the risk-taker, telling him to be cautious. "I will."

"I love you."

He kissed the top of her head. He couldn't bring himself to say the words. The wound she'd inflicted still bled.

He wove his way through the maze of humanity. This was worse than the obstacle course he'd run at prep school. How he'd hated it then, but maybe it had been good for something in the end.

As he pushed and shoved, he kept Patrik, who gestured and shook his head, in his sights. There. Ernő caught a glimpse of Éva's blond hair. She was with him.

Maybe that was a good thing. Maybe not. Perhaps it wasn't the man dressed as a German soldier who had infiltrated the Zionists but Patrik.

Pulse pounding, Ernő picked up his pace. He reached Patrik and Éva just as the Nazi grasped hold of Patrik. "Halt."

"Who are you?"

Ernő spoke in German. "Where are you taking this couple?"

The Nazi gazed down his nose at Ernő, who had to peer upward. "What is it to you?"

"Do you know you're taking in one of our best informants?"

Patrik, Éva, and the German stared at Ernő, their brows furrowed.

"Informants?"

"*Ja*. He's undercover right now as a doctor attending a conference in Nagyvárad. You standing here chatting with him is a good way to blow his cover."

"I don't believe there are any Jews remaining in Nagyvárad for him to ferret out. Most of the countryside has been cleansed of the vermin, who have been forced into ghettos before transport."

Ernő crossed his arms and narrowed his eyes. "You said

something interesting. You don't believe there are Jews remaining. You don't know for sure, do you?"

The man pursed his lips and shrugged.

"That is the precise reason why Herr Mueller is on his way to Nagyvárad. Release him this instant." Ernő held his breath.

"How do I know this isn't a trick? Do you have anything proving this man is an informant? I saw him at one of those Zionist meetings, and he appeared to be quite involved in the organization."

Ernő's knees weakened. "Pfft." He put on an air of confidence he lacked. "That's why he's one of the best. No one suspects him. Of course we wouldn't have any documentation. This isn't a kindergarten exercise. No one worth their salt would have anything on their person that would give them away."

The Nazi nodded and stroked his chin, which sported several days' worth of blond stubble.

Patrik jumped in. "Now this delay is quite unacceptable. We must be on our way."

"Wait a minute." The German poked Patrik in the chest. "Why didn't you tell me about this in the first place?"

"Because it's confidential, you dolt. I would have told you as soon as we were in private. Now this man has saved me that trouble. We'll be on our way."

With that, Patrik turned on his heel and marched away, Éva and Ernő following in his wake.

Éva, Patrik, and Ernő returned to Zofia. Drained from the encounter with the Nazi officer, Éva sank onto the bench beside Zofia, her hands still trembling. "That was too close."

A muscle jumped in Patrik's jaw. "What you did, Ernő, was crazy. He could have, and probably should have, arrested us all."

"A simple thank you will suffice." Ernő's words had a bite to them.

"Next time, don't interfere."

"Trust me, I didn't do it for you. I did it for my sister, and her only."

Éva jumped to her feet and stepped between the two men. "Enough. Now is not the time to argue."

Patrik's heavy breathing slowed. "You're right. My apologies. I don't know what got into me. Our journey was almost over before it began."

Éva sat again. Zofia distributed the *langosi* she and Ernő had purchased. Though not even a little hungry, Éva bit into the fried bread and choked down several bites.

If they faced such perils before their journey started, what would the rest of the trip be like?

A train clanged into the station on the track where they were scheduled to leave. As the passengers disembarked, Patrik addressed the group in a quiet voice. "It's best that we split up and don't acknowledge we know each other. You know what to do if something happens to the others. God go with each of you."

Chills raced up and down Éva's arm. She turned to her brother, who squeezed her hand and then Zofia's. He ambled away from the group, hands in his pockets as if he didn't have a care in the world. Éva's throat ached when he disappeared into the crowd.

Zofia walked away next, in the opposite direction. She'd just returned to their lives. Éva couldn't lose her now. Neither could Ernő. Losing his wife a second time would break him. *Apu* had reminded her that her hope was in God. *Lord, I'm trusting You. Protect us. Reunite us.*

Patrik nudged her. Without a backward glance, she strode toward the end of the train, not far from where she'd watched Ernő vanish from sight. Not that she would jeopardize them by interacting with her brother but because seeing him would bolster her as they took this first part of their journey alone.

Not long after she left Patrik, the call came for their train. Éva clutched her bag and her clarinet case close and, on shaking legs, climbed the steps. She only moved in a few rows until she picked her spot and sank into the plush red velvet seat.

Leaning against the back of the bench, she closed her eyes. Maybe if the other passengers believed she was sleeping, no one would sit beside her.

A few minutes passed, and footsteps shuffled by her. She allowed herself to relax her shoulders. This wouldn't be so bad.

"Excuse me, ma'am. Is this seat taken?"

A whiff of musky cologne drifted over her. She opened her eyes to discover a man with light, straight hair, blue eyes, and dimples in both cheeks leaning over her.

"Well, um, I—"

"Thank you." He plopped beside her.

She focused on the scene outside the window. People milled around the platform, a few hurrying for the train. Nazi soldiers with creased caps on their heads and rifles at their sides mixed in with the travelers. One even tugged on a German shepherd's leash.

"Are you going all the way to Nagyvárad?"

Éva whipped around to face her seatmate. "*Igen*, I am." A curt response to discourage further prying questions, though *Apu* and *Anya* would have been shocked by her rudeness. Her parents. What were they doing? Had they found someplace to stay?

"Do you play the clarinet?"

Her avoidance tactic was proving ineffective. "I do."

"Ah, then you must be a fan of Carl Maria von Weber."

That snagged her attention and rendered her unable to ignore the man any longer. "Very much so. Concerto no. 1."

"*Igen*, that's my favorite."

"Every clarinetist worth her weight knows it by heart."

"Do you play professionally?"

"*Nem*." Now the questions were getting too personal. "Do you play?"

"I used to." He showed her his left hand that was missing the third and fourth fingers. "After the accident at the ironworks, playing became impossible for me."

"I'm so sorry. How awful for you."

"I was no prodigy, so the world will never miss my squeaking and squawking. Fortunately, I still possess the ability to listen, and I enjoy nothing more than a fine performance by an accomplished clarinetist."

Éva gave a half chuckle. "Then you don't want to hear anything I have to play."

"But you said you've memorized Concerto no. 1."

"I have, but I never said I played it well."

A familiar figure caught Éva's attention. A larger woman with fair hair wobbled down the aisle, right in their direction.

Reka.

Éva squirmed in her seat. If only she'd purchased a newspaper while they'd been waiting. Instead of being able to hide behind that, she bent down as if searching for something on the ground.

"Are you missing something?" Her seatmate's voice sounded close to her ear.

"I, uh, I, uh, thought I heard a coin drop. Maybe from my purse."

Squeak. The springs of the seat in front of Éva protested under a great deal of weight.

Nem, nem. Reka couldn't sit there.

♪♫♪

Chapter Twenty-Three

The now-moving train car closed in on Éva until she couldn't draw a deep breath. She broke into a cold sweat, and the world spun. She had to get out of here, couldn't stay a moment longer. If Reka turned around, she would recognizer her. Reveal her true identity. "Excuse me," she whispered to the man beside her.

"Are you feeling ill?"

She nodded.

"Let me help you." He touched her arm.

"*Nem*, that's not necessary. I just need air." Blackness edged her vision. Causing as little commotion as possible, she slid by him and to the door a few steps behind her.

Once outside, she rested against the railing on the bridge between the two cars and focused on breathing. The dizziness subsided.

She turned as the Hungarian countryside whipped by. Thick, green forests gave way to lush meadows, cows grazing in the fields, munching as if all were right with the world.

Her Hungary. The land of her birth. Where she'd grown up and built a life. A good one. Neither she, nor Patrik, nor Zofia, nor Ernő had any idea of what lay ahead of them or if any of them would ever return.

She would do whatever she had to in order to come home. When the Soviets freed her beloved country and handed it to the Hungarian people, she would come back. Even if she had to fight for it. Palestine would not be her permanent home.

Apu and *Anya* were here, waiting for her and Ernő and Zofia. They could pick up the pieces of their lives, rebuild their business.

Those thoughts tapped into a reservoir of strength.

But she couldn't go back into the car. At some point, Reka would turn around, discover her, and call her by her real name. Curious that she showed up on the same train as them. Then again, she did say she went home to Nagyvárad every Thursday. And today was Thursday. Éva hadn't even thought about that until now.

Had Reka seen the others while she'd searched for a seat? *God in heaven, nem.*

Despite the danger, she had to locate Patrik and let him know. Just in case.

Steeling herself, she meandered to the next car, searching for him without appearing to be looking for anyone. She strolled down the aisle, but no Patrik.

She searched through several more cars. He had to be behind her, because she couldn't walk by Reka. Each time she stepped into another coach, she breathed a prayer for success.

The wind ruffled her skirt as she pulled open the next door. Almost right in front of her sat Zofia. Éva averted her gaze as she sped down the aisle as fast as possible without drawing attention to herself.

She stretched for the door's handle when someone reached from behind her and took hold of her by the hand. Her heart skipped a beat.

"What are you doing?" Patrik whispered in her ear.

"Come outside with me." Together they left the compartment.

They stood facing each other on the narrow coupling between the cars, Éva clutching the railing behind her. "You scared the stuffing out of me."

"Why are you up and wandering around the train?"

"Searching for you."

"Like I said before, it's dangerous for us to be seen together. Our odds of surviving are best if we are separate."

"But she's here. That's why I couldn't stay put."

At that, he leaned forward. "What are you talking about?"

"Reka."

He raised his full, dark eyebrows. "She's on this train?"

"Not only on this train but sitting in the seat right in front of me."

He leaned ever closer, so his breath brushed her cheek, sending an ache shooting through her. "Did she see you?"

"I don't think so. As soon as I spotted her, I ducked behind the seat. But I may have aroused suspicion in the man beside me. I told him I was ill."

"Good thinking."

"What if she did notice me? I might put all of you in danger."

Patrik reached out and pulled her close. Though she didn't want to, she found herself relaxing in his embrace, his cotton shirt cool against her heated cheek. As she breathed in the spicy scent of his aftershave, she was at home. *Nem*, she couldn't. She pushed away from him.

He hummed a tune, one she'd never heard before, simple yet haunting. The melody engulfed her. As she listened, she imagined the song speaking of them, telling their story, happy in parts, sad in others. Major and minor mixed together. "What's that music? I don't recognize it."

He stopped humming and touched her forehead. "When we were apart, I was so very empty. Without you, *a múzsám*, there is no music in my soul. Composing became impossible. All except for this tune. I think of it as our song."

"It's beautiful."

"Just as you are." He lowered himself until he hovered just over her, pushing in for a kiss.

Nem. She yanked herself from his mesmerizing gaze. She couldn't allow her heart to take over from her head. Couldn't let those memories of all the good they had shared cloud her judgment. "Please, don't."

His brown eyes darkened. "I'm sorry. Will you let me explain?"

"You said we can't be seen together. Especially not like we were. Just tell me what to do."

"Find another seat."

"I left my suitcase, my pocketbook, and my clarinet where I'd been."

"That's not a problem. When we arrive, wait until most of the passengers have disembarked. Then, if Reka is gone, make your way back to collect your belongings. If she's still there, you might have to leave them behind."

"My clarinet too?"

"Everything. What is more valuable—your life or your instrument?"

Éva didn't have an easy answer for that. Her clarinet was her life. Musicians understood that. "I need it."

"You need to live more. Don't take any risks just to get it." He cupped both of her cheeks. "Do you understand me? This is crucial. If you put yourself in jeopardy over the clarinet, you put us all in danger."

She nodded.

"Good. You're right, we can't stay together any longer. Sit somewhere else. We'll meet at the rendezvous spot later tonight." He kissed her hands. "And be on guard."

She would. She'd protect her heart from loving him again. But she wouldn't leave the train without her clarinet.

No matter how hard he tried, Patrik couldn't settle back into his place after his encounter with Éva. Part of it had to do with the narrowness of the space between the seats. Even though he stretched his legs underneath the bench in front of him and into the aisle, no position proved comfortable.

The other part had to do with Éva herself. She'd waltzed right by him. When he'd caught up to her a couple of cars later, she'd been surprised to see him.

Having her and Ernő on this trip was perilous. The Zionists had trained Patrik and Zofia to elude authorities. Though not perfect, they did possess a few skills. Ernő and Éva didn't.

At least no one sat on the seat beside him as he wrestled for a position that didn't cramp his legs.

How good it had been to have her in his arms once more. Nothing compared to holding her small, trembling body close. They had almost been husband and wife. Then he had let her slip through his fingers.

He restrained himself from banging his head on the seat in front of him. Why had he pushed her so hard just now? Embracing her, almost kissing her had been the worst thing he could have done. Before they could resume any type of relationship, they had to rebuild their trust. Or rather, he had to help her trust him again.

After she'd been hurt and lied to by Károly, that would be next to impossible.

If only they could get a chance to talk alone. If he could explain to her everything, all of it, every little bit, including his identity, she would understand.

He leaned against the back of the seat and closed his eyes. The train rocked as it raced through the countryside. Not much longer and they would be in Nagyvárad. Then the most dangerous part of the journey would begin.

He must have dozed, because the screeching of the train's brakes sent him bolting upright. A murmur passed through the car. Patrik rubbed his eyes.

The conductor rushed through. "Everybody off. Run as fast as you can. Get away. Then hit the ground. Soviet planes." By the time he'd finished his instructions, he was halfway out the door.

Nem, not the Soviets. They had almost made it. And now they ran the risk of Reka spotting any one of them. He shook himself and popped to his feet. What about Zofia and Éva? They must be so frightened.

He couldn't worry about that now. *Lord, protect us.* With the other passengers, he rushed to the door, down the steps, and across the field into the night. A full moon hung in the sky, a single candle shining through a darkening cloth. Beams of light streamed down, illuminating the Soviet's target. Overhead, their planes' engines buzzed, closer and closer until the sound shook his very bones.

"Get down! Get down!"

Like marionettes, everyone around Patrik collapsed. He too fell to the warm, damp earth, the grass tickling his face, mosquitoes biting his arms.

In the light of the full moon, the Soviets had their choice of targets. The ground reverberated as bombs struck the train. Explosions on the heels of explosions.

Other planes chose to target the civilian passengers. With their guns, they rained bullets on the groups of people strung throughout the meadow. Women screamed. Children cried. Men moaned.

Patrik's body went clammy. A burning pain shot through his left leg. He clutched his calf, sticky blood coating his hands. There was nothing he could do about it now. He had to stay low while the aircraft remained in the area.

As suddenly as the planes arrived, they vanished. The skies above quieted until no sound remained save that of the crickets.

Their chirping stirred a solemn, somber tune in his head.

A few at a time, people rose to their feet. Voices carried on the evening breeze. How many had been injured? Killed? His gut clenched, and the *langosi* he'd consumed in Budapest threatened to come up. He bit back the queasiness.

He turned to investigate the damage to the train. Not much of it remained. A few of the cars toward the back were intact, but the engine was a smoking shell.

They wouldn't be taking this train to Nagyvárad.

Nor could he, Éva, Ernő, or Zofia remain with the other passengers while the tracks were cleared and another train sent from Budapest. That could be days.

He rose to his knees, his leg throbbing. At the sudden movement, he wobbled. In the moonlight's glow, he caught sight of Zofia's red head. She stood out in a crowd almost as much as he did.

Unable to call to her, he struggled to his feet. He whipped off his jacket and unbuttoned his shirt. He folded it then wrapped it around his injured leg. Though he was no Florence Nightingale, it would do the trick.

After testing his weight on the leg, he limped in the direction he'd spotted Zofia, keeping his head down to minimize his height. Ah, there she was, standing in the middle of the field. He came from behind her and touched her arm. She jumped and squeaked.

"It's just me."

"Thank goodness. I don't know where the others are. I didn't know what to do."

"Are you hurt?"

"*Nem.* You?"

"Just got nicked. Flesh wound." Though it burned like a thousand beestings. "We can't stay here."

"I know."

"The rest of the way we'll have to go on foot. We're close." He wobbled.

She caught him by the elbow and nodded.

"See those woods?" He pointed.

Another nod.

"Hide in there. I'll locate Ernő and Éva and meet you."

"I was just reunited with my husband. I'm not going into the forest until I find him and know he's safe. You're in no position to argue with me."

"I'm fine." Though the earth tilted at a crazy angle. "Think about your baby. If the Russians come again, you won't make it to the tree line in time. You'll be like a deer in the open, prime for picking. Please, go now. Ernő would want you safe. I promise to find you as soon as possible. We have to stay apart, at least until we're under the forest's cover."

Tears shimmered in her eyes. "Please, bring me my husband."

"I will. Don't worry." He prayed he'd find Ernő in one piece. If not, Zofia didn't need to see it.

She headed toward the stand of trees a short distance away. He straightened, his world around him spinning, and scanned the area for any sight of Ernő or Éva. Was that them there? The woman was blond enough to be Éva.

One step toward them. Two. His leg buckled, he collapsed to the ground, and darkness consumed him.

Chapter Twenty-Four

After the Soviet planes departed, chaos struck the train passengers. The living wept for the dead. Dirty, sooty children wandered alone. Shell-shocked women sat with blank faces.

What had the world come to? Perhaps the second coming was near.

Éva scanned the countryside bathed in moonbeams and flickering firelight. Flames licked the dark sky, casting an eerie glow over the scene of devastation. The hulking engine shell smoked on the tracks, and the rest of the cars were a tangled, mangled mess. She skimmed the wide-eyed faces for signs of anyone she knew. Familiar red hair or a lanky figure.

Nothing. No one she recognized. Where were they? She choked out the thought. They had to be okay. They couldn't be injured. Or . . .

Nem, nem, nem. She would find them. She had to. *Apu* said she had to put her hope in God. How hard that was, though, in such circumstances. For all she knew, she was the only one of their group who had survived. She'd lived through two bombings in a matter of days. How many more times could she cheat death? And the others? Only God knew what had happened to them.

Wait a minute. There. A tall, dark-haired man. That had to be Patrik.

But as she headed in his direction, he tumbled to the ground.

Éva's heart jolted within her. She might not trust Patrik, but she didn't want anything bad to happen to him. She picked her way toward him as fast as possible. People were stepping over his body as if climbing over a downed tree in the forest. Humanity had become calloused. Thick-skinned from the hardships of life.

Close, closer, and now there was no mistaking that head of dark hair. It was indeed Patrik. Gasping, she dropped to her knees in the soft, damp grass beside him and checked his wrist for a pulse. Its steady beat throbbed beneath her fingers. Praise God. A quick examination revealed he'd wrapped his shirt around his leg. Blood had soaked the clothing.

"Wake up. Come on, open your eyes. Can you hear me?"

Zofia came and knelt beside Éva. "I met him and he told me about his leg. Said it was nothing. I was headed to the forest but turned and saw him stumble."

"Am I ever glad to see you." Éva kept her words low. "Where is my brother?"

"Right here." Ernő's voice sounded behind her.

"Thank God we're all alive."

"That's nothing short of a miracle." Zofia leaned back on her haunches. "So many weren't as fortunate. The Soviets did their job."

Éva gave Patrik's cheek a few more gentle slaps. Still no response. "We have to get out of here. Reka was on this train."

"She what?"

"Shh, Ernő. Not so loud. She was sitting right in front of me. I ducked out when I spied her, but if she spots us, she'll give away our identities. And probably cause a ruckus. Patrik told me if anything happened, I had to go to the woods and meet him there."

Zofia nodded. "Staying in the open until another train arrives will only increase the likelihood of us running into Reka. If she's even alive."

Ernő moved to Patrik's other side. "We have to assume she is. If he doesn't wake up soon, we may have to carry him."

Éva slapped Patrik a little harder. This time, he moaned. His eyelids fluttered open. "Éva, *a múzsám*."

He reached up, but she backed away before he touched her

cheek. "We have to hurry to the woods so we aren't so exposed. Do you think you can walk?"

He nodded. "So dizzy."

Ernő lifted him to a sitting position. "Probably from blood loss. Take a few seconds for the world to stop whirling, then we'll get you to your feet."

The fire's ghostly glow reflected off Patrik's pale face. He'd never be able to cross the meadow under his own power.

Patrik blinked several times and nodded. "Okay, I'm ready to move. I'm going to need a hand."

Her brother assisted Patrik in standing. He grasped Ernő by the shoulder and steadied himself. "We'll have to keep low to avoid being seen. We can't draw attention to ourselves, or people will wonder where we're going, why we aren't on our way to the town like most everyone else."

Ernő grabbed Patrik under one arm, and Éva positioned herself under his other. Together they supported Patrik's weight. Keeping their heads bowed, they stumbled across the grassy field, Zofia close behind.

A few others straggled toward the woods. Most moved in the direction of the nearby village.

After a short distance, Éva's arms burned under Patrik's weight.

"Sorry I'm so heavy." He pinched his lips together.

"I'm just grateful you're not dead."

"Ah, you don't despise me." His eyes twinkled in the dim light.

"Incorrigible."

Only with God's strength did they make it into the tree line. Sweat poured down Éva's face by the time the branches and leaves hid them. Several meters in, they halted. Patrik slumped against an oak. Little of the moon's brightness seeped through the canopy. The air hung thick and heavy, and the acrid odor of smoke permeated even the forest.

Ernő rubbed his eyes. "I suggest we sleep for a while, and

come daylight, figure out where we go from here." He and Zofia sat down and huddled together against a tree.

"Good idea." Éva settled against another tree. The bark was rough and the trunk hard on the back of her head. Shutting her eyes, she prayed she'd wake up and find out the last forty-eight hours were a nightmare. She would be back in her pretty pink bedroom with *Apu* and *Anya* in the other room. She would get up and go to the music studio and teach her students. Nothing would have changed.

But everything had changed. And nothing would ever be the same.

The adrenaline drained from her body, and she fell into a fitful doze.

Crack.

Éva woke with a start. What was that sound? She sat still, taking shallow breaths. Nothing.

Snap.

Nem, something was there.

Or someone.

"Zofia, Ernő, wake up."

Éva's quiet, insistent voice and her shaking Ernő's shoulder roused him from his slumber against a nearby tree. "What?"

Crack. A twig snapped not far away. Zofia's eyes flicked open.

"Shh." He rose from Zofia's side.

Nearby, Patrik stirred. Ernő motioned everyone to stay put. Then he melted into the underbrush.

Éva's pulse pounded in her neck.

Silence descended again. No more breaking branches. Even the crickets quieted their night music.

After a long, long while, just as pink brushed the eastern sky, Ernő returned. Éva, who hadn't been able to fall back to sleep, sat up straight. "What did you find?"

He shrugged. "Nothing."

"Is that good or bad?"

"The noise might just have been an animal. Or it could have been other people. There isn't a way for me to tell."

"Must move." Patrik croaked the words.

Éva was at his side in a flash. "What's wrong?" She touched his burning cheeks. "He's running a fever. A high one." If he died out here, they would be in a bad way without anyone to get them to the border. Zofia may have been part of the organization, but as far as Éva knew, she hadn't been to Nagyvárad and didn't have the contacts there that Patrik did. *God, protect him.*

"Must move."

Zofia shushed him. "You aren't going anywhere until you've healed. We're going to have to stay until you're stronger. Right now, you should have something to drink."

Ernő nodded. "When I was searching for the source of the noise, I came across a small stream."

Éva bit her lower lip. "We don't have anything to bring water back."

"I can go." Patrik's words were labored.

"Where? To the river?" Éva glared at him. "Absolutely not."

"Must go."

"You are in no condition to move. We can't risk losing you." Éva cleared the sudden wave of emotion from her throat. "You're the one who knows where we're going and has the contacts we need."

Zofia nodded. "I'm in agreement. Until you're stronger, we stay put."

"Too dangerous."

Éva huffed. How stubborn could one man be? "If we tried to travel with you as sick as you are, we would draw too much attention to ourselves. *Nem,* the best course of action is to try to find some water, food, and medicine. Patrik, do you have any idea where we are?"

He pulled his eyebrows together for a moment. "There's a town not too far. Remember passing it. East. Not far from the train."

"I'll find it." Zofia rose to leave.

Ernő caught her by the elbow. "I won't allow it. You're pregnant, not to mention that with your red hair, you stand out in a crowd."

She pulled a silky scarf from her skirt pocket and covered her head. "Better? There are risks involved with exposing ourselves. But right now, the risks are greater if we don't do anything to help Patrik. Besides, I have been trained for cases such as this. I have my false papers. The only one we really have to worry about is Reka."

"*Szerelmem*, please don't do this."

She kissed her husband's scruffy cheek. "I learned my lesson in Budapest. I won't be rash this time, I promise." She placed his hand over the spot where their child grew. "This time, I have too much to lose."

"That settles it." Éva stood and brushed away the dead leaves that clung to her lightweight skirt. "I'll go. It's too risky for Zofia, and Ernő should stay with her."

"But—"

She cut off Zofia's protests with a wave. "You know it makes the most sense. Ernő needs to be here, especially if you're forced to move Patrik at the last minute. I'll take your scarf so I can hide my hair and face. I'll blend in more."

"Thank you." Ernő kissed her hands.

She kissed his cheek.

"Éva."

At Patrik's weak call, she knelt beside him.

"Watch out. Don't take chances. Get out if you have to."

"Of course. There's not too much that can go wrong." She said the words to herself more than to him.

"*Köszönöm*."

Staring into his brown eyes, a tug-of-war raged inside. A pull toward him. A pull away from him. A dissonance between two instruments. Which side would win? She didn't have time to analyze it.

Before any of them could protest further, she set off through the thicket toward the tracks.

Brambles snagged at her skirt and scratched her legs. Had she known she would be tramping through a forest, she would have worn trousers. But she hadn't had time to think about what she packed when they had fled Budapest. And saving Patrik's life was worth a few scratches.

The sun rose higher. Heat penetrated the leafy ceiling, and not a breeze stirred the air. Plenty of rocks and exposed roots made the going difficult, and in her haste, she tripped several times. Just about the time when she couldn't take another step, out she popped onto a road. Shielding her eyes from the bright daylight, she spied an old farmer atop a donkey cart overflowing with maize plodding in her direction.

Maybe there was room for her amid the corn. She stepped into the road and waved him down.

The old man reined to a halt. "Can I help you?"

"I'm headed to the village. Are you going that way?"

"Do you need a ride? Looks like you've about had it."

She nodded. "A ride would be wonderful." She hopped onto the back of the cart and nestled into the maize.

"You can sit up front if you'd like."

"*Nem, köszönöm.*" A few stray strands of straw stuck to her clammy skin. No one would want to be near her if they could smell her now.

A short time later, they pulled into a small hamlet of red-roofed medieval buildings surrounding a central square. When the man stopped to allow a handful of pedestrians to cross the street, Éva slid from the wagon. She wished she could give him something for his help, but she had to save her money for more important needs.

Like the bribes at the border.

She hunted down the odors of yeast and flour that tickled her nose to the bakery. A few ration coupons would get each of them a bit of bread in their stomachs. From there, she could decide how to find a doctor. A trustworthy physician.

"Éva? Bognár Éva? Is that you?"

Dear God in heaven, nem. Reka had spotted her.

Chapter Twenty-Five

For the fourteenth time that morning, Zofia checked Patrik's fever. No change. His forehead still burned.

She unwrapped the dirty shirt from around his calf. A red line ran from the wound to his knee.

Leaves crunched underneath Ernő's feet as he reached them. "That doesn't look good."

"I'm afraid it's not. With every passing hour, the infection is worsening. Where is Éva? We need water and medicine now."

"She'll be back."

"She should have returned long ago."

Ernő smoothed back her hair, now loosened from its pins. "It hasn't been that long. Worry is making it seem like time is moving slower."

"What if he dies?" She needed Ernő now, but he stood back, arms crossed.

"Doesn't the Bible tell us not to worry about the future? You're borrowing trouble."

"We have to be prepared."

"I thought you were. That's what you've been trained for." He stared at her with such intensity, she gazed away.

He knelt beside her and turned her so she had to face him. "Why? Why did you leave me?"

He still didn't understand. "Because I love you. That's the best answer I can give. Can't you trust in that? Believe in that?"

"I want to. I truly do. For you, me, and our child."

"You won't desert us, will you?" She hugged herself.

"*Nem*, you don't have to fret about that. But I can't fathom how a wife could leave the husband she claims to love. What drove you to it?"

How did she explain it to him? "What I saw in Poland was terrible."

"You've never told me, not in detail."

"Because it's too awful."

He sat on the ground and pulled her beside him. "Share with me. Don't leave me wondering about your past anymore."

"When the Nazis arrived in my hometown, not too much time went by before they began rounding up Jews. Old men, children, the infirm. My father knew the situation would only grow worse. He devised a hiding place in the attic of our home.

"Because of my father's work with the Polish resistance, the Germans targeted us early on. They took him to a labor camp soon after the invasion, leaving just me and Mama. Though it was dangerous, I continued Papa's work. Each day was like waiting for a bomb to explode. You never knew when it would happen, only that it would someday."

She closed her eyes and allowed the images to flicker across her mind, to transport her to that day she hadn't revisited in years.

She had been out that night, working on printing anti-Nazi pamphlets. Mama didn't know what she was involved in or why she didn't come home at night. Maybe she guessed. They never spoke about it.

As she crept home at sunrise one day, Germans stood on the front step, their transport trucks idling on the cobblestone street. They pounded on the door. Mama passed the front window. From her hiding spot in the bushes, Zofia heard Mama's call. "I'm not even dressed."

"Open up, or we'll break down the door."

Mama cracked the door, not wearing a wrap.

The Germans pushed her out of the way with a *thunk*. "Ah!"

Mama lay at the threshold cradling her ankle. With her heart pounding even harder than the Nazis at the door, Zofia raced to Mama. "Are you hurt?"

"Just my ankle, a little bit. Go. Get out of here. Don't let them see you."

"I can't let them hurt you."

"My daughter, you must listen to me. Run as fast and as far as you can. I'll deal with them. They'll go away."

"No."

In a voice Mama hadn't used since Zofia was seven, she commanded, "Go."

There was no arguing. Zofia fled and once again hid in the hedge bordering their small plot of land.

Mama stood and disappeared into the house. Harsh shouts came from inside.

Mama shouldn't be alone. The Nazis weren't there for her mother. They were there for Zofia. To spare Mama, she should turn herself in. Then they would go away and wouldn't hurt Mama.

Before she could make a move out of the hedge, someone grabbed her and pulled her back.

"What—"

The person covered her mouth. "Hush." Their neighbor, a young man her age, Jan.

Every muscle in Zofia's body tensed. "Let me go."

"Not on your life. They will kill you for sure. I saw your mother send you away. I'm going to make sure you stay away."

Jan had always had a crush on her. She loved him like a brother. Nothing more. But he outweighed her by almost double and stood a head taller. She would never break from his hold.

"Please, I have to help Mama."

"She wants you safe. Stay put."

Her heart almost burst from between her ribs. She shook from head to toe.

Then the voices, the boots, Mama's cries faded. The front door slammed shut. Silence descended. Zofia held her breath.

Several lifetimes later, the door opened, and two Gestapo soldiers led her small, frail mother from the house, one on either side, supporting her.

Before she could call to Mama, Jan covered her mouth, stifling her shouts.

The Germans threw Mama to the ground and towered over her as she lay on the street. "Where is your daughter?"

"I don't know. I haven't seen her for weeks."

One of the large men kicked her in the stomach. Zofia hugged herself, still straining against Jan's hold.

"Tell us where she's hiding."

"I don't know." Another kick to Mama's stomach and face. She writhed on the stony road, blood pouring from her nose.

The tallest, skinniest of the soldiers pulled Mama up by the hair. Her wails tore into Zofia's soul. She couldn't stem the torrent of tears.

"You will tell us." A short, stubby German raised his gun next to Mama's head.

"But I don't know. I don't know." Mama sobbed.

Tears gushed down Zofia's cheeks, wetting Jan's hand over her mouth, blurring the scene in front of her.

"That isn't an acceptable answer."

"It's the only one I have. She's not here, and I don't know where she went."

The short soldier cocked his pistol.

And shot Mama in the head.

At the sound of Reka's high-pitched voice, Éva froze. She avoided all movement, including blinking. How had she even recognized her? She'd worn Zofia's scarf.

Pounding footsteps sounded behind her, then huffing and puffing, the tickle of breath on her neck, the odor of cabbage. "Bognár Éva, whatever are you doing here?"

Éva didn't turn around. She lowered her voice an octave. "You must have me mistaken for someone else."

"Don't be silly. I'd know you anywhere."

"I don't know you." Éva took two steps in the opposite direction.

Reka grabbed her by the elbow and spun her around. "Why are you pretending not to know me?"

What did she say? How much should she tell? "Let's go somewhere less busy." Éva led the way to a quieter residential side street.

Reka frowned, dimples appearing in her full cheeks. "Now will you explain what's going on? I thought I saw you on the train, but you didn't acknowledge me, which rather offended me."

Éva winced, both for hurting Reka's feelings and for almost getting caught. "I couldn't."

"Why not, Éva?" Reka scrunched her eyebrows together.

"Don't use that name."

"You're doing a lousy job of explaining yourself."

Why couldn't Reka let the matter go? Éva held herself back from stomping her foot. "I've said too much already. Please, do as I ask and pretend you don't know me."

"Why were you taking the train to Nagyvárad?"

What excuse would Reka believe? "I'm going to play there."

Reka sucked in a breath. "*Nem*, you're not. You're running away, aren't you? Taking Zofia over the border. I've heard of people doing that. They get the Jews to Palestine."

"I have no idea what you're talking about. Zofia is missing, remember? I don't know where she is." Éva leaned closer to Reka and spoke in a conspiratorial whisper. "The man who sat next to me, he was too friendly. I was so happy to lose him when we had to evacuate. But here in town, I don't want him to find me. That's why you mustn't use my name."

"Why do I have to pretend not to know you? It's very strange."

"Because he recognized you from university in Budapest. I told him I was from another town. If we know each other, my story falls apart. Please, for my sake, for my safety, keep my secret. I beg you. He gives me a funny feeling." For good measure, Éva added a note of pleading to her voice and grabbed on to Reka's arm.

For a long moment, Reka studied Éva, her blue eyes narrow. "I suppose if it helps you out, I'll do it. But don't come crying to me if you need a hand." Reka turned on her heel and marched away.

Éva sagged as Reka disappeared around the corner. How many had heard Reka call her by her real name? Anyone she'd given her false name to? Any Gestapo or police riding the train with them?

The situation had grown too dangerous for her to stand in line for bread with the horde of stranded passengers. Most important was locating a cup or mug to get water for Patrik. Even if he didn't eat, he had to stay hydrated.

Once she'd peeked around the corner and assured herself no one else she knew was visible, she returned to the main thoroughfare. There, a block in front of her, was a little café, most of its tables occupied by people sipping their ersatz coffee as if life-and-death situations didn't surround them.

One table was open. No one had cleared it yet.

She scurried toward the café, but before she could swoop down on the table and swipe one of the delicate coffee cups, the busboy appeared and gathered the dishes.

Oh, she'd been so close. She could sit and order a cup herself, but a little voice in her head warned her to hang on to every bit of remaining cash.

So she moseyed up and down the block as café patrons enjoyed the early morning breeze.

There, another couple stood and dropped a few *pengő* on the table. This time, Éva was better prepared. She dashed to the table, grabbed the gold-rimmed cup, and sped away.

"Hey, that woman just stole something from that table."

Éva closed her ears to the accusation. Never in her life had she dreamed she would resort to lying and stealing.

But Patrik's life depended on it. And that depended on people not knowing who needed it or where they were.

She closed her mind to everything except racing down the street and out of the village. The forest edged right up to the outlying homes, so she didn't have to sprint far before the trees swallowed her. Once out of sight of anyone who might be following, she stopped to catch her breath. The world around her spun. How long had it been since she and the others had eaten?

And because of her run-in with Reka, it would still be awhile.

Here she was, telling more lies in the past forty-eight hours than in her entire life. Since she was little, *Apu* had drilled into her how wrong it was to tell a falsehood. The Bible demanded that she always tell the truth.

But what if lives were on the line? Others besides your own? What did you do when you were faced with either lying or murder?

This must be what Patrik wrestled with when he took Zofia into hiding. Either he had to lie to them or he had to put them at risk.

But was it right? Could you ever know for sure?

She moved on. Deeper into the woods, she located their makeshift camp. Zofia and Ernő came to her as she appeared in the small clearing. Her brother took the cup from her. "This will require several trips to the creek."

"It's all I could find on short notice. And you won't believe what happened to me."

"Where's the bread?"

"There isn't any."

"What do you mean?"

"Reka spotted me. And called out my name."

Behind Ernő, Zofia paled, her green eyes wide. "*Nem.* Didn't you have the scarf over your head?"

"I did. The worst part is that she also spied me on the train."

Zofia tapped her foot. "This isn't good. We have to move."

Éva gazed at where Patrik lay on a bed of leaves, covered with Zofia's shawl. Sweat broke out all over her. "Don't worry. I have a plan."

Chapter Twenty-Six

Éva knelt beside Patrik and wiped his fiery forehead with a handkerchief she'd found stuffed in the pocket of her skirt. If possible, his fever rose with every passing hour. She kissed his warm brow. "Don't die. We need you." They did. But was she ready to admit that *she* needed him?

Nem. Not yet. Maybe not ever. Who knew?

Ernő and Zofia hadn't wanted to hear her plan. The longer they sat here, though, the more she solidified it.

"Éva."

She leaned closer. "You're not alone. We're taking care of you the best we can."

"Doctor." Patrik closed his eyes and drifted away.

Igen, Patrik needed a doctor. The sooner the better.

Slumped against a nearby tree, Zofia slept. Éva shook her shoulder.

Her eyes flickered open, and she yawned and stretched. "What is it?"

"Patrik is worse. His forehead is hotter than ever. He needs a doctor. Can we trust anyone in this village?"

Zofia gazed at the trees, as if they could provide the answer. "I don't know. The time may have come that we have to take the risk." She rose and moved to Patrik's side, checking the fever, watching his chest rise and fall. "He may not live until morning if we wait any longer."

Éva pulled Zofia away from Patrik and over to Ernő, who had curled up on the forest floor, his hand under his head, sound asleep. They woke him, and he rubbed his eyes. "What is this plan of yours?"

"Very late tonight, I'll slip back into town. I did locate the bakery, so I'll go there first to purchase some bread."

Ernő pursed his lips. "He'll have nothing left."

"I have this way of convincing people to help me."

Her brother gave a wry chuckle. "That you do."

"I can test the baker's trustworthiness, and if I deem him not to be a threat, ask him for a reliable doctor. We do have false papers. For all he knows, he's helping a group of stranded friends on holiday."

Zofia shifted on the hard ground and rubbed her expanding belly. "I wish you would allow me to go. I know what to do."

"Absolutely not." At Ernő's harsh words, Patrik stirred, then settled down again.

"Then at least let me teach her."

"There is no other way. If I would happen to run into Reka, at least she knows I'm here. But if she spies either one of you, she will get suspicious very fast. Zofia, we have a few hours for you to coach me. Teach me what I need to know."

So Zofia sat with Éva as the night deepened and the crickets and frogs sang their bedtime songs. Éva got a crash course on how to act when approaching strangers, what to say, and what to do and not do if she was captured.

Éva trembled at Zofia's words.

Then their stomachs growled in unison. They laughed, but the levity of the moment was short-lived. As she prepared to leave, Éva returned to Patrik's side.

She rubbed his cheek as he slept. "I don't know what tonight is going to bring. I pray that God will watch over me, but He may have different plans."

Staring at him, flush with fever, something stirred inside her. What had drawn her to him in the first place. His kindness. His thoughtfulness. His loyalty.

She had thought his truthfulness too. But his lies were different from Károly's, weren't they?

Patrik didn't lie to her with the intention of harming her family or anyone else. Just the opposite. He told falsehoods to her to keep them safe. Did that justify him?

She closed her eyes and recalled the camp at Kistarcsa. So much suffering. So much death.

An image of Ernő the day he returned from his interrogation flashed in front of her. What they had done to him. His bruised face. His broken ribs.

That was what Patrik had wanted to keep them from.

Like a symphony rising to its grand finale, her love for Patrik swelled. All he had sacrificed for them. He had even been willing to let go of her so she might live.

She bent over him once more. "The funny thing is, this trip has taught me that I still love you. I suppose I never stopped. I don't know if there can be a future for us, even if we manage to survive. But I do still love you.

"Anyway, you can't even hear me, but I wanted you to know. The words bring me some measure of courage and confidence, at least." She kissed his cracked lips and slipped into the darkness.

Thank the Lord, it was another clear night with a bright moon. They had no flashlights, no torches. Even if they did, they wouldn't be able to use them. On soft, gypsy-like feet, she crept through the forest until the trees gave way to the village.

No light emanated from any of the buildings. Most families were asleep, and those that weren't had drawn the blackout shades.

Following the main road, Éva came to the bakery. Was that a thin sliver of light peeking through the blackness? Of course the baker would be up at this time, busy preparing the coming day's bread. She scampered to the back door and, leaning against it, stood still so she could hear any sounds from inside.

There. Humming. A little tune, "Fly, Bird, Fly." With its turns and tone, it was more Asian than European in its influence. Beautiful and haunting at the same time.

She rapped on the door, not loud at first so she didn't wake the neighbors. But the baker must be busy, so she knocked harder.

The humming cut off, and a moment later, the door opened. An old man, short, stout, and bald, blinked at her through round spectacles. "Get out of here. Shoo. I don't need any beggars coming round."

She stood her ground. "Please, I have money. But I, we, need your help."

"I'll call the police. You don't want that."

"I'm begging for your assistance. If you could just let me in."

The baker, his white apron even whiter with its fine coating of flour, tried to shut the door.

Éva stuck her foot in the way. "I'm not leaving until you help me."

"Then you're leaving in the back of a German car."

Even though her tongue stuck to the roof of her mouth and her breath came in short spurts, she managed to squeak out her next words. "Don't you have a wife? Someone you love with all your heart?"

The hard edges of his face softened. "Don't try to dissuade me."

"The man I love," Éva almost choked on the words, "is very ill. We need bread and a doctor."

"Then why not get one?"

"We were on the train that was bombed. Please, sir." She made her voice low and shaky. "I'm frightened for him. Just by looking at you, I can see you're a good man, kind and caring. If you had a daughter in my circumstances, wouldn't you want a stranger to be kind to her?" A tear trickled down her cheek.

The man rubbed the top of his bald head. "I don't want any problems."

"What kind of problems could there be? You're helping out your fellow countrymen."

"But you come in the middle of the night. That part I don't understand. Are you hiding something?"

"*Nem*, of course not. I've been tending to the man I love, too busy to come. But I see now we need help. He's not getting better. Please, for the love of everything good, help us."

The baker sighed. "You remind me of my own daughter, young and innocent. I wouldn't want her to come to harm. While you get the doctor, I'll pop some rolls into the oven. I can deliver them when they are baked."

"We don't have a place in town. He collapsed in the woods and can't go farther. I can get the rolls on my way out of the village with the doctor."

The old man nodded and gave her directions to a house around the corner where the doctor lived.

She took off to locate the physician and came to it in short order. But she skidded to a stop at the German flag hung outside the upstairs window of the square brick house. Its angry black swastika mocked her.

Her hands trembled. Her entire body shook. But did she have a choice? Not really. She couldn't go back to the baker and ask for a different doctor. Patrik needed help. They all had their false IDs. With her red hair, Zofia didn't even appear Jewish. Patrik had dark hair, but he was Aryan. At least, she believed he was. She wasn't sure.

Steeling herself, she knocked on the door. No movement from inside. She pounded harder. What if he was on a call? Did he have an associate?

Once more, she banged on the door with all her might. Finally, a middle-aged man of average height and average weight answered. "What can I do for you?"

"Are you the doctor?"

"I am. And you are?"

She explained the situation. "I think his wound is infected. His fever is high. Please, come right away."

"I'll come with you, but I'm warning you, this could be serious. There are no antibiotics available. Everything is siphoned to our poor boys on the front."

Éva's throat stung. "I understand. But there has to be something you can do."

"I'll try my best, but I make no promises."

Pain wracked Patrik's leg. No matter how much he shifted position, nothing eased the agony. One minute he was on fire and the next, he shivered until his bones rattled. He couldn't help the moans that escaped his lips.

Where was he, anyway?

If only this searing pain would ease, and his thirst would be quenched. "Water." Could anyone hear his pitiful attempts to speak?

Zofia stood above him, her red hair disheveled, falling around her pale face. "Here you are." She raised him to a half-sitting position and trickled a few drops of water into his parched throat.

Just the effort of swallowing exhausted him. She laid him down again, and he drifted off . . .

Anya. Where was his *Anya*? She took such good care of him. Whenever he called for her, she was at his side. When *Apu* died, he had promised to take care of *Anya*, but she was the strong one. She held the family together.

He would get better so he could fulfill his promise to *Apu*.

"*Anya!*" he cried in agony. But she didn't come. No matter how often he called her name, screamed for her, she didn't come.

Where was she? Had something bad happened to her like what happened to *Apu*?

He couldn't breathe. "*Anya, Anya,* where are you? Please, I need you."

A soft hand touched his forehead. Quiet words whispered into his ear. Words like a gentle breeze.

But they were not *Anya*'s words. This was not her voice, not her touch.

He clutched the person who was caring for him. "*Anya*. Where is she? Why isn't she answering?"

He couldn't understand everything the woman said. Only one word caught his attention. "Gone."

Gone. Gone where?

A dull ache grew in his chest until it matched the pain in the rest of his body. He remembered.

Anya was gone.

Years before the war, those men had come. Kicked down the door to their house. Grabbed *Anya* and dragged her by the hair to her bedroom. They slammed the door.

Anya screamed and cried. For a very, very long time, she yelled at the top of her lungs for them to stop.

He huddled underneath his bed, unable to take a deep breath. What were they doing to her? Thank goodness his sisters were at a friend's house for the night.

He'd promised *Apu* he'd take care of her, but he couldn't. The men were very big and strong. There were two of them and only one of him. He was tall but not very strong. The kids at school teased him because he was nothing but skin and bones.

He couldn't fight men with such big muscles.

At last they left.

Anya stopped crying. He attemped to console her, but she pushed him away. From that day on she didn't sing to him, play with him, or talk to him. Her blue eyes, usually the color of the chocolate mousse cake *rigó jancsi*, were cold and empty.

Then one day, he tried to wake her up. She was cold and stiff.

The bottle of laudanum sat empty beside her . . .

"Patrik." Someone tapped his cheek.

"Patrik. Patrik." A woman's voice, calling.

Calling me. But I'm not Patrik. Who is Patrik? "My name is Friemann Avraham."

Chapter Twenty-Seven

Éva's heart somersaulted at Patrik's announcement. *Friemann Avraham*. The name couldn't be more Jewish.

Why had he uttered it? Perhaps due to the delirium. That could be. He'd helped Jews, people like Zofia. Maybe he'd helped others. This could be the name of a man to whom he'd given aid.

Perhaps this was the secret he'd hidden from her. She studied his features, his dark hair, olive skin. Maybe it was true. He wasn't the perfect German version of Aryan, that much was clear. But what blood flowed in his veins? Jewish? Magyar? A little of both?

She had trusted him once enough to want to marry him. He'd broken that trust. Little by little, she'd come to forgive him, to move past the hurt. But now this. Just when she understood his motivation for lying, yet another falsehood. He hadn't needed to keep his very identity a secret from her. She wouldn't care if he was Jewish.

What else was he lying about? Maybe even his belief in Jesus? That would be enough to destroy them forever.

The doctor with the Nazi flag in his window knelt on Patrik's other side.

The older man glared at Éva, Zofia, and Ernő. "That's a Jewish name. What is going on here? What is this all about?"

"He's delirious. I . . . I can prove that's not his name." With shaking fingers, Éva drew Patrik's identity card from his pocket, the one that labeled him as an Aryan.

The doctor waved her off. "That could be forged. Half the Jews in the country have false papers these days."

"You have to believe us and help us. We have to get to Nagyvárad as fast as possible. My, uh, my mother is dying. But I won't leave this man. Please, please."

The doctor shrugged and lifted the pants leg from Patrik's wound. "Just as I suspected. Infection. But I don't have penicillin." He reached into his black bag. "Here's some gauze and bandages. Use alcohol to clean the wound. I'll leave some aspirin for you to give him."

The doctor all but threw the items at Éva. Then he clicked his bag shut, came to his feet, and brushed off his pants. He glanced around their little group, blue eyes narrowed as if memorizing their faces. Then he tromped off through the woods.

Éva released a pent-up breath. "That was close."

Zofia brushed her burnished bangs from her eyes. "More than close. He knows the truth."

"He does?" Éva clutched her chest. "I thought we covered well. Is he going to turn us in?"

"As soon as he can."

"Then we have to get out of here. Now." What was going to happen to them? Not a labor camp. They hadn't come this far to get caught.

Zofia tottered to her feet. "Get ready."

"Where are we going to go? And how are we going to transport Patrik?" Éva fought to keep the tears at bay. Everything, absolutely everything, had gone wrong.

Life was a mess. And possibly at its end.

Ernő rubbed Éva's shoulder. "Listen to me, both of you."

Éva relaxed under her brother's ministration. Her heart ached for *Apu* and *Anya*, but at least her big brother was here. By her side, just as he had always been from the time she was little. He would take care of them.

"This is what we're going to do. I'm going back to the train. There have to be blankets. The bombs didn't obliterate everything. We'll make a stretcher for Patrik and transport him to the train. That's a place no one will think to search for us. After we get some rest, we'll decide what to do."

With a quick kiss on Zofia's cheek, Ernő raced off, his footsteps in the woods fading to nothing.

Éva used the water in the teacup and a piece of her slip to bathe Patrik's hot face. Where were they going to get alcohol to treat the infection? The doctor had given them the other supplies, but not that.

She sat back and rubbed her gritty eyes. Zofia sat beside her and drew her into an embrace. Such a motherly gesture. "God will take care of this. He's in control. All we have to do is trust."

"Trust what? Who?" Éva faced Zofia. "Is it true, what Patrik said? Is he Jewish?"

"That's not for me to say."

"If it weren't true, you would deny it." Éva jumped to her feet and kicked at the dirt with the toe of her oxford. "Why would he hide it from me? Why not tell me?"

"Please don't ask me questions I can't answer."

"Can't or won't?"

"Save them until Patrik is better. When he is awake and strong enough, he can give you the information you want."

So it was true. Dear God, it was true. Yet again, Patrik hadn't trusted her with the truth.

Ernő's arms ached from carrying Patrik from the woods to the burned-out train. The black monstrosity sat twisted and mangled on the torn-up tracks. Even the grass around it was singed and pockmarked by the bombs, but smoke no longer rose from the shell. It was safe to return.

They had made it just before sunrise. Now Ernő kept a lookout while the rest of them slept. Not that they had anywhere to go if the Germans or Reka came searching for them.

Pink tinged the sky above the eastern horizon, where the

Soviets edged their way ever closer to Hungary. If only the four of them could wait here until the Russians liberated them.

But it might be too late.

A scent of honeysuckle tickled his nose. Even after all they'd been through, Zofia still smelled beautiful. He turned to her as she came and sat beside him on the edge of the boxcar. She wrapped the blanket they had found among the debris around her shoulders.

"You couldn't sleep?"

She shook her head. "Between your child kicking me and the thoughts running through my brain, slumber has proven elusive."

He longed to reach out and touch her belly, to feel his child growing in her womb. But he held back. Her betrayal still stung.

And there was a question he had for her. "Is it true?"

"Is what true?"

Ernö ground his teeth. "Please don't act like you didn't hear Patrik."

She studied her hands as she twisted them in her lap. "That is for Patrik to tell you, not me."

Heat rose in his chest. "So you will not share it, even with your husband?"

"It's his story, not mine."

"I think I have my answer." He returned his gaze to the wooded scenery in front of him, the trees' leaves now touched with yellow and gold from the sunrise.

She brushed his arm, and he flinched. "Don't pull away. We're about to have a baby together."

"We share the most intimate of relationships, but I don't have any idea who you are."

"I'm the same woman you married." There was a catch in her voice.

"You aren't."

"Don't you see? They could do to you what they did to my mother. And I couldn't bear another loss. I begged Patrik to tell you I was in hiding. That I was alive and well. He thought it best not to. That's why I sent you that note."

He turned to stare into her shimmering eyes. "The Gestapo came after me anyway."

"I know. Maybe it wasn't the best choice, but at the time, Patrik believed it was my only one. Over my better judgment, I allowed him to persuade me."

"What about Patrik?"

She sighed and blinked several times. "He has his own story, his own trauma from his past. To survive, he took on an Aryan identity years ago. Many of the Zionist Youth do the same. I would have if I could have. But there were too many other requests ahead of mine, and they never got around to me."

"So he withheld his identity to protect Éva?"

"Éva and himself and many others. Even I didn't know his true name until tonight."

"But you knew he was Jewish."

"*Igen.* The Zionists all are."

Ernő took some time to digest this information. Had her motives been pure? Patrik's too? Could there be room in a marriage for deception of this kind?

"What I did, what he did, was out of self-preservation and love for those around us. Nothing is black-and-white these days. Who is to say what will or won't save us?"

"Isn't God able to do that?"

She twirled a lock of her red hair. "Yes, He is. But sometimes, to accomplish that, He uses us, much like He used Rahab to protect the Israelite spies. When He asks us to trust Him, He doesn't call us to be foolish."

He grunted in half-hearted agreement. The first rays of the day crested the tops of the trees and illuminated the ground in front of them.

His wife took him by the hand and guided him to feel the child moving within her. "We have this little one to think about. We'll be parents in a few months. He needs both of us to love him, to nurture him, to teach him. I can't do this alone. I don't want to."

The baby kicked. What an amazing sensation. Together, with the Lord's help, he and Zofia had created new life. Inside her rounded stomach was another tiny human being.

This child would need both of his parents. "No more lies."

"I have shared with you all of my secrets, the ones closest to my heart, the ones hardest for me to express." She nuzzled against him. "I have bared myself for you. There is nothing between us now."

From his pocket, he pulled out a pamphlet she had written. He shouldn't carry it on his person. In fact, he should have destroyed it. But something made him hang on to it. He unfolded the paper, the black ink barely visible in the half light. "You really wrote this?"

"I did. And many others like it."

"I never knew I was married to such a talented writer. What you've penned has made me see the world in a different light. The Jews haven't been treated well in this country for a long time, many years before the alliance with Nazi Germany."

He smoothed the creased sheets. "What does it matter what blood flows through our veins? Did God not create us all the same? Do we not all have the same father in Adam? The differences between Jews and Gentiles are in our genes, not in our characters. There is good and evil in the Jewish race. There is good and evil in the Aryan race. When the Lord judges us, He will not judge us on our ancestry but on our belief and faith in Him."

"I believe every word of it." She pursed her lips. "Do you?"

He pulled her close and kissed her lips. "I do. Until I read this, until I really opened my eyes and looked around me, I never understood my prejudice. When I see you, I don't see a Jewish woman. I see my beloved wife."

"Can we move on from here?"

"I would like nothing better."

Someone stirred behind them, and Éva appeared, dark bags underneath her eyes. "You two are early birds."

"How's Patrik?"

"The alcohol we found on the train and doused on his wounds helped. The infection is receding, and his fever is down."

"That's good." Ernő nodded. "We can be on the move soon."

What was that sound? He pricked his ears. A hum. The hum of a car. Many cars. And machinery. In the distance, an armada appeared, including trucks and cranes.

Everything needed to remove the train.

With them inside.

Éva sat transfixed as the machinery moved in the train's direction.

"We have to get out of here." Ernő pulled Zofia from her spot on the edge of the car.

Éva turned back into the train. "Wait. There's something I need to find."

"*Nem*. Not now, Éva. We must leave. It will take us a while to get Patrik moved."

"Just two minutes. That's all I need. Please." Without waiting for her brother's answer, she sped away.

From behind her came Zofia's soft voice. "Let her go."

In which of the burned-out cars would she discover her clarinet? Where had she been sitting? The cars were all the same, and now not much of them remained.

She picked her way around charred seats and twisted metal. *God, lead me to it.*

Her original seat had been near the middle of the train. That's about where she had to be now. Luggage and belongings filled the aisles, blown all over the place and burned.

Wait. A flash of yellow and green caught her eye. Her favorite dress, the lemon-colored one with a leaf pattern. This was the right car.

Careful of the jagged shards of train sticking up, she knelt on what was left of the car's floor and sifted through the items. A man's shoe, or what was left of it. Her fuzzy pink sweater, covered in burn holes. A blackened strand of pearls. Perhaps Reka's.

And then she found it.

Her clarinet case.

Nem, nem. The heat of the fire had burned through the lid. The instrument's wood was charred. No longer could she distinguish her family's stamp, the rock with a cross on top of it.

Ruined.

Unplayable.

A sob caught in her throat. "Why, Lord, why? Haven't You taken enough from me? This too? I don't understand. I have no home. I may never see my parents again. I'm not sure I have a future with the man I love. You can't take my music from me, too. Don't do this to me."

As great sobs rushed over her, she covered her face. Too much loss. Too much destruction. Though she almost never cried, this time she gave in to the tears.

"Éva?"

She wiped her eyes and peered up. Like a vision, there—the early morning sun streaming behind him—was Patrik. Hunched over, he limped toward her, stopping now and then. To save him the effort, she hurried to his side. "You shouldn't be up."

"We have to move. When Ernő said you'd run off, I knew where to find you."

"It's ruined." She pointed at her clarinet's remains.

"I know. You can get another one."

"*Apu* made that one especially for me. Fashioned it the way I liked it. That instrument was his masterpiece. All I had remaining of him. Now it's gone. How much more are we going to lose?"

"We don't have much left to give. Only our lives."

"That's why I'm so afraid."

"You still have me."

Having cried out her entire store of tears, Éva wiped her face. "Let me help you back to the others. We have to leave."

Chapter Twenty-Eight

$\mathcal{P}$atrik limped between Éva and Ernő, leaning most of his weight on them. No longer did his leg burn, but it did ache with a fierceness he never imagined possible. At least his mind had cleared. The fog and haze that had enveloped him had lifted.

Behind them came the clacking of cranes and bulldozers along with the ring of hammers as the train's remains were cleared and the tracks repaired. They hadn't gone more than a kilometer, and already he was breathing hard. If only they could travel by coach as they did before. But Reka was still around.

In their quick getaway, a strand of Éva's hair had escaped her pins and brushed his cheek. She brushed it away and turned to him. "Last night when I brought the doctor, in your delirium, you said something strange. Friedmann Avraham. Is that your name? Your given name?"

Patrik went cold all over, and probably not from his weakened state. He couldn't utter a single word.

"That's answer enough for me."

Patrik's heart skipped a beat. There could be no more denying of the truth. Éva had learned his secret. And though he had been the one to tell her, he didn't do it in the way he wanted. It was a wonder she was speaking to him at all.

He grimaced as he turned his ankle on a rock and leaned on her shoulders. "I'm sorry."

"For tripping? That is nothing. For lying about your name?" She shrugged her shoulders and gazed at him, her eyes asking the question as much as her lips, their fragile trust hanging in the balance.

His stomach was in knots. She needed the truth. She deserved it. "*Igen*, I hid my name."

"Once again you deceived me."

"Do you truly not understand why I would take an Aryan identity? Do you think I did it easily?" He'd never spoken the awful truth, and he wasn't about to in front of Ernő and Zofia. Even Zofia didn't know.

"More secrets and lies."

"*Nem*, just things that are very difficult for me to speak about." He panted as the sun rose higher in the sky along with the temperature.

"Just answer one question. Are you even a Christian? Deep in your heart, not on your identity card."

"I was raised in the Jewish faith and didn't begin to attend church until I changed my name. With that, I thought I owed it to myself and to my guise to learn more about what I was supposed to believe. When I did, true faith came. All that has happened in my life, including being forced to change my name, was God's way of drawing me to Himself." By the time he finished speaking, he was gasping for breath.

Ernő called a halt. He and Éva and Zofia were tired as well, dragging Patrik along with them. They ate the bread Éva had procured and took turns drinking from the single teacup.

For the next few days, they pressed forward in much the same way, resting as often as Patrik needed relief from his pain and making slow progress toward Nagyvárad. Their promised land.

On the fourth day, they saw it at last, rising above the plain. Patrik stopped and closed his eyes, just for a moment. In his mind, he could picture the Sebes-Körös River running through the town, and the Black Eagle palace with all its rounded windows and roof lines, and the city hall with clock towers at either end.

And beyond, Romania. Freedom within grasp.

The sight of Nagyvárad in front of them brought a surge of strength Patrik hadn't experienced since the night of the train bombing. They were so close to their liberation, the word sweet on his tongue. "Here we are."

"Now what?" Éva shaded her eyes against the late afternoon sun. "I'm in need of a bath, and you should have a clean place to sleep so you can fully recover."

"I have some contacts here we can get in touch with."

Éva clasped her hands together. "What about Reka? She lives here, you know."

"Thankfully, Nagyvárad is a big city. Not too much chance of running into her. It would be good, though, if we could get to our contact's house as soon as possible. The less time we spend on the street, the better. A little bit to rest and regroup, and we'll cross into Romania."

He wouldn't breathe easy until they had.

Éva picked up her pace to match his. "Do you know where you're going?"

"I've been here before."

"You mentioned coming here a time or two with some of your orchestra members to play concerts. Were you really . . . ?"

"I was." More times he hadn't been truthful with her.

"Doing this very thing?"

"This very thing. And urging my sisters to leave the country."

"Did they?" She whispered the question.

"*Nem*."

She fell silent, and they made their way through the city's back streets until they came to an unassuming house on a dead-end road. Patrik's leg burned. What a relief it would be to take his weight off it and get it cleaned out.

He knocked on the plain door. Not much time elapsed before a young man Patrik only knew as H opened the door.

"Wait. Stop."

The sound of that voice behind them. It was like someone had thrown a bucket of ice water over Patrik. *Nem*, it couldn't be. It just couldn't be.

Ernő and Zofia gasped. Éva shrank against Patrik. He pivoted and stared into those eyes. The eyes of the woman he had come to dread. "Reka?"

"Imagine running into you here." Pinned to the collar of her dress was that red rose brooch.

The one the woman wore who had watched him watch his sisters herded into the trains. That's how she'd known about him.

While she made it sound like a coincidence, it was anything but. Patrik chuckled a tight laugh. "What are you doing here?"

She touched the back of his hand, sending goosebumps up and down his arm. "You know I live here."

Patrik eyed H's home, then Reka.

"Not here here. In Nagyvárad. I've been waiting for you to arrive."

Patrik didn't dare to breathe. "Arrive?"

"I want to invite you to stay at my home until the concert." For the first time, she directed her attention to Ernő and Zofia. "Imagine my surprise at seeing you here too. Éva said she didn't know where you were, Zofia. How fortunate you have run into each other. Have you come for the concert?"

Ernő stared narrow-eyed at Reka while Zofia gave a slow single nod.

"Zofia, congratulations on the little bundle of joy. Now, why don't you come to my home and stay? You'll be much more comfortable than here."

Patrik's skin prickled. "*Köszönöm.* But we have accommodations already arranged. And not at this place." Did he say that too fast? "Um, elsewhere."

"I insist."

Éva clung to Patrik by the hand. "We don't want to be an imposition."

"You wouldn't be." Reka's syrupy tone curdled Patrik's blood. How had she known where to find them?

There was only one answer. She had been tailing them. Or

had someone do it for her. She was the one who had tipped off the Gestapo to Zofia. The one who had been watching at Tóth *Asszony*'s house. And his flat.

They had to get out of here. He squeezed Éva's hand. "We really have to be going. You've been kind." He almost choked on that sentence. "We're expected elsewhere."

The worst part was that they had led her right to their contact. The Gestapo was probably waiting around the corner to cart them all away to prison. If they didn't do away with them on the spot.

He made a move to wriggle around her. She blocked him with her bulk. "Not so fast."

At Reka's command to stay put, Éva could no longer move a muscle. "What?"

"I said you're coming to my house."

Patrik moved in front of Éva. "We have other plans."

"You don't."

Éva attempted to peer around Patrik, but he pushed her back. "We're leaving now."

"Not if you value the Bognárs' lives."

Her heart forgot to beat.

"At this moment in Budapest, I have operatives ready to take Bognár *Úr* and *Asszony* into custody. And don't think that because they are older, the interrogators will go easy on them."

"My parents?" Everything inside Éva was mixed up. What was going on?

"*Igen*, you little Jew lover. If you value the lives of your mother and your father, you will come with me. There are two ways we can do this. We can have the soldiers who are waiting around the corner come and take you to Gestapo headquarters for questioning, and have the ones in front of your parents' house arrest them, or you can come with me to my house where you'll be much more comfortable. The choice is yours."

Éva's throat tightened, as if she were trying to change the tuning of her clarinet. "How do we know you are about to arrest them?"

"How do you know I'm not? But don't worry. We've been watching the house since you left. You're sneaky. Slippery, the lot of you. You couldn't get away forever, though. Do you want to play Russian roulette with your parents' lives? I know how dedicated you are to them. What a close family you are. Something I never had. A love like that is too strong to take any risks. Whose lives do you value more? Those of your parents, who have given you everything, or your own?"

What an impossible choice. How did you price one life above another? Who had more worth? "We don't have much of a choice, do we?"

Reka crossed her arms. "Not really."

Patrik turned to Éva, his eyes misty, his voice low. "I'm sorry."

"We can't let anything happen to my parents."

Ernő grabbed Patrik by the shoulder. "But Zofia."

"*Apu* and *Anya* have always been there for us. Now it's our turn to do the same for them. We don't have a choice."

"She could be bluffing."

"Do we take that chance with our parents' lives?"

Ernő cradled his head. In that moment, he resembled *Apu* more than ever. "*Nem. Nem.*"

Zofia rubbed Ernő's back. He gazed at her with such warmth, such love, such devotion, it stole Éva's breath. He kissed her forehead and turned and nodded at Reka.

At least they weren't going to prison. Not for now, anyway.

She herded them to her large, yellow house near the center of the city. Reka unlocked the carved oak door and motioned for them to enter.

Her home was beautiful, from the dark wood in the entrance hall and on into the lounge, to the well-maintained antique furniture in the living area, to the tasteful art on the walls. Where had she gotten the money? Growing up, her family had been middle class at best.

Éva glanced at Reka, her mouth set in a hard line. Of course. This well-appointed place was paid for with Jewish blood.

A little girl, maybe three years old, with curly, white-blond hair and pudgy little legs came racing to Reka, demanding to be lifted.

"Who is this?"

"My daughter, Marianna."

Éva furrowed her brows. "I'm sorry. I didn't realize you were married." Reka wore no ring, and from the impression her house gave, she could afford one.

"I'm not."

"Oh." Éva stood dumbfounded. Marianna could well be the offspring of a German man.

Reka pointed to the davenport in the living room. "Sit."

Ernő drew Zofia close to his side. "We're pretty dirty, and we'd hate to ruin your fine furnishings. If you show me to the bathroom, I'll see to getting Zofia settled. She's quite tired. And Patrik needs to have his leg tended to."

"I said to sit."

The four of them, as filthy and as smelly as they were, plopped to the sofa. Éva settled beside Patrik. "How is your leg? Maybe you should elevate it?"

"I'm okay."

"Silence." Like a general reviewing his troops, Reka marched in front of them.

Éva swallowed hard. "What do you want with us?"

"Information."

"You won't get any." Patrik clasped the edge of the flowered cushion.

"Cooperate with me and it will go well for you. And for the Bognárs. All of them. Give me trouble, and you'll find yourself in more trouble yourselves than you could imagine. I have connections. I have ways of getting what I want."

Éva clasped Patrik's hand, his own palm moist. He wasn't as calm as he appeared on the outside. Or was it another fever spiking?

"I don't understand any of this." Éva sat forward. "I never knew you to be unkind."

Reka spun and faced Éva, her features hard in her round face. "You never knew me. Never. All you had, I wanted. It was within my grasp. A few years ago, I had an audition with the Budapest Symphony as a clarinetist. And then that Jewish boy you had taught slithered in and stole my spot. The place that should have been mine." She spat the words. "Then Ernő, the man I wanted, fell in love with a Jewess. The lowest of the low. I have this way of discovering what people are hiding, though. I found out her secrets."

Next to her, Zofia stiffened, her belly protruding.

"If you are so good at detecting secrets, why do you have to question us?"

"I don't know it all. I need names. Places. Details."

Zofia shot to her feet. "Which you will never get."

Reka stormed closer, her nose almost touching Zofia's. "Sit down."

Zofia obeyed.

The little girl peeked around the corner, and Éva gave her a faint smile. She popped out of view. Marianna shouldn't be subjected to this. Shouldn't see her mother's bitterness and hatred.

If Reka noticed her daughter's presence, she didn't acknowledge it. "Let's start with an easy question. Why are you all here? And why weren't you together on the train?"

Éva jumped in to answer. "I told you already. We're here for a concert. You need to let us go, so we don't miss it."

"Where is this concert?"

"Um—"

"At the State Theater Hall." Patrik came to the rescue. "Éva is right. If we don't get going, we'll be late. We need time to make ourselves presentable and get organized."

"Why were you traveling so early, so many days ago, if the concert wasn't until tonight?"

Reka was clever, you had to give her that.

Again, Patrik came to the rescue. "Ernő had some business prior to the concert. We all thought we'd come early and spend time together."

"How fortuitous that you found Zofia. I think I need you to fill in some details for me." Reka licked her full lips.

"She was in custody. And now she's not." Patrik clenched his jaw.

"Liar!" It was a wonder her shout didn't rattle the crystal chandelier. "She's not even wearing her star."

Éva jumped up and stomped toward Reka. "Please, don't turn her in. You can see she's pregnant."

"Did I tell you to move?" Reka shoved Éva, and she stumbled into her seat once more. If only she had her reed knife. She should have grabbed it from her charred clarinet case.

But no matter what Patrik or Zofia or any of them said, Reka wasn't satisfied. She badgered them, the questioning dragging on throughout the day. Éva had long since passed the hungry stage. Her stomach didn't even rumble anymore.

At last, as the twilight softened into evening, a broad man in a German uniform marched into the house. He pecked Reka on the cheek. "Well done, my dear. We have that pesky smuggler in custody too. Why don't you get us some dinner? I'll keep an eye on them. Finish with them for you."

His words sent Éva trembling from head to toe.

Chapter Twenty-Nine

*S*ofia woke from her restless slumber in the hot, close, window-less pantry where Reka and her German friend had locked them, and reached for Ernő, who slept beside her, snoring. The months she'd been in hiding, she'd missed that so much. Missed him next to her in bed, his body warm against hers.

She kissed him on the cheek, but though he stirred, he didn't wake. He needed the sleep. All the time since the train bombing, he'd been the one to keep the night watch. At last he could rest.

She sat up and rubbed her stomach. Where there had once been a little mound, there was now a large bump. From somewhere came the steady ticking of a clock.

On the other side of Ernő, Patrik stirred and sat. "The house is quiet." He kept his voice to a whisper.

"Did you get some rest?"

"*Igen.* You?"

"Some. I had a difficult time turning off my mind. What are we going to do?"

"Get out of here before they take us away to someplace much worse. All I want is a future with the woman I love more than anything."

"Does Éva want the same thing?"

Patrik rubbed his chin. "I don't know."

"What don't you know?" Yawning, Éva stretched and sat up.

Patrik cleared his throat and turned his attention to the dressing wrapped around his calf. "How we're going to get out of here. It's only a matter of time before we're formally arrested."

Ernő stirred and sat up next to Zofia. How she adored him. Their child moved within her. They had to fight. Had to do whatever it took to become a true family. To survive this madness and regain their lives.

They would raise their little one in Palestine. The promised land, flowing with milk and honey. They could be a beacon for her fellow Jews, shining a light on the Christ who had trod that very soil.

What a thrill it would be to walk the ground He had walked. To see what He must have seen. The hills must echo with His words. Sing with His presence.

"Darling?" Ernő broke her musings.

"Hmm? I'm sorry. Lost in my own thoughts. But I agree. We need a plan. A way out of here. There are two of them and four of us. We have the advantage."

"Not with Patrik injured," Éva said.

"I can hold my own."

Ernő got up, fumbled for the light switch by the door, flipped it on, and a dim glow lit the pantry. Then he tried the door handle. Locked.

"Whether we outnumber them or not doesn't matter." Ernő shook his head. "The man is armed, I'm sure. If we could break down the door and make a run for it—"

"Again, Patrik can't sprint."

Zofia rubbed the back of Ernő's leg, just to have contact with him. "An opportunity will present itself. We have to be patient and wait."

Éva pulled up her knees and covered her face. "I'm scared."

Patrik hugged her from one side and Zofia from the other. "I know, I know. We all are."

"Right before we left, *Apu* reminded me that God, our salvation, is our only comfort in this life and the next. But it's what happens between here and there that frightens me." Éva, the woman who almost never cried, wiped away a single tear that trickled down her cheek. Then she clung to both Zofia and Patrik and wept.

Zofia's hormones kicked in, and she cried sympathetic tears. How had things gotten turned upside down?

Patrik pulled a handkerchief from his pocket and handed it to Éva. "None of this has been easy. Did I make the right decision by withholding information from you and Ernő? Who knows? What I did, I did out of love for each of you. You have to believe that."

Zofia borrowed Éva's handkerchief and wiped her own eyes. "Patrik meant well."

"If I had to do it over again just the same way, I would."

Éva turned toward him, her eyes still watery. "Why do you say that?"

"Sometimes we have to lie to protect those we love. These aren't normal circumstances. Life is precious and worth preserving, and there are times when misguiding people is how we have to go about it."

Zofia's stomach twinged, and she inhaled and released the air a little at a time, the pain easing. "Can you understand that?" She rubbed her belly.

"*Apu* and *Anya* always taught us never to tell a falsehood. Lies spoil what is good and beautiful." Ernő stared into her eyes, his expression intense.

She shifted her own gaze to the shelves groaning under the weight of foodstores they hadn't seen the likes of since the war began. "In a normal world, I would agree. But you have to understand that right here, right now, this isn't normal. People like Patrik and I are fighting every minute of every day just to survive."

Fighting for survival. To see each new dawn. That's what life had come down to for them. *Please, Lord, protect us. May we be among the remnant that survives.*

Patrik touched Éva's cheek, soft, like the whisper of the wind. She smiled at him. "I remember a time not too long ago when I couldn't fathom that humans could be so cruel. Now that we know the truth, now that I've seen it with my own eyes, I understand. They have no heart, no soul. Why can't everything go back to the way it was just a few months ago?"

"Life is always moving, changing, like a kaleidoscope." Patrik sighed. "We have to learn to change with it."

"What will it look like a month from now? A year from now?"

He chuckled. "That's my girl. Always wanting to skip to the end of the story. God will unfold it for us in His perfect timing."

"And you have hope in that?"

"He's the only one who can offer hope. As much as I'd love to say I will never disappoint you again, will never lie to you again, it's a promise I can't make. I can promise never to keep such a big part of my life from you, but I can't vow that I will never lie to you about your cooking."

A fleeting light pierced the darkness of her soul. "That might be a good thing." Her heart thumped. Could she see a future with him? Envision them married?

He had told her falsehoods from the purest of motives. Here was a man willing to risk everything he loved, even their future together, to keep her safe. She would be fibbing to say that didn't touch her. Though her love for him had wavered, it never came close to going out.

She was his *múzsám*. He was her refrain. And those weeks without him had been the most miserable of her life. Now she was trusting him with her physical well-being. If she could do that, couldn't she trust him with her heart?

"We misjudged Reka. Me more than anyone." Éva pressed her chest, as if that would ease the pain.

"She didn't mention her child when she was in Budapest." Patrik's voice was gentle. "She's made no mention of the father."

"You don't think . . ."

"Think what?"

Éva shook her head. "Nothing. I'm letting my imagination run away with me."

"The child clearly belongs to the German. Reka has gotten in good with them to provide herself with the life she never had before. But I feel sorry for her."

Éva stared at Patrik. "Sorry?" She furrowed her brow. "How can you be?"

"Soon this war will be over. She will end up on the wrong side of it. In the long run, she isn't getting what she always wanted. She's going to wind up in a worse position than where she started."

Éva pushed Patrik's dark waves from his forehead. "How can you have such compassion for her?"

"She is a lost soul."

In that instant, every bit of the love she once harbored for Patrik flooded back, and then some. She kissed the back of his hand. "I love you."

His eyes widened. "And I love you, *a múzsám.*"

Time crawled by. No noise came from the rest of the house. Were they sleeping? Were they even here? Éva was about to go mad. There wasn't even room to pace.

Music. She needed her clarinet. If she couldn't have it in her hands, she could have it in her heart and head. She relaxed and imagined playing it—a happy tune that recalled her carefree childhood days, summer trips to the countryside, splashing in the lake, wandering in the woods with Ernő, both returning home hot, sweaty, and beyond content.

Another melody sprang into her imagination, this one in a minor key. The clarinet cried along with her spirit for everything they had lost. Peace. Home. Love. All of it ripped away in the space of a few months. So much gone, never again to be.

By the end of the piece, she was mentally exhausted, but she allowed herself to imagine one more tune. This one was upbeat, though not like the first—a more sedate joy. The kind she would experience when she returned to Budapest and her parents and picked up the pieces of her life.

Éva rested against Patrik's firm chest and closed her eyes.

A while later, she was awakened by voices coming from the living room.

"That's enough, Reka. You've had your fun with them. I want them out of my house tonight."

"I know there is more information I can get out of them. Patrik and Zofia are higher-ups in the Zionist Youth. They can tell us details about the organization. They're a gold mine."

"The Gestapo has much more persuasive techniques for garnering information."

The voices faded away. There was the faint sound of a door opening and closing, and then silence.

Patrik swallowed hard. "There's no time to waste. We must run now. Once we get to our contact's house, we'll let him know we have to get across the border tonight."

Zofia shook her head. "The moon is supposed to be full."

How well he knew. "We'll have to take our chances. There's less danger crossing the border in the moonlight than there is in staying here. We can't hesitate." He blew out a breath and struggled to keep calm. Having Éva alarmed wouldn't help matters. Already she was trembling beside him.

"I can try to kick the door and break it open." Ernő stood. "The splintering noise is sure to bring them running, but we might be able to get a jump on them."

Patrik surveyed the group. "Keep your heads down and sprint like you've never sprinted before. Don't stop, not for anything." He pinned his stare on Éva. "I mean not for anything. Even if only one of us makes it out alive, it's worth it. Do you understand?"

She gave a shaky nod. Then she stood on her tiptoes and brushed a light kiss across his lips. Fire raced through him. In that one gesture, she'd spoken so much. If he didn't survive, he would die a happy man.

I'm trusting You, Lord. I commit myself and those I love to You.

He drew in a deep breath and nodded to Ernő. With one swift kick, Ernő broke a hole in the door. Two more kicks, and he'd created a gap wide enough for even Zofia to crawl through.

"Go, Ernő." He could stop Reka or her boyfriend when they came to investigate. Then he shoved Éva and Zofia through. Finally, he surged through the opening himself, fresh air rushing to fill his lungs.

Could Reka hear Patrik's blood pounding in his ears? To have come this far, Romania within sight, and not make it. *God, nem.*

"Hurry, hurry." In a heartbeat, they reached the front door. Surely they'd been heard—but no one came behind them. Amazing. A miracle, really. He all but pushed Ernő, Zofia, and Éva out the door.

"Run!"

As he took off, a canvas-covered truck turned onto the street two blocks down, headlights glaring, and tore in their direction.

Chapter Thirty

With her blood pounding in her ears, her feet pounding on the pavement, and jackboots pounding behind her down the street, Éva ran like she'd never run before.

She glanced over her shoulder at Ernő and Zofia. Heavy with child, her sister-in-law lumbered along, Ernő holding her up. Even so, she moved like a penguin as she clutched her unborn baby. Three Nazi soldiers raced a block behind them.

God, don't let anything happen to that baby.

"Keep going. Don't stop." Patrik's shouts redirected her focus in front of her.

"We have to wait for them."

"I told you. Just run."

She stumbled on the uneven sidewalk. Patrik clutched her hand.

"We can't stop. Even if they're caught, we keep going."

Even if the Gestapo arrested Ernő and Zofia?

"*Nem!*"

"*Igen. Igen. Igen.*"

It was so wrong. Yet onward she ran, her lungs burning, over the river sparkling in the moonlight and through the grassy city square. "How much farther?" she gasped.

"Don't stop."

He zigzagged through town. Ernő and Zofia nipped on their heels. What of their three Nazi pursuers? How much ground had they gained?

"In here." Patrik half dragged her into a shop. From the almost empty glass display cases with only a few simple watches inside, she gathered this must have been a jeweler.

Ernő and Zofia ducked inside after them. "They're right behind us."

"Come with me." With his breathing heavy, Patrik whisked her behind the counter, into the workshop, then out the back exit and into an alley. Patrik allowed the door to click shut behind them. Ernő and Zofia—where were they?

"Ernő!" She fought to free herself from Patrik's grip.

He refused to release her. "They'll come."

Together they scurried down the dark alley but not far. At the fourth door down, Patrik stopped and turned the knob. "Get inside."

She glanced over her shoulder. "I don't see them."

"Just move it." He pushed her into the building, then followed and closed the door.

"What about . . . ?" Tears clogged her throat.

Patrik pulled her close and rubbed her back for a few seconds. "Relax. Nice deep breaths."

Spots marred the edges of her vision. She leaned on his sweaty chest. Drops ran in rivulets down her own face. He stroked her back, her hair, her cheek. "This is a safe place," he whispered in her ear.

Just then, a wrinkled, gray-haired man tottered into the room from the shop. "Since H's arrest, I've been expecting you. My name is György. I'm glad you made it."

"The hiding place. Now. The others are coming."

The man nodded and, without a word, led them up an ancient wooden staircase. It creaked under their weight, but there was no other noise. Shouldn't they have heard Ernő and Zofia by now?

"Patrik—"

"Shush."

"But—"

He spun around and glared at her, motioning for her to be quiet.

At the top of the stairs was an empty third-floor attic, lit only by moonlight filtering through a circular window. The heat was stifling, but the window didn't open to let fresh air in, and the roof was so low that Éva couldn't stand upright. But here they stood a chance.

The elderly man slapped Patrik on the shoulder, then headed back downstairs.

Patrik let out a breath. "We can hide in the floor if that's necessary. I'm not sure it will be." He spoke at half volume.

"What about the others?" As the words left her mouth, her arms and legs weakened, and she sank to the floor.

"I don't know what happened to them."

"We should have waited. Stayed with them."

"This is what I warned you about before we fled. It was a long shot that any of us would make it out of there, much less all four of us. But it was our only chance."

"They've been arrested. I just know it. I'm going to lose them." What would the Gestapo do to her brother and sister-in-law? Those false papers wouldn't help them. Reka had exposed them.

That would seal their fate.

She covered her face and moaned, biting back the tears. Patrik knelt beside her, but she pushed him away.

"In times like these, choices need to be made. Difficult ones."

"Why am I safe when they aren't?"

"You are by no means out of danger. We have no guarantee the Nazis didn't see us enter this building. Or that they won't search this block house by house."

The well of tears pushed higher, threatening to erupt. "I've lost my parents and now, maybe, the rest of my family."

"We've all lost. No one is a winner in war."

She gazed at him. "Your family. Do you truly have two sisters? Are your parents living?"

"What I told you about my family is true, except for the blood flowing in their veins. My parents are dead. I watched my sisters herded onto a train right here in this very city. It's another reason I visited numerous times. To check on them. To try to get them out. Whether they are alive or not, I can't say. But I fear the worst." His always-steady voice cracked.

This time she drew him to her side. A few silent tears trickled down his stubbled cheek. "I'm sorry. You're right. No one will come out of this unscathed."

A small piece of her heart broke, never to be mended.

From the alley below came the screech of brakes. They peered out the small window. The truck that had pulled up to Reka's house came to a halt in front of the jeweler's shop.

At gunpoint, Ernő and Zofia emerged from the building, their hands in the air.

The black-clad Gestapo soldiers shoved them inside the truck and sped away.

♪♫♪

Chapter Thirty-One

Zofia crouched in the damp, chilly, windowless cell. Absolute silence. When she'd imagined what it would be like to be imprisoned, she'd always heard voices. Moans. Screams. But not this suffocating stillness.

At least she wasn't alone. She rubbed her stomach, and her baby moved in response to her touch, stretching and kicking. Ripped from Ernő's arms for a second time, Zofia at least still had her child.

Another presence flooded the room. She couldn't see it, hear it, taste it. But she could feel its undefinable closeness. Deep within, she understood it was the Holy Spirit.

A peace like she'd never experienced before overwhelmed her. While they'd been running, the Gestapo a hair's width from them, her heart had been in her throat, and she'd clung to Ernő with sweaty hands.

But now, none of that. For the first time since the Nazi occupation, maybe even since the blitzkrieg in Poland five years earlier, a calmness bathed her.

What a strange sensation.

The cell door squeaked open, and a large, buxom woman with a creased cap on her greasy hair and a dark stain on her green uniform dress stood on the threshold. "Come with me." Her Hungarian was perfect.

She led the way down a cement block hall, painted a brownish green that turned Zofia's stomach. Still no sound other than the squeaking of the woman's rubber-soled shoes on the shiny gray tiles.

Not far down, and the female warden brought Zofia to a small office, furnished with only a gray metal desk, a matching gray filing cabinet, and two gray metal chairs.

Zofia sat, the seat cold on the back of her legs. Time passed—how much, she couldn't be sure. In her head was the ticking of a clock. Only in her mind, like a metronome.

With no noise coming from the hall, she scooted her chair closer to the desk. The music that lived in her bones and muscles begged for release.

Without prompting, her fingers remembered one of Mozart's little etudes. They danced across the desk as if she played the finest grand piano on the stage at the Budapest Symphony.

Heedless to her surroundings, she played on, this time choosing "Rhapsody in Blue." At first, she heard Éva performing the wonderful clarinet warm-up to the piece. Then the piano came in, and Zofia banged out the staccato chords, dissonant and harmonic at the same time.

The door swung open.

With a gasp, she sat back.

A short, brown-haired, brown-uniformed man strode into the room and shut the door behind him. He sat across the desk from her and studied her, his eyes warm and blue. "You teach piano, do you not?"

She swallowed hard. "I did."

"My mother did also. All her life, she could never sit still. If she had nothing in her hands and no piano available, she would practice her music on the table, or the back of the pew in front of her, or even on her own legs." He gave a lazy smile, a single dimple indenting his right cheek.

One might think they were old acquaintances.

Zofia stilled her hands.

"You've been busy with other things, have you not?"

She put on her most innocent face, the one her father could never resist. "I don't know what you mean." Then she laughed and pointed to her expanding middle. "You mean my child?"

His grin faded. *"Nem*, that is not what I meant."

"Then I don't know what you're talking about."

He slapped three of her pamphlets on the desk and pushed them toward her. "This."

She squinted as if to read them. "This says it was written by Katona Marika. That's not me, which I'm sure you know from my identity papers."

"Come, now. I don't want to hurt a pregnant woman. I'm sure you can understand that. But you aren't either of those names, are you?"

"I have no idea what you're talking about."

Some of the warmth fled his eyes. "Make this easy for all of us. You're Bognár Zofia, aren't you? Isn't that your name?"

She'd been careless, pretending to play the piano. That had been the tip-off. Zofia played the piano. Marika produced pamphlets. Only the woman listed in the fake identity booklet was innocent.

"Isn't it?" The man banged on the desk.

Zofia startled. Unbidden tears welled in her eyes. Mama told her expecting mothers cried easily. Why, oh why, would it happen now? "Please, you're frightening me."

"Good." His words were as steely as the furniture in the barren room. "Then maybe you'll give me the information I desire."

"But I have nothing to tell you. I'm a woman from the Polish border area."

"What are you doing here?"

Now her hands trembled. "Despite the war, life goes on. I'm here to attend a medical conference. As you can see, I'm a physician." She forced herself to breathe. As long as he didn't test her skills or knowledge, she'd be fine.

The Nazi stood, the medals on his chest clinking, and leaned over the desk. He clipped each word. "That is a lie."

A knock came at the door. Zofia gripped the edge of the chair. The man opened it.

"Hello, Zofia."

Reka.

❧

Ernő paced the small room like the caged lion he'd seen at the circus as a child. He rubbed his aching temples. Where was Zofia? What had they done with her?

Those monsters had ripped her from his arms. For a time, he'd believed they couldn't hurt her here. Not in Hungary. People couldn't be that cruel. Yes, Jews weren't always the most liked, but never did he dream the Hungarians would allow the Germans to sweep in and cleanse the country of every one of them.

Including his beautiful Zofia.

Why hadn't they left when they had the chance? She had never asked him, and he had never offered.

How blind they both had been. This was not what they'd imagined for their lives. Right now should be their happiest time ever. Newlyweds, about to have a baby. A precious new life.

But for their child to be born into such a world as this, where people couldn't live in peace, in quiet and comfort.

His pastor's words, ones he'd heard a thousand times, rattled in his head. This was a sinful and broken world. "Curse you, Adam."

"All men are cursed," Pastor would say.

All because of Adam. He broke it, ruined life for everyone born after him.

Why did this have to happen now? They were so close, so very close. The Romanian border was right there, within reach, within touching distance.

And Palestine. Their new dream, to bring the gospel to the Jewish people in the promised land, gone. Shattered.

"Just one thing, Lord, just one thing. Can't you allow one good thing in our lives?"

The door behind him creaked open and shut. He didn't turn around.

A deep voice by his shoulder asked, "Do you want to know about your wife?"

This was a trick. Nothing more than a twisted trick. Though his muscles ached to turn around, though his tongue tickled with the question about Zofia, he refused to acknowledge the man.

"The strong, silent type I see. Fine. We can play the game that way. I'll sit here, and we'll stare at each other, and whenever you're ready, you can ask me how Zofia is."

They knew her name? How?

Reka. The only possible answer.

"Have a seat, Ernő."

They knew his too. He stayed on his feet and stared at the gray concrete block wall.

"I said to have a seat."

Still, Ernő didn't move.

The man's hot breath on Ernő's neck sent shivers chattering down his spine. The Nazi twisted his left arm behind his back until, with a pop and an explosion of pain, the German dislocated his shoulder.

Ernő screamed. He sank to the seat, cradling his arm. The razor-like pain was worse than anything he'd ever experienced.

What kind of man was he for giving in to it?

A Nazi with a long, angular face and dirty brown eyes sat across the metal table from him. "From now on, I expect you'll cooperate more willingly. Now let the waiting game commence."

Fine. That was a game Ernő could play. When he was a boy, he had been his primary school's staring champion. During recess, he and his classmates would challenge each other to competitions to see who could look into someone's eyes the longest without blinking.

Ernő won every time.

Not even Éva could challenge him.

He perched on the edge of the chair, unable to rest his painful shoulder against the back. Big breaths were impossible. But he sat and didn't move.

"She's in the same building. A meeting could be arranged if you answer a few questions about her."

Never in his life.

The Nazi drew a silver cigarette case from his pocket, plucked a long, paper-wrapped smoke from inside, lit it, and puffed away.

Ernő didn't stir. Moving would cause too much agony.

Who knows how long they sat like that? Judging by the number of butts in the ashtray, it must have been a good while, though the Nazi smoked one cigarette after the other.

Every part of Ernő screamed to know about Zofia. What were they doing to her? Did they consider that she carried a child? *Nem*, he couldn't torture himself with such thoughts. They cared nothing for the new life growing within her.

The hard-edged man crossed his legs. "If you won't inquire about your wife, I'll ask you about your sister and her friend Patrik. What do you know about them? Where are they?"

Ernő suppressed the sigh that built inside him. One of relief. Éva and Patrik had escaped.

A hot bubble expanded in his chest. Why Patrik and not Zofia? If two of them had to be caught, it should have been the men. The women should have been released.

"I saw that muscle jump in your jaw."

Ernő steeled himself. He'd thought he hadn't moved. Maybe the Nazi was trying to bait him.

More time passed, and the number of butts in the ashtray grew until it almost overflowed. By now, it must be morning. His weighted eyelids closed of their own accord. His head bobbed, sending pain shooting throughout his torso.

He righted himself and willed himself to remain alert.

Did the German nod off too? *Igen*, he was growing weary of the game.

The man, almost as tall as Patrik, jumped up and made a circuit of the room. "You will see your wife again if you answer one simple question. If not, I assure you, neither she nor your child will live to see the sunrise."

Ernő's grasped the edge of the seat until his fingers numbed. The room tilted and whirled. *God, nem. Nem, nem, nem. You can't take them from me. Don't do that to me.*

The man leaned over the table, his jutting chin almost touching Ernő's. "It's an easy question. Nothing too taxing on the mind."

Flashes of Zofia as he'd first seen her, thin, large eyes, beautiful but frail. How her voice was like music, like the velvet tones of the clarinets his family had crafted for generations, rich and full. The softness of her skin against his, warm, smooth, luxurious.

Their unborn child. If he was a boy, would he be another instrument maker like his grandfather and his *apu*? If a girl, would she be as beautiful as her mother, with a soul as gentle?

These vile men would commit unspeakable acts against the two people he loved more than his own life. Only he could stop them. "What do you want to know?"

"How were you going to cross the border?"

♪♪♪
Chapter Thirty-Two

Patrik knelt on the hard wood floor as Éva wept. "Hush now, hush. You must be quiet. It's likely they'll conduct a search of the block and come looking for us. We have to be quiet."

She gazed at him through tear-stained lashes but quieted her sobs. "Why, Patrik, why?"

"I don't know."

"He's my brother. And I love her like my own flesh and blood. And the baby. Oh, the baby." Fresh tears coursed down her pale cheeks.

Patrik cradled her close to his chest and allowed her to weep. His own throat swelled. Too much pain. Too much heartache. Too much loss. "They'll be fine."

"We have no guarantee. Not of anything anymore."

"We never did." To lose one of their own was always difficult. Unfortunately, it happened way too often.

Once spent, she sat upright and stroked his own damp cheek. Had he been crying?

"You have to help them. Isn't there something you can do?"

"I don't know."

"You have connections. What about the man who owns this house?"

"I can speak with him."

Her countenance brightened.

"Don't get your hopes up." He didn't want to crush her, but they had to remain realistic. "I'm not sure what can be done. We've managed to get people released from custody before, but it's not easy, not without its dangers."

"You have to try. Please. If not for my sake, for Zofia's."

His chest tightened. "Don't you know I would travel to the moon and back for you?" She was so delicate, so vulnerable. If only he could protect her, keep her from this craziness. Her brown eyes. Her smooth skin. Her red lips. He leaned in.

Then pulled back. Not when they were hunted. Not when her brother and sister-in-law were in the hands of monsters. Not until he could fulfill the promise her kiss had asked for.

They sat together in the darkness. As the minutes dragged into hours, he stroked her hand, her back, her hair. She dozed against his shoulder. So good. So right.

No pounding at the door, no Germans demanding entrance. How strange. Very unusual. What was going on?

Deep in the night, György crept up the stairs. "I think you're in the clear. I can't believe they didn't stop here. From my window, I watched them. They raced away with the others and never searched for you."

A coldness settled in the pit of Patrik's stomach. This wasn't right. "It doesn't feel good to me."

"To me either." György scratched his messy beard.

"Do they have a plan to draw us into the open?"

Éva stirred and awoke. She rubbed her eyes. "What's going on?"

"We don't know." Patrik smoothed her blond hair from her cheek. "It's odd they didn't come after us." As he spoke the words, the truth dawned on him. They were torturing Zofia and Ernő for the information.

Pain throbbed behind his right eye. Whatever he did, he couldn't let on to Éva. Already, she was too upset.

"What do you plan to do to rescue my brother and sister-in-law?" She directed her question to György.

"We've never sprung anyone from the prison. Other prisons, yes, but not this one. They don't take chances this close to the border."

"You have to do something. At least try."

Her pleas stirred Patrik. "Bram had a German uniform."

"But he's in Budapest."

"If we could get one, maybe some false papers to go along with it, we might be able to get them out. Just maybe." Hope flickered in him. For her, he'd risk it all. Prove to her he wasn't a deceiver and a betrayer but a man who loved her and would travel to the edge of the universe for her.

György nodded. "I could get my hands on one."

Éva knelt, leaning toward György. "How?"

He waved her off. "No questions. Didn't you teach her, Patrik, to never ask? It's better you don't know. Let me get to work on this." He retraced his steps out of the room.

Silence cloaked them for a while. They had blankets and pillows, items they could take with them into the floor cavity if they needed to hide. Had Éva fallen asleep again?

If only he could. His mind whirred with the thousand possibilities of what tomorrow might hold. With a uniform, he could infiltrate the prison, but then what? His German wasn't perfect. Maybe it would have been better for him to go as a member of the Hungarian police. Then he wouldn't have to work on his accent.

He should tell György. He reached to move Éva from his shoulder to one of the pillows.

"Patrik?"

"Oh, I didn't mean to wake you."

"I wasn't sleeping. I was thinking."

"About?"

"What György said. It's better that I not know. I can . . . can see the truth in that now."

"What do you mean?"

"Is that why you did it?"

He could again ask her what she meant, but he already knew. Is that why he had lied to her? "I didn't want to, but for your own good, I had to. These days, the less we share with each other, the better. Hard as it is."

"You said difficult decisions needed to be made."

"The hardest. Ones that rip your insides out."

"Did you have to make difficult ones?"

"More than you care to know."

"Ones that involved your family?"

She was ripping off a scab and baring the wound. "*Igen*."

She stroked his cheek. "Tell me."

"When the men came and hurt my mother, I hid. I was only twelve. But I should have been braver. *Apu* was gone. I was the man of the house. I chose to protect myself instead of her. If I had, maybe she wouldn't have—"

His voice broke. And suddenly, there they were—the tears he'd held off so long.

"It's not your fault. You were a little boy."

"I knew my sisters were in the camp here. I came to see what I could do. What was there to be done? I should have tried harder."

The drops coursed down his cheeks and dripped from his chin. "I should have gotten them papers at the same time I got them for myself. I failed them. Failed them all.

"So now I try not to fail anyone else."

She drew him to herself and stroked the back of his head. "It's not all up to you. There are others working. And God is taking care of everything."

"*Igen, igen, igen.* He is. We both must remember that."

"Trust not in ourselves, but in our God." She kissed his neck. "Choices of who lives and dies are impossible. Soul wrenching."

"And there may be even harder choices ahead."

She answered with a strangled sigh. "I know."

Every muscle in Éva's body protested her movement as she awoke on the hard floor. Where was she? She raised herself to her elbows and peered around the room. Thin shafts of light poked through the small window.

Like a wave against a rocky shore, the events of the last few hours crashed around her. Her heart bled. Here she was, sleeping, safe, as safe as anyone these days, while Ernő and Zofia were facing—what?

Patrik had tried to put a good face on it last night, but she wasn't naive. She'd heard the rumors. She had eyes. Remembered the camp at Kistarcsa.

The Nazis were not gentle.

And Patrik was willing to put his life on the line to help her.

Where was he? His pillow and blanket remained folded beside her. Had he slept at all last night?

Her head ached, probably from crying. And the strange events. Never had she dreamed she would be running from the Germans. Never had she imagined Ernő in mortal danger along with his pregnant wife. Never had she imagined she would do what she was thinking about doing.

She couldn't allow Patrik to go into the Gestapo headquarters as a German. His accent was terrible. Hers wasn't any better, but her plan was far different.

She rose to her feet. She had to find him and speak to him. Tell him what she had in mind.

Wait, what had György said last night? That it was best she didn't know. That must go both ways. If it was best Éva didn't know what Patrik was up to, then it must be best if he didn't know her plans.

Here she was, withholding information from Patrik. His deception was what had broken their relationship. Now she understood. That was how war worked.

And she had a plan for what she had to do if there was any chance of getting Zofia and Ernő out of that miserable place and across the border.

Freedom lay so close.

They couldn't allow it to slip through their fingers.

She descended a flight of stairs and discovered a small water closet with a sink. Just what she needed to splash water on her face and run a comb through her hair.

She pushed her hair back with a couple of combs and allowed it to flow over her shoulders. What she wouldn't give for a tube of lipstick. That would make this charade easier to pull off. Well, she couldn't worry about things she couldn't change.

Her soiled yellow dress hung on her frame, but that was another thing she couldn't fret about. She leaned on the sink and stared at herself in the mirror. "You can do this, Éva. You have to do it. For Ernő, Zofia, and the baby. Think of them. This is all for them."

For Patrik too, though she refused to allow those words to cross her lips. She understood. Difficult choices had to be made. He hadn't wanted to lie to her. What he did in not telling them about Zofia was a good and honorable action. So opposite from Károly's betrayal.

How had she been so blind? She inhaled long and slow and let the breath out little by little. While trust would take time to rebuild, she could show him she now understood.

Life never turned out the way you dreamed it would. Difficult choices needed to be made, and sometimes that involved secrecy.

God, I need You more than ever. Show me what to do.

She knew what she had to do.

She descended the final flight of stairs to the ground floor and discovered Patrik and György sitting at a round kitchen table, leaning close to each other, speaking in low tones.

"Good morning."

They both startled and stared at her, their eyes large. Patrik came to his feet. "You look like you slept well."

"I did get some rest, thank you. From the sight of you, I'd say you didn't." Dark bags hung underneath his bloodshot eyes.

"We've been working on the plan all night." He needed a shave. "Let me get you some fake coffee."

She flashed him her best effort at a genuine smile. "*Köszönöm.*"

"And a slice of bread to go with that."

"*Nem.*" She wouldn't be able to keep anything in her stomach more than the bitter brew that passed for coffee.

A few minutes later, she sat at the table, sipping the warm liquid, fortifying her insides. Her hands, though, refused her command to stop shaking. "I've made a decision."

Again, the weight of their stares pressed on her shoulders.

"I'm going to be the one to rescue Zofia and Ernő."

Patrik stuck out his neck. "You're what? *Nem.* I won't allow it."

"What have I done other than bring bread to a child in a camp? In the end, what good did that small action do? Nothing. But I can be of assistance here." She touched Patrik's hand. "On a good day, your German is poor."

"I've been up all night practicing."

"A few hours aren't going to make a difference. Let me do it."

"And what's your plan?"

"It's best you not know."

Chapter Thirty-Three

The Nazi's question about the border crossing hung in the air. *Talk to the man.* Part of Ernő screamed that was the reasonable thing to do. Tell the man how they were going to escape, and he would let Zofia go. A few words. Move his mouth a couple times and secure his wife's and his child's futures. Except. . .

This is a trap.

That was the reality. If he told the officer how they had planned to cross the border, they would lie in wait for Éva and Patrik, arrest them, and all four of their lives would be forfeit.

"Ah!" Ernő grabbed at his hair with his right hand and pulled. "You know what to do."

He did. God help him, he did. But how could he do it? Sacrifice his wife and his child to save his sister and the man who they believed had betrayed them?

"Sleep. I need to sleep."

The Nazi's blue eyes glinted in the harsh light of the lone incandescent bulb. "None of that now. Later. When you've given me the information I desire. Is this your first child?"

Ernő groaned.

"I have three of them."

Then why ask such an impossible thing of Ernő? The man understood the preciousness of life. Understood the love a father has for his infant before that child even takes his first breath.

"They're beautiful. All golden-haired, with the brightest blue eyes. And smart, each one of them. Brigetta plays the piano, just like your wife does. My daughter is very talented. Given the chance, she'll be quite successful. Max excels in math. You should see that boy with numbers. A genius. And little Angelica. Sweet as frosted cake. She wants to be a nurse."

What would Ernő's child become? Perhaps he would carry on the family legacy in the instrument-making business. He would have his mother's musical ear, his father's deft hands for making clarinets from wood.

Music. The melodic music of his child's cries. *Anya* told him his first squalls were the most beautiful sound she'd ever heard. Oh, to nestle his own little one and hold him close.

His heart ached no less than his left shoulder. "Please, I beg you."

"Beg me to do what? Save the lives of your wife and child?"

"*Igen, igen, igen.*"

"You know how to make that happen."

What if he lied? Though he hated the thought of telling a falsehood, it might be the way out of the predicament. The only way to save five lives. Even a small fib had to be less of a sin than murder. He'd be rescuing the innocent. Surely the Lord would approve.

Would it work? That was the gamble. He'd never been one to bet on cards or horses.

His torturer reached into his cigarette case only to find it empty. "I need more smokes. The timing is good. Think about the question. Let me know your answer when I return." As he sauntered by, he leaned to whisper in Ernő's ear. "I'm running out of patience. Do us all a favor and tell me your plan."

The metal door clanged shut as the German exited the room. Ernő expelled his breath with a shot of spit. "God, help me. Help me! What am I to do?"

He fell from his chair to the floor and held his painful arm close. Tears coursed down his cheeks, splashing on the concrete.

For the first time in his life, he understood the Lord's agony in Gethsemane. "Let this cup pass from me."

But it would not.

He crouched on the ground until his knees ached and then went numb. When that brought no answer, he beat his chest.

The heavens remained silent.

He hugged himself and rocked back and forth, forcing himself to breathe in and out. Stay calm and clearheaded. If he lost his mind, he would say or do something he would later regret.

No regrets.

No regrets.

That left him with one simple choice.

His heart rate dropped into the normal range. No longer did he fight for air. He knew what he had to do.

For what must have been thirty minutes, he paced the tiny room, completing the circuit a hundred times or more. When would the guard return so he could get this over with? He'd made up his mind. There was no going back.

Get on with it.

He might go crazy with the waiting. Then the door swung open. Tall and regal, the Nazi returned to the room and took his place. "What is it you want to tell me?"

Ernő relaxed and sat across from the beak-nosed man. "I'll tell you what you want to know. How we were planning to cross the border. In return, I want your guarantee that if I do so, my wife will be released and allowed to continue the trip to Romania."

"You have my word."

Ernő tapped the table. "In writing. On a piece of paper, with your pledge. Otherwise, you won't get the information you seek."

"You are in no position to be making demands, Bognár Ernő. I hear your wife is in some distress. I have the power to make it better for her. Or worse. Now give me the information."

It wasn't supposed to happen this way. Before it even got off the ground, his plan crashed and burned.

He had to take the chance. There was no other way to save

Zofia's life and the lives of the others. "We were going to pay a smuggler."

"Names." The German pounded on the table, the sound reverberating in the tiny room like the ring of a gong. "What is the man's name, and where can I find him?"

He was going to make up a name, but just as he opened his mouth to spew nonsense, another idea struck him with the force of a bullet. "But this is a woman. And I believe you already know her. Lakatos Reka."

The oppressive summer heat bore down on Éva as she marched along the street toward Gestapo headquarters dressed in the navy-blue wool uniform of the Hungarian police. The weight of the air had nothing to do with the reason why she couldn't draw a deep breath.

This was the one and only chance they had at securing Ernő's and Zofia's release. Bribing the officer to part with the uniform had cost them dearly. And jeopardized them, leaving them with too little to pay a smuggler. Once they had Zofia and Ernő in their custody, they were on their own to cross into Romania.

The building loomed like a giant over a flea. With each step echoing the pounding of her heart, she climbed the steps and headed through the heavy wood door. The click of her oxfords resounded on the sterile white tile floor.

She approached the main desk where a man dressed in a dark blue suit sat shuffling paperwork.

"Sir, I require your attention."

At her authoritarian tone, he whipped his focus to her, eyeing her uniform. "What is this about?"

"You have to let me do this."

He crinkled his forehead. "Do what?"

Right. She couldn't rush ahead. "I must speak with two of your prisoners immediately." She worked to keep the warble from her voice, though her entire body trembled. "Bognár Ernő and Bognár Zofia."

He frowned and sorted through a couple stacks of papers. "I don't have record of them."

"Of course you do. Do you want me to report you to your superiors as lazy and unorganized?"

"But, but—" His flaccid face flushed crimson.

"Now."

"I cannot allow that without written authorization."

This was the toughest part of getting in, and she'd prepared for such a challenge. "There will be a great reward in it for you if you allow me to speak with them." She withdrew a large wad of cash from her pocket and thumbed it before tucking it away.

His countenance brightened. "Let me make the arrangements."

The bribe constituted the entirety of their remaining funds. But she did what she had to do.

Five minutes later, she sat in one of the interrogation rooms, the gray walls, gray floor, and gray furniture weighing down her spirit. What did they do to people here? She shivered. If they discovered who she was, she would learn the answer.

Another few minutes passed before the door opened and the bespectacled Gestapo officer led Ernő in the room. Her brother's eyes widened, but she shot him a warning glance. Any sign of recognition between the two could sign their death sentences.

Ernő cradled one arm close to his body and winced as he took his place across the table from her.

The guard remained in the corner.

"You may leave us now."

"I will stay." He set his lips in a straight line.

"That was not part of our agreement."

"You got your way, now I will get mine."

"If you would like your payment, you are in no position to negotiate with me."

"In that case, I'll return the prisoner to his chamber."

Éva's mind scrambled to devise a way to get rid of the guard. "I only need a few minutes with him, but I demand that you leave. Your superiors will be very disappointed in the way you handled this situation with the Hungarian police, and a woman at that. Besides, I do not see Bognár Zofia. You must get her for me as well."

"Three minutes. That is all." The guard backed out of the room and clicked the door shut behind him.

In a second, she was around the table and pulling Ernő into an embrace. He released a howl of pain.

She recoiled. "What happened to you?"

"They dislocated my shoulder. You've never imagined torture like this."

"How are you otherwise?"

"It's horrible. The men are stuffed into a few cells. Not enough to eat or drink, not enough sanitation. Why are you here?"

"Where's Zofia?"

"I haven't seen her." His voice broke. "I don't know if I will. They demanded to know our plans to cross the border, and I fed them false information. Implicated Reka, actually. They're probably discovering this about now."

"Cheeky of you. I'm going to get you out."

"How?"

"And Zofia. Don't worry about it. When the guard returns, follow my lead."

The few minutes they had alone together flew by much too fast. Before Éva knew it, the guard returned to the room. Without Zofia.

"Where is she? You promised to deliver her to me." Éva stood.

"She isn't here. According to the records, she was transported by train first thing this morning."

Éva stomped toward the man and stood on her tiptoes to stare him in the eyes. "You *dummkopf*." She screamed in his face. "Do you know who that was? She was to be under my control. You had no right to send her away. Where is she headed?"

"I don't know." He assumed a position of surrender. "Don't ask me, because I can't find out. Now give me my money."

"I will walk out of here with Bognár Ernő, especially after you botched the arrest of his wife. We have charges pending against him, and he is to remain in our custody. Once we are outside the building, then you will get what was promised to you."

The man pushed his glasses up his nose and nodded. "I'll escort you personally."

"*Köszönöm.*" Surely he knew she wasn't who she claimed to be. He must suspect her true reason for being here. But no matter, as long as he aided in their escape.

True to his word, he led the two of them down the hall, through the lobby, and out the door, gripping Ernő the entire way.

The three of them stood on the front step. The German motioned for Éva to pay him. "Time for my reward."

"You've been somewhat helpful, though you only delivered one of the two I needed." She fingered the money in her pocket and peeled off a number of bills. Without Zofia, she wasn't about to hand him her last dime. They might need it later to rescue her.

He grabbed the money and released his hold on Ernő, then disappeared inside the building.

"My Zofia." Ernő collapsed to the ground.

Éva yanked him to his feet by his good shoulder. "We have to get out of here before we're both arrested."

"My Zofia."

That same pain tugged at Éva's heart. Only God knew what was happening to her sister-in-law.

o you see him there?" The Nazi's breath stank of cabbage and onions as he whispered in Zofia's ear. Her stomach turned.

She peeped through the window in one of the rooms as Ernő and Éva exited the police station. They didn't get far from the door before Ernő dropped to his knees and covered his face, his shoulders shaking. The sight took Zofia's breath away.

"He believes you are no longer here. I told him you were taken away by train this morning."

"Why lie to him?" The baby picked that moment to kick.

"They didn't tell me the truth, so why should I tell them the truth?"

Had all men become this ruthless, this heartless? "He is all I have left in this world."

"How sweet." The man's tone was anything but syrupy. "Spoken like a woman who loves her husband. Who would do anything for him."

What did he want from her? If she didn't ask, maybe she would never find out.

"Your husband tried to play a game with me, feeding me the name of one of our informants as the smuggler they were going to pay to cross the border. You didn't marry the brightest man in the world."

She bristled. Ernő may not be able to write a dissertation on the effects of music on the human psyche, but he could take a piece of wood and carve an instrument that would play the richest music. That was far better.

"He made his choice."

Ernő came to his feet, and Éva led him away, out of Zofia's sight. She whirled around to stare at the pock-faced soldier.

"That's right. I laid his hand out for him. Either he could walk away from this prison on his own, or you would both be arrested. Look what he chose." The Nazi's breath hissed in her ear.

Goosebumps broke out on her arms. That wasn't true, couldn't be so. Ernő would never do such a thing. He would never betray her. Then again, she had walked away from him. Perhaps he hadn't forgiven her. She'd thought he understood, but maybe she was mistaken.

She shook her head. *Nem.* Her husband would never make such a choice. The German was messing with her, trying to make her believe words that weren't true.

That couldn't possibly be true.

She advanced toward him, her pregnant belly almost touching him. Without flinching, she stared him in the eyes. "You are a liar." She enunciated each word.

His cackle chilled her to her very bones.

"You will be sorry. Very sorry. You think you can write eloquent words against our Führer and get away with such vicious propaganda? We know who you are, Katona Marika. This time, you won't get yourself free from our grasp."

He spun on his heel and marched from the room. An eerie silence covered Zofia. Her baby hiccupped, and she patted the place where he nestled inside her. "Don't worry, little one. Mama will keep you safe. And soon we'll be reunited with *Apu.*"

Ernő. Her captor's words rattled in her brain. Had he given her husband a choice? And what was Éva doing here?

The pieces of the puzzle fell into place. There was no way the German told Ernő he could walk out of here. He'd said he told him she'd been taken away this morning. Her husband believed her to be gone. Or worse.

She huddled in the corner of the small cell as the shadows lengthened across the room. Was she the only one here? Why did no one else cry out? Moan? Scream?

The walls closed in on her, and darkness fell. To be rid of this misery and at home with the Lord. This world had descended into a madness that had no end. She was tired. Bone weary. Sick of fighting a losing battle.

Yes, the Soviets marched ever closer. The day of liberation neared. Perhaps within a matter of weeks or months, the country would be freed. At least from the Nazis. But throughout this war, from the very beginning until today, she'd witnessed the evil men harbored in their hearts.

Even an armistice wouldn't cure hatred.

God, help me. I don't know what to do. I'm . . . I'm afraid, Lord. Afraid to live. Afraid to die. Where and when will it all end?

"And God shall wipe away all tears from their eyes; and there shall be no more death, neither sorrow, nor crying, neither shall there be any more pain: for the former things are passed away.

"And he that sat upon the throne said, Behold, I make all things new. And he said unto me, Write: for these words are true and faithful."

The words from Revelation 21 that she had memorized as a child. Yes, that was the final victory.

The little one turned a somersault, or so it felt. His tiny hand kneaded her stomach. Her one remaining tie to this world.

Was that the heavenly Father's answer? He'd entrusted her with this precious life. Maybe he could make a difference when she couldn't. Perhaps because of his testimony, God would use him to win souls for the kingdom.

She cradled her belly and hummed to him, and the reverberations inside her calmed the little one. He listened. And now she sang.

She sang so that when she was no longer here, he would remember her voice.

Patrik paced the tiny living area in György's home. Outside, a storm broke. What was taking Éva so long? She should have returned. Something must have gone wrong. He should have never let her do whatever it was she was doing.

Her stubbornness. It was one of the first things about her he loved. Also one of the things about her that drove him the craziest. When she got an idea in her head, there was no getting it out.

That trait could either serve her well or destroy her.

György turned from the desk where he sat writing. Patrik kept from glancing at it so he didn't learn too much about György's activities.

"Stop your pacing. You're making me nervous. You said you were a composer. Sit down and compose some music. I can't concentrate with you creaking across the floorboards."

"It will be worse when I start humming." Patrik gave a wry grin.

"That I can deal with. Write a happy song."

The man didn't understand. Patrik couldn't put music to page on demand. The process took inspiration.

And his *múzsám*, his Éva, was in harm's way. Where was she?

Her image flashed before his eyes. Her silken hair, her full mouth, her sweet disposition. The way she puckered her lips when she pouted. He chuckled.

"See?" György returned his attention to his work. "You're halfway there already."

The music flooded him. It overtook him the way a wave might overtake a swimmer. A lilting, skipping tune. "Paper. I need paper and a pen."

From the desk drawer where he sat, György pulled the requested items. Patrik took a place at the kitchen table and scratched away. A breezy melody for the way Éva's hair caught the wind. One that laughed along with her. One that sparkled as much as she did.

Whatever she was up to, she would have to use every bit of her wit and charm. Dealing with the Nazis wasn't as simple as teaching clarinet to young children. She'd have to think on her feet.

Could she do it? Had she done it? Or had something gone wrong?

The music turned dark. The tempo plodded, heavy, weighted down. The cellos, trombones, and tubas added their rich deepness. Patrik couldn't draw a breath. The tune haunted him.

As suddenly as the inspiration hit, it ebbed, a tide against the sand. The piece remained unfinished. He couldn't write the ending until he knew what had happened to Éva.

His Éva. The woman he loved more than his own life.

He wiped the ink from his fingers and gathered his sheets of music. Part of the song was missing. Just as part of him was missing without her.

Much to György's consternation, Patrik resumed his pacing. "Please sit before someone sees you in front of the window and asks questions. My neighbors know I live alone."

Patrik plopped on the supple leather couch and tried to relax. No luck.

Then the kitchen door flew open. Éva stumbled in, her eyes red, her cheeks drained of all color. Behind her came Ernő.

The air whooshed from Patrik's lungs. Wait. One of their party was missing. "Where's Zofia?"

Tears shimmered in Éva's eyes. "Oh, Patrik." He rose. In a moment, he had gathered her to his chest. Her shoulders heaved in silent sobs.

He cast a glance at Ernő, who clenched his hands together and touched his forehead.

The floorboards creaked, this time under György's weight. The four of them hardly fit in here. "Something went wrong."

Patrik shook his head. Let Éva and Ernő have their grief over whatever had transpired. It was obvious the plan had been only partially successful. He hugged Éva long and hard.

Finally she stepped back from his embrace.

Patrik's arms ached to hold her longer. "Sit down. Both of you. I'll get you some water. Ernő, are you hungry?"

"No, but my shoulder is toturing me. They dislocated it."

Patrik and György worked on Ernő's shoulder as he buried his head in a pillow to muffle his screams. Once the joint was back in place, though, some of his color returned.

At last they sat at the table. Patrik brought them their water, and he waited while they sipped it. Then he sat beside Éva and rubbed her hand. "Tell us."

Her whisper was so soft, he had to lean in to hear it. "They took her away this morning."

"Where?" György's question was sharp and demanding.

Patrik glared at him before returning his attention to the two at the table. "Do you have any idea where she is?"

"*Nem.*" Ernő's voice cracked, and he rubbed his chin. "They refused to give us that information."

During the months he'd worked with her and had gotten to know her through Éva, Patrik had come to care for Zofia a great deal. Like a little sister.

"We'll get her back." They had to. To let her go was unthinkable. Forget what he'd said to Éva the day before when they were running for their lives. They had to find a way.

Ernő held up his hands. "It's not so easy. They pressured me. Told me if I gave them the information they wanted, they would release Zofia."

Patrik's stomach hardened. "What information?"

"How we were going to escape."

He clutched the back of the metal and vinyl kitchen chair. "What did you tell them?" The words squeaked out of his throat. Their entire plan hung in the balance.

"That Reka was going to smuggle us across the border."

A chuckle escaped Patrik. "Reka? Did they accept your answer?"

"Of course not. If they did, Zofia would be here. Instead of me." Ernő covered his head.

God, when will this all end? Patrik clapped Ernő on the shoulder. "Stand firm."

"How can I? My very foundation is shaken."

"God doesn't move." He clung to that. Held with all his might, though his fingers slipped.

Éva grasped him by the elbow. "We have to do something to free Zofia."

"What?" Patrik shrugged. "What? You tell me." If only he knew.

György cleared his throat. "You got one out. That's a victory in itself."

It sure didn't feel like it. "Not completely." Éva sniffled.

"You have a bigger problem."

All three of them stared at György.

"Were you followed?"

Éva blanched. "I don't know. I never thought about it."

Ernő banged on the table. "How stupid of us."

"We have to get you across the border. Tonight."

"*Nem*. Not without my wife. I go nowhere without Zofia. She's carrying my child, for goodness' sake."

"We'll work on getting her out. Probably at a different crossing. But you've been compromised. The guards will be looking for you. The Gestapo has your false names."

"We don't have much money. Not enough to bribe anyone." Éva's eyes shimmered once more.

Patrik turned to the wall and rested against it. "How are we going to manage to escape?"

Chapter Thirty-Five

György was adamant about their leaving tonight. His words stole Éva's breath as she stood in his kitchen. This was one of the difficult choices Patrik had spoken about. Why did it have to involve Zofia and her unborn child?

To protect four lives—Patrik, Ernő, György, and herself—they had to sacrifice one. *Nem*, two.

Why, God? Why? Nothing made sense anymore. She fisted her hands and rubbed her eyes.

Patrik touched the small of her back, his hand warm. She unclenched her fingers.

"If we're compromised and have no money, how do we get across? There has to be a way we can sneak over without being detected." Patrik glanced at György.

Éva drank more of the water Patrik had brought her. She was thirstier than she'd realized. "I don't want to do this. Not without Zofia."

"We've been through this. There is no other way."

Ernő wiped the condensation from his glass. "We'll do what we have to do."

What was he saying? "Without her?"

"This is ripping my heart from my chest. How can I walk away from my wife and child? Every part of me screams this is wrong. You don't leave loved ones behind. You fight for them. Do whatever you can for them. But I want you to be safe."

She eyed him. "You are coming with us, aren't you?"

"*Nem*. She's no longer in Nagyvárad. With transports no

longer leaving for Poland, they likely sent her to Budapest. That's where I'll search for her."

What? "If you don't go, I don't go." She clung to the table.

"Be reasonable. Could you walk over that border without Patrik?"

From the corner of her eye, she gazed at Patrik. Memories washed over her, but she put them on hold, like a cinema show when the flim breaks. "Patrik, can I have a word with you in the other room?"

He raised one dark eyebrow but trailed her to the living area and sat beside her on the sofa. "What is this about?"

"Do you remember the day we met?"

He scrunched his forehead. "Huh?"

"The day we met at the orchestra hall."

A slow grin crossed his face, much as it had that day, the first time they saw each other when she came with a student for an audition. "You were the most beautiful woman I had ever seen. You still are."

He'd been the handsomest man. And still was. With his towering height, he stood out in a crowd and drew her attention like no other before or since. "What we had . . ."

Her lightweight yellow dress had hiked above her knee, and he touched her bare skin. Her entire leg, entire body, tingled. *Igen*, she remembered what had been. What almost was. "How are we supposed to leave them behind?"

"We leave them in the Lord's hands."

"The words slip from your tongue, but how do you do that?"

"I don't know. This situation is eating at me too. Ernő is a grown man, though. He can make his own decisions. If you love a person as much as he adores Zofia, you don't abandon them."

"That's what I'm asking you. What would you do?"

He rubbed her thumb and studied her, his gaze intense, questioning, revealing, full of love. "In Ernő's position, if you weren't with me, I wouldn't leave."

What did her heart have to say about that?

"I've never stopped loving you. Can you accept that what I did was out of love for you?"

She opened her mouth, and the words tumbled out. "I know."

With a tender touch to the back of her neck, he drew her close, so she rested against his shoulder. Like that, she was home. "Oh, Patrik, I've missed you."

He kissed the top of her head. "I've missed you too. We can repair our relationship, make it better than it ever was."

"*Igen*, we can."

"I have a question to ask you."

Her pulse pounded in her wrists. He was going to ask her the question with the impossible answer.

"Do you love me with the kind of love that will risk everything?"

Could she leave Ernő and Zofia behind? This, in addition to her parents. Where was her place in the world?

The answer was plain. Hard but clear. "Promise me we will come back here. When this is over and Hungary is at peace again, we will come back to our homeland. To my parents, to your sisters, to Ernő and Zofia and my niece or nephew."

"I make no guarantees. Life with me will be unpredictable. My vow to you is to love you and take care of you. If there is any way I can reunite your family, I will do it."

She reached up and pulled him down until his mouth met hers. Her soul ached with the sweetness of his kiss. "Then I will follow you, Patrik."

"There is risk in leaving."

"There is greater risk in staying. I wish it didn't have to be this way."

"This is what is best for us. Ernő has made his decision. We have made ours. God will watch over all of us."

"Now that's settled, I have an idea."

"Hmm. Will I like it?"

"A way to get us across the border. Unseen."

A dimple appeared in his cheek. "Tell me more."

Patrik held tightly to Éva's hand as they slipped through the door from György's house and into the night, clouds partially shrouding the full moon. In the back alley stood a cart and donkey. The animal raised his head and brayed.

"Tell that thing to shut up," Patrik hissed at György.

He allowed the donkey to sniff his hand, stroked its muzzle, and the animal calmed. Inside the cart were several instruments and cases György had managed to get his hands on. He didn't offer where from, and they knew better than to ask.

Patrik surveyed all of them. Was this really a good idea? At first it had sounded fine. Now he couldn't be sure.

"I hope I haven't gained too much weight." Éva smiled bravely.

Ernő emerged from the house. Éva dropped into his arms. For the longest moment, they clung to each other. Silent sobs shook both sets of shoulders.

A gaping wound opened in Patrik's heart. One that bled for all that had been. For all that might have been.

For the love, the laughter, the loss.

The siblings whispered to each other, words Patrik couldn't make out. Secrets between brother and sister, like those he had shared with his sisters. The sisters he would never see again.

How difficult this was on Éva. On all of them. Once he and Éva crossed that border with György, leaving Ernő and Zofia behind, they would lose everything and everyone they loved. In all likelihood, Éva would never go back to her music studio. He would never again lead the Budapest Youth Symphony.

Though he had told her they would try to return, that was one vow he might never be able to fulfill. The Soviets knocked on the door of Hungarian territory. Patrik had heard rumblings about meetings between Roosevelt, Churchill, and Stalin. Rumors that the Americans and British were willing to hand over large parts of eastern Europe to the Russians in exchange for their help in ending the war.

If that happened, Hungary might fall into communist hands. In that case, he and Éva might never be able to return. He shook away the thoughts.

Éva extracted herself from her brother's embrace as she wiped the tears from her cheeks. He kissed her hands.

Patrik lifted her into the cart. "So, which instrument do you want to be?"

She peered at the cases for the violin, the trombone, the bass drum, and the double bass. "I'll be the bass." Her fingers trembled as she unlatched the black case to reveal the red velvet interior. "Can you lay it down so I won't be standing on my head?"

"That's the fashionable way to travel these days."

"My brain will explode by the time we're in Romania." She gave a tentative smile.

He rubbed her tense shoulder. "I was only kidding. It's going to be cramped, but it's not far. Before you know it, we'll be free."

"I'm not sure what that word means anymore."

"You'll relearn it."

She came to him and pulled him close to her, so close her heart fluttered. He stroked her hair, which glowed white in the moonlight. "I know you're frightened. But I'm going to be right beside you. Everything will be fine."

"Things aren't fine. They never will be again." She glanced at her brother.

"You're strong. Look at what you did getting Ernő released. That took courage and determination. If you did that, you can do this."

"I'd hoped that would be a start. This is an ending."

If only he could encourage her otherwise. "Beginnings and endings have this way of getting muddled. To start a new puzzle, you must finish the last one."

"But this one isn't complete. There are so many pieces yet to fit together. We're leaving work unfinished. Don't you feel that way? How about everything you've done with the Zionist Youth? And what about your family?"

If he dwelt too long on either of those matters, the darkness would become unbearable. There was much he was leaving undone. Much he wished he could do yet for the Jews left behind. The tens of thousands still in Budapest.

And his sisters. Had he fought hard enough for them? "One thing I've learned in my dealings with the Zionists is that there comes a time when your useful work ends and it becomes necessary for you to disappear. My time is now."

"You're not going to leave me?"

"Not ever, *a múzsám*, not ever." Without her, his life would be devoid of music. He could never compose again.

"With you and God by my side, I can do this."

He bent down and kissed her, the passion rising and swelling like a song. He tightened his grasp on her waist and drank in the way she brushed his cheek with her soft hand. The melodic moan that emanated from her parted lips.

He broke away, gasping. "The rest will have to wait until later. For now, you will be a contrabass." He assisted her as she stepped into the case, and he tucked in her silky yellow dress. She bent and twisted until she was inside. After one last, lingering kiss, he shut and latched the case.

"Are you finally ready?"

György. Patrik had almost forgotten he was standing there. "Of course."

"I thought you'd never finish with the sentimentality."

"When you're in love, my friend, it's more than sentimentality."

"Whatever you want to call it, I'm glad it's done. We have to get moving to make the crossing at dawn."

"*Igen*, before they catch up to us but not so early it's suspicious for someone to be transporting instruments across the border."

György unfastened the screws around the bass drum's calfskin head, and off it came. Patrik gave Ernő one last handshake. "Godspeed, Ernő."

"Godspeed, Patrik."

There was no more to be said. Not without both of them losing control of their emotions.

Patrik clambered up into the cart and inside the drum body, which lay on its side in its case. The fit would be tight for an average-sized man. Patrik had to scrunch tighter than he ever had, even as a child playing hide-and-seek.

"Are you in?" György leaned over Patrik.

"As much as I ever will be." The wound in his leg burned. "Drive fast."

"I will. I'll leave the case lid unfastened so you can get out quickly on your own."

"*Köszönöm* for doing this without charge. Somehow I will repay you."

"Stay alive and be successful. That's all I ask." György secured the drumhead lightly in place and set the lid on the case. Then he took his seat in the cart, slapped the reins against the donkey's rump, and the cart groaned forward.

From beside him, Éva wept. "You have to be quiet. No matter what, you can't make a sound."

"Pray for me, Patrik."

"I will. We'll pray together. But silently." And so they did for long minutes as the cart rolled toward the border.

At last, György reined the donkey to a halt. A deep voice spoke in Hungarian. "Papers."

Silence for several moments. The guard was probably inspecting György's documents. He had several false ones.

"Our Father, which art in heaven, hallowed be thy Name." Patrik breathed the words. His skin tingled and felt clammy. He couldn't form a coherent thought. "Thy kingdom come. Thy will be done."

Oh Father, may it be Your will that we cross without incident.

"What is the nature of your business?" The voice was harsh.

"There's to be a concert tonight in Aleşd. I'm delivering these instruments there."

"I'll need to see them."

291

Chapter Thirty-Six

Ernő strode away from Éva and Patrik without looking back. It took all his willpower. Deep in his gut, he knew this was a permanent parting, at least until glory.

Éva had called this a difficult choice, but though it was hard, it was easy too. He loved Zofia with every bit of his being. He would never, never turn his back on her and their child. The day he married her was the day that became his destiny.

György and Patrik had popped his shoulder back into the socket, but it continued to throb. That ache was nothing compared to the pain in his heart though. His Zofia, his *szerelmem*. So beautiful. So sweet. Carrying his child. Where was she? *God, what is happening to her?*

Keeping to the back alleys and side streets, Ernő wound his way through the unfamiliar city. The stunning Baroque architecture, the river shimmering in the early dawn, the pastel-colored homes waking from their slumber—under other circumstances, he would have been moved by their beauty. Now he was focused on surviving and finding Zofia.

György had told him the general direction to head. For a while, he followed the misty moon. Once the sun burned off the haze, his way was less uncertain.

By the time he reached the edge of the city, his feet screamed. Why was he even on this quest? It was nothing more than chasing after the wind. He had no idea where Zofia might be, just that the soldier told him she had been taken by train. Where should he even start to search?

He meandered down the road until it crossed a railroad. Then he pursued the tracks as they ran parallel to the street. Perhaps there was an open boxcar or a flatbed where he might hitch a ride. He could find his way back to Budapest.

To home. That was the logical place to begin, on familiar territory where he could think. The Gestapo might have taken Zofia to their main headquarters in the capitol for questioning. She was a key in the Zionist organization, after all. That made sense. *Igen*, that's what he would do.

He had to collect his thoughts and devise a plan. No matter how difficult or how dangerous, he wouldn't give up until he held Zofia in his arms once more. He would never let her go. Never allow those Nazis to rip from him the most precious things in his life.

Suddenly a convoy of German trucks was upon him. He'd been so absorbed in his thoughts, he hadn't heard them approaching.

He glanced around, a quick survey. He couldn't jump into the ditch or hide in the woods. They'd seen him. No other option remained besides continuing forward as if their presence didn't send adrenaline rushing through his body, weakening his legs.

The first canvas-covered truck passed. As it did, he searched the back of it for signs of Patrik and Éva. Had they been picked up at the crossing? Were they being transported to a camp?

His tongue stuck to the roof of his mouth. But the truck was empty. He didn't release his pent-up breath, because another truck whizzed by. Another empty truck. Where were they headed?

The third truck slowed as it pulled alongside him. "Where are you going?" The raven-haired man spoke Hungarian heavily laced with German.

What should he say? What answer would keep the Nazi from asking for his identification, would satisfy his curiosity about himself and the others? Perhaps these trucks were out scouring the countryside, attempting to locate them. He swallowed hard. "Budapest."

"Why do you want to go there? The Soviets are bombing it day and night. There's very little left of the city."

His breath hitched. His parents were there. Already they had lost one home. Were they safe? Was it only a week or so ago that he and Zofia and the others had left? "I've received word that my father was injured in a blast. I have to see him, but I don't have enough money for the train."

Ernő didn't dare move while the man examined him, even though his hands trembled. He pressed his arms against his body to still his quaking. How did an instrument maker from Budapest end up in a situation like this?

"I'll need to see your identification."

Tightening every muscle in his body so the Nazi didn't see his shaking, Ernő pulled the book from his pants pocket. He dropped it on the ground.

"Let's go. I don't have all day."

Ernő retrieved the papers and handed them to the pointy-chinned man. He flipped through the pages, scanned the information and Ernő's photo. Finally the man snapped the book shut and tapped it against his palm. "What hospital is your father in?"

"Hospital?" Ernő's voice squeaked.

The Nazi narrowed his deep blue eyes. "That's what I asked."

"He's not in a hospital. They're all full." That much he remembered. "My mother is caring for him, but she needs help."

"You planned on walking to Budapest?"

"I'll do what I have to in order to reach him. No matter how long it takes. I've lost my sister to this war already." And probably his wife, but mentioning that might not be a good idea. "I can't lose any more of my family. *Apu* and *Anya* are all I have left."

The man handed the identification to Ernő. "Good luck to you." He hit the gas pedal and zoomed away.

With a *pft*, Ernő exhaled. That had been close. Too close. Only because of God's watchful care was he still a free man.

Not long afterward, a train's whistle sounded in the distance, echoing throughout the countryside. The rumble of the engine intensified. Ernő picked up his pace. A small town lay in the distance, the church's spire reaching into the sky, now darkening with clouds. Perhaps he could sneak on board this train while it was stopped at the station. It could be his ticket to Budapest.

He sprinted toward the town until he had a stitch in his side as the train's rumble grew to a roar. The engine thundered past him, followed by a string of boxcars and flatbeds that clackety-clacked along the rails beside him and then left him behind. And still he raced. Was the train slowing? How long would it stop? The town ahead wasn't large. It wouldn't require much time for the train to unload and reload.

Ernő's lungs were burning. This was for Zofia. For Zofia. For Zofia. He ran to the rhythm of the words in his head and gained ground until, finally, praise God, he entered the village. It was nothing more than a few red-tiled roofs, a church spire, and the small brick station. The train's rearward cars hung beyond the platform like a snake too long for its cage.

He arrived as the conductor gave the last call for passengers to board. *Nem*, he couldn't risk trying to get into a coach. Not that he had money for one. He tugged on a few boxcar doors. Locked tight. Wait. Up ahead—an empty flatbed. That was it, his ride home to *Apu* and *Anya*. And, hopefully, to Zofia.

The whistle blew, the engine chugged, and there was a clattering of cars as the train lurched forward. Tapping into the last of his energy, Ernő sprinted after the flatbed as it gained speed— and caught up with it. Not a second too soon. There was a step mount for the railroad workers. He grabbed it and, half leaping, gained his foothold and then hoisted himself onto the car.

Patrik's heart pounded like the bass drum in which he was hiding. The German was demanding to inspect the cases, including the ones that concealed him and Éva.

What was György going to do?

Unfazed as if he were going on a drive to the country for a

picnic, György conversed with the guard. "Are you a musician yourself?"

The cart shifted as someone climbed into it. Not the Nazi! Patrik's pulse shifted into cut time. Whom would the German discover first? If he found Patrik, would he be satisfied and leave Éva alone? Perhaps Patrik should turn himself in and give her a fighting chance.

"This clarinet was crafted by one of the finest manufacturers in Hungary. All of Europe, really. Have you heard of the Bognárs?"

György must have gone insane, feeding Éva's family name to this German. That was the only explanation.

"I think I've heard of them." Off in the distance, a roll of thunder sounded, nature's own bass drum.

Of course the German had heard of the Bognárs when he'd been briefed to be on the lookout for Bognár Ernő and Bognár Éva attempting to cross the border. What was György thinking? Had they walked into another trap? Perhaps György wasn't who he claimed to be. Perhaps they had entrusted themselves to the wrong person.

"Sure you have. Finest clarinets money can buy. Shall I play for you?"

György must have lost his mind. If the situation weren't so dire, Patrik might laugh out loud.

In a matter of moments came the *toot toot* of the clarinet as György warmed up. Could he even play?

Again a rumble of thunder, this one much closer. The storm was moving in fast. And then came another sound, the sweetest, richest melody ever. "Serenade" by Schubert. The haunting eastern-European music awakened each one of Patrik's senses. The green lushness of the land planted in wheat. The fishiness of *halászlé*, soup loaded with carp and paprika. The sweet headiness of spring lilacs. The soft grass between his bare toes on childhood holidays.

Part of him would never leave this place. He would always

belong here, a Hungarian to the core. György was a master. As he played, a tear tracked down Patrik's face. He was leaving home.

When the last note of the music died away, a clap of thunder was the only applause György received. Errant droplets tapped on the lid of Patrik's drum case.

"Impressive." But the impassive tone of the German's voice told a different story. He was anything but impressed.

"Ah, do you prefer the flute?"

"Not another concert. Just open the case." The soldier's rapid-fire words were like the rat-a-tat-tat of a machine gun. The rain was picking up at a matching tempo.

"Very well." The latches on the flute case clicked open.

"Satisfactory. What about this bass?"

At that moment, the heavens opened. A downburst of rain and wind assaulted the cart, and a volley of bullet-like drops lashed the top and sides of Patrik's hiding place. Overhead, thunder cracked.

"Sir, I cannot open the bass case in this deluge." György shouted as the thunder boomed across the heavens. "Any water would ruin the instrument. It's a Testore and is more than two hundred years old. Any moisture would warp it and ruin one of the finest double basses in the world. In fact, I need to throw a canvas over it. Please, excuse me."

A moment later, complete darkness enveloped Patrik, snuffing out the little light and air that had been reaching him. Was this a miracle like Moses and the children of Israel when the plague of hail fell over Egypt?

Patrik suppressed the laughter that bubbled inside him, a lilting, jaunty melody begging for release. Of all things, rain would save them.

Nem, not rain but God. *Köszönöm, Lord.*

"If you would pull to the side, we will complete the inspection once the storm passes."

"Please, sir, I must be going. The canvas will protect the

instruments, but I cannot be delayed any further. If I am, the concert cannot go on as scheduled. The group is playing for some very important people tonight. People who will not be happy to sit in an empty concert hall."

"Pull over or I fire."

A lump stuck in Patrik's throat. They had been so close, so very close. In the end, the rain hadn't done them any good. This guard was proficient at his job.

The donkey hee-hawed, and the cart groaned as György drove to the side of the road. Or more likely, beside the guard station.

"Can I come inside, out of the rain?"

"I thought you weren't bothered by traveling in bad weather."

"Not traveling in it, but sitting in it when there's shelter is another thing."

"Come on, then."

"I have a bottle of *pálinka* in my pocket. It may be early in the day, but it's never too soon for a drink. You men will join me, won't you?"

Ah, that's what György was doing. Patrik should never have doubted him. The man was good. If he managed to draw all the guards inside, Patrik and Éva could come out and get across while the storm raged.

A crash of thunder shook the ground beneath them, and a series of lesser booms confirmed that storm was far from over.

For several minutes, Patrik didn't dare move. If he made a sound, any sound, before the guards were tipsy, he and Éva would never get away. Rain pelted the cart, and the donkey brayed. At last, laughter floated above the din of the storm. The alcohol György had plied the Germans with must be working.

No other noises came. The rain kept the guards tucked inside the gatehouse. But how was he to get out of the drum? He had no way to unscrew the head, and breaking it would render the instrument useless. Such a waste. But he and Éva were much more valuable than a bass drum.

He waited for the next round of thunder. Ah, there it was—a rolling cannonade that sounded as if the very sky were at war with itself. Now! He fisted his hand and punched at the calfskin head, trusting the roar of the elements to disguise his own noise. Off came the entire head, which György had secured only loosely, and with it the top of the drum case.

Fast as a sixteenth-note run, Patrik scrambled from the drum, swept aside the tarp, and, with trembling fingers, opened the bass case. Éva flew out of it and into his arms, quivering from head to toe. "Patrik—"

He shushed her with a quick kiss, then whispered, "We have to get out of here. Right away." He hopped from the cart and helped her down.

Together they sprinted, slipping and sliding on the muddy road.

Suddenly from behind them came a shout. "*Halten sie. Halten sie.*"

Stop? Not a chance. "Keep running, Éva. No matter what, keep going."

Soaked to the skin and chilled to the bone, they raced down the street. A truck engine turned over.

Shots rang out.

Patrik sucked in as deep a breath as possible. "Don't look back. Forward, forward." Searing pain sped up the back of his leg.

The truck bore down on them. They could never outrun it. But what could they do? There had to be another option, some way to save themselves.

He spotted it on the side of the road. "The field. Let's go." It was nothing, one chance in a million they wouldn't be discovered.

He grabbed Éva by the hand and tugged at her.

The truck was on their heels. They dove for the wheat.

Prayed for the best.

Waited for the worst.

♪♫♪

Chapter Thirty-Seven

Eva dove with Patrik headlong into the wheat field. This was crazy. Surely the Germans had seen them duck in here. In a matter of moments, they would be on them.

"Crawl."

At Patrik's command, she wriggled forward. The wheat stalks must be shaking with their movement.

This was how the end would come. In a field in Romania. How long before their bodies would be found? *Apu* and *Anya* would never know how their daughter died.

"Just a little farther."

The mud stuck to her dress, now thoroughly drenched, and strands of hair fell over her eyes. Maybe the end would be a blessed relief. She was so very, very tired.

"Don't give up."

Had Patrik heard her thoughts? Or maybe she'd spoken the words aloud.

For him, for their future, she would move forward. If not for Patrik by her side, she would give up. Surrender and take the consequences.

"Okay, now be still."

She halted and cleared her mind. As sunlight pierced the rain clouds, birds twittered in the trees at the edge of the field. In the distance, a cow lowed, and somewhere, an infant gave a lusty cry.

No sounds of motors. No vehicles. No boots clomping through the crops.

Where had the Germans gone? Could it be?

She dared to gaze at Patrik. He turned to her and shot her a small smile. So she wasn't dreaming. He didn't hear the Nazis coming either.

Nem, she wouldn't allow herself to hope. It might still be too good to be true. The guards could be playing games with them.

Patrik pulled her to his side, and she snuggled against him. If they were discovered, she would die in Patrik's arms. That meant she would die a happy woman.

"How are you?" His whispered words sent a wave of heat through her.

"Tired."

"We'll sleep for a while."

"What if they come back?"

"They won't. Trust me."

After all they'd come through, *igen*, she could trust him. Trust him enough to sleep in a wet field in Romania while being hunted by the Germans.

Her eyes flickered closed, and she dreamed of gowns of spun gold, warm breezes, and fireworks lighting the night.

She awoke to the sun blazing overhead. Beside her, Patrik snored. Is this what it would be like to wake up next to him every morning? Oh Lord, that it would be so. She sat up and surveyed him—the streak of dried mud that crossed his cheek. The caked-on dirt that covered his hands, his worn blue oxford shirt, his too-big-for-him tan pants. His sloped nose, his square chin, his long eyelashes.

How could she have ever doubted him? Not believed in him?

He stirred in his sleep and woke. She smiled at him. "Good morning. Or more likely, afternoon."

He reached up, pulled her down, and kissed her. Though he tasted of dirt, heat raced through her. She returned his kiss, the music of it speaking of her unending love for him.

He responded, drawing her closer, tasting more deeply of her.

With a groan, she broke it off. "I'm sorry."

"*Nem*, I am. I shouldn't have started something I couldn't finish. When I opened my eyes, there you were, like in my dreams, so beautiful, the sun behind you."

"I don't know who you're looking at. I'm sure I'm a mess."

"You're lovely because you are with me and you are mine. Never doubt that."

"I was wrong to ever doubt you. How could I have done that? How could you have forgiven me?"

"Hush now, no more of these questions. No more blaming yourself. I don't blame you. The situation looked bad. These days, you don't know who to trust. You had to protect yourself. I understand. There was never anything to forgive, because I love you. I always will."

"You are too good for me."

"Never, *a múzsám*, never. It's the other way around."

"Where do we go from here?"

"There is a farmer on the edge of a small town not too far from here. He's one of the contacts I was given in Romania."

"I forget we're in a foreign country."

"Not so foreign. Anyway, we'll go to him, and he'll be able to get us to Bucharest."

"We have no money."

He scrubbed his stubble-covered face. "That is a problem."

To come so far and to get stuck because they had run out of funds. "What are we going to do?"

"I don't know. We have to get out of here. We're still in German-held territory, and the Soviets will be here any day."

"How can we go anywhere when we don't have cash? We can't get to Bucharest, and we certainly don't have the money for a ship to Palestine."

"First things first. Let's meet my contact." Patrik helped her to her feet. "If we stick to the edge of the road, we can take cover if we need to."

"Do you think they're still searching for us?"

"I doubt it. But that doesn't mean we don't have to watch out."

They strolled down the road almost devoid of traffic. A couple of farm carts passed but nothing else. Shadows had lengthened by the time they came upon a small thatch-roofed timber cottage in the midst of a barley field.

Patrik rapped on the back door. A gray-haired woman answered shortly and, with hands spotted with age, motioned them wordlessly inside.

"Sit, sit," she said, pointing at two chairs behind the kitchen table. "Don't tell me your names. I'd rather not know. Now, you both need a bath. I'll draw the water and get it heating." She peered at the filthy bandage around Patrik's torn pants. "And I'll take care of that wound. How about a hot meal?" The entire time she spoke, she bustled about the kitchen.

Patrik grasped the back of his chair. "*Nem.* I'll draw the water. We thank you for your hospitality, but I have to let you know we have no money. Not a *pengő.*"

"For me, that's not a problem. I don't have much, but I'll share what I have. For the rest of the journey? That is an obstacle for you to overcome. It may not be possible for you to go on."

Éva rubbed her forehead. Not more trouble. Not after they had come so far.

Patrik relaxed in the metal tub of warm water, hid behind a curtain strung around this part of the kitchen to provide privacy. He scrubbed and scrubbed with the rough washcloth and the lye soap. Ah, how good to be clean.

He couldn't wash away their one remaining barrier to true freedom, though. No cash. No resources to purchase food or train tickets or to bribe any guards should they be arrested.

He lathered his hair, dirt falling from it in clumps. When he rinsed, he was no closer to a solution. Neither was he when he stepped from the tub, dried himself, and dressed in the woman's late husband's clothes. At one time not long ago, they would have fit him, but now they hung on his bony frame.

When he pulled back the divider, Éva sat at the table with a mug of ersatz coffee in her hands, the bitterness of the brew stinging his nose. Her eyes had lost all their luster. This strong, determined woman was on the brink of collapse.

He knelt in front of her. "*A múzsám*, don't be so sad. We will find a way out of this."

"How?"

"We'll earn the money."

"But my clarinet. My music is gone. Teaching music is the only way I know to make a living. I don't have any other skills. Not to mention that we're in a foreign country in the middle of a war."

True enough. The Soviets pressed in from the east. He'd heard reports of terrible Allied bombings in Bucharest. There were even rumblings of a coup. The conflict surrounded them.

Then, as if someone had suddenly pried open his eyes, he had the answer. "A concert."

Éva stared at him, her eyes wide. "A what?"

"A concert. Think of it. We'll play for the people in the village. Earn enough to move to the next one, and so on. We may have to creep and crawl along, but it's the only solution we have."

She slapped her thighs. "It's no solution. We don't have instruments."

The woman breezed in from the back bedroom. "Did I hear something about a concert and instruments?"

There certainly was nothing wrong with her hearing. Patrik nodded. "Do you know of someone in the village we could borrow some from?"

"You go see the man at the tailor shop. He has a violin and a clarinet."

Éva straightened. "A clarinet? Really?"

Patrik restrained himself from jumping up and down. "See, God provides." While it may not be the most conventional pairing of instruments, it would do, especially for some good Hungarian and Russian folk music.

A half smile graced Éva's lips.

"What a fine concert these villagers will have."

The woman shuffled to the stove and pushed the kettle over the fire. "They don't have much money, but they will give you what they can. Here, they are good people."

The tailor was more than happy to lend Patrik the violin and clarinet. He examined the violin and stroked the smooth tigerwood base. What a fine instrument. Though it had been a while since Patrik had picked up a violin, he should be able to coax beautiful music from this one.

Even better, stamped on the clarinet's barrel was a rock with a cross on top of it, the mark for the Bognárs. Éva would be thrilled.

Patrik hurried to the cottage to present the instrument to Éva. As soon as she saw it, her eyes filled with tears. "Oh, Patrik. I never dreamed they would have one of *Apu's* instruments."

"How can you tell it's his instead of Ernő's or your grandfather's?"

"See the way the barrel is curved? I recognize that line as unique to *Apu*. Ernő makes his just a little different, and so did Grandfather." She swallowed hard and inhaled several times. "What a wonderful sign. When I'd begun to lose hope, God reminds me not to give up." She caressed the gold-embossed mark.

"Hope. Trust."

"I will. No more wavering."

"The tailor gave me more good news."

"I'm not sure my heart can take it."

"No doubt, it will. He has no need of the clarinet anymore. It belonged to his daughter, who passed away. When I told him about you, he gifted it to you."

She gasped and fingered the nickel-plated keys. "This is mine?"

A lump swelled in his throat. "Yes. To keep for good."

"What a kind man. I must thank him, but I can never repay him."

"He'll be at the concert tonight. I'll introduce you."

"Then we had better get practicing. He gave you a violin?"

Patrik sat and flipped open the case. "A beautiful one at that."

"Perfect. Let's practice."

This was more like the Éva he knew and loved. *Köszönöm, Lord.*

She pieced the clarinet together, lining up the parts just right. From a paper wrap, she drew a new reed, moistened it in her mouth, and fastened it on the mouthpiece. Meanwhile, Patrik plucked the strings of the violin to tune it.

He nodded in her direction. "Are you ready?"

She gave her assent, and they began, the bright tune bringing to mind Russian dancers doing the Hopak dance.

But only a few measures into the music, Éva stopped. He gazed at her. She held the clarinet across her lap. Great sobs shook her slender frame. "I can't do it. I can't. This was one of Zofia's favorites."

Patrik scooped Éva to himself and held her as she cried out all her pain and loss. In all the time he'd known her, he'd never seen her shed so many tears as in these past few days.

Her weeping dissolved into hiccups. "She played it all the time, the piano almost rocking."

He wiped the tears from her cheeks. "What would she want you to do?"

"Play the music. Get to safety. Live a happy life."

"Not five minutes ago, that's what you told me you would do. Tonight we play for Zofia. For Ernő and your parents. For each member of my family."

"Sometimes I forget you lost everything too, including your identity."

The pain gripped him as hard as it gripped her. The sisters he had grown up with. Their laughter. Their beauty. Their love. Gone, probably forever. Would he ever discover their fates? If not for Éva, he would be alone in the world.

"This concert will be for them. About them. For all those who have loved and lost."

Chapter Thirty-Eight

A thousand butterflies had taken up residence inside Éva's stomach. She peered over the small crowd assembled in the church. The early evening sun streamed through the stained-glass windows and exploded into a rainbow of colors on the stone floor.

She'd never been nervous for a performance before. But this was no ordinary concert. *Nem*, this was for the dead and the might-be dead. For the living who would forever be haunted by the events of the past months and years. And for the generations to come, that they might never forget.

As the audience of farmers and laborers and shopkeepers quieted, she licked the reed on the clarinet and blew warm air through the ebony instrument.

"Ready?"

She turned to Patrik and nodded.

He counted the beat, and they came in together, working in perfect harmony. The Russian Cossack tune got the crowd involved. They clapped their hands, and many tapped their toes. At the end of a long workday, music uplifted the spirit, reminding the soul that God gave both joy in labor and rest from work.

This time Éva managed to get through the song without crying. Ernő and Zofia would have been proud of her. Often in the evenings, the lovebirds had pushed the furniture in the living room against the wall and waltzed to whatever might be playing on the radio. How happy they had been in each other's arms.

That is what they would want for Patrik and Éva. Joy, not sorrow. Love, not discord. Peace, not hatred.

So those left behind would live the lives others couldn't.

When they reached the end of the piece and Patrik gave the cutoff, the audience stood and cheered. They too recognized that survival called for celebration.

Patrik reached over and squeezed her shoulder. This next selection would be the hardest. A requiem. So far today, she hadn't played it through without breaking down. He'd told her they didn't have to perform it, but she had insisted. The music was an important part of the story they told tonight.

On Patrik's cue, they began. The minor key squeezed her heart and closed her throat to where she had difficulty supporting her tone. As the music carried her along, a wind-swept hill came to mind.

She stood on top of that rise, searching the landscape for something. *Nem*, for someone. All the someones. *Apu* and *Anya*. Ernő and Zofia. Those she prayed lived.

Then she gazed at her feet, and there were headstones, names carved deep into the brilliant white granite.

Her place to mourn all who hadn't survived.

So she did. In the heavy, painful music, she thanked each of them for their sacrifice. Told them she would always carry a bit of them within her. Assured them she would make it.

For a moment after they concluded the song, the audience sat in absolute silence. You could have heard the squeak of a mouse inside the ancient church walls.

Then thunderous applause drowned out all thought. Éva swayed, overcome, spent. She set her clarinet on her seat, then leaned over to speak to Patrik. "I need a break. Can you do a few songs without me?"

He grasped her by the hand and pressed it to his face. She nodded. "I'll be fine." Then she sped out of the building into the late-summer evening. Leaning against the warm, rough stone of the church, she prayed.

"How can I do this, Lord? How can I not break into thousands of pieces when I have so little left?"

That still, small voice whispered to her, in the depths of her being. She whispered along. "That I with body and soul, both in life and death, am not my own, but belong unto my faithful Savior Jesus Christ."

She clung to the rocks protruding from the old church exterior. "I trust and hope in You, Lord." Like the thirsty ground drinks in a spring shower, so her soul absorbed that truth. "In You."

The Nazis could arrest her brother and sister-in-law. The Allies and their bombs could destroy her home. Reka could rip away her belief in humanity. But neither principalities nor powers could separate her from the love of God in Christ Jesus the Lord.

She covered her eyes and slid along the wall until she crouched on the ground. "Thank You, Father. Strengthen me and keep me from being tempted to despair."

She inhaled and exhaled, drawing in and letting out as much breath as her lungs could handle. For the first time since the Germans had taken possession of her homeland, every muscle in her body relaxed. She leaned against the everlasting arms.

And the music of thanksgiving swelled within her.

Though the train ride back to Budapest in the open flatbed was far from comfortable, Ernő was grateful he had transportation. And had it to himself. If the rumors were to be believed, that's not the kind of trip the Jews on their way to the camps experienced.

At least deportations from Hungary had stopped in July. Zofia would not be part of them. That didn't mean the Nazis couldn't still send her away.

Or worse.

As the train slowed on the outskirts of the city and the land flattened, Ernő took the opportunity and hopped off. Had only a week or ten days passed since he'd seen this city? If possible, the destruction was worse. The devastation magnified as he moved deeper into Budapest.

Bombs had sheared off the fronts of apartment buildings, exposing the flats inside. The families still occupying them went about their days as if their lives weren't on display for the world. Everywhere he meandered, he dodged rubble that clogged the roads. The streetcar no longer ran, its tracks missing in many places. Not that Ernő had money for it.

He ended up in his old neighborhood, the one he'd lived in his entire life. Nothing more than a large, brick-filled hole marked the spot where he'd been born. He'd almost forgotten about the bombing the night they fled.

His parents had promised to stay with friends from church, so he headed in that direction. He rounded the corner, and a machine-gun-laden Gestapo officer patrolled the avenue a few feet ahead of him. His breath caught in his throat, and he ducked around the corner.

The officer crossed the street without so much as glancing at Ernő. After a minute or two, Ernő's heartbeat resumed its normal rhythm. Why had he been so frightened? The Gestapo had what they wanted from him—his wife. They no longer had any use for him.

He continued his trek to where his parents had said they would be. How different this neighborhood was from theirs. A few of the buildings had missing bricks, and a green-and-white-striped awning sported a hole through the center of it, but otherwise, the bombs had not touched this section of Buda.

The cream-colored brick building where the Bognárs' friends lived remained unscathed, just as it had been before all this craziness began.

He climbed the two dark, narrow flights of stairs, his aching knees protesting each step. His legs might as well have been cast from concrete, they were so heavy. A hot bath, a soft bed, and a long sleep were all he required.

Exhausted, he knocked on the plain door.

And there was *Anya*. "Ernő! My boy! You're back." She pulled him inside, shut the door, and hugged him until he was about to burst.

"*Anya, Anya.*" Safe in her arms, he gave in to the tears that had threatened to spill the entire way home—great, heaving sobs as the pain over losing Zofia ripped his heart from his chest.

What was he going to do without her? And their child. Oh God, it wasn't fair that he lived while his wife and child might not survive. One so innocent, not yet drawing this earth's air into his lungs. And Zofia, so much a part of him. How could he even breathe without her?

When his tears finally subsided, *Anya* reached into her apron pocket and produced her handkerchief. He lifted it to his face, the scent of flowers wafting from it. At that, he relaxed. Whatever else happened, he was home.

"*Édesem*, come and see. Ernő has returned to us."

Apu burst into the hall and embraced his son, slapping him on the back. "So good to see you, my boy. Where are the rest?"

"Can I sit before I tell you? It's been a long few days."

They led him into the cluttered living room, furniture and knickknacks everywhere, and *Anya* bustled about, getting him cabbage soup and a cup of ersatz coffee. Once satiated, he spilled the entire story.

Tears ran down his parents' cheeks by the time he finished. *Anya* shook her head. Were those a few more gray hairs? "That poor, poor girl. And our grandchild. There has to be a way we can locate her and get her freed. Now that you're home, you'll have access to our resources. We'll do whatever we can for you."

Apu rubbed his knees. "Of course we will. Do you know what you're going to do first?"

"Sleep. I'm so tired, I can't think straight. After that, I'm going to contact some of Patrik's friends. They'll know better how to go about this."

Anya drew him a bath, and he relished it for a short time until he yawned so much he feared he might fall asleep in the tub and drown. But though *Anya* afterwards tucked him into a clean, soft bed with a down pillow, sleep refused to come.

Then he closed his eyes, and there was Zofia, so beautiful, her red hair rolled like she had always worn it, her cheeks ruddy, her smile large. In her arms, she held a small bundle. Ernő pushed the blanket aside, and there was the face of his son, his eyes green like his mother's, small red lips, Ernő's own distinctive chin.

A pounding on the bedroom door jolted him awake. Where was he? What was happening? Oh, that was right. He was at their friends' in Budapest.

"Ernő, are you awake?" *Anya*'s voice was insistent.

"Come in."

She burst in, breathless. "A man just delivered this for you." As she passed him the small, folded piece of paper, her hands shook.

The outside of the note bore his name and this address.

In Zofia's handwriting.

♪♫♪

Chapter Thirty-Nine

*E*rnő set the note on the tangled bedsheets and wiped his sweaty hands on the brown pants he'd slept in. For the longest time, he stared at the letter, though it was so small, it could hardly be called that. What did it contain? Good news or bad? Did he even want to know?

He stared at Zofia's curly handwriting. So like her. Full of vitality.

Finally he could stand it no longer. He unfolded the letter. Just a small scrap of paper, but she had squished her words together to maximize space.

My dearest,

He closed his eyes and traced the words as if his fingertips could conjure her voice.

> *I don't know when or if you'll get this. A kind guard brought me this scrap of paper and a pencil and promised to deliver my words. I wanted to share what was on my heart. I'm in Budapest, in prison. By the time you receive this, they will have come for me.*
>
> *I have loved you since the first time we met. You were so handsome and so kind to a Jewish Polish refugee. In your eyes, I found the acceptance and love not many people afforded me. I was home.*

Our ending is not what we wish it might have been. Our child will never see the sunrise, never feel the grass on his bare feet, never shape an instrument with his hands. But he knows he was loved. Our heavenly Father will be a father to him.

Though I could wish for more time with you, I am anxious to be home. Soon my feet will tread the streets of gold. Though you may be hungry, I will feast. The music on my lips will never die.

These three years we've been married have been the happiest of my life. Thank you for loving me. Thank you for strengthening me. Thank you for giving me a child.

I hear their footsteps. Farewell, sweetheart. Until we meet again. Remember, I will always love you and cherish the memory of you.

May God bless you and grant you the peace I have, a peace that surpasses all understanding. I kiss your hands.

Your beloved,
Zofia

October 1944

Éva and Patrik stood side by side at the ship's railing as the salty water of the Mediterranean Sea sprayed over them. Behind them, Istanbul rose above the water, the spires of St. Sophia jutting into the blue sky.

Éva had never seen anything like this before. The exotic scenery, the crystal water, the topaz heavens stole her breath. She clutched her clarinet case to her chest, the one piece of Hungary she'd never relinquish.

Beside her, Patrik hummed a tune.

"A new composition?"

"I have a symphony brewing inside me. One I started at György's house. When we get to Palestine, I'm going to finish it. Perhaps I'll get a position in Jerusalem. Is there an orchestra there? Maybe I'll have to start one. That's what my mother always wanted for me. I'm sure there will be plenty of talented musicians to work with." He resumed his humming.

She strained to hear him over the din of the crowd in the overloaded boat. The song moved along, crescendos peaking and crashing, much like this ship slicing through the waves.

From what reached her ears, it would be a glorious piece. His best yet.

Their future held so much potential in the promised land.

Playing several concerts had raised enough money to fund their trek through Romania to the Black Sea port. Thank goodness Patrik's contact in Bucharest had forged papers that were good enough to fool the authorities. Many Jews were turned away from Turkey or denied passage on ships to Palestine. But God had blessed the two of them. They were among the fortunate. Who knew what awaited those who were turned away.

As the land faded behind them and nothing but water surrounded them, the number of passengers on deck thinned. Still Éva shielded her eyes from the hot sun and drank in the adventure.

"Are you sure you don't mind settling in Palestine?" Patrik furrowed his brow in a deep V.

"To live in the land where Jesus lived and taught, where He died and rose again, that is a privilege. I can't wait to get there." If only the rest of their families could join them. Word had reached them that the Germans had removed Hungary's more moderate prime minister Horthy for negotiating peace with the Allies, and now the ruthless Arrow Cross party was running rampant. Conditions had deteriorated a great deal since their *tiyul*.

Lord, protect my family. All of them.

Perhaps when this whole sordid affair ended, they would be reunited. They could return to Hungary. *Please, Lord, let that be the case.*

Next to her, Patrik moved. She turned to him as he dropped to one knee. "What are you doing?"

"Bognár Éva, you are the strongest, most determined woman I have ever met. Through everything, you have shown immense fortitude and resilience. When I proposed the first time, I thought I could never love you more than I did in that minute. But I was wrong."

She sucked in a breath, her pulse fluttering in her wrist.

"My love for you has only grown brighter every day. I need nothing else in this world other than you and God. He brought us together and has granted us our lives. I want us to live them together, as one, as man and wife.

"I promise I will love you until the very end of my days, whether that be tomorrow or, Lord willing, fifty years from now. I will treat you with the kindness and respect you deserve. Even when we disagree, I will never stop loving you.

"As far as it is possible, I will never lie to you again. I will protect you but also be your helper, your guide, your lover, your husband.

"Will you marry me?"

As the ship plunged through a wave, Éva squatted beside Patrik. Her heart almost burst through her chest. She caressed his face. "Patrik, I love you more than my own life.

"I will trust you, depend on you, and help you. Never will I leave your side or forsake you. I will always think the best of you. I commit our relationship to the Lord, who has been so gracious as to preserve our lives and to give me you as my husband.

"I will be your helpmeet, your companion, your lover, your wife."

As the ship carried them toward their new life, Patrik drew her close and kissed her.

From within her flowed the refrain that would never cease.

Acknowledgments

Thank you to the team at Kregel for their hard work on this book. Janyre Tromp, it has been a privilege to work on this book with you. Your insights helped so much and made the story so much stronger. Bob Hartig and Sarah De Mey, thank you for helping me to make the book tighter and stronger and for catching all those little things I missed. To Katherine Chappell and the marketing team, I appreciate the hard work you've already put into marketing.

I owe a great debt to my critique partners, Diana and Jen. I love you ladies. Thank you for your feedback. This book would have been a hot mess without you. You are fabulous storytellers in your own rights.

To the Pencildancers Readers and Review Crew, thank you for cheering me on and supporting me. I have enjoyed getting to know you all. As long as you keep reading, I'll keep writing.

I would be nowhere without my fabulous agent, Tamela Hancock Murray. You are my biggest advocate. Thank you for your belief in me, for never giving up on me, for encouraging me. You're the best!

My family, I cannot repay you for what you have done for me and how you have helped me fulfill my dreams. Doug, my beloved, you are God's gift to me. Even all these years later, I cannot believe you are mine. The Lord knew what He was doing when He sent you to me.

My children, three gifts from God. Brian, Alyssa, and Jonalyn, I love you all to the moon and back. The Lord has granted each of you special gifts. I pray you will use them well and for His glory.

To all of my readers, I thank you. My stories need those who appreciate them, and I thank you all for your loyal support over the years. Without you, I couldn't do what I do. Thank you for allowing me to work at my dream job. Not many people get to say that. I'm very blessed.

Thank You, Lord, for all You've done for me. You are my only hope in this life and the next. *Soli Deo gloria.*

Author's Note

One of the books I read to research this book was *I Kiss Your Hands Many Times* by Marianne Szegedy-Maszak. It introduced me to the beautiful Hungarian custom of saying good-bye in which a man kisses a woman's hand. In fact, the Hungarian word for *good-bye* means to kiss your hand. You'll find I included this custom in several places, especially in the more poignant parting scenes.

Hungary has a complicated history that began long before 1944. In an attempt to keep his country from being overrun by the Nazis, President Horthy allied with Germany. Until March 1944, the Hungarians remained largely unscathed by the war. Though anti-Semitism was fairly prevalent and had been for many years, Jews from all over eastern Europe, including Poland and Czechoslovakia, felt that Hungary was safe enough to take refuge there after the Germans invaded their countries.

Out of this was born the Zionist Youth movement, made up of young, idealistic, often socialistic Jews. They organized resistance, especially getting Jews out of the country through Romania, Switzerland, and Sweden. Some prominent foreigners assisted in this effort.

Their work became more desperate when, in March 1944, after President Horthy refused Adolf Eichmann's orders to round up the Jews, Germany invaded. Within a few short months, the Nazis cleansed much of Hungary's Jews. The only relatively safe place was Budapest, where the Jews weren't herded into ghettos but were segregated into "yellow star" houses. Horthy halted the deportation of Jews in July. By this point, it was becoming difficult for the Nazis to move them by train as the Russians had bombed many of the rail lines. This didn't deter the Germans, who forced many to march on foot to Auschwitz. Because of the already overcrowded conditions in the camps, most of the Hungarian Jews were gassed upon arrival.

Nagyvárad was a real city on what was then the Hungarian-Romanian border. Today, this beautiful city is known as Oradea, Romania. As told in the book, the cleansing of the small Jewish ghetto there took place on May 28, 1944. The description comes from an eyewitness of the events. Patrik's family would have been gassed upon arrival at Auschwitz.

The camp at Kistarcsa was also a real place. For years before, it had been a prison for political dissidents, and it reverted to its original intention in the postwar communist years. The camp is now gone. The description of it again comes from an eyewitness.